WOLVERINE HILLS

ESPIONAGE
SCOUT

For more information contact L. Gordon Kesler at
25838 S. New Town Dr., Sun Lakes, AZ 85248

ISBN 9781549942204

Credit for back cover photo – Robert D. Flaherty / energy landscapes

Printed in the United States of America.

WOLVERINE HILLS ESPIONAGE SCOUT
BY L. GORDON KESLER

SYNOPSIS

This story is based on a very real and little-known world of oil field espionage. In the oil and gas industry, the politically correct term for spying is Oil Field Scouting and it is an integral part of oil companies exploring and acquiring oil and gas leases.

The current situation in the Middle East, as well as the politics surrounding exploration of hydrocarbon fuels, makes this story extremely relevant and intriguing.

2008 – An international terrorist group headed up by Syria's president has declared war on its Middle Eastern neighbors for supporting U.S. sanctions against his regime. Assad's people have blown up oil facilities and have blocked the shipping lanes effectively stopping the flow of oil to North America.

The chapters in the story move alternately from major events in the oil field between scouts and counter-scouts to the conflicts in the high-rise executive suites in downtown Calgary, Alberta, and Houston, Texas.

Max is a field scout with seven years' experience. He has a tan complexion which is reflective of his Native American heritage and is extremely handsome with a muscular build from years of hard labor on the drilling rigs. He is married to an attractive blonde women and they have five children. Max is one smart and ambitious guy who initially got into field scouting so that he could acquire enough money to start his own oil field supply company. He is working for a junior upstart oil company. In the field, Max encounters opposition scouts as well as counter scouts.

Tom Hughes is the main protagonist in the field. Hughes is a 35-year-old baby-faced blond who considers himself a super scout and has a huge ego. Whatever it takes to stop Max from getting information from his client's well, he is prepared to do. Kidnapping and using explosives are all a part of Hughes's modus operando.

Hughes has a partner in crime named Bill, nickname Polecat. Polecat has been spying for 30 years and his ambition burned out years ago. He is an alcoholic who spends more time in the local bars trying to get laid than he spends in the field. Age and alcohol have made him careless and he becomes a useful pawn.

The second conflict occurs in the high-rise offices with marble floors and brass doors of the many oil companies on Sixth Avenue in downtown Calgary, the oil capital of Canada.

At the West end of Sixth Avenue on the sixth floor, there is a junior upstart oil company made up of a small group of people all with special skills necessary for success. Wayne Stadwell is president and leader of the group. Stadwell is quiet and reserved almost to the point of being shy, but when it comes to business, he is a no-nonsense guy. At 37 he is greatly respected by his coworkers. In order for the company to succeed, Wayne has mortgaged everything and for him failure is not an option.

At the other end of Sixth Avenue stands a tower of granite and marble with bronze tinted windows. The tower is 42 stories high. On the 41st floor is the drilling superintendent for one of the top three oil companies in the world.

Roger White is in his sixties and has been with the company since he started as a roughneck 40 years ago. Roger is a throwback to the old days of oil field executives. He is rugged and foul mouthed even in the company of woman. Roger always wanted to be important and so expensive cars and fast women are all a part of his persona. The cigar stub that he chews on and rolls from side to side is a constant fixture even when it isn't lit. The potential for getting credit for a major oil find would mean a huge promotion and would be a great feather in his hat. What Roger doesn't know is his anger and abuse of people will catch up with him and cost him grabbing the brass ring.

BACKGROUND

Within the oil and gas industry, there is a special designation of professionals known as "Scouts". The departments, in most oil companies, affiliated with scouting, are usually the Land Department or the Exploration Department both are involved with the evaluation of lands that may hold the potential to produce oil and gas. There are two distinctly different types of Scouts: first are Company Scouts and second are Field Scouts. This story involves those Scouts designated as "Field Scouts".

Company scouts are members of a professional group known as the International Oil Scouts Association (IOSA) and a companion organization in Canada (COSA). The function of the company scout is to negotiate and trade information on oil and gas wells, those previously drilled and those currently being drilled. All member companies assign their ledger of wells each with a special status for the purpose of determining how much information will be shared with another company.

One day each week the scouts meet for the purpose of exchanging well information with other companies who are members of IOSA. Each oil company has the right to designate a particular well with a "Tight-Hole Status". On these wells, they are not required to report information. However, if a company decides not to share information without the proper designation they are suspended from meeting for a time; decided on by all of the other members. The suspension can be from one week to several weeks plus a fine may be imposed by the organization.

This body of company scouts provides a valuable service to its members because they can obtain data on wells that help them evaluate their own exploration programs.

Wolverine Hills Espionage Scout is a story centered on the second designation of scouts; these are "Field Scouts".

When a well is given a tight- hole status, oil companies are unable to secure information on the drilling operation of that particular well. This is when the Field Scout comes into play.

Field Scouts are independent and work as contractors for the oil companies who hire them, they are actually oil field "SPYS", men with a multitude of special skills. The Field Scout must have years of experience working on drilling rigs. They also must have a high degree of ingenuity when it comes to high-tech listening equipment and they must have the ability to work in isolation in the wilderness for weeks and sometimes months at a time. The most important qualities, however, are courage and perseverance.

This is a story based on years of working as an Oil Field Scout. However, none of this story is intended to implicate any company or person in the activities of this story and all of the characters and companies are fictitious.

THIS BOOK IS DEDICATED TO THE MEMORY OF

MY SON SHANE KESLER (1971 - 2002)

WHO LOVED THE OIL INDUSTRY.

Thanks to all those scouts who worked for me over the years. Because of their many experiences this book was possible.

Thanks to my wife Joyce for her patience as so many nights I would wake her as I flew from bed to write down new ideas. Thanks to her also for her assistance in finding this cowboys many punctuation mistakes.

OIL WELL DRILLING RIG

CUTLINE

TIMBER LOGGING TRUCK

OILFIELD LOGGING TRUCK

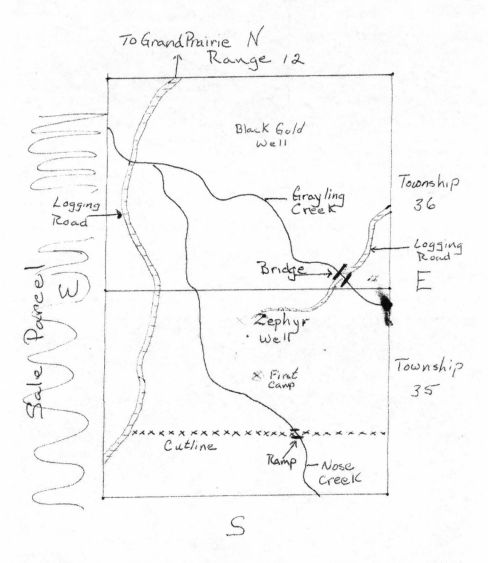

AREA MAP

CHAPTER ONE

Max Cardova slapped another coat of varnish on the side of the pine dresser and paused. Looking across the snow-covered backyard, he could see his wife doing the dishes through the kitchen window.

Probably cleaning the kids' cereal bowls, he thought. Knelt down next to the dresser he was finishing to surprise his daughter, his eyes remained on his wife. He sure was lucky to have such an ambitious, beautiful, and faithful wife.

Max knew the last quality was a rare attribute, especially for spouses of all those working in the "oil patch."

It's a hard life in the oil patch. Not just for the men who went away for weeks and months on end to work the oil rigs, but for the wives and girlfriends, as well. Being alone so long and having to take care of all the at-home business starts to take its toll. Maybe not as much as working back-to-back 12-hour shifts in freezing cold, grueling conditions, but difficult, nonetheless.

Problem is, many oilmen don't understand or appreciate what's going on at home while they are away. When they return they expect nothing but constant attention and catering to, and when that doesn't happen, trouble ensues.

Max saw this happen all too much throughout his 20-plus years working the rigs. More friends than he could count went from single moms and dads on a temporary basis due to deployment to the rigs, to permanent singlehood due to divorce.

When you spend too much time apart and only argue when you come together, an unfortunate and irreversible rift evolves. And, as was the case with many of his colleagues and acquaintances, eventually someone filled the void through the comforting arms of another.

Max was determined that would not happen to him. For one, he truly loved and appreciated his wife, Carmen. He knew the amazing things she did for him and the family while he was away. He also loved his children too much to jeopardize their happiness. He would do anything for his four sons and one daughter.

While nobody knows for certain, Max knew he didn't have to worry about Carmen's faithfulness. He could see it in her eyes each time he came home. She smiled and giggled at his jokes and goofy demeanor in the same heartfelt passion as the day they first met. Unbeknownst to Max, it also helped that he was ruggedly handsome with a dark complexion and a chiseled build reflective of years of hard work.

Max smiled to himself as he looked through the window at Carmen. Yes, he thought, he was a very lucky man. With more energy and excitement, he slapped another coat of varnish on the cabinet. As he dipped his brush back into the can, the slight smile on his face suddenly disappeared.

His thoughts of being home and enjoying the company of his family quickly changed to the fact that he knew he would soon be headed back into the field. And things were different these days. In order to make more money, a few months back, Max decided to become a "scout."

Part detective, part investigative reporter, scouting involved garnering as much information as possible about drilling operations of competing oil companies. In an industry of intense secrecy and false information, more and more oil executives were turning to scouts to dig up, literally, the dirt on the drilling operations of rivals in the vicinity.

In the big money business of oil, knowing how far down a rival is drilling and what formations may be producing crude oil or natural gas; can easily save millions. It can also make or break a company. The last thing anybody wants to do is put in a bid on a lease that only produces dry holes.

That is where scouting came in. And over the years it had become a popular, but cutthroat business. While some didn't mind information getting out about their drilling results, most take great offense to this practice. After all, it usually involved trespassing, spying, listening in on phone calls, and other illegal and immoral activities.

For those reasons, scouting was not for everyone. While the substantial pay raise lured many into it, very few were truly good at it. It took an incredible wealth of knowledge of the industry, as well as a great deal of patience and physical and mental stamina.

Considering the main source of data gathering was surreptitiously setting up camp next to an oil rig and watching the activity for days on end without being seen, it also took stealth and ingenuity. One must have nerves of steel, as well, since being caught could mean a severe beating, or worse, from rig workers.

Despite knowing all this, Max decided to give it a shot because he knew it was his best chance at making the money needed to start his own business. An engineer by trade, his true passion was building oilfield equipment and there were some technical modifications he knew that could be done to current machinery that would greatly improve efficiency in the industry.

It helped, too, that in his many years of working the rigs, he had built up a pretty long list of managerial contacts. Still, it took money, a lot of money, to turn his ideas into reality before he could hit the sales trail, and scouting seemed his best path to get there.

Despite his scholarly background, surprisingly Max was very good at scouting. In fact, in his four years, the reports he presented were so detailed and accurate, he had become the "go-to" guy at his company, Wildcat Scouting. Quite often Max would get calls from his boss, Phil Graves, before anybody else, even veterans who had been doing it for years longer.

Knowing this was a relief to Max because he knew it meant he was doing a good job. Yet, there were days when he regretted leaving his drilling job. Not only because it was less stressful and he had more fun doing it, but also because even with the nice raise to $650.00 per day, he wasn't saving any money.

You would think a man could get ahead, Max thought, but with double-digit inflation, the cost of living was killing him. Feeding and clothing five kids was an expensive proposition and, on top of that, he hadn't worked 10 days per month over the last six months.

This caused Max to look at his watch. "Damn I wish Phil would call," he said to himself, the words barely audible.

Max liked working for Phil. It was Phil who had lured him into scouting in the first place, after seeing Max's work ethics while scouting one of his rigs. What Max liked about his boss was he was a man of his word. He paid on time and was considerate of his family needs, something most scouting outfits didn't give a shit about.

Deep in thought, Max continued to lather the cabinet. He was probably over-doing it, but his mind was far from the task at hand. It was on scouting.

It suddenly switched back to the hard, rough life of working as a oil rig hand. Divorce was common in the industry, but even more so in the inner-scouting family.

Thankfully, Max wasn't one to take to the bottle. On occasion, he may get a little tipsy at a holiday or Stanley Cup party, but it was rare. Heavy drinking, however, was the norm among scouts.

Bringing that home after a few days or weeks in the field definitely didn't help the family situation. While common sense, this was a revelation to Max and he nodded to himself.

A loud shout from the patio door suddenly rang out.

"Max! Max, you're wanted on the phone honey," his wife shouted. "It's Phil."

Max laid the brush down on top of the varnish can and stood up. He brushed off his hands as he walked toward the house. The varnish was too sticky to come off, but he continued to rub them on his pants anyway.

"Thanks," he said to his wife as he reached for the phone. With her hand cupped over the receiver, Carmen whispered, "Let's hope it's a job."

Max hoped so, too, and gave his wife a confirming smile and nod.

"Hi, Phil, what's up?" Max asked.

"How ya doin' Max? What you been doin' to pass the time?"

"Just building a new cabinet for my daughter's room. Trying to surprise her, although not too sure how excited she'll be for new drawers to hold her socks."

"Ha! You're always building somethin'," Phil replied with a chuckle. "Personally, I couldn't pound a nail unless it was my thumbnail!"

There was a brief pause until Phil continued. "Listen Max. I apologize for not calling sooner, but I've got a short job up north if you're interested? This oil well may already be down and the rig may be off the hole by the time you get up to the location, but it's worth a go if you're game."

Phil started up again before Max could answer.

"These cheap son-of-a-bitch oil companies, they want all the good information: tests, tops, logs, geology, everything, but they never want to send a guy out soon enough to get the fuckin' job done right. Sorry for the language but it just pisses me off. How do they expect a good job at the last minute? Anyway, sorry for the diatribe, but it's you guys I feel bad for. At any rate, let me give you the information on this well you'll be scouting."

As Max could hear Phil fumble through his paperwork, he smiled wryly. It was like this every time with Phil. He would call asking if he was interested in a job, then profusely apologize about how short it was. Max knew Phil genuinely cared about those that worked for him and truly meant what he said, so this repetitious pattern didn't bother him. It actually had become quite amusing, especially since Max knew there were no small jobs in this business.

Through talking with veteran scouts and through his own arduous work, it was evident a solid report could not be compiled without ample time.

"Sorry, Max, I can't find the information that I just put it in this pile of rubble. Bear with me."

By experience, Max also came to realize as long as you filed a detailed, thorough report, management didn't care if a "short" job took a few more days than expected. Especially if that report meant there was black gold to be had.

"OK! Here it is," Phil suddenly chimed in. "Looks like about a six-hour drive from your place. It's Alpine Drilling - Rig 6."

Phil gave Max the well coordinates, the proposed total depth and all the other pertinent information he had on file regarding the oil operation. Max was careful to write the data down clearly and accurately, as he didn't want to end up at the wrong location.

Not only is that just shoddy work, something that could easily cost him his job, but also if other scouts found out about it, he would never hear the end of it. Several scouts are still getting razzed about that exact fiasco, Max knew, even though it had happened years ago.

"OK, Max, that's it. Say, if the well's down when you get there, I'll figure a way to pay you a couple of extra days, sound good? The sooner you get on the road the better."

Max chuckled to himself. Another typical Phil maneuver – making Max wait for what seemed forever for the next job, then reminding him of the urgency to get on location.

"Good luck! Get some good info," Phil concluded.

"All right, Phil! Thanks! I'll try calling you tomorrow with my first report." Max hung up the phone.

"Let me guess," Carmen said. "You have to leave right away and it's only a short one?"

Max looked over at his wife and nodded. The last-second call was annoying, but the irritating feeling was quickly overridden by the fact that he had work again.

"I know honey, it's frustrating, but you know these short jobs sometimes turn into weeks. Maybe when I get to the rig they'll be stuck in the hole."

Max chuckled, that quiet chuckle he quite often did with his wife. He smiled and gave his wife a quick hug, before turning and heading out the door to get his equipment ready.

It was always sweet revenge, Max thought when the oil companies tried to skin the job down to two or three days and it lasted a month or so. Max was hoping this was one of those situations.

Always on call, Max had his equipment in good shape and ready to go. He was religiously committed to going through his checklist to make sure when he arrived at the job he could jump right in. Considering some of the best scouting is done under the cover of darkness in the wee hours of the morning, he must be ready to go at a moment's notice.

A check at his watch revealed it was already almost 3:30 in the afternoon. Doing the math in his head and knowing it would take him another hour to get ready, Max estimated his time of arrival to be close to 10:30. That was if he drove straight to rig, too, which was never the case, as he would need supplies.

Plus, nobody ever drove straight to a rig. The closer he got, the more back roads and off-road he'd have to travel. And, eventually, he'd have to ditch the truck altogether and hike in the rest the way in order to remain undetected.

Probably looking more like midnight once I get all situated, Max thought, as he opened up his trusty equipment box.

Inside, staring right back at him was the checklist he always went over. Things had really changed in four years, Max thought, as he scanned the ever-growing list. Soon he'd need a U-Haul for all his stuff. The thought of driving a U-Haul through the dense forest made Max chuckle.

Starting at the top, Max ran a finger over each item: spotting scope, scanners, antennas and adapter, tape recorders, a line of stars – this was code to remind him of the special equipment he used that he didn't want any straying eyes to know about.

Max continued down the list: rifle and shells, chainsaw, tire jacks, generator.

"Yep, everything accounted for," he said aloud. It always was, but Max never took anything for granted. Once out in the bush, a scout rarely turned back for supplies.

As Max was finishing packing his truck, Carmen came out. "Got time for an early supper before you get on the road, honey?"

Max threw a duffel bag into the back and glanced at his watch. After a short pause, he turned to his wife.

"Well, H-O-N-E-Y, we have a few minutes before the kids get home from school, so I'd say there's time for dessert, too!"

Max smiled at his wife, then reached out and grabbed her with both hands and pulled her close. Carmen loved the mischievous tone of Max's voice. He never ceased to amaze her even after 18 years of marriage.

In one fell, seemingly effortless swoop, Max picked up his wife and plopped her down on the tailgate. Looking lovingly into her eyes, he once again realized just how lucky he was.

He lowered his head and gave her a long, passionate kiss.

CHAPTER TWO

Max's Chevy 4x4, was in good shape, but through all the off-road use it had its share of brush scars from traveling too many cutlines. Most scouts bought a new truck every year because they beat them up so much on the bush roads, but not Max. He couldn't part with his baby. It was running well and it had gotten him out of way too many serious jams.

Max drove down the main road and headed to the west side of Fox Lake. Checking the map, he knew that he was getting close. He spotted a well-used logging road and headed south. As the 4x4 headlights swept across the road and the thick branches of the mixed-conifer forest, it was just as he had expected – a ribbon of twisting ice.

Max navigated the hazardous conditions with the skill that only came from many years of experience. The road narrowed in spots, causing the brush and tree branches to scrape the sides of his truck. As he slid on the dirt and ice around a narrow bend, Max spotted the twinkle of a rig through the shadows of the snow-covered trees.

This was a familiar sight. And one that gave Max a surge of relief since it meant he was indeed heading in the right direction. Maybe it was more a feeling of anticipation than of relief, Max contemplated.

By now it was 1:00 in the morning and Max would have to hustle if he was going to find a cut line and get a status of the operation before daylight. The cover of darkness was always best and he only moved during the daytime when it was absolutely necessary.

The old cliché "out of sight out of mind" had proven to be true in the world of scouting.

Since Max could now see the rig through the trees that meant someone on the rig could most likely see his lights, as well. Thus, he slowed down and hit the off switch on his headlights. The moon was nearly three-quarters of the way full, which made it light enough to see the outline of the logging road in front of him. Max let out a slight smile knowing it would be a fairly safe last mile or two in.

His eyes opened with more excitement when he noticed a cutline to his left.

Cutlines were common in the patch. In order to find the most optimal geological structures, seismic crews drilled a series of holes in straight lines, and then loaded them with explosives. Once the dynamite exploded, the shock waves were recorded, giving an idea of the exact type of formations underground. The seismic work was almost always done in straight lines for logistical purposes and all trees and brush were cleared away in order to get the blasting equipment in and out.

These clearings were called cutlines and they are a scout's best friends. Not only were they easy to use because they were either cleared away or only filled with small, new-growth trees, like willow, but also they usually led right to the prize – the working oil rig.

The cutline Max spotted in the moonlight was easy to see. In fact, the new growth of brush and willow was but a few feet high, making it look like a glowing hallway amid the giant silhouettes of the towering spruce and fir trees.

Max wheeled his Chevy off the road, over the bank, and onto the cutline. About 100 yards down, he pulled his beloved 4x4 between two large spruce trees and parked. This cutline was extremely easy to use, too easy, thought Max. He knew this would be the first place the rig workers would look for approaching scouts.

Seeing the light of the moon reflecting off the pick-up hood in front of him was the last straw. This told Max it was time to hide the truck and go the rest of the way on foot. More than once, a scout had been spotted because he forgot to pay attention to the small details.

The second Max climbed out of the warm cab; the -30° temperature stung his face like a swarm of hornets. He didn't know how long he'd have to spend in the shadows of the rig to get a detailed status report, so he dressed extra warm to be safe. Still, in these temperatures, nobody is truly safe, he thought, and the frigid numbing feeling on his cheeks was a constant reminder of that.

Only three pieces of equipment were needed at this stage, deduced Max, a high-powered spotting scope, a high-powered rifle with cartridges, and his mini scanner. Course, he also needed food and water since he wasn't sure how long he'd be in the bush.

With all items neatly tucked away in his backpack, Max extracted a camouflage tarp from the back and covered his truck. It was pretty well hidden behind the trees and brush, but one can never be too careful. Especially with the ease at which to travel on this cutline, Max knew.

In just a few short steps, Max noticed the set of tire tracks in the snow. They looked fairly fresh. Most likely surveyors, he surmised, as no scout worth his salt would drive this line into the rig.

With his trusty Sako 300 magnum over his shoulder, Max resumed his walk toward the six-diamond formation, shimmering in the distance. It was a mile or so away, but in this darkness; the rig lights looked much closer.

The Northern Lights danced hauntingly across the star-spangled heavens before him. Max loved the Northern Lights. Someone once told him if you were very quiet you could hear them crackle. Max had listened many times before but never heard anything. He suddenly stopped in his tracks, closed his eyes, and strained his ears. Nothing! The only sound was his breath crackling in the sub-arctic air and in the distant the haunting howling of a pack of wolves.

Max smiled. It was probably just folklore, but he didn't mind. He loved the silence, anyway. He enjoyed being out in nature and felt one with his surroundings. The crackling sounds of his breathing were quickly joined by the crunching sound of ice under his feet.

As he got closer, Max could hear a subtle "clang-clang" in the distance. It was a sound he recognized right away, one that had become part of his life long ago. It was soon joined by a whirring noise.

"The normal, everyday sounds of an operating rig," Max said with a smile as he continued his trudge down the cutline. Another, louder "clang-clang" sound joined the melodious chorus, and Max knew this was from the elevators being latched as the crew made a pipe connection.

Max checked his watch. Twenty-five minutes since he left his 4x4 hidden in the shadows of the trees. Another five minutes and the rig would be in full view. The lease would be lit up like high noon and Max knew that just the sight of it would make him feel warmer.

As Max moved in closer to the opening where darkness gave way to the lights of the rig, he could hear another soft engine sound. Even as his trained ear heard the soft throbbing in the frigid air, Max began to warm all over. But, this wasn't a pleasant warm feeling, this was warmth caused by anger.

He stopped in his tracks. Right in front of him, almost as clear as day thanks to the reflection of the moonlight and the lights of the rig off the metal, was a truck! Not just any truck, but the beat-up Red Ford half-ton of Bill Emerson, known as Pole Cat to fellow scouts.

"That fuckin' lazy bastard"! Max said aloud.

Max was livid. The idiot had driven straight down the cutline almost to the rig itself! Some fucking things never change, Max thought. Shaking his head, Max continued down toward the Ford. As he got within 20 feet, he slowed down his gait and crept forward.

The truck was idling and Max ever-so-slowly peeked into the partially frosted window on the driver's side. Lying on the front seat, completely sprawled out, was Pole Cat. He lay motionless. Fast asleep, Max knew.

Max looked over at the rig in the distance. He shook his head, then looked back at his fellow scout sleeping soundly in front of him. Max's anger suddenly gave way to humor. He chuckled to himself, then raised his hand and banged on the dented door panel.

"Hey! Get outta here, ya stinkin' low-life, scum-sucking scout! Get outta here before I kick your fuckin ass!"

As Max banged on the window, Pole Cat jumped to a vertical position on the seat. His eyes shot wide open and bounced around staring off in every direction as if he had stuck a finger in a light socket.

He squirmed mightily to try and find the keys to the pick-up. Finally realizing they were in the ignition and his truck was already on, he frantically scrambled to throw it into gear. He looked like a scalded cat, Max thought, rather than a pole cat.

Usually, a very reserved, quiet individual, Max couldn't help but bust up. He laughed so hard it caused him to damn near piss his pants. Just as he found the gearshift and threw it into drive, Pole Cat heard the bellowing through his frosted window.

He quickly put the truck back into park and immediately rolled down his window. He could see Max buckled over still laughing loudly. His scared, panic look turned to a mix of relief, embarrassment, and annoyance.

"You son of a bitch, Max, you nearly gave me a heart attack!" Pole Cat yelled.

Max continued to laugh. He then stood back up and took a long, deep breath. Pole Cat stared at him, then shook his head. "Shit man! I thought for sure you were some damn rig hand comin' to fuck with me!"

Max sighed loudly. "Well, of course, you did, ya idiot! You practically parked on the damn hole itself! What the hell ya thinkin' driving this close! I can see your truck from way up there on the hill!"

Pole Cat looked out the window and back down the cutline where Max had just come from. He looked back at Max and shook his head again.

"Shit, Max, are you crazy? It's way too fuckin' cold to walk in!"

Max just looked at Pole Cat, unsure what to make of his lazy ass.

"Damn man! You're lucky nobody's keeping an eye out. Otherwise, the cold would be the least of your worries."

Pole Cat didn't answer. He just sighed loudly and repeated his relief. "Fuck, you scared me."

"Well, since you're already here, I might as well join you for a spell. Open up, so I can get warm, will ya?"

Pole Cat nodded reluctantly, as Max walked around the front of the truck. He hit the unlock button, and then quickly started searching for his bottle of whiskey.

As Max opened the door and climbed in, the foul stench immediately overwhelmed him. A mixture of body odor and hard liquor, Max deduced. Also, there was an over-powering smell of cigarettes. Probably a whole lot of farting mixed in, as well.

Max immediately regretted getting in. Battling the cold was much more inviting than fighting the nausea brought on by the putrid, stale air.

"How long have you been here"? Max asked.

Max had to wait until Pole Cat finished another long swig from the bottle. "Two days," he replied with a slight gag and grimace.

That seemed about right, Max surmised, from the musty odors in the cab. "Have you been sitting in here the whole time or did you get in any recon?" Max already knew the answer.

"Nope. Just watching from here and checking the scanner for any talk on the radio waves," Pole Cat said with a nod to the scanner on the dashboard. "Pretty good vantage point, if I do say so myself! I can see that they are drilling at a rate of 10 minutes or so per foot."

Course it's a good vantage point, Max repeated in his head, you practically drove right into their damn camp ya lazy bastard. Max decided to let it go.

"Any idea how deep they are?" he said continuing the conversation.

"Nah. They haven't pulled her out of the hole since I got here. I figure they must be about 9000 feet from the information I got from the scanner and the communication back and forth between the rig and HQ back in the city. But, hey, those pricks might be lyin'."

As Max eyed Bill, he suddenly remembered why they called him Pole Cat. It damn sure wasn't because he was agile or crafty.

The two scouts passed the next hour watching the rig hoping the drill bit would need replacing so the crew would have to pull out of the hole. This would give Max a chance to count the pipe and get a good depth for his client. Max always liked to have an accurate depth when he phoned his client with the first morning report.

As time went by and daylight approached, Max knew he wouldn't be so lucky. He also knew it was time to bid Pole Cat adieu. He knew that unless Pole Cat's scanner was fortunate enough to pick up a morning conversation between the engineer and his bosses, he was going to have to find another place to count the pipe.

The fact that Max was starting to get used to the smell inside the truck was also reason to go.

"All right there, Pole Cat! It's been fun!"

Max threw open the door and immediately put on his extra-thick parka.

"Wait! Where ya go'in?"

"I gotta keep moving. Need to get some information for my client so I can get paid."

"What are you talking about? It's all right here in front of you! We can see everything from here."

"Yeah! Except we can't see the important details!

"It'll happen," snorted Pole Cat. "Just a matter of time."

"As is them seeing you, my friend; all it takes is them to stop what they're doing and take a quick peek to the west. You're sitting here like a naked jailbird. But I appreciate the info! Take care"!

Max shut the door and threw his backpack over his shoulder. With the sky turning a grayish, pink, he jogged toward the closest trees between the truck and the rig. The cold was piercing, but the air refreshing.

When Max reached the forest, he was suddenly overwhelmed by a feeling of relief. He was back in his element and back scouting the way he liked to do things – alone and by his rules. Despite that, he turned around to look back at Pole Cat.

For whatever reason, Max suddenly felt sorry for him. As the sun slowly rose in the east, the run-down Ford idling in the middle of the cutline said it all. Max studied the image for a few seconds and a sense of loneliness and melancholy overwhelmed him.

The feeling was quick and fleeting, however, and in an instant, Max had disappeared into the woods.

If Pole Cat was right and it had been two days of straight drilling, Max knew they'd be changing the drill bit soon. Seeing them "come out of the hole," as they called it would give Max the ideal time to count the pipe sections. Seeing the amount of pipe come up would give Max an accurate depth of their drilling. This was vital information to his clients because they would know how far down they were drilling and in what formation.

In the oil patch, everything was classified by formation. Thanks to time and geology, the earth was segmented in different rock strata. While tilted and uneven, these different strata crisscrossed beneath the ground like layers of a cake. A company could discover oil and gas in a number of different formations, but it was the porous ones that yielded the best results.

Course, the true grand prize for any scout is getting the oil and gas test results for each formation. Certainly, something Max always had his mind on but knew getting it was rare. Sort of like hitting the mother lode when prospecting for gold, Max concluded.

On occasion, this information would leak out in a phone call from the rig, but people were usually not that careless. To get specific details like that for a client, it usually required incredible stealth and patience and occasionally sneaking onto the lease to garner it physically from the engineer's shack. It also took, Max knew in his heart, great timing and dumb luck.

Which was something Max was hoping he would have on this job if the client required that much data? According to Phil, the client owned property just to the southeast and was hoping to find out all they could about the drilling operations, so they could compare it with their own drilling results. Normally if a company was having great results nearby in the same formations, that meant there was great potential for adjacent lands. Course, the opposite was true, as well.

Until Max talked to Phil again, he would hang back and attempt to get a pipe count. That in itself was risky because he needed to get close enough to watch it rise out of the ground. And for that to happen, Max needed a nice vantage point clear of foliage, snow, and other obstructions.

As he searched for the best view through the towering spruce, a big booming sound suddenly interrupted the silence. Max knew what it was right away: it was the intermittent roar of the big Caterpillar, or "Cat" as they called it, in the patch.

Despite the snow, Max quickened his step. He knew things were springing to life at the rig and it was imperative he found the ideal spot to get settled and watch. Sliding to his left, Max was in luck. Between two extra-thick blue spruce trees was a perfect three-foot wide clearing. He could see the rig just a few hundred feet in front of him and was camouflaged on all sides thanks to the thick brush and towering pines.

The snow depth also allowed for him to dig down, creating a nice oval hole to hide his backpack and the mini-scanner. Like a war bunker, Max was ideally covered all the way around. It was the perfect spot to watch the days', and most likely nights', activities unfold.

He placed the four AA batteries inside his scanner and turned it on. Making sure the volume was turned down, he tested the frequencies. Satisfied it was working well and was on a potentially good channel, he reached into his backpack and pulled out a sleeve of crackers. Ritz crackers and cheese were a necessary staple in the world of scouting.

Max took his knife from his belt and reached in and pulled out a nice chunk of Swiss. Carmen thought Swiss had an odd, pungent taste, but it was Max's favorite. He sliced off a piece and placed it between two crackers before throwing the whole thing into his mouth.

He smiled to himself as he ate in silence, staring at the rig hands working laboriously in front of him.

That used to be me, Max mused, concentrating on the derrick man working 120 feet above him. Probably couldn't see me from there with the naked eye, Max deduced, but if the man decided to take a scan with binoculars, things might be different.

This thought caused Max to break off a few branches from the spruce tree and further camouflage himself. He then took out his own scope and lightly placed the tiny tripod on the flat snow surface in front of him. As Max was leveling it and adjusting the focus, he could see they were preparing the rig floor to pull the pipe out of the hole, or "trip" as it is called in the industry.

As someone who spent years working the rigs, Max knew the routine all too well. It was clear they were preparing to pull out and Max sighed loudly with relief. He hadn't missed it and he didn't have to wait two days like Pole Cat.

Black smoke billowed into the cold, crisp air as the powerful Cat engine groaned in an effort to initiate the 9000 feet of pipe skyward. Max had his trusty chrome counter in his hand ready to begin the monotonous clicking that would occur with each 90-foot column of steel.

The hole appeared to be very tight and the tripping process was slower than usual. This was normal, but never fun and Max could tell this was going to be one of those long days. In such monotony, it was easy to fall asleep. Already exhausted from the all-night trip to get to the rig, Max was fighting to stay awake.

An hour into it and they've only pulled 10 stands of pipe, Max exclaimed in his head. Once again the Cat engines bellowed across the vast expanse of forest, as Max continued to watch the long, silver pipe ease skyward.

Max's eyes slowly closed but sprung back open. Again, his heavy eyelids were too difficult to combat and they ever so slowly started to shut. Suddenly, there was a loud shout from the rig and Max was wide-awake. The very loud yell morphed into several anguished shouts of the same nature. What the hell was going on? Max strained to see.

He even risked exposure and stood up to get a better look. Not seeing anything, he reached down and grabbed his scope. Peering through the lens and adjusting as fast as he could, the object of all the chaos came into focus.

Pole Cat.

With no shirt on and stripped down to his underwear, the lazy bastard was being pushed across the rig location like a prisoner of war. Max knelt back down, while still staring through the scope. More and more rig hands came into view. They were all hollering with surprise and joy at the fact that their fellow workers had caught a scout. Even the workers on the rig floor were screaming down with excitement.

One of them gave Pole Cat a hard push and he went flying to the icy ground in what looked like a very painful landing. He tried to get up, but another rig hand kicked him back down. Max could see Pole Cat throw up his hands and muster an innocent, harmless smile.

Reeling on the ground with hands raised, he was desperately trying to plead with them to let him go. It was futile as everyone in camp was having way too much fun. Several more workers came over and Pole Cat was now completely surrounded, as the rest of the roughnecks, looked down at the action with sadistic glee.

Max couldn't hear what they were saying, but they were having a good ol' time. Max heard someone yell "tar and feather the bastard," from up on the rig.

Poor ol' Pole Cat Max thought as he watched him squirming in the icy dirt. He may give scouting a bad name, but nobody deserved this. Max watched as Pole Cat once again tried to get to his feet, but immediately was knocked down again. He was then encircled by the men and disappeared from sight.

Holy shit, Max said to himself, who knows what they were going to do with him? They already removed his clothes in near -20-degree temperatures and now they were toying with him like a mouse.

Up here, what happened to a scout after he is caught is anybody's guess. Some outfits simply escorted them off their property, usually without their equipment and truck, while others held them until the local police arrived and charged them with trespassing or disturbing the peace.

Then, there were those that took the law into their own hands. In such a remote region, the law was whatever and whoever you wanted it to be. Max had heard some pretty gruesome stories of scouts being beaten, arms and legs broken, and left abandoned by the roadside. He also knew of a few who were held captive, tied up and bound in an old outbuilding, until the drilling was done.

Yeah, what happens to a scout up here in the patch if he's caught is truly anybody's guess, Max surmised. In Pole Cat's case, it didn't appear that he was going to get the preferred treatment of being escorted off the property. These men meant to teach him a lesson and Max knew he had to do something.

That meant blowing his cover, and most likely putting an end to the vital information on this job.

"Sorry, Carmen," Max whispered to himself and angrily reached for the 300 magnum propped against the trunk of the spruce.

He pulled out the high-powered rifle and checked it for ammunition. He then got to his feet and started through the snow toward the rig.

It didn't take him very long to make his way onto the permafrost, flat plateau of the drilling site. As he made his last high step over the two-foot snow bank, he could see the rig hands still toying with Pole Cat.

They were taunting him and taking turns kicking him. "Come on guys!" he could hear Pole Cat plead. "I won't tell anybody! Honest! You have my word! Just let me go!"

His begging fell on deaf ears and was answered with perverse laughter. Suddenly, someone on the rig spotted Max and screamed. "Hey! There's another one! "Behind You!"

It took the men a few seconds to hear the loud shouting over their merriment, but eventually they turned and looked right at Max. Max quickly raised his rifle and pointed it at them.

"All right, fellas! You had your fun, now let him go." Max tried to remain calm as he took aim at the men. They simply stared back at him; some with concern, others with amusement.

One of them closest to Max took a step toward him. "Oh, look what we have here, another scout coming to the rescue. Now ain't that sweet."

The rest of the men stepped away from Pole Cat and all stared at Max. Max said nothing and continued to point his gun right at the men. The one closest to him took another step toward him and let out a hollow laugh as he glanced around at his co-workers.

"What are you going to do? Shoot all of us?" he said confidently.

Max quickly pointed the rifle right at his head. "No. Just you," he replied coolly.

This caused the man to stop. He could see Max meant business and the quiet, daunting way he held the rifle told him Max knew how to use it. The two stared at each other in silence for what seemed an eternity.

Suddenly, a loud, terrified shout rang out.

"Everyone get out! Get out!"

The scream was quickly followed by a loud rumbling sound that shook the ground. Everyone turned to look back at the rig. Max lowered his rifle and looked on in horror.

"Out! Everyone Out!" someone screamed.

All the workers on the rig started running down the stairs toward the ground as the earth shook even harder. Workers were running for their lives as the pipe soared skyward in what looked like spaghetti spiraling onto the location in a twisted, lethal nest of steel. Two workers tried to run down the stairs but were sent flying through the air by hurling metal.

The entire rig started to break apart and huge sections came crashing to the ground. The ghastly screams were gut-wrenching.

"Oh, Dear God," Max said, as he watched with wide eyes and mouth agape. As everyone ran for safety, Max could see Pole Cat lying motionless on the ground with hands still in the air. It was an odd scene among all the chaos.

As the grisly sights and sounds echoed throughout the forest, another sound caught Max's attention. It was the sound of running engines. A whole new horror befell him.

"Shit! The engines! You need to shut off the engines!" He yelled it so everyone could hear him. Nobody did.

Max dropped his rifle and ran for the rig. He knew that in the case of emergency, the engines were supposed to shut down automatically to prevent gas from igniting. Hearing those engines meant that didn't happen and all the flammable gas surging to the surface was now free to ignite.

Max ran across the icy ground toward the bank of big Cat engines. But before he could get halfway there, he was knocked off his feet and sent flying backward.

The explosion was deafening and Max found himself on his back with an extremely loud and painful ringing in his ears. He lied there motionless staring straight up at a massive torch shooting 300 feet into the sky. The orange and yellow contrast; against the morning light and pale blue sky were beautiful and hypnotic, Max thought. He stared at it in wonderment and confusion as the ringing continued to roar in his ears.

The throbbing ache slowly began to fade and was replaced by low, muffled sounds of screaming. His moaning quickly turned into louder, shouts of fear and Max suddenly realized, again, what was happening.

As fast as his body would let him, he climbed to his feet and stared off toward the nearby rig. It was completely engulfed in flames.

Max had been involved in a blowout only once before. He looked across the yard at the chaos and knew someone had really screwed up. At the far end of camp, Max spotted a few of the rig hands at the water truck desperately trying to unravel the hose.

It was futile, Max knew, as the water would do nothing against the huge flame of natural gas spewing straight toward the heavens. But he couldn't help but admire their bravery and efforts. Just to his left and slightly in front of him, Max again spotted Pole Cat. He was in the same position on the ground as he was before the explosion and he still had his hands up. He shouted over to him.

"POLE CAT! You OK?"

Pole Cat didn't respond. He simply laid there on the ground, staring at the burning rig.

"Bill! Are you hurt!" he repeated.

With an odd, dumbfounded look on his face, he slowly turned to Max. Must be in shock, Max deduced.

"You OK?"

"Yeah…Yeah…I think so," he finally answered slowly.

Pole Cat put his hands down and started to climb to his feet. Just then, there was a loud cracking sound and the ground began to shake. Starting at the rig, tiny fissures started forming in every direction.

Max looked at the cracks emerge in the ground. He quickly turned to Pole Cat. "We need to get outta here! The whole place may blow!"

Just as Pole Cat got to his feet, Max looked across the yard and saw a lone pickup truck trying to flee the scene. As it zoomed by the rig, a fairly large crack in the ground opened up right in front of it. In an instant, a clear, but visible gush of natural gas shot into the air.

The truck didn't have a chance. The second the gas hit the hot metal engine, it ignited. The explosion sent the truck high into the air and it came crashing to the ground cab-side down.

"Pole Cat, Help me out!"

With no time to waste, Max rushed to the truck. The front end was a giant fireball and Max knew it was only seconds before it would reach the gas tank. Taking off his thick parka, Max glanced to his right expecting to see Pole Cat alongside him. Instead, as he wrapped his hands inside the parka, he saw the chubby, mostly naked body of his fellow scout running away into the woods.

"Typical." It was all Max could muster, as he reached out with his thick parka to pull on the singed door handle.

It took several attempts before he was able to open the door and it took a huge yank to get the partially melted door open enough to get the driver out. Gagging at the smoke and attempting to keep his face away from the searing heat, Max blindly reached in and grabbed the driver.

He was forced to pull him by his rugged flannel collar, but it worked. With both hands, Max was able to get him out of the cab and onto the ground. Fortunately, he was the only one in the truck.

Max threw his parka to the side and dragged the man away from the truck as fast as his adrenalin strength and the friction of the ground allowed. With all his might, he kept pulling. Then, all of a sudden, the gas tank exploded.

Max was once again knocked off his feet, but this time he hit hard on the cheeks of his ass.

Sitting there in a daze, Max watched what was left of the truck somersault in the air and land right where it started in one giant fireball. He watched the flames for a few seconds, trying to catch his breath; he then turned his attention to the man in front of him.

He quickly dragged him off the drilling surface and safely away to a nearby snow bank. He turned and knelt down beside him. He was unconscious and his clothes and face were jet black from the smoke, but he was breathing. Yes, Max thought, he was alive!

A feeling of elation came over him as he saw the man slowly move. All right! Max smiled. The man slowly opened his eyes and looked up at Max. He tried to say something, but Max could not make it out.

Just then, he heard shouts from behind him.

"Hey! Over there! It's Sampson!" Max turned around to see three guys bearing down on him. Just as they all ran up, Max stepped to the side.

"Sampson! Can you hear me?" one of them asked.

"Is he alive? Is he OK," asked another.

"Yeah. He's alive. He's alive!"

As the two looked him over the third man, hunched over Sampson, looked over at Max. "Dude! You saved his life."

Max didn't say anything. He was too tired and disoriented. He looked back down at the man as the three men continued to care for him. The man's eyes slowly turned toward Max again, as the others stared at him in jubilation.

As they did, one of them suddenly got curious.

"Hey! Who the hell are you"? he asked, turning around.
He never did receive an answer. Max was gone.

CHAPTER THREE

Al Wallace sat behind his big oak desk staring at a newspaper in his hands. One article along the side panel of The New York Times was of special interest to him. The headline read: "OPEC to cut supplies drastically, US scrambles to find new sources." The sub-headline read: "Radical Islamic Terrorists Threaten Oil Fields in the Middle East."

As president of Zephyr Petroleum, Al had threatened to retire every day for the last two years, but even at the age of 70 his love for the industry and the company was too great to walk away. After donating fifty years of his life, just the thought of leaving was too emotional.

Despite climbing the corporate ladder to the top, Al always referred to himself as, "just a rig hand." Since he had started rough-necking at the age of 18, it was ingrained into him. At age 20, he had gone to work for Zephyr organizing rig crews. His intelligence and ingenuity quickly led him out of the fields and into the boardroom. It didn't take too long until he was part of the management team, and then president.

Today, he was considered by many, as one of the shrewdest executives in the oil business. Even so, Zephyr had fallen on hard times of late. All oil companies were under serious threat thanks to an overabundance of international oil supplies and the extra-low prices.

Zephyr, however, was worse off than the rest. While most multi-national oil companies went into protective mode due to unfavorable market conditions, Zephyr decided it would take a giant risk and expand operations. The thought by Al and management was, the down market would quickly rebound, but that didn't happen and the strategy had backfired. The result of which was leaving scores of drilling rigs high and dry across the globe.

The industry leader for the past sixty years, Zephyr now had only two offices open, company headquarters in Houston, where Al worked, and in Calgary, Alberta, also known as "the oil capital of the north."

With several board members calling for his resignation, Al was determined to save Zephyr from the brink of bankruptcy.

As the silver-haired executive sat at his desk with the hot Texas sun warming his back, he continued to stare at the newspaper. A slight wry smile emerged on his concerned face. He threw the newspaper onto his desk and sighed.

He took a moment before leaning forward in his chair to peruse all the geological data on his desk. He eyed the material closely, then picked up one piece of paper from his geologists in northern Alberta.

If a huge discovery was to be found, and the company rescued, this was the region that was going to do it, thought Al. Since the area was synonymous with huge oil reserves and had been void of any serious exploration in the past fifteen years due to environmental restrictions put in by the Canadian government, it was ripe for the picking.

Al decided to get more input from his local geological staff, so he leaned over and hit the intercom on his phone.

"Hey, Sally! Can you get Moe on the horn and tell him I'd like to see him?"

Al leaned back in his chair and waited. "Right away, Mr. Wallace," came the reply through the speaker.

Moe Hamilton had been with Zephyr for 15 years. He was a damn good engineer, Al thought. The only drawback was his lack of experience and knowledge of the oil fields of Canada. Shit, Al said in his head, oil is oil. He would bounce it off of Moe and his staff, anyway. Time was of the essence!

Al looked at his watch. It was Friday morning 10 A.M. his time. That meant it was 8 A.M. in Calgary. He leaned forward and picked up his phone.

Roger White had just put the key in the lock when he heard the phone ringing through the office door.

"Shit!" he said aloud as he scrambled to get the door unlocked. He finally pushed the door open, but as he did the tiny cigar stub in his mouth fell to the carpet. Knowing the call may be important, Roger simply looked back at the butt burning on the carpet. He continued passed the receptionist's desk and straight into his nearby office.

"Hello, hello, Zephyr Petroleum," Roger said breathing heavily.

"Hello, Roger, this is your old buddy Al in Houston. What's happening? You sound, out of breath."

"Uh, hang on one second will ya, Al? Dropped my cigar on the carpet and it's burning a damn hole on the floor."

Roger didn't wait for a reply and quickly put the phone on the desk and jogged over to get his stub. He picked it up and inspected the damage. A tiny black hole in the carpet, no big deal, he thought. He blew on the stub and put it back in his mouth, as he casually walked back into his office.

"Okay, got it," he said into the phone "Sorry bout that!"

"That's all right," Al replied. "Hell you feel plumb naked without that stub in your mouth, don't you?"

Roger chuckled. "It's a little too early in the morning to be talking about my naked body there Al. Now if I were a hot young coed that might be a different story."

The two shared a quick, little laugh.

"That may be true, there Roger. At any rate, this isn't a social call," Al said, suddenly changing his tone. "Your geological group sent us information on all areas it thought had the potential to be an elephant up there in northern Canada and, well, we got our eyes on one in particular."

"Oh really, which one catches your fancy, Al?" Roger replied with anticipation.

There was a long pause. Roger wasn't sure if Al needed to look up the information again or if he was stalling for effect.

"Wolverine Hills," finally came the calm, collective answer.

Now it was Roger's time to be silent. The shock of it left him speechless for a few seconds.

"Are you kidding me, Al?" It was all he could muster.

"Why would you think I'm kidding, Roger?" Al asked with a bit of annoyance.

Roger was silent, but his mind was racing.

"It's just that we thought for sure you'd reject it. Out of all the plays we sent you, that is the one we believe has the most potential, but there's just so much baggage that comes with it."

"What do you mean"? came the quick retort.

"Well, first and foremost, I highly doubt the government will ever let us drill there. We've tried for years and they've turned us down each time! Not even as much as a hearing thanks to all those environmentalists!"

Roger paused before quickly starting again.

"And second of all, the terrain up there is extremely rough. Lots of steep gorges and cliffs, it would be a pain in the ass, not to mention a ton of money, just to get in there. Also, we'll need special drilling equipment because if memory serves me correctly all our seismic data says the best potential for a big oil discovery is in the Granit Wash formation. Course, the data is like 20 years old."

Roger eagerly awaited Al's response to his thoughts. He had to wait a few seconds as Al pondered what he just heard. With each passing second, Roger got more and more nervous.

"Look, Roger. We know all that. I have the report right in front of me," Al finally said. "You let me worry about what we need to do to get the drilling done, you just make sure we get the OK to drill! Got that?"

Roger was quiet. He was letting the direction from his boss settle in.

"Um! sure, Al." You're the boss! But if I may say, I wouldn't get my hopes up. We've tried getting the Energy Board to put a Wolverine Hills parcel up for a land sale like a dozen times in the past and we've been turned down each time. Not even a hearing."

"Well, we're going to try one more time," came the slow, but very assured response.

Roger was dumbfounded. He shook his head to himself.

"If you say, so, but I'm telling you right now it's a waste of time. The Energy Resources Conservation Board will never go for it! Not a chance in hell!"

"Well, Roger," Al replied. "We may be close to hell, but I think our luck is about to change."

Roger stood there, speechless. He wasn't sure what Al meant by that or why he was so confident. It didn't matter, as Al was his boss and it was obvious, he was determined to get an answer.

"You're one of the good ole' boys up there, you get a hold of someone on that Energy Board and you do what you have to to get the deal done, got it? I'm thinking you'll have better results this time around with all that is happening in the Middle East."

Roger still couldn't muster a response. It didn't matter, as Al didn't give him a chance.

"All right thanks there Roger! Talk to you soon!" And with that Al hung up.

Roger stood there, behind his desk, holding the phone in his hand. All that Al had said was too much to digest in one quick phone call. He was racking his brain as he stared out the window rolling his cigar stub side to side in his mouth.

He slowly hung up the phone but continued to stare out the window. How on earth was he going to get that land posted? It's been pretty much off limits for years thanks to all those eco-freaks out there trying to save the grizzly bear, salmon, spotted owl, three-toed fuzzy-navel banana slug, whatever stupid reason they could come up with, Roger concluded.

He slowly plopped into his chair, still deep in thought. Al wanted him to check in with the Energy Board, but that would be a waste of time. Typical bureaucrat jackasses with egos much larger than their dicks, Roger thought.

As he sat there pondering, he heard his secretary come in through the front door. His head slowly moved toward the open door as he listened to her plop her stuff on the desk.

"Morning, Shelley! I see you are in early," he yelled sarcastically.

Roger looked at his watch. 8:22 am. She was supposed to be at work at 8 am sharp. In fact, she was the one who should have been answering the damn phone, not him. Nearly cost him one of his prized cigar stubs, he thought. Not to mention a damn carpet!

"Hey!" he began again. "Once you get that cute, tight ass of yours all settled in, do me a favor will ya? Get me the Energy Minister's phone number at the Capital in Edmonton!"

Shelly Thompson shook her head with disgust, as she reached over to the corner of the desk and started twirling the Rolodex.

Such a chauvinist ass, she thought, as she zeroed in on the contact card. She plucked the card out and walked it into Roger's office.

"Here you go, sir," she said politely, placing it on the desk right in front of him. He smiled and nodded at her as she placed it down. She mustered a half smile back. As she turned and walked back out, Roger concentrated on her tight young ass. A big smile came on his face, nice he thought.

"Close the door behind ya, will ya honey? Try not to hit that great-looking ass on your way out."

Shelly said nothing; she just rolled her eyes and grimaced. Why she put up with Roger's bullshit, she didn't know. Probably because it was so hard to find work in the industry downturn, she concluded.

After watching the door close, Roger's smile disappeared. His countenance suddenly went serious. With determination, he picked up the card with one hand and the phone with the other.

"Here goes nothing," he said aloud as he punched in the number.

"Hello. Mr. Handy's office," came the voice on the other end.

"Hello there, sweetie! Name's Roger. Roger White. I'm president of the exploration department over here at Zephyr Petroleum. I'm sure you've heard of us. I need to speak to the Energy Minister right away."

There was a brief silence before the reply came. "I'm sorry. Who did you say you were?"

The question irked Roger. He shook his head and muttered to himself. "Just tell your boss it's Roger White! He knows who the hell I am."

Roger could hear the annoyance of the woman through the phone. He chewed hard on his cigar stub, as he waited anxiously for her response.

"Please hold," came the cold, direct answer.

Roger looked at the clock on his wall. It had been nearly five minutes since she put him on hold. Probably hasn't even told the minister he was waiting on the line, Roger thought. Probably getting him back for that 'boss' comment. It didn't help, too, that the music playing was some irritating roaring 20s-style blend of operetta and jazz. It made him more irked and uneasy.

The silence was finally broken. "Hello, this is Mr. Handy. How can I help you?"

"Hey there, Mike! It's Roger over at Zephyr. How are you doing today?

Roger took a deep breath and waited for the typical indifferent reply that always came with a call to the Alberta government. They knew he only checked in with them when he needed something and each time his inquiries were met with the same vexed attitude given to any unwanted solicitor.

"Oh! Hi there Roger! Your ears must have been burning."

The semi-energetic, positive response was a huge surprise. He wasn't sure how to answer. He was all prepared to make a quick, solid sales pitch before being dismissed for other business. He fumbled to find the right words.

"Um, uh. I'm not following," he replied.

"Your ears. We were all just talking about Zephyr and the other oil companies in our area since we are in deep discussion about opening up new areas for exploration."

"You are"? came the slow, baffling question.

Roger couldn't believe what he just heard. He also couldn't believe he had just questioned the opening of new lands for potential drilling. It was usually he who was demanding, prompting, and essentially pleading for this sort of political action.

Yet, here it was, served up to him on a silver platter. It was an odd feeling, one that Roger had not felt in his 30 years working in the industry.

As he sat there speechless, Mr. Handy continued.

"Yeah. As you are well aware, oil imports to North America are going to be drastically reduced. OPEC has voted to cut ties with the West due to its support for Israel and Assad has turned his terrorists loose for the same reason. I really don't know all of OPEC's reasons and quite frankly I really don't care, it's happening and therefore we may have an oil crisis on our hands. Simply put, we have got to stay ahead of this situation!"

Roger was completely awe-struck. Those were the exact words that have come from his mouth each and every time he talked to the Energy Board. And every time they rebuffed him and accused him of being melodramatic! And now they were telling him! Now that's irony, Roger surmised.

"Well, yeah! I've been saying that for years! I..." Roger stopped. He knew it wasn't the time to say "I told you so." It was time to stay level headed and just go with this incredible, unbelievable new flow.

"Um. At any rate, I totally agree. And, of course, we at Zephyr are here to help any way we can."

"Of course you are," said the Energy Minister with a laugh. "Now, we are going to have an emergency meeting in the coming days. But now that I have you on the line, are there any regions, in particular, you wanted to discuss? I'm assuming that is why you are calling?"

Roger was still in a state of shock. This was by far the easiest, most agreeable call he has ever made to the Energy Board. He thought about pinching himself to make sure he was not dreaming.

"Um, uh, yeah! Yeah, it is," he said fumbling for the right words. "And we have the ideal location that can solve all our energy needs. You know that wilderness area up there south of Grand Prairie, the one called Wolverine Hills? We are hoping to get a 120-day land posting on it."

"You mean you want the minerals posted for sale, right"? came the correct, by-the-book question.

"Yep! That's right! Down to include the Granit Wash," he replied as he anxiously mashed the cigar between his mandibles.

There was a pause as Mr. Handy mulled it over.

"All right, let me write that down. I know that is currently designated as a protected area, but everything is on the table right now."

There was another long pause as Roger could hear him writing down information and moving around papers. "OK, Anywhere else?"

In all his days, Roger had never been asked to list regions he'd like to drill. It was either responding to the slim offerings the government put up for land sale or it was he futilely requesting specific regions that never opened up.

Yet, now, it was happening – an open invitation to choose any region he wanted. He had often dreamed and joked of scenarios this easy. He was overwhelmed with a feeling of elation. It was like a boy in an ice cream parlor checking out all the different flavors he can choose from. Roger couldn't help but smile.

The smile quickly faded. Like the ice cream parlor, he knew you can only pick one, and Al had his sights on Wolverine Hills. Best not to screw with his boss' wishes.

"No," he said with a feeling of regret. "That's it. Just Wolverine Hills."

Roger knew there were other areas that could be the "elephant" that Zephyr was looking for, so he felt a bit of a failure for not requesting more. Probably nice, too, to have backups in case Wolverine Hills is not approved, he thought.

Still, he opted to stick with the one. Those were his marching orders and best to do what he's told. To help ensure this request was approved, Roger attempted to sell this play some more.

"It was from 20 years ago, but our geological data shows that Wolverine Hills is extremely promising," Roger said, half talking just trying to convince himself this was really happening. "Should be very good for all of us!"

"Yeah, that could be true, Roger," Mr. Handy said half-listening, half writing down information. "OK! Give me two days."

With that, he hung up and for the second time that morning Roger was left holding the phone in amazement. What had just happened? Why was it so easy? Al was right, he suddenly thought.

This time was different. Roger's shock faded into a state of happiness. It was a feeling he hadn't felt in a long time; a feeling nobody at Zephyr had felt for a few years.

Suddenly, he was also confused and a bit angry. He was the one that told people how this industry worked and why it was vital to drill. He was always the one in charge.

Roger shrugged. Who gives a shit, he thought to himself, they were going to drill in Wolverine Hills! And Roger was going to be in charge of it!

CHAPTER FOUR

At the offices of Black Gold Resources on 6th Ave in downtown Calgary, the staff had gathered for its weekly morning exploration meeting.

The offices of Black Gold were scaled back to only the necessities and were operated by a skeletal staff of its former start-up days. Like so many other small resource companies, Black Gold had great expectations of making it big in the oil industry.

The staff consisted of former employees who became expendable in the eyes of management when two of the biggest Canadian oil companies merged. Rather than try to find a job with another natural resource entity or change professions, the group of engineers, geologists, and accountants decided to pool their funds and skills together to start their own outfit.

Out of the ashes of the massive layoffs that took place in the region three years ago, rose Black Gold Resources.

At its origins, Black Gold had thirty employees. Today, twenty of those employees had moved on. Because the conditions were so bleak, a few went back to school vowing to learn a trade that was as far away from the oil industry as possible.

Headed by a soft-spoken geologist, Wayne Stadwell, only ten full-time employees remained. Wayne had short blond hair, light blue eyes, and a tight smile that was merely a straight line across his face. The smile was deceiving. Behind the quiet, conservative demeanor was an extremely intense, competitive man who was willing to go down with the "ship" if necessary.

At the age of 45, Wayne had mortgaged everything he had and put it all into Black Gold. He simply could not afford to fail and he tried to convey that same sense of commitment each and every day.

The mood of the meeting was highly charged with excitement; a rare sight to see of late. Everyone was buzzing over the recent news – the Energy Board had recently put up a new area for lease: Wolverine Hills.

"OK," Wayne started, "let's get down to business. First of all, does anyone know why on earth they posted Wolverine Hills for sale? I mean, out of all locations in all of northern Canada, why this one? Why now?"

Joe piped up. "Not sure, but who cares? The fact that they chose a land parcel right next to our own land is a God send!"

Everyone at the table nodded in excited agreement. Everyone that is, but the grumbler Gerry Flanders.

"Well, it's not a God send yet! Not until winning the bid," he jeered. This pessimistic attitude was typical of Gerry and the fellow employees let it go as if they didn't hear him.

The 47-year-old geophysicists always showed up with his own brand of sarcasm and sour sense of humor. He had been with Black Gold for two years and never appeared to be satisfied with his decision to join the small outfit.

The staff at Black Gold had been working on the Wolverine Hills play since it was founded, but like all others really did nothing about it due to the strict environmental regulations and the fact that there were other, more accessible drilling prospects to go after.

But, deep in his heart, Wolverine Hills was the number one place Wayne wanted to drill. Unbeknownst to his colleagues, he deemed it "his baby."

He had a vision of a huge discovery in that region ever since he led an exploration team for his former company, Oilcom. That was ten years ago when he was just a young buck working as part of a survey team. When he was suddenly let go three years ago, it was the first thing that came to mind.

There were both good and bad things that came from his time at Oilcom. While some of his current colleagues would disagree, the one good thing was his knowledge and familiarity of Wolverine Hills. He knew there were vast riches hiding deep down in that terra firma.

That is why his first move as head of Black Gold was to purchase land adjacent to it in the hopes that one day the Energy Resources Board would open it up for drilling.

Since it had always been considered a protected area due to its rugged terrain, dense thick forests, and bounty of wildlife, many did not understand his passion or his desire to make this the first purchase as president of Black Gold. Not only was there little geological or seismic data to base the purchase on, but also it butted up against an area some thought would never be leased for oil and gas exploration.

It certainly was a tough sell to management at Black Gold at the time, and Wayne could remember the angry debate that ensued as if it were yesterday. Despite all that, Wayne was able to convince enough people to get the deal done. At the time, he thought he had made a real coupe, but so far it had only been expenditure with zero revenue.

He certainly took a lot of flak for it over the years, too, especially after Gerry came on board. It was his decision and all the risk lay on his shoulders. Because Black Gold was eking out revenue in other sites, the razzing mostly came in sarcastic, passive-aggressive comments.

But all of that was coming to an end, today, Wayne knew. His gamble could now pay huge dividends for the company. A slight smile fell onto Wayne's face as he looked across the table at everyone.

"OK!" Wayne said abruptly. "As you are all very well aware, we have a huge advantage over all other oil companies when it comes to Wolverine Hills since we own land right next to it. This allows us to drill on our land to test if there is anything indeed down there. This is exactly why we, as a company, decided to purchase this parcel in the first place."

Wayne emphasized the word "we" and "company" to give everyone credit for this intelligent forward-thinking. He knew where the credit truly lied, but as a leader, it was important not to gloat and to build camaraderie and a sense of teamwork.

"As our geological data shows us, there could be some really big oil reserves in this area, so we are definitely serious about putting a bid in to lease these lands and acquire the mineral rights."

Wayne paused to make sure everyone was listening and clearly understood what he was saying.

"But, to make sure the preliminary data and our gut instincts are correct, we want to drill as close to the Wolverine Hills boundary as possible. That means drilling a well on our property as soon as possible."

Wayne again emphasized the phrase "our gut" to again give off a sense of unity. He nodded to everyone before turning straight to Gerry.

"Gerry. I need you to get all the seismic data you can get your hands on and pick the best place to drill. I certainly have some valuable information in my files that I will forward you."

"Sure," he said casually, half listening.

"Good. Get me your results in three days."

With that, Gerry let out a huge gasp of disapproval. Before he could complain, Wayne shut him down. "I don't want to hear it, Gerry! We don't have the time. Just get it done."

As Gerry continued to mumble disapprovingly, Wayne turned to Joe Swanson on the other side of the table. "Joe! I need you to find me a drilling rig, one that is capable of going down to say…14,000 to 15,000 feet!"

Always the positive dutiful one, Joe simply nodded as he took notes.

"That's pretty tall order, Wayne, but you got it!"

Wayne simply acknowledged his concern with a nod as he scanned everyone's faces.

"All right people! The way I see it, this is boom or bust time for us! You all know what we're up against. We've got 120 days to get a license approved, build a lease, and drill a well to test what's down there. That is all the time we have before we must submit our bid to tie-up the mineral rights."

Wayne paused again to ensure they understood the situation. He slowly and purposely studied each and everyone's face.

"OK! Let's get to work people!" he abruptly said.

With that, he smiled and nodded as everyone anxiously rose to his and her feet and energetically headed out the door. As usual, Gerry was slower and less enthralled than the rest. Wayne watched him closely, as he finally waddled his rotund body out the conference room doorway.

Wayne leaned back in his chair and enjoyed the solace of the empty room. His slight smile slowly gave way to a more serious countenance.

Normally, at their weekly meetings, they discussed finances. Seeing how the atmosphere was finally electric with excitement and anticipation, he opted to cut the meeting short and not broach the subject. Wayne knew that while Wolverine Hills would most likely result in a huge discovery, which could quite possibly save the company. If this latest venture failed, it would mean the end of Black Gold.

That realization took some steam out of his enjoyment.

There are no guarantees in this business and there are a lot of risks, Wayne knew. The entire bidding process alone was enough to scare most people away. Not only is it blind, meaning you have no idea what another company offered to lease the land, but you can spend millions of dollars just getting a rig up to drill to the formations to garner the vital data necessary to make a bid. A bid you more often than not, lost.

Shit, Wayne thought, even if you're lucky enough to win a bid, there is the chance there are not enough hydrocarbon reserves in the ground to offset the expenses. In this business, we are essentially high-stakes gamblers, Wayne surmised, as he leaned back in his chair, staring up at the ceiling.

The fact that Black Gold was about to embark on this precarious venture; sent a quick, cold chill down his spine. He suddenly shook his head to clear his mind and leaned forward in his chair. "Stay positive, Wayne," he murmured to himself.

He turned his focus back to the meeting. The excitement in the room was certainly refreshing; a sight for sore eyes, indeed. It was important to keep that energy going, Wayne concluded, and to do that he needed to focus on one thing: financing.

Getting into that rugged region and setting up a drilling rig, one that had the ability to go down to 14,000 feet was not going to be easy – or cheap.

In fact, it was going to be far more money than Black Gold currently had available. That meant he needed to find an investor.

This caused Wayne to lean forward in his chair. He perused all the paperwork in front of him. Looking at the information disseminated by the Energy Board in Alberta, Wayne could see that the block of land posted for sale included 48 sections and totaled in excess of 30,000 acres.

In the government land-leasing world, that was a lot of land to put up for bid. A whole shit load of land, Wayne thought. He sure wished they had posted a much smaller, more affordable size.

Why would they put up so much land? Wayne understood the dire situation the world was about to face thanks to OPEC's decision to play hardball, but still, this was far greater an area than he had seen. As he sat there pondering, the answer suddenly came to him.

It was to weed out the smaller players, such as Black Gold, and ensure only the bigger, well-established oil companies put in a bid.

"Things keep getting better and better," he said sarcastically to himself, as he grabbed a calculator.

He knew that if the geology held true, as it should, a formation could hold a substantial oil and gas reserve for miles in both directions.

Quickly, Wayne started pounding at numbers on the calculator in front of him.

"Thirty thousand acres at, say, $250 per acre," Wayne said as he hit the equals sign. "$7.5 million!"

He leaned back in his chair and let out a pensive sigh. He knew a bid at $250 per acre was conservative and it still came to $7.5 million. That was a lot of money to any company, especially his. Wayne also realized it was going to cost them a lot more just to get in there to set up a rig and clear roads for access.

This caused him to return to the calculator and punch more numbers. He did this frantically, then stopped and stared at the number. He was concerned and it looked as if he was perspiring. He leaned back in his chair once again and resumed staring at the ceiling.

We are going to have to come up with a shit load of money if we are to pull this off. The thought echoed in his head over and over again.

Wayne was guessing, but he estimated Black Gold's net worth to be about $8.5 million. That included roughly $700,000 in cash. He also knew that the company's line of credit was in the neighborhood of $2 million.

Small potatoes in the oil patch, Wayne acknowledged. As he sat there deep in thought, Joe suddenly burst into the room.

"Wayne! You are never going to guess what's happening!" Joe was red in the face and looked exhausted.

"Simmer down now, Joe. Just take it easy," Wayne said. "I'm sure whatever it is, it's all going to work out."

Joe looked at Wayne and did start to settle down. Wayne's cool, collective demeanor always had a calming effect on Joe.

"I started calling on drilling companies, per your request, and none of them have a rig we can use! I mean none!"

Wayne looked at Joe, as he processed the news. "OK, well, that is to be expected given our short notice."

Joe was still trying to remain calm, but his chest was heaving in and out.

"I agree Wayne, but there's something else going on! The first two I called said they couldn't help. I mean didn't even discuss it. And the third one said they couldn't come up with one either! "Hell, I know they didn't even bother to check inventory!"

Wayne simply replied with a "Hmm," as he knew Joe was to continue.

"I tell ya Wayne, there's something fishy going on here! I'm sure of it!"

Wayne sat quietly. He agreed something didn't seem right with all the short, curt responses. Black Gold was certainly a small player in the province of Alberta, but they had a good reputation and always found the equipment necessary to get the job done.

"All right Joe, have you tried R&R Drilling? We've used them on a couple of holes and always paid our bills on time. They should want to help us."

"Already tried," came the quick response. "They've fallen on hard times and have been selling off their equipment just to survive."

"OK, what about Comanche Drilling? We've done some great business with them," came the calm reply.

"They were the second company I called. Told me they don't have anything that can go down that deep."

Wayne had no reply and thought about it some more.

"There are only like 10 companies that I know of that have drilling equipment to go down 14,000 feet, Wayne. There aren't many left that I can call on."

Wayne nodded, still seeing that Joe was clearly upset and overly concerned. "I wonder if we have time to look south of the border for a rig?" he said aloud, even though it was more of an inner-thought.

"Not possible! Wouldn't be enough time to get a rig brokered and sent up here fast enough," Joe quickly retorted.

Wayne took a deep breath and mulled it over. He finally leaned forward in his chair and stood up.

"Well, Joe, it's your baby! I'm sure you'll find a rig somewhere."

"Damn it, Wayne! I'm telling you we can't get one in time!"

Wayne stopped gathering up his papers on the table, and turned and looked Joe straight in the eyes.

"Don't can't me!" he snapped. "The only can't around here is if you can't cut it, you can't work here. This is a small problem, Joe; please show me you have the grit and experience to handle it."

The sudden change of moods startled Joe. It wasn't like Wayne to lose his cool or to bark at his employees. He was the consummate leader; the level-headed, mild-mannered commander-in-chief. He was the one guy everyone looked up to and looked to for support and guidance.

"Sure Wayne. I will," replied Joe rather sheepishly. "But I'm telling you something stinks out there."

"Take an early lunch, Joe," Wayne said with a sigh, knowing it wasn't very wise or nice to show his annoyance in such a manner. "Maybe that will clear your head and you can get back at it this afternoon."

Joe nodded and turned to leave. Just then the phone on the table began to ring. Wayne reached over and hit the intercom button.

"Yes, Connie, go ahead."

"Hello, sir! Is Joe in there with you? I thought I saw him go in."

"Yeah, he's here," Wayne said, turning to make sure Joe was still nearby.

"What's up?" Wayne motioned Joe back into the room.

"I have a Riley from Sonoran Drilling on the line. Says it's urgent and wants to speak with you and Joe." Joe looked at Wayne with surprise as he stepped up next to him.

"OK. Put him through," Wayne replied, as the two waited anxiously to hear what he had to say.

"Wayne Stadwell here. Is that you Riley?"

"Yeah, it's me, Wayne."

"Good. I have Joe here, as well. What can we do for ya"?

"Hey Joe, I know I just talked to you about a rig, but I…"

"You changed your mind, after all"? Joe quickly interrupted with excitement.

"No, not really, I called to tell you all something kinda odd that just happened."

Joe and Wayne just looked at each other with curiosity and confusion.

"I got a call from management over at Zephyr."

"OK. But what's that got to do with us"? Joe asked.

"Joe, what they want is to tie up all our deep hole rigs for the next three months! Offered to pay us $2,000 a day, per rig, just to let our rigs sit in the yard."

"Riley, what the hell you telling us"? quipped a suddenly angry Wayne.

"What I'm saying is I think Zephyr may be trying to corner the market on rigs so nobody else can drill!"

"I knew it," cried Joe, as he immediately started a nervous pace around the room.

"That's impossible, Riley, nobody's going to go for that," said Wayne as the pigment in his face slowly turned more crimson.

"I could be wrong about that, of course. How many rigs did you secure today"?

Wayne and Joe didn't answer Riley. They just looked at each knowing he was right.

"Those bastards!" screeched Joe, as he continued his aimless roam.

Wayne watched Joe in silence desperately trying to assess the dreaded situation. Suddenly, Riley broke the silence.

"Listen, guys. My guess is you want to drill a well on your property next to Wolverine Hills, am I right?"

Wayne glanced at Joe, as he suddenly stopped and looked at his boss.

"Yeah, Yeah, we do, Riley. How'd you know"?

"Well, they just opened up the new territory, to which you guys have an adjacent plot, and you are looking for deep-well drilling equipment. It doesn't take a rocket scientist to figure that one out, Wayne."

Wayne chuckled to himself and nodded toward the phone. Riley started back up before anybody could comment.

"Look! You both know we're straight shooters here at Sonoran. This is a small community, all our kids go to school together, and we all have BBQs, sports, and just hang out together throughout the year. I sure as hell ain't gonna just sit back and let those assholes at Zephyr run everyone out of town! Hell, we could be next! It's just not fair or right!"

Joe had stopped pacing and with both hands on the table was staring down at the phone. Again, Riley started where he left off.

"Joe, I know I told you I couldn't get you a rig put together in time, and that may still be the case, but if you guys want to go with Sonoran, I'll give it my best effort and scavenge everything I can fuckin' find to try put a decent rig together for ya."

Wayne and Joe looked at each other and both couldn't help but let out a slow, but confident smile.

"That's great, Riley, That's just great!" Wayne commented, still leaning over the phone.

"There is one condition, however," Riley added.

"What's that"? Wayne answered cautiously.

"If this play is successful and you win the bid, you promise to give Sonoran first crack at future drilling and back us at the bank if we need more rigs to keep up with the demand."

The smile on Wayne's face grew even wider. "You got a deal, Riley."

"Great! All right, gentlemen! I'll see ya later! I've got a rig to put together!" said an excited Riley.

"Thanks, Riley!" Joe and Wayne said in unison.

Wayne hit the button on the intercom to hang up. He then stood up and took a deep sigh.

"Can you believe those rotten bastards over at Zephyr"? Joe exclaimed.

Wayne was somber. "Now we know who we're up against."

Joe was slow to answer. "Yeah. Zephyr Petroleum," he said dejectedly, as his head slumped slightly down.

CHAPTER FIVE

It's amazing how time flies when you're having fun. Or was it because you're working around the clock to try and meet a deadline? The latter, Wayne surmised.

It was January 12, still more than three months until the land posting on April 28, but Wayne was already stressing about time. Things would have to go without any glitches or you might as well have the bids be due tomorrow, he concluded.

While the issue of time was constantly on his mind, the one element in all this that kept nagging him was Zephyr Petroleum. No matter how well and efficient Black Gold worked over the next 100 or so days, it had the upper hand.

It had the size, the influence, the power, the money.

Wayne called a meeting of the entire staff for 10:30 that morning. Despite the recent excitement, it was time to discuss financials. Sooner or later reality would set in and Wayne decided it might as well be now. Best to get everything out on the table!

Literally, Wayne joked to himself, as he looked at the swath of financial reports in front of him.

Experienced oil personnel always thought about dollars and cents. Well, maybe just dollars. Projects lived and died based on how much cash was available. Even in cases of relatively inexpensive plays, many geologists had seen months of hard work die on the drafting table due to a shortage of money.

Timing was everything in the oil patch: oil prices, land sales, finances. In this business timing was life or death, and the timing of this posting couldn't have come at a worse time. Black Gold's cash flow was down and investment dollars had dried up from Wall Street to Bay Street.

There just wasn't any glamor in $30.00 per barrel of oil. But, the market was suddenly about to change, and Wayne was hopeful that would be Black Gold's trump card moving forward.

Wayne deliberately scheduled the meeting for 10:30 instead of the usual 8:30 because he needed more time to gather his thoughts. He didn't want to dampen the enthusiasm or slow the momentum of the project, but the bottom line was Wolverine Hills was just a fantasy in everyone's mind unless Black Gold could garner a financial partner or loan from the bank.

One way or another, this opportunity had to happen. Wayne would not let his dream die now; not after years and years of anticipation and hope.

As Wayne surveyed the room, the boyish grin crossed his youthful face. The mess of paper before him was refreshing to see. The scattering of paper strewn across the big oak desk was a sign that great things may soon be coming to Black Gold.

The boardroom table was covered with maps and charts and financial statements, and logs and seismic charts practically hid all four walls. Everything was a collage of color, from marking pens hi-lighting critical points of data to red graph lines showing the latest trend in oil supply vs. demand. Despite the obstacles ahead, Wayne was suddenly overwhelmed with anticipation.

This was the way it had been in the past, the Good Ol' Days, Wayne reflected.

"How's Wayne this morning"?

Wayne snapped out of his deep thought and turned to see Chuck walk into the room and take a seat next to him. Chuck Braden was the financial officer for Black Gold. They may be called bean counters, but a good financial officer could make or break a company in good times or in bad.

After 30 years of dealing in oil, Chuck had seen all the boom and busts cycles and had learned the art of survival.

"I'm good! Thanks for asking, Chuck," Wayne replied. "You bring the current financials with you?"

"Got 'em right here," Chuck replied.

Wayne knew it was a superfluous question to ask. Of course, he had them with him; it was why he called the meeting and why they were all there.

"Great!" Wayne said. "Feel free to add them to my collection here."

Wayne motioned toward the plethora of paper sheets and maps in front of him. They both smiled as they scanned all the data.

Chuck was a typical first-born child; very conservative, organized, and methodical. He had the perfect demeanor to be an accountant.

Chuck placed his briefcase on the floor next to him and took out a binder. He placed it on the table in front of him.

"Just so you know, Wayne, I don't have our final figures. I'm still crunching numbers on the road and lease construction."

By now, the rest of the staff had started to enter the room.

"Just take a seat and enjoy the mess," Wayne said to his fellow employees, before turning back to Chuck. "That's fine, Chuck, just present us what you have and we'll revisit as soon as we can."

Chuck nodded as Wayne watched everyone get settled in. Of course, Gerry was last. As if he had a piano on his ass, he slowly shuffled to the last chair available. Probably a metaphor, Wayne chuckled to himself, to illustrate the burden he was carrying since joining Black Gold.

Gerry was good at what he did, however, so Wayne just rolled with it; for now anyway. As Gerry trudged to his final destination, Wayne's adrenaline began pumping.

"Let's get started." Wayne stood up and leaned on the table.

"Let me first thank each of you for the superb effort over the past few weeks. This isn't an easy task, as you all know, but because of a joint effort, it is coming together. We are few in number compared to our competition, but what we lack in numbers we will make up for in drive and dedication. This is our company, we're not merely employees, we are partners, and hopefully we can pull this project off together as a team."

"Amen to that!" Joe echoed.

Wayne knew that Joe would be the cheerleader and he didn't disappoint as everyone in the room cheered loudly.

"All right, Joe! I know you have some good news for us, so I'll let you have the floor."

It was technically a financial meeting, but Wayne wanted to throw in some positive project news so it wasn't all fire and brimstone. Wayne took a seat, as Joe shuffled some papers in front of him.

"Hope you all don't mind if I stay seated. I talk better from my butt cheeks than I do from my feet," he said with a nervous smile.

"Are you saying you talk better out of your ass"? Gerry said with a smile.

Others smiled too, despite their better judgment. Joe just glanced at Gerry because he didn't quite get it.

"At any rate, things are great on my end…"

This drew a chuckle from Gerry, but Joe just continued. He rapped his knuckles nervously on the oak table, as he spoke.

"I talked to Riley over at Sonoran Drilling again this morning and the rig is coming together quite nicely. He's having some minor problems, but figures it will be ready in a week."

Gerry nearly spit out the coffee he was drinking.

"A week! Seriously? If it takes any longer we can scrape this whole fuckin' project!"

"That's enough Gerry!" Joe shot back. "Riley's doing everything possible to have the rig ready and I'm confident he'll have it ready to move onto location in no more than 10 days."

"Oh, now it's 10 days? What will it be tomorrow? Two weeks?" came the cold, sarcastic reply.

Joe's face turned red and he starting grinding his teeth. "Look, Gerry! You worry about your department and I'll worry about mine."

Gerry just scoffed. "The way that timeline is working out, we should all worry."

Joe's face turned beat red and he pointed at Gerry. "Now, see here! I..."

The calm, collective voice of the leader quickly ended what could have erupted into a full-blown argument.

"OK. OK, guys. Let's take it easy now. We've got enough competition already without the internal bickering. Remember, we sink and swim as a team."

Everyone glanced over at Wayne and like two schoolboys; both Joe and Gerry felt embarrassed at their actions.

"Please continue, Joe," Wayne added after a pause and deep sigh.

Joe shot Wayne a nervous look, and then glanced down at his notes.

"What else? Um, the two D9 cats are completing the lease today, the six miles of road construction needed to get to the drilling site went great and we've got a good road in place to handle any lousy spring conditions."

Joe moved a piece of paper to the side and continued reading.

"There was actually about three miles of old, abandoned logging road in place that we were able to use, so that was great news! That cut our costs, considerably, as Chuck knows. In fact, we are about 40% below budget so far on the lease and road construction, but I'll let Chuck talk about that," he said, looking up with a smile.

Everyone but Gerry nodded and smiled back.

"Let me see, here. Oh, yeah," he continued. "The Forestry Department made us get permits to cut some of the timber on the access, but that didn't set us back too much or take too long. We should be able to get a little revenue back when we sell the timber. Won't be much, but it all adds up."

"You got that right," Chuck quickly remarked. The two shared a smile of agreement

"So, that's basically it so far. Our next step will be to dig the rat hole and set the conductor barrel. I've got a company lined up for Thursday. Once that's done, we'll be waiting on the rig. If the weather holds and there are no blizzards it should all go as planned."

Joe pushed his papers slightly to the side and looked up. "That's it from my end." He quickly shot Gerry a cold look. Gerry just rolled his eyes.

"Great! Thanks for that, Joe. Val, you got something for us"? Wayne said as he turned to the other side of the table.

Val Robinson was a tall, slender brunet with green eyes that seemed almost out of place. At 43, she looked more suited for a job modeling fashion design on 5th Ave or doing ads for high-end perfume than she did as a geologist working on 6th Avenue.

Val was more than just a beauty, however. She had major-league geological smarts and when Black Gold started, Wayne had recognized her talents right away. She joined Oilcom straight out of college and Wayne was the only boss she ever knew.

In this business, there were a lot of geologists that came and went. Wayne knew that Val had what it took and was determined to hold on to her as long as Black Gold was in business. Not only was she technically solid, she was tough in a tight squeeze.

She could handle pressure and that would be a necessary asset on the Wolverine Hills' project.

"Thanks, Wayne," she began. "I don't have much more to offer than I did last time. I will say that I'm very optimistic about our drilling location. The one small problem, however, is the Resources Board made us move our original pick from the Northwest quadrant to the Southwest portion of the section. Apparently, our location of preference was too close to a small stream, but we're still looking good and we've cozied up as close to the border as possible."

"How did they manage to change our drill site after they issued the license"? The question came from Joe.

"I have no idea. It's the government. They're like banks, right, Chuck? They change the rules at will." Val shot Chuck a look, who nodded and smiled to acknowledge he agreed.

"At any rate, it won't hurt us that much," she continued. "We will have to drill down a bit more, but we'll still hit the target."

Val scanned the faces of the room. She then smiled.

"I really am optimistic, everyone. As Gerry and I were compiling data from logs and seismic charts, there are two zones that have the potential to be extremely rich. One is the Banff Formation and the other is the Charlie Lake. Oh! I almost forgot! Gerry and I have identified another zone of interest that could be a positive surprise. The Cadomin Formation! The well of reference, for some reason, was never completed. Looks like they had problems or they may have run out of money. Anyway, the preliminary results show this could be a real sleeper!"

Showing his overwhelming approval, and to show everyone in the room he was instrumental in finding this potential gem, Gerry nodded profusely and grunted "That's right," over and over again, as Val talked.

"Sounds good Val, you've done a great job- You, too, Gerry." Wayne was sure to look over at Gerry and acknowledge him, as well. Adding to his ego was never fun, but if that's what keeps him working hard through this project, Wayne was sure to do just that.

Joe gave Val an extra wide smile. He had the utmost confidence in Val. He knew she could carry the ball once the tough decisions had to be made, as the well progressed. He also had a secret crush on her. If that's what you could call it at his age. She made something in him come alive every time she entered the room. And it wasn't just the amazing, scrumptious perfume she wore.

Joe had gone through a divorce three years ago and Val was dealing with the ramifications of her own split just months past. Because of personal situations and company pressure, the timing never seemed right for Joe to do anything more than maintain a professional relationship.

He sure was looking for the opportune moment, however, to change that.

"OK, Chuck," Wayne said with a giant sigh. "Give us the straight goods!"

"Thanks, Wayne," Chuck said.

Joe's mind quickly shifted back to business. He turned to Chuck to hear what could mean the end of the entire project.

"Despite all the great news from you guys, I'm afraid things don't look so bright and cheery on the financial side of things." With a solemn look on his face, Chuck looked up and scanned the room.

"I'll be quite honest with you. We're behind the eight-ball when it comes to funding. As you all know, on paper we're worth $8 million. Well, that's in good times. Right now, we're worth less than that and our cash flow is way down. You all know that because we've all taken pay cuts. There is roughly $700,000 in cash on hand and we have a two million dollar line of credit, give or take."

Chuck again looked up from the paperwork in front of him and peered at everyone over his reading glasses.

"To put it into perspective, let's assume we have $2 million for now. Near as I can figure, this well is going to cost $9 million to drill and the land sale will be another $10 million minima. Then there are all the operational costs."

Chuck looked up again. He threw his reading glassed onto the table and leaned back in his chair.

"As you can see, we will desperately need some funding to not only continue, but to even put in a competitive bid. With Zephyr in the mix, who knows what that will come to"?

Chuck's news had the exact negative effect on the group that Wayne expected. Maybe he should have had Chuck go first, so Joe and Val's enthusiasm could be the last impression. The room was dead silent and it was almost as if you could feel the energy escaping out the door.

"That's all the good news I can share, now. Sorry to kill all the optimism in the room," concluded Chuck.

Wayne eyed the room. The faces staring back at him said it all. OK, he thought, this is rock bottom, time to be the good leader and raise spirits. Wayne stood up with confidence and determination. He looked from side to side before starting.

"Thank you, everyone, I want to share with all of you some information I received early this morning. When Joe started looking for a rig, one of the first companies he contacted was Comanche Drilling. The response they gave Joe was simply, 'no!' Didn't even check inventory or give us a reason. You all know we gave Comanche all the work we could in the past. Well, you soon find out who your friends are in this business, don't you? Turns out they contracted their best rig to Zephyr for their own Wolverine Hills' project."

Wayne scanned the faces and saw even more despair. OK maybe now we were at rock bottom, he thought to himself. "All right, all of the downsides have been aired! Now! Time to move onward and upward to more positive things! Chuck and I are going to go to the bank to get the necessary financing needed to get this done. We also have a few companies in mind that are very interested in partnering with us."

Wayne again surveyed the room. He thought he could see a little more color and hope returning to their skin and eyes, respectively.

"The worst that can happen here is we run out of money trying to win this bid or we win the bid and find a dry hole. The best thing to happen is we win the bid and we find the discovery of the century. We are all banking on the latter and the preliminary data points to it! Thus, we are going to bust our asses to make sure we get this done!"

There was more hope in the air, Wayne could feel it. Or maybe it was just his unfounded wish. He nodded and smiled at every single person in the room. He then turned to Chuck.

"Chuck"?

"Yeh, Wayne"?

"I have two bank meetings set up in the next few days. I need the most optimistic numbers for them and our potential investors. With OPEC refusing to ship any oil to the West and with terrorism in the Middle East on the rise, the price per barrel is now up to $40. By tomorrow, it could be $50!"

"The last time we were in an oil supply crisis was the Gulf War and oil skyrocketed to $42 a barrel. We could start there?" Chuck responded. "Although that price was short lived and it dropped like a rock, putting a lot of small companies out of business. So, that may be too high."

"Nope! That number is great, Chuck, Keep in mind, if this doesn't work, we'll probably be out of business anyway."

Wayne turned back to the table. He had a serious countenance.

"With the numbers, Chuck and I will be presenting we should be able to bring in partners. Thus, I've taken the liberty to contact three companies to get a feel for interest. I'm assuming that is OK with everyone"?

While it was a question, Wayne phrased it more like a statement. He noticed a concerned look on Val's face.

"Val, you got something on your mind"?

She was hesitant to speak up. "Well, I have some companies in mind, too, that may also want to partner, but maybe we should try to deal with financial institutions first? Partners always mean complications, as we all know. Also, if we take on partners they have to be quality operators."

Wayne nodded and thought about it.

"Thanks, Val! Duly noted and agreed!" Wayne said as he surveyed the room. "OK! I'll let you guys know about the banks and then we'll meet back and discuss the partnership options. If any of you have any ideas, please don't hesitate to speak up. We are going to make or break it as a team!"

Everyone at the table seemed to perk up a notch with the team comment. Or maybe it was the fact that there may be some additional financing coming in, Wayne wasn't sure. But at least they were all on the same page and all still diligently working for one, common goal.

"Meeting adjourned!" Wayne said, mustering a wide, confident smile. "Let's get at it!"

As everyone started to stand, Val again spoke up.

"Oh! One more thing, Wayne, If I may?"

"Sure! What is it?"

Everyone stopped heading for the exit. Joe sat back down and listened intently as did Chuck. Gerry remained standing with a look on his face that stated he'd rather be elsewhere.

"This may be premature, but maybe we should start thinking about security for the rig? And perhaps talk about scouting, as well."

"Scouts! Are you serious? Why the hell would we do that?" Gerry blurted. "Those guys are nothing but deadbeat spies that cost a lot of money!"

Val looked nervous. "Maybe," she stated timidly. "But we do know Zephyr will be scouting our rig. That is if we get one up and running. You can also bet they'll have security in place on their own rig, as well."

There was a brief silence until Joe came to Val's defense. "That, actually, may be a good idea. Face it, Gerry, security, and scouts are a necessary evil, in this business. Those guys can help us save millions if they can somehow get accurate information on Zephyr's well. Shit!, Could be our only option if we don't get our drilling rig up and running."

"I disagree!" Gerry quickly snapped. "Those guys are lying, cheatin' bastards! They are nothin' but blight on our whole industry!"

Gerry was adamant and everyone was quiet as Wayne mulled it all over. Finally came the calm, collective answer.

"Can't hurt to investigate and have that ready, too, when the time comes, just in case. Did you have anybody in mind, Val"?

"Not really, but I have heard some good things about a tiny outfit called Wildcat Scouting."

"Yeah. I've heard of them," Chuck chimed in with surprise. "Actually, met the owner awhile back at an industry trade show or conference. Phil Graves, I think his name is. Really good guy! I bet he could handle the security and the scouting for us. I believe I still have his business card somewhere in my office if you want it"?

"It's nothin' but a waste of money, Wayne," chimed in a grouchy Gerry. "We need to save every penny we can, you said it yourself!"

Wayne pondered everything he heard and then nodded.

"That may be true, but can't hurt to talk to the guy. Val, get the card from Chuck and set up a meeting, will ya?"

"You bet, Wayne."

"Good. Good. All right! That's it! Let's get to work!"

With that everyone headed for the door.

CHAPTER SIX

Roger was rarely late to work. He took great pride in being on time, but this morning was an exception. With so much to do and so much on his mind, he suddenly found himself driving through downtown Calgary at 8:15 am.

"Damn it," he said aloud as he pushed down on the accelerator of his Mercedes 380SL. He ran two yellow lights on 6th Avenue, which were probably more like orange, he surmised. Thankfully there are no traffic cameras, he thought.

His mind was methodically organizing what lay ahead for the day. He knew there were at least 10 calls to be made to get a status of their rig going up on their land location adjacent to the Wolverine Hills land parcel. He was hoping to get the absolute up-to-date information before talking with Al in Houston.

Sure hope he doesn't call me first thing this morning. Roger mulled that over as he slowed down to make a right-hand turn. In the distance, Roger could see the 46-floor tower that housed Zephyr's Calgary office.

It was a beauty to behold and made Roger smile each time he saw it.

Zephyr had the entire 40th thru 46th floors and he occupied the North West corner on the 44th floor, which gave him an amazing, panoramic view of the entire city and miles and miles of rolling hills and forests beyond it.

In its prime, Zephyr had the top ten floors. but now, thanks to the sagging market, it was down to seven. The three floors below them were still vacant, and it was one of Roger's tiny side goals to once again fill that space with employees.

Wolverine Hills was going to be the catalyst.

As he hit the brakes to turn right into the underground parking garage, the hordes of people out front quickly came into view.

"What the fuck is going on"? He murmured with surprise.

Roger applied the brakes even more to get a better view of the event. Standing outside the main entrance were hundreds of people all yelling and pointing. Many of them carried signs, and they were flanked by at least three camera crews.

"Holy Shit! Fuckin' environmentalists!"

Roger slowed to almost a stop as he scanned the protestors crowding the front entrance of the building.

"Stop the Drilling – Save Wolverine Hills," read one of the signs. "Save the Grizzly Bear," was written on another.

"Get a life you sorry, Marxist bastards," Roger said aloud and he shook his head and surveyed the chaotic scene. Just as he started to turn and head down into the garage, a reporter jumped at his car and knocked on the window. It scared Roger and he slammed on his brakes.

"Fuck, man!" He couldn't help but yell it out, as he turned to look at the passenger-side front window with wide eyes.

"Hey! What are Zephyr's thoughts on drilling in Wolverine Hills? "He could hear the muffled voice of the reporter, as he pounded on the window to get his attention. "Come on! Can I get a quick statement"?

Fucking vultures, Roger thought. No way are you getting a statement out of me, he added, as he hit the accelerator and disappeared into the confines of the dark parking lot. Looking in his rear-view mirror, he saw the reporter stop abruptly as the gate closed in front of him. "Thank God he didn't follow me in," Roger sighed.

Upset by the events on the street, Roger was not in the best of moods when he disembarked the elevator on the top floor.

"Great timing, Mr. White," came the voice of his secretary. "Mr. Wallace from Houston is on the line. Would you like me to put him through or would you prefer calling him back?"

It was a nice, pleasant voice. But Roger's wasn't.

"No, I won't call him back! You don't ever put off the boss! Put him through!" he ordered, marching right past her and into his office.

Roger was pissed. Al had beaten him again. Why can't he give me some fucking time to get settled in, before calling? Roger shook his head in frustration.

Shelley once again took a deep breath, knowing Roger was in one of those moods again.

"OK, Mr. White!" she simply answered. "I'll tell him you're on the way to take the call."

"Oh, there's a bright idea!" Roger said sarcastically, as he closed the door behind him.

Shelley shook her head and rolled her eyes, as she completed the transfer. What a jerk. Why on earth do I put up with it, she thought, feeling anger swelling within herself.

Roger threw his briefcase onto his office chair and immediately checked the ashtray on the desk for cigar butts. He found two worthy of a good chew and threw the larger one into his mouth. It was a nervous reaction of his, but it always calmed him down; that and a big drink of whiskey.

"Hello, Al! Roger here."

"Afternoon, Roger!"

Roger didn't say anything. The sarcastic comment only fueled his acrimony.

Knowing Roger probably didn't like that snide comment, Al continued. "I haven't heard anything for a couple of days, so I thought I'd call and get an update. There is growing anxiety down here in Houston."

Roger was hoping for more up-to-date information from his crew in the field, before calling Al, but now it was too late. I'll just give him the latest from yesterday, he thought, close enough. As he was about to give the update, his secretary buzzed in.

"Mr. White! I'm so sorry to interrupt."

Roger could feel his blood boil and his face turn red. What the hell was she thinking to interrupt a call with the boss?

"Mr. White! Are you there!" came the voice again. This time with a little more panic. Roger knew something odd was up.

"Sorry Al! Can you hold on! My secretary keeps buzzing me. Have no idea what's going on."

Roger bit down hard on his cigar. "What? What is it? I'm in the middle of a conversation with Houston!"

There was a quick pause before the trembling voice answered.

"So sorry Roger, I really am, but I just got a call from security. Apparently, some reporters snuck past them and somehow managed to get on the elevators! Security says they are on their way up here now! What should I do?"

There was desperation in her voice. "Say nothing and tell them everyone is tied up in meetings!" Roger's reply was curt.

"I'll try, Mr. White!" It was all she could muster.

"Don't just try, do it," Roger snapped as he turned off the button on the intercom.

"Hey Al! You still there?"

"I'm still here. So, what was that all about?"

"We've got fucking watermelons on the rampage here."

"You've got what?-Watermelons?"

"Yeah "Watermelons!" it's what I call these freak eco-terrorists; green on the outside and communist red in the middle. They're outside our offices now, causing a full-blown media circus."

Al chuckled. He was stubborn and arrogant, but sometimes Al could only laugh when it came to Roger's view on the world. His sense of humor was beyond words. Al took a deep breath.

"OK," Al said, suddenly getting serious. "How bad is it?"

"I don't know yet, Al. She tells me some reporters crashed security and are on their way up. Probably outside my doors right now."

"Roger!" Al quickly and sternly replied. "Whatever you do, don't lose your cool, even if you have to swallow that cigar of yours."

Al couldn't see it, but Roger couldn't help but nod to show he understood.

"Actually, screw that! I have a better idea. Get your secretary there – what's her name, Shelley? Get Shelley to pluck out the first two or three that come in and have her tell the rest to hit the road. I'll field a few questions."

"Really, Roger replied with skepticism. "You sure you want to do that, from Houston?"

"Yeah! Let's nip this thing in the butt, right here and now! Just like that cigar of yours."

Al didn't wait for Roger to reply.

"Once she gets them into your office, have them take a seat and put me on speaker. Got that?"

Roger paused to think it all over. Not having to answer any questions, especially since they would all be directed toward the environment was music to his ears.

"Sounds good to me, Al! Just hang on; it might take me a few minutes."

More relaxed now, Roger pushed the button. "Shelley, you got company out there"?

"Yes, Mr. White! There are a bunch of reporters here wanting to get a statement from you regarding Wolverine Hills."

Roger nodded his head.

"OK, pick the three closest to you and send the rest home. Tell them we're sorry, but we're making a statement on a first-come, first serve basis."

There was a long pause before Shelley answered.

"Um, OK, Mr. White! If you say so."

Damn right, I say so, Roger snapped. "Hang on Al! She's lining up the media nuts for you now."

"Careful Roger! Diplomacy is key at this time."

With a chorus of disappointment and displeasure in the background from the other journalists, Shelley escorted three of the reporters into Roger's office.

Roger whipped the unlit cigar from side to side in his mouth as he directed the men to take a seat. He explained who was on the other end of the phone and said they had ten minutes to ask questions.

"OK, Al! The Nut Jobs…Err, I mean, the reporters are all yours."

Roger overly smiled to show he was kidding and took a seat. The reporters went well over their 10-minute allotment of time as Al calmly and collectively fielded each one of their questions. It was closer to thirty minutes when it finally wrapped, but it didn't bother anyone at Zephyr because, in Roger's mind, Al was doing a wonderful job.

He quickly spun the conversation away from the environmental damage that may come from the testing and drilling to the critical global economic situation that would soon come if a major discovery of domestic oil was not found soon.

Roger was impressed as Al laid out all of the precautions Zephyr would take to ensure as little environmental impact occurred as possible. How could he guarantee these precautions would be implemented? That was the last question of the day.

"Well," Al said. "Roger in the Calgary office knew how critical Zephyr's public image was and was a devout outdoorsman who held the environment close to his heart, so if they had any concerns, they could call on Roger, personally."

Roger couldn't believe those last comments. In fact, he damn near swallowed his cigar. "Outdoorsman!" Cared about the environment? What a bunch of bull shit, Roger knew.

At first, it irritated him to think he'd have to deal with a bunch of questions from these biased, eco-freaks, but he also knew he would never return any calls. The fact that Al's assurance actually worked and the reporters were satisfied was all that mattered.

Who knew how they might twist the information by the time the story hit the newsstands, but, for now, they seemed pleased with the official response from Zephyr.

Shelley politely escorted them to the elevators where a few of the straggling news lemmings from other papers and TV networks desperately pleaded with them to share their notes.

Roger leaned back in his chair. "Quite a morning, Roger!" Al said.

"Sure as hell is!" Roger calmly replied. "Nothing like running into a buzz saw to start your day, no cup of coffee can give you a jolt like that!"

"Guess not. Look," Al said, wrapping things up. "If you get any more problems with these 'watermelons,' as you call them, give me a call."

"You got it, Al. I have to say, I am pretty concerned about these jokers showing up at our drill site. They start fucking with the roughnecks out there, who knows what will happen?"

"That's a good point! We should probably talk about security."

"Yes, we should. Speaking of which, did I tell you about our gnat? "

"Our what?" Al questioned.

"Our gnat! It's what I call our competition at Wolverine Hills."

There goes Roger again with his own vernacular and spin on things. "No, you didn't mention it. Just one outfit so far?"

"Far as I can tell, it's just us and a tiny company called Black Gold. They are right down the street from us here in Calgary."

"They going to be a problem, Roger?" Al's tone was extra quiet and concerned.

Roger laughed.

"Highly doubtful! They're nothing but a speck on our radar. My guess is they don't even have the capital to put in a competitive bid."

"I don't like taking any competition lightly, Roger," came the sage advice. "You never know in this business."

"You are right about that, but just in case I put the word out to all the rig contractors in the area not to lease to them. They got an old junker that won't do the job. Cost me a bit of cash, but better safe than sorry, I think."

"Winning this is vital to the longevity of this company that is for sure. That's good thinking, Roger," Al replied.

"Oh, and by the way, not sure if I told you, but we secured that new Comanche rig I was telling you about. Best iron around; should eliminate a lot of issues with drilling in that remote, rugged region."

There was a brief pause as Roger leaned back in his chair with a smug grin on his face.

"Sounds like you're on the stick there, Roger. Very good to hear."

"I'm trying, Al. I'm trying," he said, knowing full well he was doing better than that. "Oh! And another thing while I have ya. I had my buddy over at the Resources Board make Black Gold move their location- cited some old rule about riparian zones. If they ever do get a rig up and running, at least that should slow them down some."

"You're doing a hell of a job, Roger. Keep me informed. Hopefully, they'll never get going and we'll be the only one bidding. How's our road coming anyway?"

"It's about finished. We had some problems getting across Grayling Creek, had to bring explosives in, to blow some rock. Took a couple extra days. We're also bringing in some extra equipment to help secure the temporary bridge. It's real steep and rough out there, as you know."

"Sounds good Roger, save time where you can," Al commented. "Getting back to security, for a moment, you think this other outfit, Black Gold; will want to bring in scouts?"

Roger scoffed at the notion.

"They are the least of my worries, Al. Only Black Gold and Zephyr have a position to drill a well on adjacent lands next to Wolverine Hills, so if any of the bigger companies want to make a bid they'll have to do so blindly or by getting the sneaky, underhanded way – by stealing our data."

"That's what I was thinking, too," Al slowly replied. "Thus, we should get in a security crew as soon as we can."

"Yup! I think we should try and kill two birds with one stone."

"What do you mean by that?"

"We get a license of occupation from the Forest Service on the 6 miles of road from the main logging road to our location. That stops anyone other that Zephyr employees from accessing that location. They don't issue them too often as they believe the forest is public domain, but I think I can make a strong enough case to get one. Especially now, that we have all these Greenpeace whackos causing such a stink about our project."

"Good idea, so who should we hire to enforce it?"

"We've got an ex-cop in charge of security here at the building, who is perfect. The guy's 6' 6" and 260 pounds and really knows how to manage a team. I'll have him set up a security check on the main road access with phone lines to the rig to stay in constant communication."

There was a brief pause before Al chimed in.

"I cede to you, Roger, as the man in charge up there, but have to say this so-called security expert didn't do so hot with the white-collar, pen-pushing journalists this morning! Just think what a real outdoor, experienced scout can do!"

It was true, Roger thought. How on earth did these guys get past security? Definitely not great timing on Roger's part to endorse this security contact, but he knew that he had the experience and there was just no easy way to get around in those woods."

"I will definitely check in with him on what went wrong this morning, for sure. But, in the case of our rig, Al, the good news is there is no way around up there! We're sitting right between Nose Creek and Grayling Creek. The banks are sheer cliffs except where our road crosses Grayling Creek. It's a bitch to get back in there, but once we're set up, it is the perfect place to drill without being bothered."

Roger's ego didn't have to wait long before being even further inflated.

"Damn, Roger! I knew there was a reason we kept you around all these years! Good to hear!" said an enthusiastic Al.

Roger smiled even more. Knowing Al was in a good mood and he was looking good, he thought to keep on sharing information.

"There's more Al. I've got a company lined up to scout the Black Gold rig if we decide it's necessary. That is if they ever get to drilling."

"I'm an old-school guy and like focusing on our own work and data gathering, but if you feel it's needed, I'm all for it."

"I do, sir. The good scouts are worth their weight in gold! Wish we could say that about oil, but they can sure add the finishing touches on a bid come sale time."

"Well, listen, Roger do what you think is best. Sounds like you've got things under control up there. Do me a favor and keep us posted on every-thing. And I do mean everything. When things get really going, I plan on coming up to see you and the rig, first hand, OK?"

"Sounds good Al! Look forward to your visit," Roger said lying through his teeth.

He hated when the big shots from Houston came into town. They always flaunted their knowledge and power, as if they were experts on oil opera-tions any everyone else was just a country bumpkin. Truth of the matter, they knew jack-shit about how to drill up here in the Great White North. It was a whole different ball game.

The last thing Roger wanted was for them to come in here and flex their muscle and call the shots. This was Roger's baby! He was going to run the show and save Zephyr all on his own.

Course, he would never tell them that. As good as he was, he could be shit-canned at any moment for disobeying or going rogue without approval, so he knew to keep his mouth shut and fall in line like a good little soldier.

"I'll call you on Monday, Al! Thanks for the call and dealing with those pesky reporters," Roger said kowtowing to his boss.

"All right, talk to you then."

Roger hung up the phone and felt a surge of adrenaline. He was in control and this was his domain. Sure they will come up and look around for a few days, but Roger could handle that. What're few days in the grand scheme of things?

His big office chair swiveled deliberately toward the massive window that looked west down the long alley of towering buildings on 6th Avenue. From his lofty perch, he could see the small structure that housed the offices of Black Gold Resources in the distance.

A smirk crept across his face as he rolled the cigar from check to check.

"Wonder what the small people are doing right now," he mused out loud.

CHAPTER SEVEN

Wayne stood looking at the bold letters across the top page of his notepad. It read "94 Days until Sale!"

He wished he could make the number read 184, but that wasn't in his power. Best to not even think about it, he mused, as he surveyed the conference room. Here we were again; about to discuss a project that may never materialize or, worse yet, bury the company entirely.

Why was he thinking this way? This was everything he pushed for; everything he always wanted. Sure, there were many hurdles in the way, the biggest of which was the distinct possibility that underneath the lush forest of Wolverine Hills was nothing but rock and water.

That was the constant reminder of naysayers over the years. But Wayne never listened to it. He was sure there were large reservoirs of oil and gas and it was only a question of how big. Despite everyone fearing they could be on a fool's mission to bid on a useless parcel of land, Wayne's only concern was Zephyr Petroleum.

That bigger, much more lucrative company was the only thing that stood between him and his dream. To outbid them and win the rights to extract the region's oil and gas, he had to convince everyone, his own employees, the bank, investors, that there were indeed riches to be had.

As he looked up, he could see everyone already seated at the table staring at him. Oh, wow, he thought, how didn't I hear anyone come in? Must be all the extra stress and worry he surmised.

"Morning gentlemen and Val of course!" he stated.

"Morning to you Mr. Stadwell," Val responded.

"All right, let's get into this. We have a lot to get through in a short time. First I would like you all to know I've invited Phil Graves from Wildcat Scouting to be here about 9:30. That gives us a few minutes to get through our internal business before he arrives."

"You really think that's necessary"? Gerry grunted curtly.

"I think so, but won't be sure until we hear him out." Wayne was surprised at Gerry's tone.

"You going to let him into the board room? Not sure that's wise, letting him see all our logs and charts in here with all our geological data all hi-lighted and marked."

"Listen, Gerry, this guy is on our side, that's why we invited him. He'll be working for us."

"Fine, but I don't trust any of those spies! For all we know, he's already working for a competitor!" Gerry grumbled.

"I highly doubt that," Val chimed in. "Seriously, Gerry, I don't know why you hate scouts so much. In all honestly, I'd get on board with this whole thing. As far behind as we are on our own rig, the only information we get on Wolverine Hills may come from Phil's scouting reports."

Gerry was about to chime in again, but he looked at Wayne glaring at him. He mumbled to himself and let it go.

"By all means, you can excuse yourself when he gets here, Gerry. I'm OK with that," Wayne said.

Gerry squirmed in his chair and mumbled a bit more to himself a little extra loud to clearly show he was not happy with the team's decision.

"Let's move on." Wayne sighed loudly before continuing, "Joe- how about an update on the rig."

Joe looked down at his notes and was slow to start.

"Things have gone a bit slower than we had hoped, as you all probably know by now," he started listlessly. "Talked to Riley at Sonoran just before I came into the meeting. He apologized for the delays but wants us to know he's going 24 hours a day to get the rig on track. As you are all aware, Zephyr spud their well on January 25. Apparently, they would have spud a couple days sooner but they had some problems with a portable bridge across Grayling Creek."

"What happened?" Val's mind was always alert to any information that might help her solve future problems she might encounter.

"The grapevine has it the bridge collapsed on one end shortly after it was constructed. Wiped one truck out and bent a bunch of drill pipe when it went into the water. Guess no one was hurt, not seriously anyway."

Joe looked Val in the eyes and smiled to make sure she was satisfied. She nodded his way, and he looked back down at the pad in front of him.

"But, getting back to our situation, Riley is having a hell of a time putting the rig together, but he says he's close to being done. He's looking for a second mud pump right now. Unfortunately, they discovered the first one had a crack in it way too wide to weld. Should have it all secured and in place on our lease within a few days."

"We've heard that before," Gerry muttered loudly.

"Hey, I know it's been slow. But the rig is about ready to spud even as I speak. I know we're three days later than we anticipated, but we can make that up. We're going to drill the surface hole without the backup pump. That gives us about a week if we set surface pipe at 1,500 feet. Hopefully, we can have the backup pump sooner."

Joe looked over at Wayne. He simply gave him a reassuring nod.

"The other problem," Joe went on, "came courtesy of the resources board. Don't know what's going on over there, but somebody doesn't like us. We had to bring the D9 Cat back in, yet again, to do some upgrades on the lease to protect the nearby creek. We had to move a whole shit-load of dirt, let me tell ya! You'd think there was an endangered species in that creek or something. Anyway, they finally OK'd it and we should be back on track."

The silence in the room was telling.

"Val you're next." Wayne's lack of enthusiasm added to the somber mood.

"Thanks, Wayne. Um, again, there's not much from me. Just waiting for that call to say we have a spud time. I've been going over formation projections and I would like to have a geologist on location when we get to about 2,000 ft."

"Who do you have in mind"? Wayne inquired.

"To be honest, I thought I might do it myself," said a nervous Val.

"Val, you're talking at least two months out there in a field trailer," Wayne quickly shot back.

Val glanced around the room to see everyone's reaction before turning back to Wayne.

"I realize that, but I really don't want any screw-ups on this one. We can't afford them. Plus, there will be running water and I'm used to camp-type conditions."

There was brief silence while everyone mulled it over. Joe put his head down and smiled. Just as he expected, when it came time to take control of things Val was there to step up. She wasn't a bra-burning feminist; she knew how to take charge and do what it took to make sure things got done. His feelings for her were growing by the day.

"All right, Val. Do me a favor, though, and think about it some more and let me know if you change your mind," Wayne said calmly. He then turned to his right and looked at his head of financing.

"Chuck, you got any updates"?

"Not today Wayne," came the quick and short reply.

"Nothing at all"? Wayne responded with eyebrows slightly raised.

"No. I'm still reworking the abstract numbers. The construction costs are running about 20% above projections because of the extra lease preparation. The other numbers I'm still working out."

"Chuck, you've had ten days to come up with these numbers, what's taking you so long"?

"I know that Wayne, but with these oil prices jumping all over the board, it's near impossible to come up with numbers that will hold true. I am waiting to see the prices stabilize a bit before I do the final numbers."

Wayne was not happy. He leaned up in his chair and turned.

"Chuck, just use $50.00 a barrel like I asked you in the beginning, please! If oil goes higher it's a bonus. I need something on paper to take to the bank or to a fund broker, or whomever!"

Wayne was frustrated. He was about to go on a rant but looked over at Chuck and stopped. He remembered the look on Joe's face when he snapped at him. Wayne just sighed loudly knowing everyone was getting frustrated.

"I just need the financial report done, Chuck. Can you do that for me,-PLEASE?"

Chuck looked exhausted. "Sure, Wayne, I can do that."

Wayne breathed in deep again, then smiled and nodded. He looked back down the table.

"Val, I know you were calling on potential financial partners. If any of them are still a possibility, I'd like to have meetings set up before you head to the field. Is that something we can do? The sooner we can identify potential players, the sooner we can make some decisions."

"I'll let you know, Wayne," Val said with a confident nod. Wayne nodded back to her, then at everyone else at the table.

"Along those lines, I talked to Alpine Resources yesterday and they've expressed a real interest. They're willing to look at any number of scenarios for participation, maybe between them and Val's companies we'll get something done; And done fast!"

Glancing down at his watch, Wayne noticed it was 9:40. Phil should be waiting outside, he surmised.

"Excuse me! I'll go see if Phil is here." Wayne abruptly stood up and went out the door.

A quick check of the main lobby found Phil sitting on the couch thumbing through an Oil Week magazine.

"Hey, Phil!" he hollered from just outside the conference room door. "Sorry, we're running a little late."

"Hey! That's OK!" Phil said, standing up. He shook Wayne's hand as the two headed back into the conference room.

"People, I'd like you to meet Phil Graves. He's president of Wildcat Scouting," Wayne said, motioning Phil into the room and toward the closest open seat "I think some of you may have had the occasion to use his services in the past."

"Hi, Phil," Val was first to say.

"Nice to see you again, Val. It's been a while." Phil waved at her across the table as he put down his notebook and pen.

"Anyone else here work with Phil before"? Wayne inquired, as the two took a seat.

"I think the last time I saw Phil was fifteen years ago," Joe laughed. "I was a green field engineer and he was scouting my rig up around Windfall. I had no idea what a scout was, so I'm sure he got all the information he wanted; probably before I got it."

Joe laughed. Phil smiled with pride.

"I do remember that, Joe. That sure was a long time ago. Personally, I don't go out into the field much anymore, but I can assure you I have some great hands that do. Trained them myself, so should provide you guys with whatever you want if you all decide to use our services."

"Is that one scout still with you? Max, I think his name is?" Val asked

Before Phil could answer, Gerry suddenly got up from his seat. "Excuse me, everyone, I have real work to do."

Everyone watched quietly as an agitated Gerry slowly waddled out of the room, mumbling to himself. Phil was unsure what to make of it. He looked around with surprise, but all eyes were on Gerry. Once he was finally out of the room, Wayne slightly shook his head and rolled his eyes.

"OK. Sorry about that. Go ahead, Phil." Wayne smiled with confidence toward Phil and motioned for him to answer.

"You bet, Val. He sure is. Have to say he may very well be the best in the business! Course, I am biased," he added with a chuckle.

"Any chance we could get this guy for our job?" Wayne asked

"Wouldn't use anyone else on this one, Wayne."

"Good. Good," Wayne responded.

""I have to say, Wayne, this is not going to be an easy job!" Phil looked around the room to make sure it was all right to continue.

"The name really does say it all! Wolverine Hills is a beast! And Zephyr picked the toughest spot of all; makes your location look like a cake walk in comparison."

Phil again looked around the room, making sure he looked each and everyone in the eyes. Providing great service was one thing, but through his days, Phil learned to be a successful owner, one must also play the sales game. It took him a while, but he eventually mastered the conduct and demeanor necessary to win folks over.

You may have the greatest scouting team in the field, but if you don't first impress in the boardroom, you can kiss your company goodbye. Got to land the sale before you investigate the land, Phil always joked to himself. He was pretty sure Black Gold would hire him. It was clear this potential project was too important not to cover all bases, but one can never be too sure.

"Seriously, they couldn't have picked a better location in terms of security unless they were drilling atop Everest. As you know their lease road comes in from the logging access east of the rig site and that logging road is the only access as near as I can tell. It is wedged between Nose Creek and Grayling Creek and completely surrounded by steep banks on both sides. I'm sure you all heard what happened on Zephyr's rig move, right?"

Phil looked around to see if they heard the news.

"We spoke about it briefly this morning," Joe chimed in.

"Yeah. They are having a real bitch of a time getting in there! Oh, sorry about that Val," Phil looked down the table to make sure he didn't offend her. Not good, Phil thought.

Val just smiled un-offended. It took way more than that in this business, she mused to herself.

"At any rate, that crossing is the only place to gain access to Zephyr's location," Phil continued. "If we do this, I'd like to propose moving a scout in as soon as we can after they set surface pipe. May take a couple of days just to find any possible way to get back in there."

Wayne looked at Val, then around the table at everyone's faces. He pondered the situation, then turned and looked right at Phil.

"I think I speak for everyone in the room when I say we trust your instincts Phil and cede to you on what you think is best. Getting information on Zephyr's rig may be the best data we get on Wolverine Hills. Actually, as stated earlier, it might be the only data."

Wayne shot Joe a glance. Joe looked disappointed, but he slightly smiled and nodded knowing Wayne was right. Phil nodded modestly; happy to know he had the full trust of Black Gold. Well, everyone but the guy who abruptly left the room earlier, he concluded.

"I appreciate that Wayne, I really do. Not everyone likes to use scouts or feels the information we provide is all that valuable. The truth of the matter is, the information is only as good as what we dig up and thankfully we've had some great success in the past. In fact, it many cases, we've managed to secure as much information as the companies paying the millions of dollars to drill the hole in the first place."

The words seemed to ease the tension and uneasiness in the room. Val and Chuck nodded with confidence.

"You can say all you want about our trade being underhanded, immoral, unethical, what have you, but in the end, we truly can get some valuable information! And as you all know, that info may lead you to the next great discovery!"

Everyone in the room was convinced hiring Phil was the right answer. In fact, it made each of them feel more hopeful and optimistic.

"On the flip side, we can also save you from making the huge mistake of bidding on what may end up being useless wasteland, right?" Phil added with a smile.

The look on the faces in the room was a sight to see, Wayne thought. Before Phil came in, they looked defeated and downtrodden. Now, the bright eyes and smiles glowing back at Phil showed renewed enthusiasm.

This could be the ideal solution to most of the problems, everyone deduced. If Black Gold was unable to get to the proposed depth for critical information, Wildcat Scouting may be able to get the necessary information from Zephyr. It was the perfect backup plan.

And, quite possibly, the only plan!

"I have a suggestion," Phil said as the room continued to process all the exciting information. "I'd like to lease a chopper in Grande Cache to spend a couple of hours checking the terrain. It may be the only way to find an access to that location."

"What's the chopper going to cost"? Chuck quickly asked.

"I'd say about $800 an hour, which I know sounds like a lot, but we only need it for two or three hours. That could end up being pennies compared to having a scout try and do it on the ground. Who knows how long it will take him on foot or on a snowmobile."

"That sounds fine. Just as long as you don't take a joy ride on our expense," Chuck said with a smile.

"We don't play games with someone else's money. We are in business to do a job and do it right," Phil said with an offended countenance on his face.

Wayne looked at Phil closely. Clearly, this was someone who took his job very seriously. He was also clearly an experienced, knowledgeable oil person. Wayne liked him immediately and knew Val had chosen wisely.

"Let's do it!" Wayne said emphatically. "Chuck, I want you to get Phil everything he needs. This scouting thing, to me, seems like the right thing to do. Whether we have the extra money or not, what we can get from it is just too invaluable to pass up."

Nobody said anything, but Wayne knew by looking at the excited faces in the room that everyone agreed.

"Sounds great," Phil said, as Wayne stood up.

"Oh! one more thing."

Wayne stopped and stared at Phil.

"I'm pretty sure the minute Zephyr hears you've successfully got your own rig in place, they are going to send their own scouts," Phil added. "If you agree, I'd like to also set up a security check station on your access road, as well as run security around the perimeter to give you some protection."

Wayne glanced at Chuck, who quickly nodded his disapproval. Wayne ignored it.

"That will be fine, Phil," he said gathering up his papers from the table. "Get Chuck here some numbers on what that will cost us and Joe will let you know when our rig is up and running. Right Joe?"

Joe couldn't help but smile looking down at the table at a confident, upbeat Wayne.

"You got it, Wayne."

"By the way, Wayne what are you doing about office security?" Phil questioned again.

It threw Wayne for a loop.

"Nothing," he said surprised. "We're a small group and everyone is pretty tight-lipped around Black Gold."

"That's good to hear. How you plan on communicating with the rig for daily reports"?

Wayne looked at Phil with slight admiration. Man, this guy thinks of everything, he thought.

"Um, I believe we use a fax system," Wayne said, looking around the table to see if anybody disagreed with him.

"That's not good enough," said Phil a bit nervously.

"You sure?"

"It's my business to be sure, Wayne. With technology today, any good scout worth one's salt can pick up a fax transmission. Unless you use satellite phones, you might as well stand on 6th Ave and broadcast your morning reports to the general public."

"Good, God! Has it really gotten that bad?" Wayne belted out with surprise.

"Well, with the likely hood of an entire company on the line? Yeah, it has," Phil politely and calmly said.

Everyone in the room knew he was right. The importance of the Wolverine Hills project and the pressure to land the bid suddenly returned.

The mood was once again somber and tension in the room hung like a thick fog.

L. GORDON KESLER

CHAPTER EIGHT

Mayhem, absolute mayhem, was the only way to describe the activity around the dinner table in Max's house. It was always the same; five kids all excited about the day's events and each one thinking his or her story was the best.

Tonight, on the other hand, was a little less chaotic. Usually, they were vying for dad's attention, but this evening, it was less so. That's probably because I've been home for going on almost three weeks, thought Max. They are probably tired of seeing my face around the house.

The sounds and smells in the kitchen made life's problems seem insignificant. It was true he had not worked in a long time and the pressure and stress were mounting on him like a vice grip. But for now, however, he was relaxed. Yes, it was noisy and hectic, but this was what life was all about.

Max managed a smile amid the amicable, but tumultuous scene in front of him.

"Move over, here it comes!" Carmen was jockeying for room to put the steaming chili on the table.

"Chili again tonight, guys," Carmen said, half apologetically. She would like to have had more elaborate meals, but with kids coming and going and money getting scarce, it didn't make much sense.

Max watched Carmen perform her domestic ritual. "What do you mean chili again, you make the best damn chili in the country, right guys"?

All five voices blurted in unison, "Right, dad!"

Just as Carmen got seated at the table, the phone gave notice that someone had timed his or her call perfectly. With a sigh and roll of her eyes, Carmen pushed her chair back.

"You sit, honey! I'll get it!" Max quickly shot up and went toward the phone as the family dug into the hot chili. Max walked out of the kitchen and into the living room to take the call.

"Evening, Max here."

"Max, what's happening in your neck of the woods?"

It was Phil. A smile and look of anticipation fell on Max's face.

"Phil, how are you?"

"Good. Hope I didn't catch you at the supper table again?"

Max looked over his shoulder toward the kitchen.

"Um, no. Well, it's OK. What's going on?"

"Max. I hope you're sitting down. I've got a big one for you." Max looked as if he just let the weight of the world off his shoulders. He slumped with relief and sighed loudly.

"That's great, Phil. Thought maybe I'd have to go back to rough-necking on a rig here soon."

"Yeah. Sorry about that. It's been pretty slow," Phil came back. "But not anymore, we have a pretty intense job ahead."

"Not another three-dayer, I hope," Max said half laughing, half being serious.

"I assure you, this is not Max; this one is at least two months long" Music to Max's ears. Again, his body relaxed with relief.

"Great, Phil. Just Great! Maybe now I won't have to eat chili every night." Max chuckled quietly as he looked back over his shoulder to make sure Carmen didn't hear him.

There was silence on the other end, causing Max to wonder if Phil was still there.

"Look, Max, I'm going to put it to you straight. This may very well be your toughest scouting job yet! The terrain is incredibly rough up there. So rough, I've lined up a chopper for us to take a first-hand look at it tomorrow at 2 pm. Does that work for you?"

Phil didn't wait to hear Max's answer.

"It's in Grand Cache, so I have to pick you up pretty darn early in the morning."

"Yeah. No problem. I'm ready to go, whenever " Max said with enthusiasm.

"Good to hear. I'm going to get an early start, probably leave by 4:00, which means I'll hopefully be at your doorstep by 7:00. I did hear the roads up there are pretty icy and a tough sled, but hopefully that gives us enough time to get to Grand Cache in time."

Max nodded. "OK. Should I bring anything in particular or is this just a quick day trip?"

"Just a one-dayer, Max, but be sure to dress accordingly. If that chopper happens to go down up there, it won't take long for us to freeze to death in those frigid conditions."

"Of course," Max said with assurance.

"Oh," Phil chimed in. "and another thing. Make sure you bring your good binoculars. We are going to have to look high and low for an access route. As I said, it's very steep and treacherous terrain. Hopefully, we find one."

Max nodded into the phone. He knew Phil couldn't see him, but it was instinctual.

"I'll let you get back to your chili," Phil said with a touch of humor. "Sorry, I interrupted dinner again. See you at 7:00!" With that, Phil hung up.

Max slowly put the phone down. He could hear the family chaos ring out from the other room. He closed his eyes and listened to it. He took a deep breath and soaked it all in. He smiled ever-so-slightly.

At 6:45, Phil was already lightly knocking on Max's door. By 7:00, they were already headed to Grand Cache with a big Thermos of hot coffee to keep them company.

The roads were as reported, icy and dangerous most of the way. The hills north of Hinton were the worst and that slowed their progress considerably. They were pushing it awfully close and with just ten minutes to spare, they pulled the 4x4 up to the main offices of the helicopter company. Max and Phil quickly gathered up a few more warm clothes and the binoculars and headed inside.

"Got any matches, Max"? Phil asked as he opened the door.

"I always have matches," Max answered with a confused look on his face.

Phil smiled at him and winked as he swung the door wide.

"Just checking."

Max finally understood. He smiled at Phil as he stepped past him into the office. Phil always liked testing his scouts to ensure they were always prepared for the unknown. For Max, it came naturally, but Phil knew he'd catch him off guard at one point. It was just another tiny side trait that made Max like Phil.

The pilot was waiting as the two scouts approached the counter.

"You timed it down to the last minute. Didn't think you were going to make it," he said, looking up from his clipboard.

"It was slower than expected, but we're here," Phil responded.

"Beautiful! I'll fire the chopper up and let her get warm. My gal here will help you with the paperwork," he said, thumbing to his right where a middle-aged woman was trying her best to type at a computer. "Good thing you dressed warm, it's going to be a cold flight today."

Phil hastily read the contract and signed "Banff Scouting" on the form next to "Rider Name." He didn't like lying, but in case someone came snooping around to see who may have rented a helicopter recently, he didn't want the evidence to point straight back to him. That would just be way too easy even for the average scout, Phil deduced.

He usually signed a different name each time in an effort to keep things random. He wasn't sure what it would be this time until a poster of Banff National Park on the wall behind the counter caught his attention.

He filled out the rest as best he could, then paid in cash so as not to leave what they call a "paper trail." The woman seemed satisfied with the contract and the down payment, then directed them out the back door to the waiting helicopter.

The turbo engine was already screaming and the snow was swirling at a face-cutting pace as the two jogged under the spinning blades to the doors of the helicopter. Phil ran around to the other side and took the front seat as Max stepped up and jumped into the back. The pilot handed Phil a headset and motioned him to put it on. He turned around and did the same to Max.

"Headed up to township 65 and 66 and range 12, is that correct?" The words came across just as Phil put the device over his ears.

"Affirmative," he answered back, "Wolverine Hills."

"Understood! I'm familiar with it," the pilot responded. "Mighty rough terrain!" Phil nodded toward the pilot, before turning and looking back at Max to make sure he was seated and ready.

The chopper began its slow vertical lift from the ice-covered pad, creating a miniature blizzard as it hovered. It then accelerated and headed in a horizontal line to the north. The chopper climbed for a good twenty minutes, then leveled out at a comfortable cruising altitude.

Nobody spoke a word since lift off. Max and Phil weren't sure the protocol of talking in a helicopter. Both felt it was best to share only important information over the headset, so each remained quiet and enjoyed the beautiful terrain below. Once the chopper reached cruise speed, the clamor settled down to a steady, almost hypnotic, whirl as the blades cut through the frigid air.

Finally, Phil broke the silence.

"We're looking for a drilling rig. Shouldn't be too hard to spot as there will be a bright fluorescent crown against the snow covered background."

The pilot turned to him and nodded to show he understood.

"The rig is set between Nose Creek and Grayling Creek," Phil added.

"Should be easy enough to spot," the pilot answered. "Couldn't have picked a more beautiful day. Looks like a winter wonderland down there, don't it?"

The two men didn't answer him, but both nodded profusely, as they scanned the terrain beneath them.

There was another long stint of silence, as they continued their way north. Looking at the horizon line, Phil became worried he may have scheduled the flight too late in the day. It wasn't quite 2:30, but this far north the light was already fading.

"What are you fellas looking for anyway"? The pilot broke the lull. Max and Phil shared a quick glance before Phil answered.

"Just checking out the terrain; looking for ways in and out in case of emergency." Phil again glanced back at Max. "Speaking of which, try to stay back, a little bit away, from the rig itself. Be great if we can fly in low and stay as hidden as possible."

The pilot just turned to Phil and smiled. He knew exactly why these two were in his chopper. He gave Phil a thumb's up.

"Whatever you want, this is your ride fellas. We can even land if you want?"

Phil nodded to show his thanks. He then looked back to at Max. He wasn't looking too good.

"Hey, Max! You OK? First time in a chopper?"

Max turned and looked at Phil. He looked a little pale and sweaty.

"No. I've flown plenty of times, especially back in my day as an arctic rig manager; although it's been a while." Max took a deep breath and looked back out the window.

"Sounds like you're used to all this then," Phil said reassuringly.

"Not really, Phil. Fact is I don't like these things at all. Too many close calls, I guess."

Phil watched Max a little more as his lead scout laid his head against the cold glass and took another deep breath. The queasy look on Max's face was a real surprise. He couldn't help but chuckle to himself. Even the best of us have our weaknesses, Phil mused.

As Max leaned against the window trying to calm his nerves, he noticed the bright fluorescent orange derrick in the distance, off the port side.

"There she is," Max shouted, pointing to the northwest.

"Yes, sir! Thar she blows," the pilot confirmed.

He quickly moved the control stick to his left and the chopper dipped toward the ground. Max made a sound as if he was going to throw up, but managed to control himself. Phil looked back and smiled again.

"Looks like two rigs down there," the pilot said. "Supposed to be two"?

"Yeah. There are two rigs!" Phil said with slight amazement. He turned back to Max. "Hey! Looks like Black Gold got their rig up!"

Max mustered a half smile and nod back to Phil. Phil again laughed at his star scout showing he was indeed human. Both fluorescent tops were showing above the timber in the distance. They looked to be very close from this high in the air but were separated by several miles of dense forest and steep terrain.

"Which one you trying to stay away from?"

Phil looked over the situation to make sure he had his bearings straight.

"The south rig," came his answer to the pilot. "Stay west of the south rig and maybe we can work our way up and back over the treetops."

Phil leaned forward and pointed. "Head to that logging road, west of the two rigs. That looks like a good place to start."

The pilot again moved the joystick and the chopper started a free fall toward the thin dirt line winding its way through the dark green outline. Max put his hand against the window and braced himself out of fear. As the helicopter leveled off again, he relaxed and resumed looking out the window.

He could see the logging road clearly visible as it cut through the heavy, thick timber.

"Let's work the road first. I'd like to see if there are any old cutlines running off it," Max said, as he intensely studied the ground. Now that they were at their destination, Max was all business.

The blue and green aircraft hovered just above the treetops and slowly followed the logging road leading toward Zephyr's rig. The two veteran scouts studied the foliage, looking for any sign of change.

"Wait! Hold' er steady, if you can," Max said abruptly. "Right there! Looks like an old line there. You see it, Phil?"

Phil had to look back at Max to see where he was pointing. Following his stare and his finger, Phil looked past the pilot to his left and strained his eyes. It was tough, but eventually, he could see a slight difference in tree species and density. "Got it Max! Really hard so see."

As the helicopter moved slightly down the road, Max blurted out again.

"We're right above it now! It's all grown over with willows, but I can handle willows much easier than the dead fall in that thick mixed conifer forest," Max said excitedly. "Veer to the left here and follow the slightly shorter trees, please."

Max leaned way up in his seat and pointed over the seat in front of him so the pilot could see where he wanted him to go.

The pilot nodded and the helicopter left the logging road and slowly hovered above the willows as it headed southeast. Phil quickly scanned all around him.

"Keep her low," he said. "Keep her real low. Don't need any rig hands seeing us checking this access."

Max's excitement was obvious and Phil knew that was good news. He looked back and could see the adrenalin coursing through his veins.

"You've got a good eye there Max," Phil added, as he looked down at the cutline barely visible amid the towering pines and spruce.

The chopper covered the six miles of line to the banks of Nose Creek in just a few minutes.

"Lots of snow down there," the pilot noted casually.

There was no response. No response was necessary, as everyone knew it to be true.

"Damn those banks on that creek are steep," Max muttered, as he moved anxiously in his seat.

"Is there any way we can get a better look at the spot where the cutline dead ends into the creek?"

"Sure enough, boss" came the response. "I can drop to the creek bed, but can't land. Way too rough down there."

The chopper dropped down between the banks of the creek and hovered over the frozen water. Max knew that while motionless now, that creek would become a roaring torrent come spring. Currently, because of the freezing temperatures, it looked passable. Just as long as there was a way down there, Max queried?

"Banks must be 40-feet high on the west, but the east side bank has a good slope up from the bottom," Max said, talking mainly to himself.

"Any chance you can ease her a hundred yards north, up the creek?" Max asked without taking his eyes off the ground.

"I'll try boss, but it's getting awfully tight down here."

Like a snail, the chopper eased ahead. "If she gets any tighter, I'm pulling out, boss."

Max was intently surveying the entire creek and the banks on both sides. He was quickly sliding back and forth on the back seat. He looked up, down, and on both sides. Phil wasn't sure he truly could see all he needed but was impressed that Max was getting a firm idea of what could be done to get back here by foot or snowmobile.

Phil knew in an instant the helicopter was a very good idea.

Max finally nodded to himself.

"OK! That's good enough! Let's check the line from the other side of the creek, see if they also cut in from the east."

The pilot slowly manipulated the stick and the chopper lifted further away from the rugged creek bottom. With a close eye on his rotor clearance, the aircraft eased its way skyward and out of the thin, steep canyon.

"Glad that's over. Don't know about you, but way too friggin cold to go for a walk today," the pilot said half-jokingly.

Everyone shared a quick laugh and nodded in agreement. The helicopter made a right-hand pivot and headed east.

Phil got Max's attention, "I don't think we should get much closer to the rig, do you?"

Max was staring out the window deep in thought.

"No, I guess not. This is good," he said still looking out the window and strategizing in his head. Max gave Phil a thumb's up.

"We can head back to Grand Cache unless you need to see more Phil."

"Nope!" came the quick, confident reply. "If you're good, I'm good."

Phil turned to look at the pilot. "All right, my good man! We've seen enough. You can take us back to base."

The pilot simply nodded and turned the lever to his left. The helicopter rose further above the treetops and away from the rig to the northwest. As they were heading away, the Black Gold rig caught Phil's attention.

"Actually, circle around past the other rig over there if you don't mind," Phil said pointing at the bright light in the near distance. "Would love to get a good look at their operation."

Without a change in his countenance, the pilot nodded and led the helicopter in a wide half circle.

"You can get close to this one," Phil added. This seemed to make the pilot happy as with more speed, he buzzed right over the lease, just feet from the rig itself.

"Still rigging up, haven't got the draw works in place yet," Max said, as he and Phil looked intently down.

"Sure wish I was scouting this well," he added.

Phil laughed. "Sure would make our job a whole lot easier, now wouldn't it?" They both continued to stare down at the rig as the pilot circled the area. "But then again, who wants another three-day'er?"

Phil glanced back at Max, who took his eyes off the ground for one second to give Phil a reassuring nod and smile.

"What d'ya think?" asked the pilot.

"I'm good. Let's get out of here!" Phil answered.

"We're gone," said a confident pilot and off to the south, they flew.

As Max and Phil left the tiny terminal, Phil gave the pilot a long, sturdy handshake and thanked him for a safe trip.

"Might need you again in the next couple of months, so I'll be in touch."

"We're here to serve anytime you need us," he replied.

Phil reached into his back pocket and pulled out two hundred dollar bills.

"Also, I'd appreciate it if you didn't mention our little trip to anyone."

Phil extended his hand again, and this time he shook it and left the two bills in the man's hand.

Without a change of expression, the pilot nodded. "What trip?"

Phil and Max smiled. "Good," Phil said. "Let's go, Max. We've got a long drive ahead of us."

Max nodded and they both waved back to the pilot. They climbed into the truck and headed back toward Max's hometown of Rocky Mountain House, or "Rocky," as the locals called it.

It was a quiet drive south toward Hinton. Phil knew Max was planning his strategy for attacking the problems ahead. Max always got quiet when he had major situations to contend with.

"A penny for your thoughts," Phil finally said. Curiosity finally got the best of him.

Max didn't turn his head; he just kept watching the ice-packed road ahead.

"You know those large fir trees along the west side of the bank?"

"Um, yeah, I think so. Lots of large fir trees up there, though?"

"True. And that's what I'm counting on."

"How's that?" Phil questioned, taking a quick peak Max's way before returning his stare on the icy road before him.

"Figure I can cut half a dozen of those big trees and drop them down that slope. If I can fall them close enough together, I can take a portable winch and pull the trunks together and tie them off."

Phil was intrigued. He wasn't sure where Max was going with this or why he would consider going to so much work.

"That way," Max continued, "I might be able to make the perfect ramp down to the creek for my sled."

"That's a big job, Max! And a hell of a ride," said an astonished Phil.

"Not sure how else I can get back there. Not with all the stuff I am going to need. I think I can get down and across, and then back up the other side. The east side isn't so bad," Max prattled on.

"If you say so; Max. Sure sounds like a lot of work, to me, though!"

"Well, when you said this was going to be a rough one, you weren't lying were you?"

Phil laughed.

"No, Max, I wasn't."

The two traveled in silence again. The only sounds heard were the tires sliding across the icy road. Getting close to Max's house, Phil decided to throw out some encouraging Monday Morning QB advice.

"Look, Max, this is your show and I don't ever want to tell you how to do things. You're too experienced for that." Phil glanced at Max quickly to check if he was listening. "But just remember don't bite off more than you can chew, OK? Do what you think is best to get back to that rig, but if things turn out to be too difficult, feel free to walk away. Bottom line, I want you to be safe. Lives are more important than money."

Max nodded slowly. He continued to stare forward. Phil was pretty sure he only heard half of what he said. "Thanks, Phil," he said somberly.

That is all Phil offered. He knew it didn't matter what he said because Max was already deep in scouting mode. They drove the rest of the way to Max's driveway in silence.

"Want to stay here tonight, Phil?" Max politely asked.

"No! Thank you for that. I've got lots of shit to do! Need to get back to the city."

"I'm sure you do. When do we start the job?"

"We already did," Phil said with a smile. "But, I do need to report back to Black Gold before proceeding. From what we saw today, however, I wouldn't get too comfortable, Max. Judging from where Zephyr is with that rig already, we need to get you out there ASAP!"

Max gathered up his belongings and reached for the door handle.

"All right, Phil!" he said as he opened the door. "All I need is a day or two to get some special gear lined up. I'm going to need a little more than usual, as you might expect."

Max stepped out and turned back.

"OK, Max! I'll convey that all to Wayne tomorrow. Oh, almost forgot to tell you, Wayne Stadwell will be your contact. He runs Black Gold. But we can go over all the particulars tomorrow. It's late. Go get some rest."

"You got it! Goodnight Phil."

With that, Max shut the door and Phil backed out of his driveway and drove off with a wave. Max watched as the taillights of Phil's pickup disappeared around the corner.

Get some rest. That last line of Phil's stuck with Max as he stood there in the dark. Not in this house of five kids, Max thought, with a silent laugh.

Max moved quietly toward the bedroom not wanting to wake Carmen so late at night.

"That you, honey?"

"Who were you expecting?" Max asked teasingly.

Max felt his way through the darkness until he reached the bed. He found Carmen's ear, "you smell delicious!"

"Come closer and I'll give you a taste," Carmen purred.

The two bodies became one as both drifted off to sleep.

CHAPTER NINE

Max worked tirelessly into the late hours preparing his equipment. With all of his years of experience, Max sensed this was going to be a test like no other.

There were the items he always brought, the portable lights, chainsaw, monitoring equipment, and there was stuff, such as his Polaris snowmobile, that he needed to rely on for the first time in years.

Max laid the large trappers tent out and carefully stitched a few of the holes he hadn't noticed in the past. How he ever put the tent away with all these small rips tore at Max's compulsive need for perfection. Just wasn't like him to leave equipment unattended to.

After a couple of hours of mending what may be his home for the next two months, Max decided to add his smaller, backup tent, as well. Can never be too safe in the freezing temperatures of the north, Max rationalized.

He went down his checklist one-by-one. Chainsaw, worked fine; the propane heater was full and valves secure; monitoring equipment functional with more than enough batteries.

As important as the actual monitoring devices were, it was easy to forget about the antennas. If they were not the proper length or broke off in transit, you might as well go home. They were the source of picking up each particular frequency and the lifeline to garnering the critical information expected by the client. Even on the tightest of rigs Max had scouted, sooner or later someone would eventually call from the rig and involuntarily divulge some sort of critical information.

Ropes, straps, and chains were packed tidily in the carry boxes. Most scouts had equipment loosely thrown in the back of a pickup truck that went unchecked between jobs. That was not a good idea and not Max's way of doing things. While much of the equipment went unused, truth of the matter is; stuff breaks. It's just a matter of time, and much better to find out about it in the comfort of your garage where you can do something about it, than off in some remote area.

It had been two days and Phil had yet to call back. Max began to think that all his preparation was in vain. It wouldn't be the first time this has happened.

Max pushed the thought aside and once again focused his full attention on organizing. His gaze fell on the new hi-tech 800 Pro RMK Polaris in the corner of the garage. This would pay for itself on this job, Max knew. It was going to be his transportation in and out of that steep canyon and had enough power to pull a supply sled with all his equipment. Or so Max hoped.

He knew this "expensive toy," as Carmen called it, was finally going to earn its keep. Still, he wondered if it would be able to handle the banks of Nose Creek. They sure looked steep and rugged from the helicopter.

One thing was for sure, he would have to make special modifications to the front of it. From the chopper, Max had identified the red willows on the cutline and knew they had many years of growth to them. They were going to do some serious damage to the fiberglass body if he didn't construct a special front-end guard.

After several hours of measuring and bending pipe, Max was able to weld the invention into place. Looks like it should be able to cut a path through the willows without smashing up the poor machine, he thought. Max looked over his handy work and smiled. He'll find out for sure soon enough, but at this juncture, he was confident he could carve out a pretty good access trail after two or three trips in.

Max checked his Timex. It was 2.00 in the morning.

"Damn," he said to himself. Once again he was so into his work he forgot to say good night to Carmen and the kids. Max quickly threw one last duffel bag into the back of his Chevy and paused to look everything over. It was all tightly packed in the back, all neatly organized around the Polaris that looked like something out of a post-apocalyptic movie with all the metal pipe crisscrossing the front.

He stood in the silence of the garage and smiled. Job or no job, he was ready. Feeling a sense of pride, he spun around and headed to the house to get some rest.

Max awoke to the normal daily chorus of screams coming from his kids at the breakfast table. Unbeknownst to him, Carmen had called him for breakfast several times, but he was way too tired to hear. As Max lay in bed staring up at the ceiling, Carmen carefully pushed open the bedroom door and peeked in. Max turned and smiled at her.

"Hey, you're missing breakfast! The kids have almost finished everything."

"That's OK. I'm just enjoying listening to the commotion, might be a while 'til I hear it again."

Carmen nodded and motioned for him to get up.

"You can enjoy the chatter at the table just as well. Come on, the kids want to say goodbye before school."

Max smiled a mischievous smile. "Sounds good, but since I may be leaving soon, any chance we can get back in here after the kids get off to school?"

"One thing at a time, honey," Carmen said, as she walked away seductively swaying her hips.

Just then, the phone rang.

"Max! Max, it's for you!" came Carmen's voice from the kitchen.

"Thanks!" Max yelled back, as he reached over to the nightstand and picked up the cordless phone.

"Max here," he said with a slight yawn.

"Morning, Max!" Phil said enthusiastically from the other end.

Max knew right away the sound in Phil's voice was a good thing. Max could always read Phil by the tone of his voice.

"Ready to hit the road?"

"Always ready," Max replied with a chuckle.

"That's great! Stadwell called this morning; early; wants you on the road as soon as possible!"

There it was again, Max thought to himself. Days with no word then the call to hit the road right away. Some things never change.

"Zephyr's been drilling for three weeks now," Phil continued. "So they should be getting down to some points of interest."

Max just nodded into the phone. "Got it," he said rising out of bed.

"Think you'll have any problems with that access, Max?"

Max had no idea. He had a pretty good idea of how to accomplish his goal in his head, but there was no way to truly answer that question without getting out there and trying.

"I'll know soon enough, won't I?" came the sleepy reply.

"I guess you will!"

Max rose and stretched. He then started for the bathroom.

"Listen, Phil. I probably won't call anyone with a report for the first few days. I'll have to play it by ear, obviously, but might want to call Stadwell and tell him not to expect a call for a while. It's so remote out there, who knows when I'll get back to a phone."

Max opened the glass door and turned on the shower.

"Already explained that to him, Max, when you think you can get on the road?"

"Should be out of here in an hour," came the confident reply.

"That's my boy! I knew you'd be ready! Call me on your cell if you have any trouble."

"You know I don't like to use the cell, Phil. Never know who might be listening in."

"All right, Max. Use a landline if you can, but if something goes wrong or your need help, you just call, got that?"

"Sure Phil, I got it," Max said with a half-smile and nod.

Phil always liked to reassure his scouts that safety always came before the job. "All right, Good Luck, Max!"

"Thanks, Phil. Talk soon."

Max hung up the wireless phone on the night table. He stood there in the dimly lit room and paused. All was silent.

"Damn it!" he said. He had missed the kids. Max felt a tug in his gut. He always made a point of spending time with his kids and saying good-bye before he left. In this business, you never know when, or if, you'd be returning. A sense of sorrow overcame him, as he dropped his boxer shorts and stepped into the shower.

Just as he was adding shampoo to his hand, the shower door slid open and Carmen was standing there wearing nothing but a robe. Max stood in awe as she seductively removed it from her body. He stared in excited disbelief as the robe hit the floor.

The two finished showering and Max gently carried Carmen to the bed.

The drive was as Max expected – treacherous. He slid and skidded up and down and side to side almost the entire way to Grand Prairie due to the ruts in the snow and ice caused by the many heavy logging trucks that used these roads.

By the time he reached the fork in the road that would take him west to the Zephyr location, it was already getting dark. Max thought about going into town for the evening, but anxiety on starting the job got the better of him. It was going to be difficult in the fading light, but Max was hoping to identify the cutline he saw from the chopper.

Driving slowly with the window down, the biting cold caused tears to run from Max's eyes. Despite the heater on full blast, Max still shivered violently. He never took his eyes off the side of the road, intently looking for the red willows that would signal the cutline.

"That's it," Max said aloud with enthusiasm, as he hit the brakes and brought the Chevy to a stop.

The shoulder on the logging road was low, so Max wheeled into the ditch, as close to the timber as he could get. The pickup flew in the air and dropped with a bang. Max hit the accelerator, but nothing happened. There was no movement and the only sound was the screaming of the tires as they spun freely in the air.

"Shit," Max hollered.

He hit the accelerator again and nothing. Jumping out of his truck, he quickly could see that both back wheels were completely off the ground thanks to a partially covered log under his truck. Max never saw it.

He stood there shivering in the dark. It was late, and he was tired. He decided it was time to get some sleep. He would deal with digging himself out in the morning. One turn and one stuck truck. Max knew this may very well be a sign that Phil was right – this was going to be his toughest job yet.

After about an hour of jacking and groaning that next morning, Max was able to pull the eight-foot long log from under his truck. What may have taken some all day, Max was able to do in one hour. That was just the type of survival skill that made Max the ideal scout.

Max decided to walk back from the logging road to inspect the beginning of the cutline. Seeing no other hidden objects under the snow, it was a quick, easy drive to get his truck further back into the trees. It was here he decided to set up a temporary camp.

He found a wide, flat area to pull the truck off the cutline and into the heavy timber for further security. He walked back to the logging road to check it all out. Hidden from the logging road and hard to spot on the cutline, Max deduced.

He systematically unloaded what he needed from the back, and then wrapped the truck in a camouflage cover. Max checked his trusty Timex. Noon! Only lunchtime, but the northern daylight was already beginning to fade.

Max was anxious to start making a reliable trail to Nose Creek, so his sustenance would have to be just an apple and few Oreo cookies. Max pulled back the camouflage and lowered his tailgate. He stood momentarily admiring his handy brush guard on the Polaris.

Won't look so fancy when I'm done cutting the new trail, he thought. He then placed two wooden planks down as a ramp and jumped up onto the back of the snowmobile. Max straddled the cold hard seat and hit the ignition button.

"Fire baby, Fire!" he mumbled nervously to himself. The engine of the big machine growled into action causing the seat to vibrate wildly beneath him. The throaty sound coming from under the hood reverberated throughout the heavy timber surrounding him.

"Piss!" Max dismounted his trusty mechanical steed and returned to his pick-up. Reaching behind the seat he pulled the 300 magnum out and slid it into the new scabbard he had fashioned on the snow machine. The 300 wasn't his most trusted friend, but damn close. Once more, Max mounted the vibrating Polaris.

Max hit the throttle again and down the planks, he rode. He didn't bother stopping or looking back, he turned and powered right through the willows. His maiden voyage to Nose Creek had begun.

It was rough, much rougher than Max anticipated. Most of the willow trees were almost two-inches thick in diameter, and each bang into the front caused a big dent in the installed metal grate. , Max was spending as much time mounting and dismounting with his chainsaw to cut through the trees as he was going around or plowing through them.

After five hours of torture, Max decided it was time to go back to camp. Max checked the distance on the way back. Coming to a halt at the side of the tent, he was very discouraged. After all that work, he had only made 1.5 miles of trail. At the rate he was going, it would take two full days to get to the banks of Nose Creek. And, he knew, that was where the real work began.

"What the hell?" Max muttered out loud as if talking to some unseen companion.

Despite the slow start, the next day went much better. Max's Polaris took a beating that morning and he lost count of how many times he had to pull out his chainsaw. But after adding another half-mile to the trail, much to Max's surprise, the soil changed to a sandy loam and the willows became smaller and sparser.

Working right through lunch without stopping, Max found himself on the banks of Nose Creek by 4:00 pm, looking back at his trail drew a huge grin. It quickly faded as he turned and looked straight down the 50-foot embankment.

"Piece of cake," Max chuckled sarcastically.

It was incredibly lucky and fortunate to get a trail formed down the cutline as he did, but now the real challenge stared him in the face. One mountain, or canyon, at a time, Max joked to himself, as he turned and headed back to camp before it got pitch black.

By morning, Max had made the decision to move his equipment to the creek bank, which took him three trips and roughly four hours. Thanks to the back and forth traveling, the access was becoming easier and more familiar. Max was already starting to memorize every zig and zag, which would prove most valuable if he ever had to escape at night.

After finding a nice place to store all his equipment, he quickly set up his tent. He didn't spend much time on it, as he knew it was once again temporary. The focus was now solely on getting down the slope, back up the other side, and finding a concealed camp location within eyesight of Zephyr's rig.

Just as he pictured it in his mind after the flyover, the giant fir trees along the edge of the canyon rim were long enough and straight enough to reach the creek below. Phil thought he was crazy, but he was pretty sure they would act as a nice ramp once he secured them together.

It took planning, but Max finally selected five trees very close to one another to fall. As he started cutting, the chainsaw noise echoed through-out the forest followed by an explosive crashing sound as each tree was dropped, spraying frozen brittle branches into the frigid air.

"Noisy bastards," Max muttered out loud as though the newly fallen timber could hear him. All the racket made Max extremely nervous. He may still be on the opposite rim as the rig, but that noise could easily be heard up and down Nose Creek canyon. The ramp had to be made, so he tried to forget about it and just go as quickly as he could.

Course, he thought, maybe nobody was even thinking about scouts. This notion caused Max to laugh and expedite his cutting, because he knew it was quite the opposite, especially with so much on the line with the Wolverine Hills project.

The work was grueling and even with the sun shining brightly it was still -20 degrees below. Max knew he had gotten lucky, it could just as well have been – 40 degrees.

Max turned off his chainsaw and once again stood on the canyon edge to survey his work. Five fir trees all lying on the steep slope with tips all lined up on the creek below. It was a thing of beauty.

"Perfect," he said with a smile. Course, now he had to winch them all together on the top and bottom. That would have to be done with the nylon cord he brought and with his snowmobile. If the Polaris couldn't move the freshly fallen logs, it would mean using the hand winch and going one slow crank at a time. Not something Max wanted to do, but something he would complete because, as far as he knew, there was no other choice.

The sun in the sky told Max he would have to hurry to complete the job before dark. Quickly, he tied the yellow nylon cord around the first stump and hooked it to the back of the 80-horse-powered machine. This would be a real test. Max didn't want to wreck the Polaris, but if it could handle the load it would save precious time.

Max mounted up with one foot on the running board and his right knee kneeling on the seat. Now, he said to himself, and he squeezed the throttle. Once the cord was tight, he hit the gas wide open and the blue Polaris lurched ahead. Nothing!

"Piss," Max shouted and bailed off the seat. The first thing he checked was the cord. It was solidly in place. A different strategy might be in order, he thought.

Mounting the Polaris again, Max gunned it one more time. This time he rocked back and forth, as he hit the throttle. Shifting his weight by half standing and half kneeling, he was able to slowly inch the log ahead so it butted up against the other one. It was critical to have all five trees placed perfectly if they were to serve their intended purpose.

Four hours had passed and it was pitch black when Max moved the last tree into place. He had worked all day and well into the night without a break. The only thing that made him realize this fact was the growling noises coming from his stomach.

Time to eat, he said, as he moved the last log into place. He stepped off the Polaris and looked down at his handy work. It all looked great. He'd have to remove the branches with his chainsaw, and carefully shinny down the slope to cut off the tips of the trees then hand cinch the tops together, but all of the butt ends were together and a primitive ramp was definitely taking shape. Looking up to the top of the embankment all Max could see was a wreck waiting to happen.

Oh, well, he thought. We only live once, might as well live dangerously!

Back on top of the river bank, Max smiled with pride as his headlamp shined down onto the frozen creek below. As has happened to almost every other smile since he embarked on this trip, it quickly disappeared.

Looking down from the rim, the steep slope of the ramp suddenly made him panic. He knew one slip could be the end of him by way of a broken neck. This far from civilization no one would ever find him. The thought of it made him shudder.

Must eat, he thought to himself, and get some sleep.

Standing on the frozen creek late the next morning, Max looked back up. All logs were tightly together and all branches removed. He may not be able to make it down, or back up, but the ramp he envisioned in his head for days was no staring right back at him.

"Take that Phil," he said jokingly to himself.

He was tired and every muscle hurt in his body. Yet, looking up the ramp, he suddenly had a surge of energy; must be from anxiety and nerves, Max thought, since it was almost time, to test out his engineering feat.

After hours of shoveling, packing, and sweating in the arctic tempera-tures, the snowpack approach ramp leading up to the start of the logs was complete. It had to be solid because it needed to hold not only his weight and that of the snowmobile, but also the sled that would carry all his stuff down. That was a lot to ask but he desperately didn't want this to fail before it ever got started.

Max rested briefly and ate an apple sitting on the cold plastic seat of his Polaris. He looked around for a moment and suddenly saw the beauty of Wolverine Hills. What made those fucking environmentalists think they were the only ones who wanted to preserve God's great work, he asked himself.

The river gorge extended far into the distance and huge, dark green trees covered the region. After this job, maybe he'd come back here in the summer and camp with his family, he thought. There certainly will be a pretty good trail for them to follow, he joked.

The respite didn't last long, as the anxiety of testing the ramp was just too great to control. Max tossed the apple core aside and fired up the snowmobile.

"Here goes nothing," he said out loud and slowly rode up the snow ramp. The skis sank noticably in the top portion of the snow, but it held just fine and he was able to get the skies onto the logs without issue.

It was a very scary scene in front of him. It was probably a 50-foot drop at roughly a 45-degree angle, all dead-ending into ice and jagged rocks below. Any miscalculation could lead to a plunge to his death.

"What I do for a paycheck," he said.

Carefully, Max eased the nose of his machine down over the ramp. It was important to run the skis in the grooves between the logs to stabilize the journey to the bottom. This was something Max knew would be close, but didn't take specific measurements. He was going down regardless.

Fortunately, the skis were wide enough to fit one of the skis into a grove and the other just off another. Definitely close enough to keep from sliding to the side. With a hand tightly squeezing the brake, Max slowly started down.

Like letting a horse take you home, he thought, managing a nervous chuckle. Heavy on the brake, Max eased her down foot-by-foot. He leaned backward so not to go flying over the handlebars. Not a single buckle in the logs. That was good because a ski could easily get caught. The winching and the nylon cords were working, Max knew.

It took him roughly 10 minutes to go the 50-foot canyon side, but soon the skis hit the flat, frozen ice of Nose Creek. Max immediately jumped off and looked back up at his course. Everything was intact. He did it!

To the music of the idling snowmobile, he couldn't help but do a little victory dance. Like paying patrons, the tall spruce trees lining the east and west banks were a great audience.

All elation aside, it was now time for yet another daunting task; seeing if the Polaris had enough power to get right back up the primitive wooden pathway. In the back of his mind, Max always knew this was the one true unknown in his plan.

Luckily, the frozen creek was wide enough for Max to complete a fairly easy U-turn and he quickly had the Polaris facing skyward. With precision, he placed each ski in the same trusty grooves that brought him down and without hesitation leaned forward and hit the throttle.

The 800 started up the ramp, chewing and spitting chunks of bark out the rear like a buzz saw. The metal cleats clawing at the timbers slipped and slid, but managed to gain traction and the snowmobile shot toward the heavens. Up the ramp he flew. In fact, he went up so fast that at the rim's edge, he completely over-shot the snow ramp.

With the nose of the Polaris pointed almost vertical, Max came down with a thud, landing first on the rear, then he bounced forward as the skis hit the cushion of snow. He was close, real close, from flipping over and landing on his back. Very fortunate, he knew. A couple more inches and he'd be lying on his back with the snowmobile on top of him.

His hands were shaking and his knees were vibrating from the wild ride, but within the traumatized body was much relief. It worked much better coming up than he ever would have guessed which was vital since the next time he'd most likely be pulling a sled.

Max thought about going up and down again, just to make sure it wasn't all luck but decided against it. No need to put undue stress and work on the Polaris, or the ramp. He may need that extra power and reliability later, especially if there were angry rig workers after him.

Instead, he opted to inspect the ramp by foot. Nothing moved an inch. Some big chunks came out of the top of the logs, which could work against him in the future, but everything else looked intact.

Max climbed back to the top of the canyon and turned around. His eyes fell onto the canyon slope on the opposite side.

"Tomorrow it's your turn," he said with confidence and headed back to camp.

Moving his equipment up the east bank proved to be pretty easy compared to what it took to get down. A few times the snowmobile got buried in heavy snow, especially near the tall bushes, but nothing a little reverse and retry couldn't handle.

Max carried most of his equipment down to the frozen creek by hand and then loaded the sled in the creek bottom. The thought of driving a heavy sled down that steep slope was just too daunting, and too much of a gamble, he deduced, in the end. He had come too far and done too much to jeopardize it now.

Don't want to push my luck, he thought; knowing full well that getting that whole canyon ramp to work was not just due to hard work, but luck, as well.

A couple full-throttle advancements with several reverses and Max was sitting on his Polaris on the rim of the east bank. In the distance, through the swaying branches of the dense forest, he could see the derrick of the drilling rig.

Max idled the snow machine under a low-hanging branch and shut the engine down. He had done it. He had made it back into this extremely remote area, through the treacherous canyon, and was now looking directly at his prize.

Leaving his trusty transportation well-hidden below the tree limbs, Max moved with the stealth of a lynx through the two-feet of snow. Like he was playing hide and seek, he darted from tree to tree, always moving closer to the rig and the ultimate goal of finding an ideal place to set up camp.

The site had to be totally invisible to the rig, yet it had to give him a line of sight with his spotting scope. Every decision had to be carefully considered, including the placement of his generator so the low rumble was muffled to anyone who might come snooping around. Max had made the decision long before embarking on the job to use propane as his heating source so there was no smoke.

Max sprang back and forth from tree to tree and grove to grove for almost an hour. After transecting the region, a camp location was selected. He was confident it was the best in that particular area and with snow to use as cover; his white trapper's tent would be perfectly camouflaged after he cleared out a nice, 15 X 15-foot square spot.

He made sure to leave his snowmobile a little further back. Not only did the sound of the engine make Max nervous this close to the rig, but having it by the canyon was a good idea in case he had to leave in a hurry.

It took that afternoon and most of the next morning for Max to surreptitiously dig out his camp and move in all his equipment. His big trapper's tent evolved into a home complete with propane heater, shelves, bed, and even a plywood floor.

Max circled the tent slowly checking every detail. He cursed under his breath as he saw several tears he had missed during his shoddy stitching session the week before.

Grabbing his pick and shovel, he moved cautiously over a small hill into a shallow dip by a large spruce tree and began digging. The 3x3x3-foot hole would be lined with insulation and a special white cover that would act as the top. Everything had to be camouflaged to make it as inconspicuous as possible. This hole would serve as his secret vault to conceal critical, expensive equipment, such as his special monitor when he had to leave camp for supplies and report back to Phil and the client.

The next task was selecting and digging out a nice hole for the Honda 1500 generator. The location had to be far enough from the tent as not to interfere with his scanning devices. Max was sure to bring the blind that was designed not only to hide it but also came with a special noise-reducing outer cover. It really did work and was one of those perfect scouting items that made Max smile.

Every detail was planned to make his camp as invisible as possible for as long as possible. He knew deep in his heart, however, that no matter how perfect his camp blended in with the surroundings, if they opted to come looking, sooner or later he would be discovered.

Surveying the camp after securing the generator in place, Max was so hoping it would be later rather than sooner. Much later, he thought, not only because he needed time to successfully finish the job, but also because he would hate to see this incredible camp left behind.

It did look perfect. The generator and storage holes were undetectable and you could barely see the top curve of the white tent above the surrounding snow. Max nodded with pride.

Finally, in place, Max decided that night would be a celebration of sorts. He would reward himself with his first cooked meal – steak and eggs. He would eat in peace with Mother Nature and her haunting breath whispering through the boughs outside, as his only guest.

He was here to scout, but scouting would wait. Well, at least until after he finished eating.

Morning came early for Max. He had trouble fine-tuning the monitoring equipment the night before and it bugged him all through his anxious sleep. Max was really hoping to catch some morning chatter. That was the time that companies scheduled their daily report with management back at headquarters and it was a popular time for workers to call their loved ones back home.

Patiently, he slowly turned the knob checking each frequency on the new scanner he just ordered from Sweden. The Swedish-made scanner gave him an advantage over other scouts because it allowed for additional frequencies to be manually programmed in. Most scouts didn't even know this mode or capability existed.

This one also had the ability to scan on its own and stop at any station that detected activity. As did most scanners, it was complemented, too, by a built-in device that automatically recorded everything it picked up.

Once he had the scanner searching all relevant frequencies, Max quickly stepped outside to get a first-hand look. He could see the red and white outline of the rig derrick through the thick brush and tall trees and he could hear every bang and clang necessary to identify any activity taking place. The "V-doors" that exposed the rig floor were facing west, which was ideal in relation to the opening in his tent flap.

In the large spruce next to the white canvas tent, Whisky Jacks were scolding the new intruder and it instantly brought a smile to Max's face. The Whisky Jacks competing for attention and the soft creaking of the spruce boughs as they swayed in the light breeze were so familiar and a sort of comfort that only someone alone in the bush could identify with.

The direction of the breeze was critical to survival. Max was upwind from the rig location. Most of the time, the winds blew westerly, which would take any sour gas away from his camp. As most scouts know first-hand, sour gas can be a dangerous and deadly part of the job. Max had been through one potentially deadly experience with it already.

Technically, the gas is hydrogen sulfide and attacks the nervous system and can instantly cause someone to stop breathing.

On that particular day, Max was eating pistachios while peering through his spotting scope. One second he was watching the drill stem test at the rig, the next his fingers and toes suddenly started tingling and his breathing became shallow. Without a second thought, he jumped up and ran.

He couldn't see it, or smell it, but he knew what it was. And he took off running to get away from it. A hundred yards up a hill, he finally got out of it. Sour gas is heavier than air and always goes to the lowest level. He was lucky there was a hill to climb that day.

So was his blue heeler, Rocky. As Max ran for his life, he looked back to see his dog desperately trying to get through the deep snow. After one leap, he tried another, but gas stopped him in his tracks. The heelers' nose went under the snow and never came back up. With shirt over his nose and mouth, Max ran back, picked him up, and again turned to fresh air.

He wasn't sure if they outran the silent killer or it just happened to dissipate enough to allow them to live, but either way they both managed to escape with their lives. Max's Blue Heeler dog wasn't the same after that, however.

Rocky was the best dog he ever had, and it made him sad thinking about how he walked slightly at an angle and wasn't quite all right in the head after that day. Max vowed never to bring another companion with him on any scouting job. It was one thing if something happened to him, but if someone else got hurt, even his dog he'd never be able to live it down.

Maybe that notion was another reason he suddenly had to leave Pole Cat's truck on the last job. Who knows, Max thought, but that smell in his truck was pretty much man-made sour gas. Max chuckled at the comparison, glad to get his mind off that sad day.

Max didn't want to dwell on the experience any longer, but he did decide to get a breathing device on his next trip to town, just in case. At $10 a day it was damn cheap to save a life, he deduced.

It was time to check out his new scanner. As much as he relished his Swedish scanner, it couldn't compare to the one item he had in the newly crafted hiding spot.

After years of experimenting and research, Max had finally developed a device that could intercept satellite calls. Even Phil was unaware of his little invention and he wasn't about to tell him or anybody else. It would be his little secret – his little industry edge.

He wasn't sure but was fairly certain nobody else had cracked the satellite dilemma, which gave him an incredible advantage over all others. Max retrieved the priceless commodity and returned to the confines of the tent.

No sooner had he entered the warmth of the tent, did a dull thumping sound ring out in the distance. Max stopped what he was doing and listened intently. It was subtle but the thump, thump, thump slowly grew louder.

"Chopper!" Max said aloud with surprise and anxiety.

Max turned and ran straight to the generator and turned it off. He quickly covered it with pre-cut pine boughs and turned to check out the rest of camp. It looked all camouflaged, so Max quickly ran back to the tent and jumped inside.

Just as he entered and shut the flap behind him, the helicopter was over him. Max watched through the crack in the flap as the bird flew right overhead straight for the rig. It slowed considerably and hovered over it, blowing debris in all directions. It finally landed between the rig and the engineer's quarters.

Max grabbed his spotting scope and pointed it through the flap. The pilot was the lone occupant and he remained seated with blades spinning. Max watched as two rig personnel, crouching down to avoid being beheaded, approached. As they neared, the pilot opened the door. Each handed him a large brown envelope and quickly retreated away. The pilot gave an exaggerated wave, then shut the door and was once gain headed skyward. It made a large circle around the rig, came back toward Max, and disappeared out of sight behind the large spruce trees.

Slowly, Max lowered his spotting scope.

"Fuck," he said ever so softly to himself.

Max couldn't believe what had just happened. In one fell swoop of the helicopter, he knew his job had gotten infinitely harder. Zephyr was delivering its daily reports to the city via helicopter.

Max leaned back onto his sleeping bag and sighed heavily. He was going to have to earn every penny on this job.

CHAPTER TEN

Roger was in a good mood. He strolled past Shelly's desk and shot her a confident, arrogant look.

"How's it going, honey? You get sexier every day!"

Roger gave his exaggerated wink and continued to his office.

Shelley said nothing. Great, she thought, I work for a jerk and now a sexual harasser. Everything about him disgusted her – his attitude, his demeanor, and his stinking cigar stench. It was always bad, but since Wolverine Hills, it had gotten much worse.

The news that Wolverine Hills was now up for bid and Zephyr was the frontrunner in landing it made Roger and the company the talk of the city.

Shelley didn't care how important he was, or this project, she was tired of his constant harassment and badgering.

"Morning, Shelley!" The voice startled her. She was so deep in thought, she never heard anyone walk in. Right in front of her was Nick Mayfield with a handful of papers.

"Oh, hey, Nick. How's it going?"

"Great! Just great! This Wolverine hills project just might be our stepping stone to bigger and better things, don't you think?"

Shelly was pretty sure she wouldn't be around to find out but managed a big smile and nod. It may have been faked, but she sold it well. Too many years of working in the customer-service industry, she deduced.

"I'm keeping everything crossed," he continued, "but my eyes because I still need them to read the geological data."

Nick laughed out loud, hoping Shelley found it funny. She giggled, again feigning genuineness. She also did it to help him relax. Nick was always nervous and uptight, even when there was no reason to be. They call geologists rock sniffers and Shelley thought Nick really did fit the description. But he was very nice and completely harmless. Unlike the asshole in the other room, she thought.

"Is Roger in yet"?

"Oh, yes the King is in, sitting on his throne basking in all his glory."

Nick wasn't sure if she was joking or being sarcastic. It wasn't like Shelley to throw out a comment like that, so Nick wasn't sure how to take it. He giggled, awkwardly, but looked at her with a slightly confused frown.

"I'll tell his majesty your waiting," she continued.

"Um, uh, great! Thanks," was the baffled reply, as Shelley hit the intercom and alerted Roger.

"Send him in gorgeous!" Roger didn't bother to use the intercom; he simply yelled it out the door so Nick could hear.

Nick smiled at Shelley and entered the posh office. As he stepped in, Roger was standing at the window looking out. There was a heavy cloud of smoke lingering all around him; it reminded Nick of Pig Pen from the "Peanuts Comic Strip. This caused Nick to grimace as he came in and took a seat. He didn't smoke and hated the smell of it. It suddenly dawned on him this was one big reason he always resented coming to Rogers office.

Without turning to greet Nick, Roger took out his cigar and began speaking.

"Come here to the window, Nick," Roger motioned with his hand. "Look down, way down."

Nick stepped up, right into the toxic cloud and tried holding his breath. It was futile and he started gagging immediately. Roger didn't seem to notice or care.

"See that speck of a building down there," he continued. "The tiny, rusty brown colored one?"

Nick knew which one he was referring to.

"Those minnows think they can swim with the big fish, but we're going to gobble those fuckers up!"

Roger put the cigar back into his mouth and inhaled. Nick didn't say anything, he just looked over inquiringly. Roger glanced at him and studied the geologist's blank stare.

"Never mind, Nick," he concluded as he blew smoke out, almost right into Nick's face. "That's not your department. No need to get you involved. Come on, let's talk rocks!"

Roger slapped Nick on the back and headed back to his desk. He put the cigar in the ashtray and stomped it out. Thank God, Nick thought, as he took a seat opposite Roger.

"Where do things sit this morning?"

"Well, Mr. White ..."

"Never mind that Mr. White bullshit! Roger, just fucking Roger."

Nick began to speak but was quickly cut off, again.

"Actually, on second thought, if this hole of ours is a raging success like we think it will be, you may call me Sir!"

Roger laughed, as he turned to Nick and took a seat in his oversized chair. That really did look like a throne, Nick thought. Nick cast that thought aside and looked down at his papers. He pulled out a large manila envelope from the pile and handed it to Roger.

"Here is the full report from the rig, but in a nutshell, we're just about through the Fernie formation. I have to say, it's been slow."

Roger glanced at Nick, as he took the report and started perusing it. Nick continued. "The shales in the Fernie are a nightmare, as you know, and we had to stop and condition mud for several hours to guard against sloughing."

Roger didn't respond as he took the report out of the envelope and glanced at the cover page.

"Any other problems," Roger asked abruptly, throwing the report onto his desk.

Nick fidgeted in his seat. "Um, not yet, thankfully, but I guess my thought is we should run intermediate casing once we get to the Charlie Lake."

"Why do you say that? You just said everything is running smoothly, there's no reason to take any unnecessary chances and waste time, is there?"

Nick wasn't sure how to respond. He shifted his weight again and swallowed, nervously.

"But the drilling program calls for casing once we hit the Charlie Lake formation, anyway, if I remember correctly," Nick said timidly.

Roger's response was a quick, rude grunt. "Let's just see what Matt Crane on location thinks about that. He'll have a better handle on things at the rig."

Nick suddenly felt a bit nauseous. He wasn't sure it was the cigar smoke in the room or the fact that Roger was challenging everything he was saying.

"Um, you sure that is wise? I thought we weren't supposed to have phone conversations with the rig regarding operations?"

Roger just laughed and looked at Nick as if he didn't matter.

"Settle down, Nick!" Roger motioned for Nick to relax. "I just want to get Matt's opinion on exactly where he wants to set the casing."

Nick still didn't feel comfortable with the idea and opened his mouth to speak, but suddenly thought better of it. Roger dialed the number to the satellite phone at the engineer's shack. Roger put it on speaker and leaned back in his chair.

After several rings, a low, growling voice responded, "Crane, here. What ya need?"

"Hey, Crane, ya old' cranky prick! Took ya long enough to answer. What d'ya got out there some bimbo or something?" Roger laughed loudly. He was the only one that thought it was humorous.

"Bimbo my ass! Workin' way too damn hard for that, Roger!" There was a brief pause before Matt continued. "Besides, how do I get a broad out here if you guys don't let us make any damn phone calls?"

Roger just shook his head. "I see your sense of humor is still intact," he answered still laughing. "Let's switch gears and talk business instead of pussy, OK? Maybe you'll be easier to get along with."

Roger paused before adding, "You got your drilling program there?"

"Yep, right in front of me," came the cold, quick answer. Roger leaned forward and grabbed the unlit cigar out of the ashtray and put it in his mouth. Nick looked at him, hoping he wouldn't light it.

Instead, he leaned back in his chair and continued talking.

"Nick, our geologist here, is concerned about the Fernie shale and wanted to confirm that we are still planning on running intermediate at the top of the Charlie Lake. I told him it was a waste of time. What says you, big guy?"

"Roger," came the confident reply. "I've been looking at that, but don't want to discuss it on the phone. I wrote up my opinion in the morning report, didn't you get it?"

Roger just glanced at the report Nick handed him and back out the window. "Yeah, I got it! I just wanted to hear it from you. Get more information and confirmation, you know?"

"Well, I stand by the recommendations in that report," Matt said, purposely trying to be vague in case anyone was listening in.

"Fine," came Roger's curt reply. "I'll just forward the report on to Houston and see what they say."

"Forward to Houston? Fuck Houston!" Matt came back angrily. "This is our well, not Houston's!"

Roger looked over at Nick and raised his eyebrows with pride. He knew that comment would rile the engineer.

"Relax there, Crane, they just want to be notified of all that goes on up there at the site. I'm sure they will go along with your ideas. What does Murphy the onsite geologist, say?"

Roger thought he heard Matt grunt with displeasure. "Never mind what that little hair-brained Scotchman thinks! His job is to check the samples and pick the formation tops, my job is to drill the fuckin well! Look, since you must know, I agree with you! We don't need to run any intermediate for a while. We don't have the time! We need to keep drilling!"

Roger smiled and leaned back in his chair. He happily chewed on his cigar. "That's what I thought."

"I don't want to discuss it anymore on the phone; you should understand that better than anyone, Roger. I'll send another package out by chopper tomorrow!"

Still smiling and playing with his cigar, Roger rolled his eyes. "Fine, Crane, fine. But before you hang up I did want to ask you how the security system is working"?

"You mean that shit house of a road block you got down there on the entry with the three stooges?"

"Listen, Matt!" Roger said suddenly getting serious. "That shit house and those so called stooges are there to do a job and I don't want you or any of your hands hassling them, you got that? All I want to know is if the phone lines from the gate to your engineer's shack are working and if the security personnel are notifying you of all entries to the rig site. Simple fucking request, Matt!"

Roger knew his change in tone would get the curmudgeon to fall into line. He did it partly because he was growing annoyed by his negative attitude and partly to show his seniority. The response from the engineer made both his smile and pride grow.

"Yes, Roger. Phones and security are in place and all seems to be working fine."

Roger shook his head as he looked at Nick and winked. "Oh! One other thing, seen any signs of scouts around?"

The old, crusty pessimist quickly returned. "No scouts!" he shouted. "They don't dare come around or they'll get what's coming to 'em!"

"That sounds good," Roger said. "If you see any, however, you let me know."

"Yeah, you bet, Roger. Right after I beat the shit out of 'em!" Matt snarled

"Do what ya have to there, Matt, as long as it's legal and Zephyr doesn't get sued!" Roger said with a laugh. Nick did not like that at all.

"Hang tuff one minute, I'll see if Nick has any questions," Roger quickly added.

Nick immediately waived him off with a wave of the hand and shake of the head. Nick was done. He only wanted to get out of the room. He was feeling extra nauseous, partly from the smoke in the room and because of the uneasiness from the conversation.

"All right, Crane, we're good here. Talk to you later." Roger hung up without waiting for Matt to acknowledge.

Nick immediately got up and headed for the door. "Hold on, Nick! Let's quickly call Houston and let them know what we recommend. You may be able to add some value."

Roger then yelled out the door. "Shelley! Get Al Wallace on the phone for me!" There was no please or thank you added.

Roger quickly scanned the report and started nodding to himself. He flipped the page and kept reading. He nodded to himself again. Nick, looking pale and sweaty, slowly plopped himself back in the chair.

"Looks like Matt wants to drill through the Charlie Lake, and to the Doig, and then log those formations," Roger said without looking up. "The logs should give us a good indication of any hydrocarbons to that point. Once we log, we'll run intermediate casing and eliminate the risk of the Fernie shale coming in on us. That should put a damper on any gas kicks from the upper zones."

"You do know that's not what headquarters requested," was the sheepish, nervous response from Nick.

"Hence the reason we are now calling them, Sherlock." Roger just glanced at Nick and laughed. Nick so wanted out of the office. He desperately wanted some fresh air – and possibly a stiff drink.

"Al's on the phone," Shelley's voice rang out from the other room.

"Put him through," came the curt response.

"Hello, Al!" Roger said with exaggerated enthusiasm, knowing that persuading Houston to change the drilling program may be tenuous.

Roger carefully explained Matt's recommendation to Al and the chief exploration geologist who was also sitting in on the call.

"Pretty risky, don't you think?" Al responded. "Things have been going along smoothly to this point, Roger, why do you want to deviate now?"

"Well, Al, it's to speed up time. Matt Crane is the engineer on location and he really feels, if we keep the hole in good shape, we can make the extra 300 feet no problem before we run intermediate."

"Crane has been known to forego safety in the past, hasn't he," Al said it as a statement, but it was also a bit of a question to everyone.

"Maybe. I don't recall, personally. He's one tough son of a bitch, though! That's why we picked him for the job."

"I certainly hope that's not the only reason," Al piped back.

"No, hell no! He's the best on these deep foothill holes! He's got fifteen years engineering experience up here in the north, most of it in foothills drilling."

Roger shuffled the cigar back and forth in his mouth, nervously. Roger knew he was going out on a limb by backing Matt's recommendation. It was a limb he didn't want to be on, however, he really did want to get all the data they could before the sale date. And he wasn't about to fail Houston.

If it played out, as he hoped, he'd look like a smart, take-charge type leader, which should easily send him soaring right into the company penthouse. If his idea and support of Matt screwed up, he'd be dropping like a turd into the outhouse, he deduced.

Roger heard some serious talk going on between Al and the geologist. He couldn't hear what they were saying, but he knew it was a pretty intense conversation. He waited anxiously.

Nick was anxious, as well, but for other reasons. He was really hoping Houston would not agree, and decide to run intermediate at the next formation. Safety first, Nick always thought.

"All right, Roger," finally was the response. "You tell Matt to use his best judgment and you use yours, as well. You guys know the geology up there better than we ever will, so we will let you make the final call on that."

Roger was excited. He quickly pumped his fist and mouthed "Yes" to himself. He not only got the green light, but it also came with a compliment, which was extremely rare. It just wasn't in the DNA of Texas oilmen, Roger thought, as they all thought they were God's gift to the industry. But there it was – a direct remark from Houston about Roger and his team knowing more than them. A double coup, he rationalized. Roger fed off the energy and rolled with it.

"Sure, sure Al! Thanks for the trust! It will all work out fine! By the way, forgot to tell you, Zephyr is the envy of the oil patch here in the city."

Roger stared out the window with a big, prideful smile.

"Yes, Roger, we're all pretty excited about the possibilities down here as well, but we don't have anything yet! Keep your eyes on the prize."

Roger's smile didn't completely disappear, but it did fade slightly. He should have known Houston would splash a little cold water on his raging excitement.

Al continued. "By the way, I'm planning on being in Calgary on April 14 and I would like to fly up to the rig and get a firsthand look at the operation. Can you make the necessary arrangements, Roger?"

Roger was still staring out the window, trying to process it all.

"Um, yeah, you bet, Al. Look forward to seeing you, maybe we can get in a game of golf." Roger said, trying to sound fun and supportive.

"Not sure I'll have time, but we'll see. Carry on, Roger. Keep me informed on the drilling going forward. Thanks!"

Before he could answer, Al hung up. Roger was immediately irked by the move, not realizing it was the same way he treated his rig engineer.

Nick sat there knowing Roger had gotten what he wanted and Zephyr was going to drill as fast and as far as they could without following proper drilling protocol. It was a hugely important project, Nick knew that, but drilling straight through the Charlie Formation without running intermediate was not a wise thing to do.

Roger suddenly interrupted his deep thought. "What d'ya think Nick? Is this our fucking show or what?"

"Yes, Mr. White, it's our show," he said barely audible.

"Damn straight! This causes for a celebration!"

With that, Roger rose and walked to the corner of his office where he had a little bar set up. He poured a shot of Canadian whiskey in two separate glasses and, chomping proudly on his cigar stub, brought them back over to the desk. He handed one to Nick.

"Oh, No thanks Roger!"

Roger ignored him and shook his head for Nick to take it. He nervously and cautiously did. Roger removed his cigar for just a second so he could take a big hard drink, then plopped it back in. Nick watched him, and then looked at his own glass. He smelled it and grimaced. He then took it to his mouth and took a very tiny sip. He grimaced even more.

Roger was oblivious. He was too self-absorbed and he walked over to the window and looked out again. Nick put the glass down on the desk and firmly gripped the mound of paperwork in his lap.

"I'm," he started nervously, "a little concerned about the shale, Roger."

Roger didn't respond for a few seconds. He was enjoying being in charge and standing up here on the top floor of the tallest building in town, looking down at all the "plebeians," as he called them.

"Fuck the shale!" he finally answered. "Matt knows how to drill wells and I take him at his word."

He then turned back toward his desk. "Where are those matches? Ah, there they are!" Roger grabbed the matchbox off the desk, took one out, and lit the little stub in his mouth.

He blew the match out and threw it and the box on the desk. Nick's face turned a shade more white and a hint of light green. Roger sucked in to get the cigar really lit, then blew out a huge puff of a smoke. It hovered over his desk like a big rain cloud.

Satisfied, Roger turned back to the window. Nick just stared at the thick smoke hovering around Roger's head and his mouth started watering. He really didn't feel well. He looked down at his papers in his lap, then nodded to himself and rose.

"OK. If you don't need me anymore I guess I'll just be getting back to work now," he said quietly, starting for the door in a speed walk.

Roger said nothing. He simply nodded and raised his glass to him. Nick slipped out the door, extremely relieved to get out of that office.

"How'd the meeting go?" a polite Shelley asked as he scurried past her desk.

"Good! Good!" he said, not slowing down and barely glancing at her.

Shelley was unsure why Nick was in such a hurry. She watched him throw open the door and exit as if the fire alarm had gone off.

Suddenly, the intercom crackled. "Shelley! Get your little tight ass in here!"

Shelley's quizzical look instantly turned into annoyance. She let out a huge disgruntled sigh, then grabbed her notepad, and headed into Roger's office.

CHAPTER ELEVEN

Meetings, nonstop meetings, were the order of business around Black Gold. Fortunately, the mood was getting livelier and more upbeat as the news coming from the field was positive. Not only were operations apparently back on schedule, but the last report from Wildcat Scouting was very promising.

Wayne was looking particularly energetic, as he stood ready to conduct the morning business.

"Morning!" Wayne greeted everyone with a smile. "You want the good news or do you want the good news?"

There was a round of giddy short laughs, as the three grinning staff members stared back at Wayne.

"Let's start with the good news!" he said, continuing his upbeat lead-in. "Looks like we have a partner on the Wolverine Hills project. The company is Global Resources. This was a lead from Val before she headed up to the rig and we'll be, hopefully, getting everything together tomorrow."

"What happened to Alpine Resources?"

"Good question, Joe," Wayne replied. "They just wanted too much in the end. They wanted full control of operations and no less than 45% interest with 30% capital input."

"Did they have guns drawn and masks on when they asked for all that?" a flabbergasted Joe asked with a hollow laugh.

Wayne chuckled.

"Guess they thought we were desperate and they were the only takers in town. Good thing that was not the case. Global came in with a much more fair and reasonable request and we ended up negotiating 30% capital for 30% interest, which Chuck and I feel is a sweetheart deal for us on a play this wild."

Wayne paused to let this news sink in. Both Joe and Gerry seemed satisfied, as they both slowly nodded back at Wayne.

"Global has drilled some shallow wells in the area and they felt this well was worth the risk," Chuck added.

"I'd like to add, too," Wayne said, "that there's a huge bonus in doing business with Global. Apparently, they have access to a major pension fund and if the well looks good near the bottom sections, they'll help finance the land purchase."

This news was very well received, even from Gerry who let out a surprised smile. One of the biggest hurdles in the entire Wolverine Hills project was raising enough capital in order to put in a satisfactory bid for the land and now it looked as though Black Gold would be able to do this. This was huge because it now meant they could compete with the likes of Zephyr Petroleum.

Wayne looked over and smiled at everyone, especially Chuck, to show his gratitude. Chuck confidently and proudly returned the nod and smile.

Wayne was a team player and knew the value of giving credit in order to keep morale high. He was also a very modest person and tried to avoid the limelight whenever possible. People of his good-mannered, quiet nature usually didn't make good leaders, but because Wayne was so good at what he did and built fabulous teamwork, he successfully bucked this corporate trend. He was a rare breed.

"With that," Wayne said, "maybe we should get a quick update on our well before I share the other potentially good news. Joe, why don't you jump in here?"

Wearing a broad grin, Joe looked down at his notes.

"Well, do you want the good news or do you want the good news first?"

He looked around the room, nervously, to see if his joke went over well. Chuck and Wayne chuckled, but Gerry just rolled his eyes. Even in those pessimistic eyes, however, Joe could see Gerry was in a good mood and almost joined in on the laughter.

"The best news comes from Val," Joe went on. "She is ecstatic over what she is seeing in the formation samples. Her report gives a great breakdown and description of the Cadomin Formation. Looks to be about 10 feet of heavily oil stained sand and the samples also show good porosity with the tops coming in twenty to twenty-five feet high, which, as we all know, is a great sign of things to come if everything holds true."

Joe paused to look up. The look on everyone's face was what he expected, silent elation. Joe smiled, confidently, then returned to looking at his notes.

"Harry Marinoff, our engineer on site, feels we should test the Cadomin before it becomes too contaminated with drilling mud. Both Val and I agreed with that assessment and told him to order testers. Harry said the zone should be tested by late afternoon and we should have results by tomorrow."

Joe paused again. This time he did not look up, as he was trying to find the next item to discuss.

"Um," he started. "Let's see here. Oh, and Harry said he wants to run intermediate casing as soon as we get through the Fernie Formation to make sure we don't have problems with sloughing shale."

Joe looked up and threw his pen on the pad of paper in front of him. "That's it from me. All is looking good and I'll update you all on what Harry finds as soon as he lets me know."

Everyone nodded at Joe, satisfied with his update.

"Now, that brings me to the other good news," Wayne said, taking over for Joe. "I received a call from the man we hired to scout Zephyr's well..."

A grunt from Gerry caused Wayne to pause. He just looked over at him and glared before continuing.

"At any rate, the scout tells me that for whatever reason, the engineer for Zephyr decided to drill past the casing depth and the Fernie shale came right at them with all its might! Now, it looks like they've been stuck in their hole for the last thirty-six hours. According to the scout, Max is his name, they only have about six feet of movement in the pipe and now they are trying to get out of the hole to run intermediate string."

Joe laughed. "That's classic. Nothing like closing the barn door after the horse is out."

There was light laughter in the room, partly because of Joe's apropos analogy and partly because of the joy of hearing Zephyr was having serious issues.

"Max is getting quite a bit of chatter over the air and it appears, shit is hitting the fan over there. Looks like management back in Texas wanted casing in the hole right away, but the locals here in Calgary talked them out of it. Bet it was our good ol' buddy Roger who did that!"

Wayne laughed at that statement and looked around the room at everyone. Their glowing faces showed they agreed.

"Man! I sure wish I was a fly on the wall when that news went down! What I'd pay to see the look on Roger's face when he got his ass chewed out," Chuck said with a laugh.

Everyone chuckled at the thought of the brash, trash-talking Roger getting in serious trouble.

"That would be priceless," Joe agreed.

The phone on the oak table interrupted the conversation. Wayne leaned in and punched the blinking light.

"Val is on the line, calling from the rig, sir. Would you like me to patch her through?"

"That would be great. Thanks!"

Everyone in the room sat in silence waiting to hear from Val. Joe got a little excited and leaned up in his chair to get a few inches closer to the speaker phone.

"Morning, Wayne! Morning, guys!" Val's voice resonated with excitement.

"Morning, Val! You're sounding lively! That bush environment must agree with you," Wayne replied.

"Sure does," Val responded. "The northern lights bring out the wild side in me."

That statement got Joe way too excited and he couldn't help himself. "In that case, I'll be there tomorrow," he blurted out.

He was embarrassed the second he finished. Joe's face turned red and looked around the room hoping people found it funny. Gerry laughed pretty hard, but Wayne and Chuck just looked at him with baffled expressions.

"Try to contain yourself, Joe," Val laughed nervously. She then went straight back to business.

"At any rate, I wanted to try and catch you all during the morning meeting to let you know the operation I mentioned in the fax is going well. Should have results in tomorrow's morning report, which I'll send to Joe. I'm on the satellite phone right now, but according to Phil, I shouldn't say much."

"How you like the engineer out there?" Joe asked, looking around the room still feeling abashed.

He didn't really care what Val thought about the engineer, he was just trying his best to look and sound professional after his earlier blunder.

"Uh, he's good, Joe," Val responded. "As an old Russian immigrant, he's kind of hard to understand, but he's super knowledgeable and very conservative, as well, but definitely knowledgeable. Guess he's worked all over the world, from the north slopes of Alaska to Saudi Arabia. I think we chose wisely with him."

There was a brief pause. Joe looked around the room to see if people liked his question and Val's answer. He couldn't read much in their indifferent faces.

"OK, guys! I gotta run. We will update you all in tomorrow's report."

"Sounds good, Val," Wayne said. "Keep up the good work."

Everyone, but Joe said goodbye. Normally Joe was the loudest and friendliest to Val, but he was now trying to look indifferent. He didn't want anyone to know how he felt about Val, although now it may very well be too late. He also wondered if it was borderline sexual harassment. He tried his best to get it out of his mind.

Thankfully, Gerry chimed in, offering the ideal digression.

"So, tell me, how's our spy doing out there in the field, anyway?"

Wayne's brow quickly furrowed, as he looked across the table at Gerry. "You mean our scout, right?"

Gerry didn't care. "You can call him whatever you want. I'll call him a fuc…."

Gerry suddenly stopped. He knew he was crossing the line with Wayne and he didn't want to do that. Wayne was a very mellow, easy-going person, but when he got upset, it was a pretty alarming and traumatic experience for all in the room. It certainly wasn't something Gerry wanted to start, or endure.

"Forget it," Gerry said quietly.

Wayne gave Gerry a glaring glance. He took a deep sigh.

"To answer your question, Gerry, he is picking up some chatter and getting some good information, but he did warn it may be tough going in the future. They're flying their daily reports out by helicopter each morning."

Gerry looked up from his slightly cowering position with a quizzical, interested look on his face. "How is this guy, what's his name?"

"Max," Joe chimed in.

"How does Max know they're stuck in the hole?"

Wayne looked at Gerry perplexingly. "Don't know. He doesn't divulge his methods, just gives me updates. My guess is with the trouble of getting stuck in a hole, someone probably picked up the phone to curse someone out or he simply observed it through his scope."

"Hopefully, Roger," said Chuck with a smile and slight laugh. Joe and Wayne quickly smiled, but Gerry still looked very dumbfounded.

He wanted to know more but thought it best to let it go.

"Well, I still think it's a waste of money and time, especially if they are flying out their reports, but hey, who am I to say?"

With that, Gerry pushed his chair back and stood up. Wayne looked at him and thought about telling him to sit back down, but the truth was the meeting was over. He didn't want to end the good day on a bad note.

"All right everyone, meeting adjourned. Oh, and by the way, the president of Global will be coming in tomorrow, so I'd like you all to be here in the conference room at 10.00 A.M. to meet him. Thanks!"

And with that, they all exited the conference room.

CHAPTER TWELVE

Max was feeling much more confident about the job now, as he headed from his new camp toward the cutline and the Chevy hidden and camouflaged in the bush. With the cutline fairly visible from the logging road, at least in his trained scouting mind, he decided to move his truck further down to conceal it better. He also wanted to make sure it could not be seen from the air. It may have just been the way the pilot liked to fly or his imagination, but the helicopter seemed to be flying much lower in recent days upon its approach and take off.

Max was always uneasy when leaving his camp unattended, but he needed supplies, particularly propane and fuel for his 1500 Honda generator. A few groceries were in order, as well, but Max could go without food if necessary.

As Max idled the tandem down the east slope of Nose Creek, he couldn't help but feel pride in his accomplishment waiting to be scaled on the opposite bank. Max had made several trips up and down the roughly made ramp and it hadn't budged an inch.

On the surface of the frozen creek, the 80 horses snorted as Max gunned the snowmobile skyward. Just like each time before, he flew right up and onto the snow-packed ramp. Exhilaration filled Max as he topped the canyon rim. Without looking back, he continued right down the cutline, zigzagging between the thick willows.

The light sled bounced along behind the Polaris on the trail back to his truck. By now, it was becoming familiar. He knew each bend, dip, and mound up and down the cutline.

He checked his watch upon pulling up to his 4x4 – 30 minutes. Not bad for the roughly six-mile trip. Every detail was important to Max and knowing how long it took to get back to the truck may prove vital. Of course, there was a good chance he may need to escape in the dark, so he did want to try timing himself at night.

Max took a mental note of that as he transferred the camouflage tarp to the Polaris.

The 4x4 groaned in the extreme cold when Max turned the key, then went dead. Max held his breath as he tried again. The engine rattled, and then slowly turned over with a ruff clattering idle.

"Phew," Max said, as he worked the steering wheel back and forth to get the fluid moving.

He slowly eased his way down into the ditch and back up onto the logging road, making sure to look both ways for oncoming logging trucks. Not much traffic up here, so most logging trucks came fast and furious around each bend, using both sides of the road to its maximum. The drivers of the big units didn't give a shit about beating their logging trucks to pieces. Shit, why should they care, most didn't own them, surmised Max?

Knowing this, Max hit the gas pedal as soon as he cleared the ditch. Dirt and rocks spewed and he was off down the road toward Grand Prairie.

The drive was rough and it felt like his insides were getting squashed as his body rattled up and down as the wheels slid in and out of the frozen ruts in the road caused by the heavy trucks back when the ground was muddy. Now, in the dead of winter, they were frozen cock stiff.

It didn't help that his truck was three years old and the suspension in need of new shocks. Still, he would never part with his trusty Chevy; not until it was absolutely necessary. It had treated him well to this point. Too well, he thought, with a smile.

Max was looking forward to giving Carmen a call from a land phone. He had called only once before to let her know he was OK, but the conversation was short and impersonal. Max never knew if another scout might be monitoring calls and he didn't want to give away his location or any details.

Grand Prairie was booming when Max rolled his truck into town. Oil companies were obviously trying to capitalize on the higher oil prices by bringing marginal wells online and as a result, there was activity all over. What used to be nearly a ghost town only months before, was again bustling with people.

More activity and more wells, meant more scouts and Max wondered how many might be lurking about town. He knew the favorite hangout, a new motor lodge and bar on the north end of town and after gathering up his supplies and checking in with his family, he found himself pulling into the parking lot.

No sooner had max pulled up near the front entrance did an old, beat-up red Ford catch his eye. Max immediately started chuckling. Pole Cat.

Unbelievable, he thought. Max got out and walked down to inspect it some more. It was a sight like no other. The top of the cab looked like a Christmas tree with aerial antennae pointed skyward and the back piled high with old, random scouting equipment. Max couldn't believe it. It was as if the guy was scouting a rig from the motel parking lot. This made him laugh out loud until the realization that he was probably right quickly made him feel sorry for the old bastard.

Max shook his head and walked toward the hotel lounge. Before he even stepped in, the loud, familiar drunken slur could be heard echoing into the foyer. Pole Cat's drunk again, Max knew, as he stepped into the dimly lit, smoky lounge.

As the stale, cigarette smell overcame him; he again had the sudden feeling that he made a mistake. Sour gas, Max said to himself, with a hollow laugh. He quickly turned to leave, but it was too, late.

"Look who's fuckin' here! I don't believe it," Pole Cat hollered across the jam-packed lounge. He was spotted. "Shit," Max said to himself, as he rolled his eyes and turned around to greet his fellow scout.

It took a few seconds, but Max saw Pole Cat's waving hands at a tiny table in the far corner. He was sitting next to a fairly big woman with long red hair. Max stepped up, faking a big smile.

"Hey, honey! I'd like you to meet a fuckin' fellow scout," Pole Cat said to the woman who was practically sitting in his lap. "Max is his name, but he also goes by asshole or little prick!"

Pole Cat cracked himself up, nearly spilling his drink as he leaned forward. The red head barely moved; she could care less about Max. With blood-shot, blurry eyes, she simply snuggled in closer to Pole Cat.

Max felt uneasy and looked around the room to see if anyone was paying attention.

"Just kiddin' there Maxy Boy. Come on, take a seat!" Bill made a clumsy attempt at kicking out a loose chair for him to sit in. His foot barely touched it and the chair moved about an inch. Max grabbed it anyway and took a seat.

Pole Cat grabbed the red head's hand and slammed it into his crouch. She immediately started moving it up and down. Pole Cat smiled broadly and leaned back.

"Meet my new girl here, Max. Name's Red. Now, ain't that fuckin' original"? The red head laughed with ditzy glee, moving one hand up and down his leg and using the other one to throw back her cocktail.

Oh, boy did Max want out of there.

"So, tell me Maxy, my old buddy, what brings you to this little cow paddy, huh? Which rig ya workin?" Pole Cat was drunk but was still smart enough to try and pry information out of Max.

"Can't tell you, you know that," Max calmly replied.

"Don't give me that bullshit! We're all friends here. Seriously, what rig they gotcha watchin'"?

Max didn't respond. He was hoping with his mental state and the nice erotic rub down he was getting, Pole Cat would simply forget the question. No such luck.

"Fuck, man! I don't mind tellin' you what rig I'm watchin'! Fuckin' piece of cake south of town. Too far out of town on such a trashy road; I hang out right here most of the time."

Pole Cat's voice boomed throughout the quiet room and Max looked around to make sure nobody was listening. Most of the heads barely moved. It was like a graveyard in there. How depressing, Max thought, as he turned back to Pole Cat.

"How far south?" Max casually inquired, trying to focus the attention away from him.

"Too far to describe," came the slurred, but purposely vague answer. He then opened his blurry eyes wide and looked directly at Max.

"Haha! Nice try you little prick! You're trying to figure out what rig I'm watchin', but I'm not gonna tell ya. Ha!" Bill again roared with laughter.

Max again turned and looked at the patrons around him to see who was watching. Nobody seemed to care how drunk or obnoxious Pole Cat was.

"Shit, Max, I'm just kiddin' ya! If you want to know what rig I'm workin' just ask! Truth be told, it's such a cakewalk I took big Red with me last time. She was a helluva lot more fun than you were last time; if you know what I mean."

Pole Cat again bellowed with self-amusement.

"It's OK Pole Cat," Max answered after Pole Cat settled down. "It really doesn't matter."

"Fuckin' right it don't matter; like I said a piece of cake down south."

Max was pretty sure Pole Cat was lying; after all, it was natural for a scout to withhold information and give false information in case anyone was working for the opposing oil company. Perhaps fed up by Pole Cat's constant questioning, or because it was just the nature of the game, Max suddenly had the impulse to give him some false information of his own.

"If you must know, I'm on a Horizon rig, south about 10 miles," Max stated casually.

There was a large Horizon sign on the way into town and Max knew Pole Cat would have seen it.

"Oh, yeah, I know that one," Pole Cat slurred. "That's down my way. How come I haven't passed you on the road"?

Max went into deceit mode again, "Just got here two days ago. I haven't even been out there yet, still gathering supplies."

Pole Cat looked over at Max and shook his head. Either he was satisfied with the answer or bored by the talk because he turned to Red and grabbed her breast. "Damn I love these big jugs!"

The redhead giggled and moaned with excitement as Pole Cat put his other hand between her legs. Red giggled more profusely as she sucked the straw of her drink. It was time for Max to go. Just as he rose to his feet, however, Pole Cat suddenly stopped and grabbed his drink and turned to Max.

"You know, that rig I'm watchin' is run by Black Gold."

Pole Cat paused to take a big swig of his drink. Intrigued, Max quickly sat back down.

"Those fuckers are too damn clueless to know how to run a tight hole," he continued after swallowing another gulp of whiskey. "They got security set up on the lease road and everything, but that's no obstacle for an old hand like me. Fact is, they are so dumb and chatty, I know they ran a drill-stem test a couple days ago and I didn't even have to get close to the rig. I got that all sittin' right here on my ass, Right where I like it!"

Pole Cat roared with laughter again.

Max wondered how much more Pole Cat knew. "So, they get anything on the test"? Max attempted to be as casual and indifferent as possible.

"Fuck how would I know? I just know they ran a test," came the muddled reply as he tried to swallow another quick drink. "I would've got more info, but Red here was calling my Manhood."

Pole Cat again turned and started getting amorous with the rotund woman. They were practically taking each other's clothes off, but nobody in the place seemed to notice – or care.

"Got to go," Max suddenly said, as he rose again to his feet. "Need to get some more supplies before nightfall. Good to see you again there, Bill."

"Later," came the muffled reply since Pole Cat had his tongue down the woman's throat. He didn't bother looking Max's way. Good, Max thought, I will sneak out while he's pre-occupied. Might not even remember he saw me, Max hoped.

Max speed walked out of the lounge. He went straight to the back of the truck to do a quick survey of his supplies. Everything was still there, thankfully. He jumped into the freezing cab, fired her up, and headed south toward the Kakwa River.

After a block, he spotted a pay phone. Whether true or not, he wanted his client to know about the hired scout and see if Black Gold did, in fact, run a drill-stem test.

Max listened to the chorus of urban sounds around him, as he punched the number pad on the phone. After several rings, a recording let Max know Black Gold was closed for the day. A check of his watch indicated it was 5:45 pm. Max didn't realize it was so late. He could call Wayne's cell phone number that Phil gave him, but it wasn't technically an emergency. The call would have to wait for another day. If he was going to reach camp before dark, he needed to get going.

The pickup was idling as Max jumped in behind the wheel and once more headed south out of town. It was 7:00 pm when Max finally idled the Polaris at the top of the canyon rim. Max had made most of the trip down the cutline with the light of dusk, but now it was pitch black. His first descent and ascent at night, always a good learning experience, he surmised.

He eased his way down the ramp with just the light of the Polaris. Everything was pitch black around him except for what was directly in front. The ramp once again held, and within two minutes, Max was throttling it up the east side and down toward the rig.

Max hid the snowmobile between two large blue spruce trees and covered it with boughs, in case the helicopter pilot was keeping a close eye out. With supplies in hand, he headed off toward his camp.

He could see the rig lights in the distance. It was quite a peaceful and beautiful sight through the trees. Very much like looking at the North Star, he thought, as he listened to the crunch of snow beneath his feet. The mournful howling of the resident pack of wolves reminded him to be more careful when storing his food. Wolves could cause serious problems; problems he would like to avoid.

It was just past dinnertime when Max threw back the tent flap. It was an ideal time to catch calls from lonely rig hands to their wives or sweethearts back home, so Max tossed the supplies to the side of the tent and went straight to the scanner.

So far, he had only caught a few calls and nothing yielded anything useful. Zephyr most likely had a no-call order issued, but even those were quite often broken. It just wasn't humanly possible to keep so many hands away from their loved ones for so long without at least a quick check-in – especially up here in the middle of nowhere.

As usual, the scanner locked on calls from other activity in the area. Some of the conversations bounced in from as far away as fifty miles, showing just how powerful Max's little unit was.

Max tapped the top of the scanner and smiled. He then leaned back, put his hands behind his head, and stared up at the stained canvas roof of the tent.

Listening at night was depressing. Max referred to the night activity as "scanner soap opera." Actually, some of it beat any soap opera you could ever find on TV, he thought. Problem was, the drama between husband and wife that he listened in on was real life, and that troubled Max greatly.

There was the constant barrage of rig hands cheating on their wives, wives cheating on their husbands, and all of them lying to each other. The saddest tragedies, probably because Max knew it was a distinct possibility in his own life since most of the divorces were caused by financial problems. What a mess the world was in!

Max thought about Carmen again and was grateful to have a solid relationship and a good family. He was so grateful to be working again, even if the job was the hardest he's ever faced.

Max monitored until about 10:00 pm, then turned the volume down low and dimmed the bright blue light so it didn't shine in his eyes. One more check through the spotting scope revealed they were finally back drilling. They were no longer stuck and with casing in the hole, it meant they would make better progress. It also meant Max would have to pay extra-close attention going forward.

Max rolled back over onto his back. Staring once again at the stained canvas ceiling, he listened to the idle chatter on the scanner and quickly drifted off to sleep.

L. GORDON KESLER

CHAPTER THIRTEEN

Max settled into a daily routine and his surroundings became more like home with each passing day. Since running casing, the drilling had gone smoothly for Zephyr. That made Max very uneasy because he had no idea if or when Zephyr might decide to test or cut a core, as they penetrated each new formation.

Without much data, it was time for him to think about going into the phase of scouting that was most challenging - sneaking onto the lease and physically gathering information. That always ran the high risk of exposing himself, and, of course, getting caught. If nothing changed, however, and he wasn't able to catch some solid information on the scanner or via his spotting scope, it would have to be done.

To this point, he stuck to a strict pattern, especially in the morning. The first hours of the day, between 6:00 and 9:00 am, were spent listening to the constant jabber coming from the scanner. Max huddled over the procession of flickering lights, stopping and starting the auto-search sequence, as he deemed necessary.

It was monotonous and laborious, but it was his best chance at gathering the facts his client coveted. It took skill to separate the important calls from the domestic bullshit that typically clogged the frequencies. It also took a lot of patience.

Max glanced at the time: 8:55 am. Time for some breakfast; he decided to turn the volume down, so he could have a little peace and quiet for once. As he reached for the volume knob, a voice came booming in. It was a voice he recognized.

Max quickly punched the monitor button to stop the auto-search and quickly reached for his micro mini voice recorder. The scanner recorded automatically but Max always wanted a backup, just in case.

"Crane, here!"

It was the engineer. Max had only heard his voice once before, but immediately knew who it was. His brash, curt tone was unmistakable. He sounded as if was going to eat the phone instead of speak into it.

"Shit! They shouldn't be making a call this late." Max was so intrigued he didn't realize he spoke out loud. In his gut, he knew calls came at all times of the day or night, but so far Zephyr was very quiet with only sparse chatter coming in much earlier in the job before the real drilling action commenced.

The other voice was coming from the Calgary office and it sounded just as pleasant as the rig engineers. Max recognized that arrogant, rude voice, as well. He wasn't sure of his role, but knew him as "Roger." The two deserved to work together, Max thought, since they both sounded like miserable pricks.

"Morning, Crane! How does it feel to be working with the cheeks of your ass missing"?

"It's too early in the morning for your fuckin' idiotic brand of humor," the engineer growled back.

Roger laughed. "Take it easy there, Crane! I got my own ass-chewed, well before you did."

Roger didn't wait for an answer. "At any rate, that was days ago! It's fuckin 'time to forget and move on."

"I don't know about you, but that's not something I'll soon forget!" Matt tersely replied.

Max knew exactly what they were talking about. He knew the problems with the hole were a result of ignoring the well plan and trying to take shortcuts. Never a good idea!

Roger ignored Matt's foul mood. "Have it your way. Hey, I got some interesting news for you."

"What's that"? was the cold, semi-interested question.

"You gettin' any information out there on the Syrian situation?"

"Not a fuckin' word, really don't give a shit about Syria. I'm paid to drill a well not worry about the fucking world."

Despite Matt's foul mood, Roger continued to inform him of events that were happening anyway.

Max listened intently to the conversation. This Crane fellow might not be interested in what was happening in the world, but Max certainly was. He hadn't read a newspaper or listened to the radio in a long while.

Roger continued to explain how a couple of Syrian terrorists came on shore in the refinery area of Louisiana, apparently, after stowing away on an Egyptian freighter that anchored offshore a few miles. They successfully blew up two refineries before authorities gunned them down. Everything is still being assessed and the US government is trying to figure out how involved Egypt was in the plot.

"Way I got it figured, the bombers are probably the President's fucking cousins," Matt snorted back.

"Well, it looks to be turning to shit out there," Roger replied, ignoring Matt's bad joke. "But on the other hand, this whole OPEC, terrorism shit storm should only help our cause, as people panic and oil prices go through the roof."

Matt said nothing, so Roger continued.

"In other news, we hear Black Gold had oil to surface on their drill-stem test. Guess maybe we should have tested, too, before we got fucked up in the Fernie."

Roger let out a hollow laugh. Crane was silent. He wasn't sure how to take the news since it ended on a backhanded insult. The last thing he wanted was to get into a pissing contest since it was his decision not to test. Like any good engineer, however, he was interested in what Black Gold had on their test.

"How do you know that about Black Gold"? he said suddenly interested. "Zephyr got a scout on their well?"

"Can't say anything on the phone! Just thought you might find it interesting. By the way, speaking of scouts, anything out your way?"

"No, not a sign," Matt answered confidently.

"You actually been looking, Matt?" Roger asked with much doubt.

"We're always looking!" Crane hollered back. It was a lie, but he didn't care. He was too focused on the job they paid him to do.

"All right. I better get back at it. Got lots to do. I just wanted to touch base with you since management was all over the two of us."

"Got it! Will update you in the morning report," Crane quickly said, nearly interrupting Roger. He then hung up the phone. The delayed second click indicated Roger was now gone, as well.

Max sat looking at the silent scanner. Not much there, but good news about Black Gold's test. That made Max smile. It disappeared the second he asked himself the very important question – how did they know? Shit, maybe Pole Cat was actually doing his job, Max thought. If so, he lied to him when he said he hadn't watched the test.

Max should have known. It didn't matter how drunk Pole Cat got, or how lazy he was, he was still a scout and capable of stealth and deceit.

Something didn't feel right, though. If the redhead was with him, no way Pole Cat would have walked to the well to watch Black Gold test. Especially not in minus 30 degree temperatures, he deduced. Maybe that was a lie, as well?

Max was now full of questions. Breakfast was put on hold. He was not hungry anymore. He also wanted to get to town to notify his client that Zephyr was getting some good "intel" on its well. As he prepared to leave camp, Max was overwhelmed with anxiety.

After the prodding from Calgary, the engineer might now decide to check the bush for scouts. The timing for the trip wasn't great, but he felt the situation required chancing it.

So far, Max hadn't gone near the rig, so there were no footprints in the snow or other signs to give him away. The normal, easy way to check would be to have the roughnecks climb the derrick to see if they see any signs of a camp around the area. Max was pretty sure this far out and hidden behind the snow bank, he would be invisible from the rig, even from the crown at the very top of the derrick.

To discover his camp, Max concluded, they would really have to get outside the immediate perimeter and into the forest and that would not only require an extensive search, but also one that required the hands to wade through two feet of snow. That thought made his uneasiness fade a little since Max knew most hands were too lazy for such as task.

Being careful not to rev the engine of the Polaris, Max slipped away from the camp keeping noise to a minimum. Good thing Nose Creek was far enough away to really open things up to get up the ramp.

It took longer than expected to reach the Chevy. Max was very nervous about sound and took things a little slower than usual. He also took extra effort to conceal the snowmobile. He made sure it was not in the same vicinity of the 4x4 because, despite the fact that he could cover his footprints in the ice and snow, the tire tracks leading to and from the logging road were near impossible to cover.

Once everything was secure, he headed down the logging road for town. This would be a quick trip, Max vowed. Call the client and get right back!

As Max bounced down the road toward Grand Prairie, a teal, Chevy truck blew by him going the opposite direction. The fancy truck grabbed his attention because not only was it, brand new, but it also was outfitted with high-range antennae on top of its cab.

A scout! Max was sure of it!

The realization of that fact blew into his mind as fast as the Chevy blew past him. He didn't recognize the spruced up truck, but it didn't matter. He knew he had company.

Max became even more worried and anxious. He thought about turning around but kept on going toward town. It was more important to alert the client that they were being watched, he concluded. The adrenalin caused Max to push down harder on the accelerator. He didn't notice or care about the extra jarring his body took as he shook his way to the main road.

The 4x4 slid to a halt at the first phone booth he found. Max bailed out into the cold and hit the booth running. He was still sliding into the opening when he grabbed the phone and began punching numbers.

"Good morning! Black Gold Resources, may I help you?"

Max was in no mood for small talk. Normally, he would chat with the receptionist – not this morning.

"Max Cardova here. Is Wayne in?"

"Yes, Max he is. How are you doing up there?"

Max slowed his tempo and composed himself. "It's going well! Mighty cold, but going fine."

"Good to hear, Max. Let me put you through to Wayne."

Max looked around the gas station nervously. "Good morning, Max." Wayne's voice was calm, yet filled with modest enthusiasm. "Have a report for me?"

"Sure do!" Max pulled out his notepad and placed it on top of the phone shelf. He turned a few pages. "OK, here we go!"

Methodically, Max went through each day's activities, giving the drilling information he had picked up.

"Please keep in mind, most of this stuff is all visual," Max explained, knowing Wayne was hoping for something more substantive.

"Understood, Max." Wayne could sense Max's uneasiness on his report. "Just keep working at it. I'm confident you'll get some good information again."

Max wasn't so sure, but he kept his feelings to himself. He concluded with the update from Zephyr.

"Caught an interesting call this morning, Wayne. I figure you would want to know about it," he said. "Zephyr HQ was talking to the field engineer and mentioned you had oil to surface on your drill-stem test."

Wayne was quiet, so Max continued.

"The guy's name at Zephyr is Roger and he sounded pretty confident about the information he received."

There was continued silence on the line until Wayne finally answered.

"Hmmm. That is interesting news. It's also accurate, so what does that mean? They have a scout watching our rig?"

Max shook his head to confirm.

"Yeah. That seems the case. Although to be honest, if the scout I think is the one working your rig, I can't imagine how he found out. He's too lazy to leave his scanner, let alone the comforts of a truck heater, so perhaps they got lucky and intercepted a phone call between Black Gold personnel. Not sure, but you should definitely start keeping an eye, and ear, out."

Wayne took some time to reply again. "OK, Max. I'll let everyone know. Thanks."

Max waited a few seconds before changing topics.

"Another thing, Wayne," he added excitedly. "Zephyr has instructed the field hands to check the area for scouts. That's not a big deal, as I'm pretty well situated out in the snow and bush, but because of it, it may be a while until I phone in my next report."

"That's fine for now Max, but once they get deeper we will need reports as often as you can," came the reply.

"Copy that. Oh, and lastly, looks like I may have company. I passed another scout on the way into town. He looked to be headed right for the Zephyr rig. Not sure which team he's working for, or why he's out there but will let you know the next time I call in."

"Sounds good, Max. I know it's freezing up there, but sure sounds like things are heating up!"

The two men shared a quick chuckle at the reference and play on words.

"Better get going, Wayne. I might have company when I get back to camp. I'll talk to you in a few days."

Max left town without calling Carmen. He was on a mission to get back to his Polaris as soon as possible. His insides were churning as he made his way to the cutline entrance. It was quickly replaced by a sense of relief. As Max slowed his truck into the ditch, there were no other visible signs of tire tracks and no sign of the teal Chevy.

Max's heart returned to a normal beat rate and he relaxed. He pulled the Chevy into the cover of the thick red willows just off the cutline. Stepping out, Max's pulse suddenly started racing again as he spotted fresh footprints in the snow. Max reached back behind the seat and grabbed the 300 magnum, then slowly walked away from his truck.

Sure enough, someone had walked in from the logging road and out again. The fresh footprints led to a melted spot where the intruder had left the vehicle running while he surveyed the area.

Max walked with a sense of urgency toward the hidden snow machine retracing the stranger's footsteps. Shit, he thought, they were leading right for the Polaris. Suddenly, the tracks came to a halt not twenty yards from the prize stashed under the white tarp.

Must have walked into the forest, saw nothing, then walked back to the warmth of his truck, Max surmised. Max looked off into the near distance and could barely make out his snowmobile.

"Man, that was close," Max said to himself.

His anxiety rushed out of him and he replaced it with a deep, full breath of cold air. He was finally able to breathe normally again.

Max returned to his truck and spent the next few minutes looking around the area. What a stroke of luck, he again thought. Whoever it was, they were short on ambition and just short of the prize. Max laughed nervously; his breath making smoke signals in the cold.

Still, the scout did find the cutline and followed the tire tracks to where his truck was hidden, so another hiding spot would be in order; if that was even possible?

Max loved his Chevy and did not want to have it damaged or worse, stolen, but it was only a matter of time until the unknown party returned, to the scene and found it again. There was just no way to truly hide the tire tracks.

The key was to make sure they didn't find the snowmobile or the sled tracks leading through the cutline. Course, even that made Max shake his head because any scout worth his weight in salt would find it eventually. The cutline and his sled tracks led straight to the west bank of Nose Creek. There, his makeshift log ramp was clearly visible.

Still, Max moved his truck to another location and concealed it under the tarp. Every little measure might prove beneficial.

It was futile at times, but by jumping from stump to stump, Max managed to get to the Polaris without making many prints in the snow. Again, any competent scout just needed to follow the cutline, but it just wasn't in him to not take every precaution.

Max jumped on the cold black vinyl seat and charged down the well-worn trail back to his camp.

Another wave of relief poured over him when he walked into camp and found it intact. He immediately took inventory. All was good.

He was lucky this time, but he knew it was only a matter of time until his luck ran out. After all, someone had already found his entry point.

Max knew he had to prepare for any trouble that came his way. He glanced down at the trusty Sako Magnum in his hands. He didn't want to use it, or get anybody hurt, but when it came to the world of scouting, all bets were off.

He just hoped he could get some valuable information before he was found and any trouble ensued. Max sighed as he looked off into the distance and listened to the sounds of Zephyr's drilling operation.

CHAPTER FOURTEEN

It was Monday morning and Max was up early. It had been five days since his last trip to town and each day, each hour, was extremely nerve-racking. Max anticipated a confrontation from rig hands or fellow scouts at any moment. So far, however, none had materialized.

Outside the tent, the Whisky Jacks were arguing over who owned the scraps Max had put out for them. He always left scraps around the camp to encourage visits from the birds. They were welcome company in the quiet of the bush.

Max was very careful not to leave meat scraps since the scent would entice animals much bigger and more dangerous. He was already expecting an encounter with other humans; he didn't want one with wolves or wolverines. He was pretty certain he could easily drive them off with his rifle, but that noise would put a target right on his camp.

The wind was whispering softly through the boughs of the spruce trees. Max loved the hypnotic sound of the breeze. He found it soothing to the soul, especially in these times of uncertainty and tension.

There was another sound outside his tent that also grabbed his attention. It was the sound of snow dropping from the branches. That indicated warmer temperatures and it was clear the westerly flow of air had moved into the region. That was good in the battle against the extreme cold but could prove disastrous if the temperatures continued to rise over an extended period of time. If the ice melted in the bottom of the canyon, there would be no way of getting across Nose Creek.

Max added some notes to his notepad, and then checked the rig through the high-powered scope mounted to a tripod he set up inside his tent. The opening in the door flap was just enough space for the optics to peek out in the direction of the derrick. Roughly 250 yards away, give or take a few yards, Max surmised.

The massive 50-ton yellow blocks that fed the drill pipe slowly into the ground swayed gently back and forth between the 8-inch steel girders. Max checked the position of the blocks against the cross beams and then noted the time on his watch. Still drilling at 12 minutes per foot, he figured and made a note of it.

The rate had been the same for the last two days. He had gotten a good pipe count and knew within a few feet how deep the Zephyr well was. Normally, Max would get an inventory of the entire pipe stacked on the pipe racks at the rig, but that would mean getting much closer to the rig for inspection and leaving footprints in the snow.

Not a good idea, he figured, and decided to just keep a close eye at a distance. Surprisingly, Max was in a good mood. Sure, he had anxiety and occasionally looked over his shoulder, expecting company, but so far nobody had bothered him.

Also, his monitoring of the airwaves had finally hit pay dirt.

He figured if he was persistent and didn't give up, eventually somebody would talk. It happened on every job in the past, but it didn't mean the next one was going to buck the trend.

At first, Zephyr seemed to be that job. It was unusually quiet, most likely because of the importance of Wolverine Hills and landing the posted land at the sale. OPEC was still playing hardball, vowing to stop shipments of any foreign oil to the West, and that had everyone on edge and gas prices were soaring. The increase in terror activity wasn't helping market stability either.

It made for an exceptionally quiet and well-secured rig, which in turn made Max extremely worried.

Yet, every tight hole eventually springs a leak, and late one night that is exactly what happened.

It was an unusual time and source for a leak and Max was fast asleep when it happened. He was fortunate to have forgotten to turn down the volume. At about 3:00 am, three nights ago, the geologist with a heavy English accent decided to call his gal back in England. The tone of the call immediately stirred something in Max and he was suddenly wide awake.

Gil Murphy was the chap's name and, at first, he was very cautious and offered nothing useful. But, as the conversation went along, he must have gained more confidence with the knowledge that everyone was asleep because all of a sudden he started boasting to his little English Bird about how important he was and how much everyone here in Canada needed someone of his rare expertise.

He eventually went into specifics to back up his claim, quite possibly an attempt to impress his sweetheart. After confidently mentioning to her that nobody could intercept a satellite call, he went into formations, depths and speeds of drilling, porosity, and other results. This was probably all boring drivel to his girlfriend, but it was liquid gold to Max.

By the end of the call, Max leaned over and hugged his satellite phone invention. The boastful geologist had made the same call, at the same time, for three straight nights. Each time he would give her, and Max, an update of Zephyr's situation and how it would all be in shambles without him.

Thanks to the old bloke, Max finally had a nice, big nugget of vital information to offer his client.

Max peered through the scope one last time, before putting everything away. He closed the scanner box, packed up the scope, and went outside for some fresh air. He had a big day ahead of him. It was time to go back into town and give his client a report.

Before he could leave camp, however, he had to safely secure all his valuable equipment. He was very concerned because this was the first time he was leaving camp since seeing the other scout. He was also worried about leaving his equipment in these melting temperatures.

The falling moisture could damage the buried electronics, so as a precaution, Max wrapped the gear with plastic garbage bags. He then deposited them into their snowy enclosures.

Fortunately, by the time Max reached the bottom of the canyon, the temperatures were still below freezing and the creek was rock hard. If the ice were ever to crack and start flowing, Max knew this creek would be impassable. He cast that idea aside. Up here, it would take several days, sometimes weeks, for that to happen. Yet, it had happened before.

Forget it, Max reminded himself. Worry about what you can control.

The ride through the willows was a soggy journey and by the time he was near to the end, he was soaked to the skin. There was no time to worry about being wet, he was anxious to see if his truck was still there and intact.

He parked the snowmobile between two large spruces. He could barely make out the white tarp covering his truck in the distance, so he knew right away nobody had stolen it. Again, jumping from stumps and open moss patches, he worked his way to the Chevy.

All was good. Nothing had been done to the truck and there weren't even footprints to be found. He opened the door, jumped in teeth chattering, and quickly started her up. He then took off most of his wet clothes and put the heater on high and headed for town.

After hitting the local 7-11 for a much-needed coffee, Max began his typical pattern of gathering up supplies. This time it took a bit longer since most of his rations had dwindled to almost nothing. He handled the most critical items first – propane, gasoline, and batteries for the scanners.

Groceries were next, but he only grabbed a few necessities, as deep in his heart he knew he may not be out there much longer. Besides, even if by a miracle nobody came looking for him, he still had to come back to town more frequently to give reports.

Speaking of which, the next item on his list was to call Wayne. Max found a secluded phone booth at the Shell station on the west side of town. As expected, the client was especially pleased.

Max never gave up the way he acquired the information, as there are some things that must always be kept secret, but he did divulge that it was the well- site geologist being careless that was the source for the extra-detailed report.

Funny enough, Wayne didn't seem to care. He trusted Max and took him for his word. That was an odd behavioral trait in this industry and Max couldn't help but hope he would get to work for Wayne again in the future.

All-important errands out of the way, Max decided to head back to camp. As he cruised down the main drag, the GP Inn in the distance caught his eye. Maybe Pole Cat was there again and maybe, just maybe, he could pry some more useful information out of him. It was fairly early in the afternoon still, so Max decided it was worth a shot.

Sure enough, the old beat-up red Ford was parked in the lot. Actually, Max thought, it was in the same darn spot as last time. Something's never change, Max thought.

As he pulled closer, Max also saw the shiny teal Chevy. Oh my, Max said to himself. Now, he would find out who the opposition scout was tracking him.

The stale, smoky, alcohol air hit him in the face before he even walked in. Sour gas, Max joked. That would be his name for any foul-related, man-made stink, especially one involving Pole Cat, going forward, Max vowed with humor.

He walked into the lounge and stopped. He needed to let his eyes adjust from the bright sun outside. Pole Cat was too busy with the same red head to notice his entry. Max stood in the shadowy room, trying to make out the husky crew-cut blond with the beard at Pole Cat's table.

Before Max was even half way across the lounge, he knew both men were heavily intoxicated. Each had a woman nestled in very close. The red head and a chunky brunette were giggling like schoolgirls, as they mauled their male companions. Not a good time to be here, Max thought. Pole Cat glanced up and saw Max approaching.

"Well, now, look who it is! Get over here ya fuckin' prick!"

Wasn't that the same greeting he gave last time, Max wondered. Probably the only greeting the drunk knows. Max was reluctant to stay but thought the agony might be worth it, so he marched up with fake vigor.

"How's it going, Bill"? he asked with an overly wide grin.

"How's it look like it's going," he quickly shot back. "Can't be going to fuckin' bad, right? Got a bottle of CC in one hand and a horny redhead in the other!" Pole Cat hollered with laughter. That self-amusement and belly laugh was really getting annoying, Max concluded.

"Hey! You know Hughes, here, don't ya?" added Pole Cat, slapping his buddy on the shoulder.

"No, don't think I do," responded Max. "Nice to meet you." Max held out his hand, while the man looked him over.

"Tom Hughes," the bearded man finally said, removing his hand from the brunette's breasts and thrusting it into Max's open palm.

"Max here is a fuckin' spy like us!" bellowed Pole Cat, taking his drink in hand. Max looked around the room to see who may be listening and taking an interest. Tom squinted and inspected Max a little more closely.

"Hey! By the way, you're a lyin' bastard," slurred Pole Cat, pointing right at Max. Max knew what was coming next, but he decided to play dumb.

"What you mean?"

"You told me you were watchin' that Horizon rig ten miles south of town," he said still pointing at Max. "Fuckin' lied to me, you did!"

Max wasn't going to change his story now. "What d'ya mean, that's the rig I'm watching."

"Don't bullshit me, Max! I thought we were friends. You're scoutin' the damn Zephyr rig! Tom here verified that the other day! Ain't that right Tom?"

Pole Cat proudly raised his glass toward Tom and took another big swig of whiskey. Hughes was paying less attention to the brunette now and focusing more on Max.

"Ah, that was you, huh?" Hughes said, staring up at Max.

Tom swiveled his chair to face Max head on. "Seen where ya been going in. Sure looks like rough access."

No use playing the dumb game anymore, Max decided. Even these two drunken morons wouldn't fall for it. Max nodded his head in acknowledgment. He was beginning to feel uncomfortable with Hughes and the situation.

"Heard the creek in there, is near impossible to cross. Guess you are walking in most of the way, huh?"

Max didn't respond, he didn't want Hughes to know about the ramp he had built, nor about his Polaris. He'd find it soon enough, just as long as he got his ass off a bar stool long enough. But might as well make them work for it.

"Turns out I'm scouting the same rig," Tom went on. "Personally, it's too soon for me to be going in, so I'll wait another week or so."

The brunette was nibbling on Tom's ear and playfully running her fingers through his beard.

"Stop talking and let's go to the room." She attempted to whisper, but in her drunken stupor, it was clearly heard by everyone at the table.

Hughes slightly pushed the woman away and ignored her. He was still looking at Max.

"Hey, listen, friend. You mind if I travel to the rig with you next time you go in. Might as well team up, right?"

Max wasn't sure what to say. There was no way in hell he was going to escort another scout to his camp. Plus, he was still hoping nobody knew there was a camp.

"Um, sure," Max said not too convincingly. "So far, I've been hoofing up and back on foot trying to find a good way in. From the looks of things, it's very difficult like you say. I can tell they are just drilling so far, nothing too exciting."

Max looked Tom in the eyes. They were blood-shot red and blurry but focused intently on him. It made Max feel uncomfortable. Time to be more convincing, he thought.

"I got an approximate depth on the rig if you need it," Max said, trying to act excited. "After all, we're on the same team, right?"

This seemed to get Hughes' attention and a tiny smile formed on his rough, wrinkled face.

"Yeah, that would be great," came the slow, slurred response.

Max quickly shot out a fictitious depth. Something that was off, but not far enough off to cause alarm. If he truly was scouting the same rig maybe that would keep him away for a few more days, Max hoped.

Suddenly, Pole Cat jumped from his chair. "Come on you big blond prick! Grab your honey, there, and let's get the hell outta here."

Max watched as the four adults rose from the table. The brunette bumped hard into the table, nearly knocking it over. One drink glass fell to the floor and she was next if not for a quick, hard grab of Tom's arm at the last second. Neither man said goodbye as they both staggered out the door with the two women desperately leaning on them for support. If one fell down, they were all going down, Max concluded.

Max stood there watching the doorway. Something stunk, and it wasn't the booze or cigarettes. Max decided to follow them.

In the parking lot, all four drunks piled into Hughes's teal Chevy. Max jumped in his truck and followed them down the main drag, knowing that their intoxicated state would give him cover. The inebriated crew traveled two blocks north to a cheap one-story motel. Nice move, Max thought, drunk as hell and risking life and limb just to travel from one fleabag motel to another. If it wasn't so sad, it would be hilarious.

Max pulled over and watched the Chevy pull into a parking spot. He observed their activity from across the street. Staggering toward the blue door with the number 14 on it, Pole Cat fumbled for the keys in his pocket. He didn't see the curb and tripped just as he pulled the keys out.

He stumbled and slammed right into the door. The four of them thought it was the funniest thing ever and even from this distance and through the rolled-up window, Max could hear their laughter.

They all eventually made it into the room and the door slammed behind them. Max sat there thinking for a minute, then had an idea.

He quickly pulled his truck into the parking lot of a convenience store next door and walked back to the motel lobby. With an extra $20, he managed to convince the clerk to give him the key to room 15, next door to where the foursome disappeared.

No suspicions were raised, as the teenage-looking young man seemed convinced that 15 was Max's favorite number. He was all ready to tell him Bart Starr was his favorite athlete growing up, but he didn't seem too concerned about the odd request. With the likes of Pole Cat and others staying here, maybe his request wasn't as odd as Max thought.

After checking in, Max returned to his truck and grabbed a small box of equipment hidden under his seat. He then returned to the motel and entered the musty room.

Once inside, Max wasted no time. He opened the small case and took out a tiny listening device.

Like an experienced investigator, he removed the cover of the electrical outlet with a small standard screwdriver and skillfully inserted the microphone. The conversation in the adjoining room was loud; almost didn't need the mini mike and amplifier he also set up.

The activity was raucous; it was obvious they all jumped into the sack the minute they got back. Max felt uncomfortable and somewhat dirty listening to the pornographic action in the opposite room.

After an hour, Max thought his idea was a lame one. The lustful appetites had finally been satisfied and now the four sat drinking and bantering loudly about frivolous matters. Knowing they'd probably pass out soon, Max was about to pack it up.

Suddenly, the conversation switched to scouting. Here we go, Max thought, leaning against the wall with anticipation.

"We sure fooled that dumb fucker back there at the bar, didn't we?" It was Tom's voice.

"Don't be so fuckin' sure," Pole Cat answered with a thick slur. "That Max is one wise mother fucker. He ain't as dumb as you think."

"Shit! Maybe, but he'll never suspect a counter scout, now will he?" It was now Tom's turn to laugh at his own joke.

The room had just paid for itself tenfold! Max looked up at the ceiling and smiled. He knew what Hughes was up to and how careful he had to be going forward.

Max stayed in the room until he heard nothing but a low, hard rumbling noise. Someone was snoring up a storm, which meant it was the ideal time to get out of there. Max put his equipment away and exited the room. He dropped the key on the front desk of the lobby and headed to the convenience store to get his truck.

As he started up the Chevy, he felt troubled, yet relieved. Things were certainly heating up, as Wayne described earlier.

It was late, much later than Max wanted to be leaving town. It meant he'd have to make the entire run to camp in the dark. And after all that snowmelt, it was going to be a treacherous, icy run – especially down the ramp.

Oh, well, he concluded, it was more than worth it.

CHAPTER FIFTEEN

It took a bit of time, but Roger White was back in the good graces of management. All indications were that Zephyr would get their well down in plenty of time to evaluate the zones of interest prior to the land sale.

Gil the geologist was excited about the oil and gas showings in the Doig and the Belloy formations and Roger knew that if the grouchy young Englishman was happy, things must be going well.

Nick had been receiving samples on a delayed basis from the field but was doing his own version of the rock sniffer happy dance. He was also taking as much credit for the success as the exploration manager in charge of the entire Canadian region. Nick knew a project of this magnitude was a team effort, but it had been some time since he had been involved in something with such potential.

There was just one problem, and Roger intended to deal with it today. At 9:00 am sharp, Roger hit the intercom button to get Shelley's attention. Shelley responded to the flashing light immediately.

"Yes, Mr. White? What can I do for you?"

Roger knew exactly what she could do for him, but decided to save the lewd comment for another day.

"Morning, there, honey bun," he said calmly.

What a change, she thought. Shelley was suspicious anytime Roger wasn't hollering.

"Do you happen to have Jack Watt's number handy?"

Shelley checked her directory. "No, I don't see a Jack Watt in the files."

"Check under JW Scouting," Roger suggested.

Shelley flipped through the directory for a few seconds before stopping at a card. "Oh, yeah, here it is. JW Scouting Company."

Shelley read the number to Roger, who wrote it down on a random piece of paper in front of him.

"Thanks, toots," Roger said before picking up the phone and dialing the number.

"Morning, JW Scouting. How can we be of service"? It was Jack Watt.

"Times must be tough Jack if you're answering your own phone these days!" Roger chided with a laugh. Jack waited patiently until Roger satisfied his warped sense of humor.

"Just trying to help out where I can. We're a team here at JW."

Jack tried to spin it into a positive in order to look good to the client.

"So, Jack. What's your lunch look like today?"

Jack quickly checked his Day-Timer.

"Um, looks wide open at present," he responded.

"That's good because we need to get together," Roger said enthusiastically.

Jack suggested a restaurant where they cooked a mean steak sandwich and he could get drinks for half price. He knew Roger would expect him to pay the bill, and with Roger's appetite for drinking, he needed to save where he could.

"No not today. We need some place quiet and a little more secluded for this meeting." Roger countered. "There's a small coffee shop call "Java" on the north side of the river on Kensington Avenue that won't be too busy. Let's meet there, say about 12:45?"

Jack agreed and hung up the phone. He knew something fairly serious must be up for Roger to pass on free drinks.

Jack made it a practice to arrive 15 minutes early for all appointments, but today he was going to try and arrive even earlier. Roger usually arrived late, most likely a sign that he was in charge, Jack guessed, but best not chance it for this meeting.

After the waitress sat him at a table next to the window, Jack checked his watch. It was 12:30. Not quite earlier than his usual time, but still well before the scheduled meeting. He ordered a cup of coffee and decided not to look at the menu until Roger arrived. Who knows if it was going to be a full lunch or a quick chat and drink, he thought.

Before he even added the cream, Roger appeared at the table. Wow, Jack thought, he's never on time, let alone early.

"Coffee over here, too," Roger hollered, snapping his fingers to get the waitresses attention.

Roger sat down and quickly started with some basics and generics about the Zephyr well. Jack spent most of the time nodding his head and sipping his coffee. Just after 1:00 pm, however, as the lunch crowd thinned to almost nobody, Roger changed his tone and focus. He leaned forward and lowered his voice several octaves.

"Got some good information on the Black Gold well yesterday," he said, looking around the room to make sure nobody was listening. "Looks like they had a serious gas kick in the Belloy and apparently they didn't have the mud weight up when they drilled into it and the hole unloaded on them!"

Roger looked over his shoulder, then turned back to Jack.

"Guess they've been fightin' to get the gas under control for the past two days. That should set them back a bit and give us a little edge. With some luck, maybe they'll never reach the main zone of interest."

Jack nodded, as Roger took a sip of his coffee.

"Course, notice I said should," he added with raised eyebrows.

Jack nodded again, playing with the plastic swivel stick in his coffee. He was intrigued by how Roger knew about the gas kick since that information, as far as he knew, didn't come from his scouts. Bill had called him from the field early that morning and never mentioned anything about the gas in his report. Something that big would have been the focus of the daily update, but Bill only offered potential depths and drill rates.

"You payin' attention"? Roger snapped his fingers, bringing Jack's mind back to the conversation.

"Yeah. Yeah, I'm paying attention. What you got on your mind, Roger? I know you didn't call me here just to tell me that."

"That is true. Here's what I'm thinking," Roger again leaned in close. "We need to do something about that Black Gold scout your boys told us about. There is a chance they won't get their well drilled in time, so the last thing we need is them getting what they need at our expense. You know what I mean? We need to take care of this right here, right now!"

Jack sipped his coffee, contemplating the situation.

"I've already got Hughes keeping a close eye on this fellow from Wildcat and, at this stage; he doesn't seem to be getting anything useful. Hughes got a depth reading from him the other day and it wasn't anywhere close to reality," Jack said slowly, lowering his mug. "You are the boss and we can do things however you want, but I think it's too early for drastic measures."

Roger's face told the story. His jaw set and his eyes squinted. He peered hard at Jack, indicating that this wait and see approach was far from the appropriate solution.

"You're right, Jack, I am the boss, and I have a plan I want you to be involved in. My engineer, Matt Crane, is going to call me from a landline at 2:30 this afternoon. I want you to be there."

Jack knew it was futile to resist. Roger was an arrogant jerk, but he was the client and he paid the bills.

"I'll be there," Jack calmly replied.

"Good! Good! I'll see you then."

And with that Roger got up and left without saying goodbye. Stuck with the tab again, Jack mused to himself. At least this one was just coffee and a cinnamon roll not a T-bone steak and five whiskey sours.

It was 2:35 pm and Crane hadn't called yet. Roger reached over to his cigar box and pulled out a contraband Cuban. He offered the box to Jack, who refused with a polite wave of his hand. Roger rarely offered one of his expensive illegal delicacies, but he secretly knew Jack didn't smoke and was certain he'd turn him down.

Roger grabbed his book of matches and lit the end. He sucked in hard until it was ablaze, and then leaned back in his chair. A huge plume of smoke rose to the ceiling. Jack couldn't believe how much smoke one cigar and one man could produce. It completely engulfed the ceiling fan.

"So, tell me," Roger said casually. "I'm not getting much in the way of info from your one scout, Bill I think his name is or is it Pole Cat?"

Roger blew another lung-full of smoke toward the ceiling and watched it billow around the light fixture.

Jack was taken back. It was the first indication of any dissatisfaction with Bill's scouting.

"Oh, sorry to hear that, I'm sure he'll get more info as the well gets deeper. It takes a little time to get a handle on these things."

"Your man has had damn near a month and a half to get a handle on things," Roger responded with a wry smile. "You would think the last time I talked to him he would have mentioned the gas blowout, don't you think?"

Jack wasn't sure how to answer. He was completely right. If that was truly the case, and Bill missed it, it would be a catastrophic mistake on his part. As Jack searched for the right answer, Roger came to his rescue.

"That's OK, don't worry about it," Roger said casually, as he once again blew smoke upward and watched it calmly.

Jack's mind was racing. He was annoyed on two levels. If Pole Cat had missed this vital information on the well, which would have been clear as day to anyone watching the rig, this was a serious dereliction of duty. So, why would the client cast it aside so easily?

Jack stared at Roger wondering what he was up to. Was he lying about the Black Gold well? Did he hire another scouting company? The latter seemed like the most logical choice. That bastard, Jack concluded, he went out and hired another scout to make sure the job got done right.

As he stared at Roger, he tried to throw ego aside and understand the situation. It made complete sense, he countered, especially in these desperate times and with a potential project this size. Still, the secrecy and the backstabbing annoyed him. I certainly picked a great business to go into, Jack thought.

Just then the phone rang. "Right on time," Roger said, leaning up in his chair to hit the speakerphone.

"Hello, Crane! You're mighty prompt this afternoon."

"Save the sarcasm, Roger!" Matt quickly snapped. "What's so important that I have to leave the rig and drive fifty miles of fucking shitty logging road, to make a call, huh?"

Roger was enjoying his cigar too much to let Matt bring him down.

"The reason you're on a landline there, Matt," he said, removing his cigar and looking at it, "is so you, Jack, and I don't end up with our oil-patch asses in jail. Now how does that sound to you?"

"Sounds fine," Matt replied sensing Roger might explode at any second. "But who's Jack?"

"Jack Watt. He runs JW Scouting. He's sitting here with me now and is the reason for this call. I asked you the other day if you'd seen any scouts and you told me, no. Is that still the case?"

Roger looked smugly over at Jack.

"Yeah, as far as I know, it is," Matt said, fearing he may be wrong.

"Well, you and those roughnecks of yours must be blind, or not even fuckin' looking, because we know you've got at least one scout lurking around the rig somewhere."

"That may be true," Matt stated cautiously, "but if he is, he is way back in the woods. The rig hands have checked at least a half dozen times for tracks and so far nothing."

"Maybe he's like the son of a bitch I'm paying for, sitting in town on his ass still working on a plan of attack." Roger laughed coldly and gave Jack a quick, but hard, glance.

Jack shuffled uncomfortably in the big leather chair. Matt didn't quite understand, so didn't answer.

"At any rate, Matt, never mind looking for tracks near the rig. Our source says he's out there. Some fella named Max. So, do me a favor, will ya? Get your damn rig hands out there, into the snow, and get rid of this nuisance! Got that?"

"Fine, Roger. If it's that fucking important, we can send a couple of hands out and we'll snuff out the rat!"

"Atta boy, Crane, I knew you had it in you," Roger said, staring at his stogie with a smile.

"What do you want us to do with him when we find him"? Matt asked.

"At this stage in the drilling game, I just want this gnat of ours spooked off! Not squished, mind you, just gone! Understand? If intimidation doesn't work, get back to me, and other plans will kick in."

Roger waited for a reply from Matt. It was far more enthusiastic than he had expected.

"All right! This actually may be fun." Matt was actually excited. Jack,…. on the other hand, was feeling uncomfortable. The sudden interest by the engineer was too much and he had to finally chime in.

"Uh, Jack Watt, here," he shouted toward the speakerphone. "Please don't get too carried away with this guy if you find him. We wouldn't want anybody getting hurt, and a lawsuit levied against Zephyr."

Not sure he was allowed to speak or that anyone agreed with him, he glanced at Roger nervously. His real motivation was to make sure no bodily harm came to this unknown scout, but he threw in the lawsuit hoping that would get Roger on his side.

Roger just stared back at him with little to no emotion. He finally smiled and nodded to show he agreed. Or was it a sarcastic nod, Jack couldn't tell.

"Sure. Sure! Whatever the brass wants," Matt said, not sounding too convincing.

Roger rocked back in his chair and sucked on his cigar again. A huge plume of smoke came out and swirled skyward. Man, that thing stinks, Jack thought.

"All right, Crane! That's it!" Roger casually said looking back up at the ceiling. "Let me know in your morning reports what you find out there, got it?"

"You bet! We'll let you know if we discover any skunks hiding out in the bush!"

Matt was annoyed at first about this whole scout thing. It was not what he was being paid to do and he had to focus on meeting the drilling schedule. But now that things were going well, and, perhaps, because everything was the same each and every day out there in the middle of nowhere, the thought of doing something different was very appealing.

"All right, talk later!" Roger leaned forward and punched the speakerphone button, hanging up.

Jack felt queasy. He'd seen violence in the patch before and didn't like it. He knew it would inevitably reflect badly on the whole industry and become just another reason to stop scouting altogether.

"Don't you think it's better to simply keep an eye on this guy and see what he's up to, instead of actually starting something that could turn ugly?"

Jack didn't want to rile Roger and was pretty sure he would disagree with him, but it was his duty as a scouting company owner to say something.

"At least not until we get further into the drilling"? Jack clarified further.

Roger didn't move or change countenance. He was too busy staring up at the ceiling at the swirling smoke.

"Relax, Jack," he finally said. "We're just going to scare the guy a little. That's all. Nobody is going to do anything to him unless I give the OK."

Roger continued to stare upward. ""Speaking of which, can you have your boy Hughes give me a call the next time you talk to him? I have a tiny side job for him."

Jack did not like what was said during the meeting, and Roger's latest request was the topper. He was now really suspicious and nervous. Roger sensed this and looked over at him.

"Come on, Jack! I am not going to have Hughes hurt the guy. I have something else for him to do. Don't worry."

But Jack was worried. He got up and simply nodded his head. "OK," he said. "I'll have him call. Talk to you soon, Roger."

"Say, Jack. That Pole Cat fellow you got out there? Just have him continue to do what he's doing. I want him to be a decoy and give Black Gold the impression we simply hired a dumb, lazy prick."

Jack wasn't sure what to make of that statement. He wanted out of Roger's office, so just nodded and walked away, leaving Roger once again staring confidently and proudly at his Cuban cigar.

He had been in business for twenty years and this was the first time he felt trapped by a situation. He truly sensed that what was about to happen was beyond the scope of normal scouting.

With stakes, this high, Jack knew things would be different – much different.

L. GORDON KESLER

CHAPTER SIXTEEN

Deflated, dejected, depressed, any of those words could be used to describe the mood in Black Gold's offices.

After years of experience, it was reasonable to expect some problems when drilling down to the Granite Wash formation, but the problem that Black Gold came across was completely avoidable.

The mud technician fell asleep at the switch. He literally fell asleep and all hell broke loose as gas came spewing out because he didn't have the proper mud weights in place. The hydrostatic pressure pushed the gas and everything else in the well, straight upward beyond the rig crown and into the heavens.

Wayne knew the derrick hand and the engineer on the site were just as much to blame as anyone, but as normal practice would have it, someone had to be the scapegoat and that someone was the mud tech. He paid the price by getting fired.

The only good thing was it could have been much worse. When gas of that magnitude pushes skyward with such force it can easily trigger a gigantic well fire that results in a huge rig explosion. All it takes is one tiny spark, which often times happens when metal crashes into metal due to everything slamming around on the drilling rig.

In that regard, Black Gold was extremely fortunate. While it had been a costly setback, a rig fire would have suspended operations and most likely put an end to the company.

An optimist at heart, Wayne chose to focus on the fact that they were still in business. Course, looking around the room, positive attitudes were hard to come by.

The only staff necessary for this morning's meeting was engineering and geology, both in the office and from the field. That meant Joe and to some extent, Gerry. Wayne knew they could go without Gerry, but it was a good political maneuver to include him.

Before Wayne made the call to the rig, he wanted to discuss another development behind closed doors. Morale was in the toilet and he didn't want to flush it down with more pessimism.

Joe was prompt as usual. He and Wayne were heavily engaged in a discussion when Gerry arrived for the meeting.

"OK, let's get started!" Wayne quickly started the second Gerry took his seat. "Besides the problem at the well, I wanted to bring you up to date on another situation."

Wayne thumbed through the documents in front of him as Gerry and Joe looked at each other completely baffled.

"Here it is," Wayne said to himself, as he pulled a legal document from the stack of papers. Wayne looked it over briefly and then continued in a quiet and subdued manner.

"I had a meeting with Global Resources late yesterday. The meeting didn't go as well as I had hoped, but I will say, we did mediate a solution that works for both parties."

Wayne looked around to make sure he had both of their attention.

"Steve Majors and the rest of the Global group are not impressed with what happened at the rig. They blame us directly for the blowout. Yes, it was the work of a couple of sloppy field hands, but in the end, we are all a team, and thus Black Gold is to blame."

Wayne sighed loudly before continuing.

"Majors wanted to replace our people on the well with Global personnel and, as you can imagine, I objected in the strongest possible way. He in return pulled the contract agreement out."

Joe and Gerry both groaned with disappointment at the same time. Wayne glanced at them, then laid the contract on the table

"It's right here in black and white. If the partner has reason to believe that the operator is negligent in any way that leads to significant problems, it has the right to replace personnel with their own."

Wayne paused, looking down at the contract.

"No way to get around it," he went on. "Our people were careless, very, very careless."

Wayne sighed again. "The option in the contract essentially gives Global the right to sever the contract with full compensation, plus a penalty if we fail to honor the demand for a personnel change."

Joe futilely protested. "Shit, this could have happened to anyone! The mud hand isn't Black Gold personnel anyway, he's a contractor!"

Each of the men looked at Joe, knowing it was superfluous. "Wouldn't want to try to win that one in court," Wayne said sadly.

"Yeah," Gerry chimed in quietly. "We'd get our butts kicked for sure! Then get handed a nice big fat legal bill."

There was silence, as it seemed hopeless.

"But you said there was a solution, though, right?" Joe asked desperately hoping for something to grasp on to.

"Yes. Yes, I did. In the end, it might all work out just fine. Steve Majors at Global is a great guy. It was the reason I brought him into this deal in the first place. I..."

"Doesn't sound too damn great, to me", Gerry interrupted.

Wayne chose to ignore the comment and continued on.

"Um, Steve has staff and shareholders to account to and apparently some of them were demanding our balls over this debacle. To help alleviate this demand, the two of us agreed to send a Global man to work alongside

Harry Marinoff. We both know Harry is one of the best engineers on deep wells in this region, so they wanted him to stay. Steve was also OK with Val staying on as lead geologist."

Joe's face suddenly perked up. "Oh, that doesn't sound so bad," he said with a bit of enthusiasm.

"Yeah," Wayne replied with a nod. "Steve is comfortable with this new arrangement and feels he can sell it to his people."

Joe glanced up and looked at Wayne. "The only thing I'll say is Harry is an old stubborn Russian bastard. He's not going to be happy with a babysitter".

Wayne let out a hollow chuckle. "That is true, but considering the alternatives, this really is an easy, minimal change."

Both men in the room nodded in total agreement.

"Plus, we're going to let Harry think he's still in charge."

Wayne smiled and he dialed the number to the rig. Joe understood what he meant; he just wasn't sure how that was going to happen.

"Hello?" The female voice on the other end sounded very tentative.

"Good morning, Val, Wayne here. I've got Joe and Gerry in the room on speaker with me."

"Morning, Joe." Val was pleased that Joe was at the other end of the conversation. "Oh! and hi to you too Gerry. How are you this morning?"

Gerry answered in his usual sour manner, "Been better, Val."

"How you makin' out up there Val, not with the grizzly bears I hope!"

Joe let out a laugh and quickly surveyed the room to see if others found his joke funny. He knew things were sensitive, but was hoping a little humor might break the tension. Wayne forced a smile. Gerry shook his head at Joe in a manner a disappointed parent would at his child. Joe's laughter quickly faded.

"Trying to kiss a bear would probably be a better situation than the one we got here if you must know the truth." Even in a crisis, Val's soft, drawn out voice sounded sexy to Joe.

Wayne patiently waited for the banter to come to an end before chiming in. "OK, Val. What's the latest"?

She was not quick to answer him.

"Um, I haven't yet finished the paperwork, Wayne. I was going to fax it to you in a bit. I guess the good news is we have the well under control, but you know that already. Thank God there was no fire and explosion."

Val threw in the last statement hoping the avoidance of a worst-case scenario would put things in perspective. And soften the ill feelings everyone had for what occurred.

"We're having trouble building volume, but Harry figures once we get the gas out of the mud system, everything should level off."

Wayne and Joe both nodded. Things were slowly getting back online, Wayne concluded.

"I'd like to add," Val went on. "Harry has really been working 'round the clock to solve the problem. The poor new mud tech has him attached to his hip. Every time he does a check, Harry's right next to him."

"Maybe he should have done that before the well blew," Gerry criticized just loud enough to be heard.

Joe was instantly pissed. "Cut the bullshit, Gerry! Enough is enough! We're all trying our hardest!"

Joe's outburst was followed by silence. Wayne was not in the mood for any useless banter or in the mood to discipline anyone, yet again. He just wanted to get through this meeting.

"Where's Harry?" Wayne asked Val.

"I'm right here, Wayne!" Harry's voice boomed loudly into the speaker box. "Thought we weren't supposed to use the phone?"

"I know what Phil told us, but circumstances make it necessary, Harry," Wayne explained.

"I s...ee. So, is this the big call? Are we all getting canned?" Harry's Russian accent was suddenly very noticeable.

Wayne situated himself closer to the speaker. "You're not going anywhere, Harry! You've got the toughest part of the well still ahead of you and we all need you."

"That's good to hear!" Harry quickly came back.

"You're not going anywhere either, Val," Wayne added. Everyone in the room could hear an exclamation of relief through the phone. Joe smiled, knowing Val was happy.

Wayne leaned closer to the phone and stared up at the ceiling trying to find the right words.

"Harry, how do you feel about doin' a little training for us in the weeks to come"? Wayne didn't wait for an answer. He knew he had to explain himself. "Our partner; Global Resources has an engineer it wants to get some deep-hole experience and they requested he spend some time on this well with you. What do you say to that?"

The line was silent. "Harry?" Wayne asked.

"I'm here. I'm just thinking." Harry's speech was slow and drawn out.

"Never been an instructor before, but I guess there's a first time for everything. I can certainly teach him what not to do, especially after what happened last week."

Wayne's eyes lowered and he looked at Joe and Gerry with a bit of relief.

"Great, Harry! That's great!"

Wayne thought about it, then laughed.

"Damn, Harry, I didn't know that. Guess I should have written that down. At any rate, just teach the guy all you know and he should be the second best engineer in the region."

"Ha-ha, good one, Wayne, I'll do my best," the Russian said calmly. "By the way, if this is the alternative to us getting shit-canned, I appreciate it."

Wayne just smiled and chuckled.

"Thanks, Harry; Switching subjects now…How long 'till you have that mud system back in shape?"

"Another day, Wayne, and we'll have 'er whipped right up," Harry answered.

"That's good! It looks like we've lost about a week's progress. Last we heard, Zephyr was sailing right along with no problems. They'll most likely have the advantage going into the sale, but with a month to go anything can happen. So let's all remain focused- Eyes on the prize!"

Everyone in the room expressed his agreement with a heavy nod.

"Harry and Val, I know you guys have been preoccupied, but out of curiosity, have you seen any scouts around?"

"As a matter of fact, Wayne," Harry bellowed. "We might have had one at the security check last night. May not have been a scout, security said the dude was stinking drunk and there was a redheaded woman with him. According to one of our guards, he nearly ran over the security shack and almost swerved right off the road on his way out. Very bizarre scene, but the only one I've heard about since getting here."

"All right, Thanks, Harry," Wayne replied. "Sounds like you've got everything under control. I'll get off the phone and let you get back to work."

"Wayne!" Val jumped back into the conversation with excitement. "I've got a bunch of washed formation samples all bagged and ready to send. With your permission, I'll put them on the chopper when it comes tomorrow with the Global guy."

"Yeah, that's fine, Val. We'll take a good look at them when they arrive. Thanks, everyone! Good luck and be safe!"

"You, too!" they both answered.

Much to the delight of Joe, Val snuck in a quick "Bye, Joe" just before Wayne turned off the speakerphone. He entered the room feeling like he was surrounded by a black cloud, but with one quick acknowledgment, he was now on Cloud Nine.

Wayne watched as his exuberant operations manager left the room. And I thought I was the optimist, Wayne thought, feeling more upbeat.

L. GORDON KESLER

CHAPTER SEVENTEEN

The westerly winds had continued their attack on the winter snow. Max surmised the average depth to be around three feet when he first set up camp. Now he figured there might be just over a foot.

He loved spring weather, but he was getting very nervous. If this thaw continued, he was in big trouble. Once the water started running, it would be impossible to navigate the rising waters of Nose Creek. Not only would that make it impossible to pass, but also meant his ramp would get washed downstream. The one consolation was the night temperatures still dipped well below freezing.

As Max crossed the creek on his way to town, he checked the river ice carefully. It was holding up well considering how warm the days have been for the last week. Fortunately, it was always a few degrees cooler down in the canyon.

Not to worry, Max thought, as he jumped up and down on the ice. There were always a few teases from Mother Nature every late winter. This was most likely one of them and temperatures would soon return to -30 below.

Again, it was a slushy ride, but a quick, easy trip to his truck, which was right where he left it and unharmed.

He drove the logging road north toward town deep in thought. The pounding his body was taking didn't bother him. Maybe he was used to it. Most likely, he was oblivious since his mind was elsewhere.

Max thought how much he enjoyed scouting. It was mostly because of the freedom it gave him. Out here, on his own, he didn't have someone always checking in and looking over his shoulder. Best of all, he didn't have to use one of those punch clocks.

Course, he did have the stress of providing results, but everyone had to do that no matter what job he or she had. At least this job was done on his time and on his schedule.

Despite his ever-looming uneasiness about leaving his precious equipment behind, Max was in no hurry today. The rig had tripped for a change of bit the day before and he felt confident with his latest depth tally. He also had the English geologist feeding him everything he needed every night at 3:00 am sharp.

Sure hope nobody catches him or sees that phone bill, Max mused. Max chuckled, even more, remembering Gil's last conversation. The poor chap just couldn't help himself; he was so desperately trying to impress his gal.

"Can't tell you too much," he said to her," but we're drilling in a zone named after the resort I'll be taking you to when you visit in July."

Max wasn't sure if the guy was simply trying to be funny, feeling extremely confident nobody was listening, or if he was truly trying to use code. Either way, Max knew right away they were drilling in the Banff Formation. Max laughed at the attempted disguise. He also knew that would be news the client would be delighted to hear.

Maybe he should take his family on a vacation to Banff at the same time and personally thank the geologist for his creative late-night geological updates, Max joked.

With the confirmed depth and the identified formation, it would help Black Gold's geologists determine how the formations were running and they could correlate Zephyr's well with their own. It really was the pay dirt Max was hoping for, at this stage.

The last thing he wanted to do was spend more time sucking Sour Gas, but Max decided to check Pole Cat's old haunt to see if the fellow scout was once again up to his old tricks.

It was a little early to be in the lounge, but for Pole Cat, no time was too early. For once, his truck wasn't in the parking lot. Max decided to check the other motel. Sure enough, the only vehicle in the entire parking lot was the beat-up, red Ford parked in front of the same blue door with the number 14 in the middle.

Amazing, he thought, at 11:00 am most people were already out doing something constructive with their lives. But not Pole Cat. Course, the teal Chevy was gone, so maybe the two ultra-scouts were teaming up somewhere. Max thought it strange he hadn't seen Hughes on the logging road since the first encounter. He certainly wasn't making much of an effort to get down that cutline.

"Who cares," Max muttered aloud. "Why dwell on the drunks Zephyr hired. The least amount of information they get, the better, anyway."

Max made one last stop to call the client before leaving town.

Wayne wasn't in, so Joe took the call. Max enjoyed giving the reports to Joe almost as much as he did the boss. He always had a sense of humor and he put the best face on a bad situation.

Methodically, Max went over the report reading each category: operation, depth, progress drilled in the last 24 hours, etc. Max saved the best for last.

"I got a solid piece of information for you this morning too!" Max said with excited vigor.

Joe could sense the added pride and excitement in Max's voice. "Thought all your information was solid," Joe said jokingly.

Max chuckled, looking for a good comeback. It didn't come, so he just said: "Well, it's all solid, so maybe I should have said juicy."

"OK, there, Maximillian. Hit me with the tender, juicy tidbit," Joe said, relishing the fact that he was getting a report that Wayne may be overjoyed to hear.

"Take a look at the depth on the morning report. It's bang on and they are drilling in the Banff formation."

There was a brief silence.

"You positive about that Max?" Joe asked with some caution and hesitation, trying to hold back his amazement.

"Gaur..an.....teeed!" Max said with pride.

"How'd you get that info? Thought they were flying the reports out with the chopper pilot?"

"Persistence, Joe, persistence! That's all I can say. A scout never reveals his sources. Or methods."

"Wow," Joe went on. "That's great news! Wayne will be happy to hear that and we'll be sure to get this juicy tidbit of yours out to our well-geologist right away. We'll most likely core and test the Banff ourselves when we get into it, but keep that to yourself."

"Shit, I'm working for you! Consider it kept!" Max was serious in his response. When it came to work and client confidentiality, Max was a stickler. It was no joking matter.

"That brings me to another topic," Joe said suddenly remembering a request from his boss.

"Shoot!"

"Wayne asked me to see what the counter scout is up to. I guess he's worried about your health and welfare. Is everything going OK out there?"

In his few short years of scouting, a client only asked about his safety once. Phil mentioned it all the time, but not the client.

"I appreciate that!" Max replied, expressing his sincere gratitude "So, far so good. I do expect that counter scout, Hughes, to come sneaking around one of these days, but maybe he's too pre-occupied with the brunette I saw him with the other day. I have to assume Zephyr knows I'm out there, though, so shit may hit the fan anytime soon."

"Hmmm. Well, glad everything is going great, for now. But you be careful, Max! It sounds like things may change right quick for you."

"Thanks, Joe! I have to get going. Need to get back to camp. I'll try to call in a few days."

Joe thanked him for his great work and the tasty morsel of information, and Max was back on the road heading to the cutline.

Joe mentioning that things may change for the worst, made Max reminisce about some of the wild experiences he had over the years.

He remembered one situation in particular that took place about four years ago. It seemed like yesterday to Max, but that was probably because it almost cost him his life.

Just like now it was late spring and the snow had been gone for days, making it easy to navigate the old trail that led to the back side of the rig he was scouting.

Max remembered just how easy it was thanks to all the cows in the area using it, as well. The trail led to a meadow just below a hill about 30 feet high. Only about 100 yards from the rig, it was the perfect location to see and hear everything without being spotted.

After three days of watching the rig hands test around the clock, Max was exhausted. Fearing he would miss the pipe count, Max only slept in quick, 10-minute intervals on the seat of the pick-up. For this job, Max had decided a camp wasn't necessary.

During one of those catnaps, he suddenly opened his eyes. To this day, he still isn't sure why he woke up, he just knew something wasn't right. When he looked up the hill out of the driver-side window, he thought for sure he was dreaming. But what he saw was a nightmare.

Heading right for him, down the hill, was a carpet of fire.

Max sat erect behind the steering wheel, as the fire burned out of control straight for him. Just beyond the 10-foot wall of flames were rig hands all laughing and backslapping each other with joy. A master of detail, even in times of emergency, Max noticed most of them were toasting each other with bottles of beer.

Drunken bunch of bastards he concluded, before springing into action. Hiding below the only hill in the area so close to the rig was a mistake, he admitted in hindsight. Course, he was just starting out as a scout, so what did he know?

The adrenalin rush he felt was like no other. As Max threw the truck into drive, the flames had surrounded him and the situation had become perilous. The smell of paint and oil burning was unmistakable, as Max stepped down hard on the gas pedal and surged forward.

He knew what had happened. Some son-of-a-bitch had spotted him below the hill and had dumped a 45-gallon drum of fuel at the top so it would flow right toward his truck. Then the bastards set it on fire. That was the only explanation for why the flames shot straight for his truck.

What he didn't know is if they were just trying to scare him or truly trying to kill him. Probably didn't care one way or the other, Max concluded.

Had he woke up just a minute later he would have died; his truck would have been engulfed in flame and most likely exploded. Max shuddered at the thought. Max also knew if the fuel had been regular gasoline instead of diesel fuel, it would have reached him much more quickly.

He'd been shot at a number of times, but always felt the shots were a scare tactic. He wasn't so sure about the fire. In his gut, he knew the answer, which meant there were definitely some in this business who would stop at nothing to get rid of a scout.

The funny thing is every time Max thinks about that day; the first thing that comes to mind is the laughing. Despite the loud popping and crackling of burning brush and the smell of burning paint, it was the thunderous howls of elation from the rig hands that he remembers most.

The sight of the cutline caught Max's eye just as he drove past. "Damn," he said aloud while hitting the brakes. He was so deep in thought; he drove right by his entry point.

He put the truck in reverse and backed down the logging road. Throwing it into drive, he hit the accelerator and drove up the ditch and back into the willows. Max camouflaged his truck and then checked the Polaris to make sure nobody had tampered with it. All was good, so he jumped aboard, and headed off through the willows.

At the bottom of the canyon, Max decided to check the ice levels of Nose Creek again. This would give him a good idea of the thaw during the day. There was a little melting snow on the sides, which was concerning, but the ice was still thick and intact.

He jumped back on the snowmobile and throttled it up the east bank. He didn't get too far over the canyon rim when warning flags in his head went up. He slowed down and cut the engine and stared forward toward his camp. Looking ahead, he could see boot tracks in the snow.

These were not his Arctic Pak prints either. Blood rushed to his temples and his pulse began to race.

Max strained his eyes all around for any sign of movement but saw nothing. He quickly fired up the snowmobile and hid it in a clump of bushes not too far away from his camp. He made sure to have the nose pointing outward in case he had to flee.

Who knows what they could have done to it. That thought made him hustle a bit faster. Always looking around, he gripped his Magnum rifle, ready for any ambush.

Max saw that the tracks were all over camp. They led straight to his hidden generator, as well, so he checked that first. He stepped over and looked into the snowy enclosure. Much to his relief, it appeared untouched. He glanced over toward the hiding spot to his most treasured invention but decided to check out the tent first. Throwing back the flap, he was sure to see it in shambles. He had seen his camp in shreds too many times before not to expect the same here.

Again, much to his surprise, nothing seemed out of place. A confused look fell on Max's face. Perplexed, he stepped away and looked about the camp. Very bizarre, he thought, until he saw something in a nearby tree.

It was a dead coyote hanging from a rope thrown over a low branch of a spruce tree. As the stiff body slowly turned in the breeze, Max could see a note stuck to its bloody torso by a small hunting knife.

Max glanced around, still expecting roughnecks to come flying out of the thick brush and attack at any moment. All was quiet. The only thing Max could hear was his own heavy breathing and the blood pounding in his head.

He slowly pulled the knife out of the coyote and cut the lifeless animal down. It dropped to the snow below. The note was bloody and the knife cut right through the words, but it was plain and simple: "Pack your fuckin' ass out of here scout! There won't be a second warning!"

Max sighed deeply. "Nice of them to at least give me a warning," he said to himself with a hollow chuckle. Max was still looking over his shoulder as he read the note a second time. He was sure he was being watched.

Looking off toward the rig, he noticed something else. Between his tent and the rig, they had pushed up a 15-foot snow and debris bank to obscure his view.

Max sighed loudly again. He knew it was time for plan B.

CHAPTER EIGHTEEN

Phil Grave's lunch meeting was a success. The new client was interested in retaining three scouts for at least six months. It was the kind of news he needed badly and it meant staying busy during the spring when the oil patch was traditionally at its low point for activity.

The prime rib sandwich was the same delicious quality he had come to expect at this restaurant and it was made sweeter with the contract that was signed right before he took his first bite. The only potential negative that nagged at Phil was a few comments that came up during the conversation.

How did this new client know so much about the Black Gold operation and such specific details regarding the recent drill-stem test and the gas kick in the Pekisko Formation? Phil queried him about it, but the client simply said no comment – a common response when trying to protect a source.

Lunch was within walking distance to his small Wildcat Scouting office and Phil found himself practically speed walking his way back.

He needed to have a conversation with Max on a landline as soon as possible, he concluded. "But how"? He couldn't afford to wait to have Black Gold tell him to contact him the next time he called in from a payphone. No, Phil decided, he'd have to risk it and call him on a cell phone.

It was Phil's policy not to contact scouts in the field unless there was an emergency. While technically not an emergency, it was worthy of breaching protocol.

Max looked around his new camp and smiled. It wasn't anywhere close to the rig, but at least he could make it out in the distance through his spotting scope.

After finding poor ol' Wily Coyote, hanging from the tree and making the decision to move camp, his hope was they'd come back, see that he was gone, and conclude, he had turned tail and vacated the area.

It took him a full day to break camp and haul his stuff away from the rig, but it had to be done. His new location was almost to the rim of the east bank of Nose Creek. Too far back in this snow, he thought, for them to search, yet close enough to still see a bit of action.

He was just putting the finishing touches on the new camp when he heard a low-sounding beep in the distance. It took a minute for Max to realize the sound was coming from only 20 feet away and by the time he reached the coat hanging on the tree branch the sound coming from the pocket had stopped.

Max checked the cell. Wildcat Scouting was the name on his caller ID. It was his boss.

He suddenly felt nauseous. Something must be wrong with Carmen or one of the kids, he deduced, because Phil never called him on the job.

Max rationalized his concerns. The last time Phil called him in the field, was when Carmen had come down with pneumonia. Oh, no, he thought, as he quickly hit the "call back" button.

After four very long rings, Max heard the click of the receiver.

"Hello, Wild Cat Scouting. Graves here."

"Hey, Phil! It's Max! You called?"

"I did!"

Max stood there anxiously waiting for Phil's reasons for the call. He could feel the heart beating in his chest.

"Nothing serious, Max," he started. Max was instantly relieved. He breathed a little easier.

"Got some shit going on here in the city, and I need some help to get to the bottom of it. Thought maybe you could help find some answers."

"Fire away"! Max said, feeling much calmer and relaxed.

"Look. Sorry to do this to you since you are working, but how long you think it will take you to get to a secure phone. I don't want to discuss this over the cell."

"I could head out right now, I guess. I pretty much got things under control here now and...." Max stopped short of mentioning the camp move in case the conversation was being monitored.

"Feeling uneasy?" Phil interrupted. "Everything OK, Max?"

"Yeah, for sure, got things under control I think. Zephyr discovered my camp yesterday and let's just say they left me a not-so-subtle warning to vamoose."

"Hmmm," Phil said after a few seconds. "I don't like the sound of that. You sure you don't just want to pull out? This is a huge project with a ton on the line, who knows what kind of hardball these people are willing to play."

"I think I'll be OK, Phil. But we can discuss it further from a landline," Max said looking at his watch. "Give me an hour or so."

"Sounds good. I appreciate it, Max."

Max hung up and stuffed the cell back in his coat pocket. He turned and surveyed his new surroundings. Should be good to go, he surmised. Highly doubtful the rig hands would venture a half-mile into the woods to look for him since not much of the rig could be seen this far away. Max nodded, then turned and headed for the snowmobile.

The pay phone at the Mobile gas station didn't look tampered with but just in case, Max twisted off the receiver cover and checked for bugs. Looks clean, he thought, then put the lid back on. His last check was the metal shelf above his head, nothing!

He dialed Phil's number and waited. "Hello, Wild Cat Scouting. Graves here,"

"Howdy, Graves! Cordova here! What can I do for ya?"

Phil smiled at Max's subtle sense of humor.

"I'll be quick Max. I hope you can help resolve a concern that came up at a lunch meeting I had today with a new client."

"A new client?" all right, boss, way to keep the sales rolling!"

"Ha-ha," Phil said with another slight chuckle. "Thanks, Max. The good news is this client should have work for you during the late spring, which, as you know, is very fortunate. But, we'll get to that when you get home."

"OK. So what happened at the lunch?"

"What happened," Phil started, "is while we were doing some small talk about the oil industry and OPEC cutting supplies and terrorists on the rise, he all of a sudden unloaded about Wolverine Hills and Black Gold. He went into specifics about the well, drill-stem tests, gas kicks, formations, the whole kit 'n' caboodle."

"That is interesting," Max said, thinking it over.

"Have you heard anything unusual, or picked up any Black Gold chatter on your scanner?"

Max thought for a minute. "No. I haven't heard much, hardly anything at all. Just one reference about the up-hole test, other than that they seem to be running a damn tight ship- at least on the airwaves."

Phil was quiet for a few seconds. "That's what I was afraid of," he finally said, sounding concerned. "They may have a leak somewhere in their organization. I'm going to have to talk to Wayne about it."

Max understood what this could mean and, if true, Phil would have to go into scouting mode on his end.

"Next question for ya Max; do you think Pole Cat or Hughes have been getting any good information from the Black Gold well?"

Max couldn't help but chuckle. It wasn't nice to laugh at other scouts because, in all honesty, it was such a secretive, deceitful industry; it was extremely hard to tell reality from fantasy. Plus, Max believed in karma and making fun of someone else may just come back to haunt you one day.

With Pole Cat, however, he couldn't help himself.

"No damn way!" he said. "The only way those two could get good information is if someone walked into the bar and dropped it into their lap! Wait, never mind that, dropped it into their drink!"

The line was quiet. Max thought he had lost the connection or Phil didn't get his reference. "Phil you still there?"

"Yeah, I'm here. I'm just thinking. OK. I'll handle things on my end. Thanks, Max."

"You bet," came the response.

"All right, be safe! If you see any sign of trouble, you high-tail it out of there! You got that? I don't want to have to file a missing person's report! You know how long those forms take!"

Phil tried to be funny, but Max knew deep down he was worried. He worried about all his scouts and was one of the reasons Phil, on occasion, opted to change professions. It wasn't that he couldn't handle the stress and pressure for himself; it was being accountable for other people's welfare that kept Phil up at night.

"Phil, I'll check in with you as soon as I can. But, if you don't hear from me in a month or so, feel free to start on those forms."

Phil laughed nervously.

"Just be safe, Max." It was the last thing Phi said. Max obliged and hung up the phone.

Max glanced at the time when he got back in the pickup. It was 4:30 pm. By now Pole Cat had to be settled into his favorite chair at the Motor Inn lounge. A smile formed on Max's face. He knew this was the ideal time to probe into Pole Cat and Hughes' activities. It was also a great time to let the double-agent know he had just been evicted from the woods and was too scared to return.

Like the permanent fixtures on the wall behind him, there was Pole Cat sitting at his usual table. The lounge was the same dingy, smoky environment when Max stepped in. Despite the no-smoking signs everywhere, it was obvious nobody cared, in an oil town.

Pole Cat was in fine form already and slouched in his chair, as Max approached. Red was again stitched to his hip.

"Mind if I join you?"

Pole Cat looked up through bleary eyes. "Not at all, take a seat, ya little prick! Buy me a drink and I'll even let you stay!" The joke followed with the usual solo belly laugh.

"No problem, Pole Cat. What's your and your sweetheart's poison?"

"Vodka and orange juice," the redhead responded with enthusiasm. It was the first time she ever said anything to Max. Perhaps even the first and only time she acknowledged his existence. Anything for a drink, Max mused.

Max waved the waitress over and placed their order, along with a soft drink for him.

"Heard you had company at your camp the other day," Pole Cat suddenly blurted out. "Scared the piss out of you I bet!"

"Yeah. It was nerve-wracking," Max said, playing on. "Might be a while 'til I go back out there again; Maybe Never!"

"Don't blame you," Pole Cat agreed with a nod. "Those bastards mean business!"

Max was quiet, as he let Bill run the conversation.

"I kinda like you, Max. Hate to have anything happen to you. Take some advice from an old drunk scout. Don't fuck with these boys. I'm serious."

Pole Cat's tone was serious and he looked Max in the eyes. It was obvious he had a direct connection with the men he was referring to. Max wasn't sure how or why. Perhaps he had a run-in with them in the past or perhaps he was familiar with them as a contract employee of Zephyr.

"Perhaps you're right, Bill. I might just work the airwaves from here in town from now on."

Max hoped when Bill sobered up, if that ever happened, this news would find its way back to Zephyr management. It should take some heat off.

It was 9:00 pm when Pole Cat's eyes closed and his head finally fell into the large breasts of Red. About time, Max said to himself. Looking across the table at the busty woman, however, he couldn't believe how wide-awake she still looked. Just in the time, he spent with them she had thrown back four double vodkas and OJs.

"Looks like you guys could use a ride?" Max asked, getting to his feet.

The red hair bobbed in slow motion. She looked at her passed-out companion, then back up at Max.

"Yea. A ride to Bill's room would be a help," she said with a thick slur.

Good, Max thought, she was drunk. Maybe she'll finally topple, he hoped, as he stepped over to pick up Pole Cat.

It took nearly 30 minutes to get his limp torso into the truck, but they were successful and Max was headed down the main drag toward the other motel. A block down the way, Max glanced over to see Red fast asleep with her head against the window. He smiled.

Sure would have been nice if just one of his passengers had stayed awake long enough to give him the key to the room, he concluded. Oh, well, nothing was ever easy.

After Max came to a stop in front of the blue door, he started his search for the key, fumbling through Bill's pockets, hoping not to wake him up. If caught with his hands in Pole Cat's jean pockets, it wouldn't look good for several reasons. Max chuckled silently.

He found nothing but lint and loose change, so he moved on to Red's purse, which had fallen to the floor. Carefully, Max snared the tattered purse and rifled through the contents.

He finally pulled out the large key with the Motel name on the plastic attachment. "Murphy's Law," Max muttered, "Keys always at the bottom and the last thing you find."

Max left the truck running with the heater on so his passengers would stay nice and warm. He then walked up to the room and knocked on it. No answer. He eased the key into the lock and pushed the door open.

It was pitch black except for the glow of the green fluorescent digital panels on the three scanners lined up on the large dresser. Max hit the light, then walked over and turned down the volume on each of the scanners so that he could hear if anyone was coming into the room.

Report forms, other paper, and empty fast-food wrappers were strewn all around the room. It was an utter mess; nothing seemed to be in order. How could any scout operate under these filthy conditions, Max wondered. It only took minutes to determine that Pole Cat had nothing of significance in the reports. Near as he could tell, most of the information Max did find was pure speculation on Pole Cat's part.

Max checked the dresser drawers and night table. There was nothing worthy of a second look. Max dropped to his knees and looked under the bed.

Jackpot!

He pulled out a black briefcase and placed it on the bed. It was unlocked and both latches snapped open. No surprise there, not with the way his fellow scouts conducted their affairs.

The first page contained a bunch of notes from Tom Hughes. They were surprisingly neat and orderly, Max thought, as he poured over them. Each page documented Tom's progress in tracking and checking Max's activity, including the meeting in the lounge and mention of the cutline entry point. No mention of the Polaris, however, or his camp.

Max thumbed quickly through the other pages. No mention of any activity on Black Gold's well, either. As he carefully placed the notes back in the case, he spotted a piece of paper in the small pouch in the top of the briefcase. Max slipped the paper from its hiding place and unfolded it.

Written on Zephyr Petroleum letterhead, in big, bold letters, was one simple sentence: "Do Whatever You Have To – But Get Rid Of That Scout!"

It was dated yesterday, indicating that Tom had just received his latest marching order. Max had one more pocket to check when he heard heavy footsteps outside the door. He quickly put the piece of paper back in, snapped the case shut, and slide it back under the bed.

The rattling keys were just outside the door, so in a panic, Max dove into the bathroom. He reached for the door to close it, then thought otherwise. He simply hit the light switch and stepped over to the toilet and dropped his pants. A second later, Tom was standing in the doorway staring at him.

"What the hell you doing here?" came the loud, angry protest.

Max wasted no time in a desperate attempt to turn the tides. "That's exactly what I want to know!" he yelled, sitting on the toilet. "Can't a guy take a dump in private, anymore? Close the damn door, will ya?"

The immediate comeback and harsh tone startled Tom. He stood there baffled for a few seconds, then stepped back and closed the door.

"That's more like it! Thank you!" Max yelled.

Max took a few seconds, and then flushed the toilet. He pulled his pants up and washed his hands. When he opened the door, Tom had the black briefcase out and was pouring over the contents.

"How the hell did you get in here"? he demanded.

Max calmly adjusted his pants and acted as nonchalant as he could.

"What do you mean? I had a few drinks with your sidekick and when that pussy passed out, I had to bring him home. I thought I'd use the john before I had to lug their drunken asses in here."

"What are you talking about? I don't see Pole Cat anywhere!" Tom took a step toward Max ready to fight. Max ignored the sign of aggression and continued his act.

"Well, if you opened your eyes, you'd see he's passed out in my truck!" he retorted. "As is that red headed bimbo he's with!"

Tom eyed Max closely. He was obviously thinking it over. Max continued his attempt to get the upper hand.

"But, hey! I'm glad you're here because you can help me carry them in. Gonna take both of us on that one; judging by the looks of her."

Max laughed, hoping Tom would buy his excuse. He continued to stare at Max with clenched fists. The hands and fingers suddenly loosened, though, and he turned and marched outside.

Max rolled his eyes and took a big sigh, as he followed him out. Max stepped through the doorway to see Tom step up to the passenger-side window of his truck and peer in. He turned to Max and his angry countenance quickly melted into an expression of contrition.

Max marched over next to him.

"Might as well get this over with."

Max opened the door and Red immediately fell to the frozen concrete. In his focus on the charade, Max completely forgot she passed out leaning against the passenger side door.

"Oops," Max said, feeling sympathetic. It was about the only thing truthful about the whole scene. Tom looked at Max and smiled. It was a great sight to see and Max knew he was in the clear. The two shared a quick laugh.

"All right! Let's get these two booze hounds to bed!" Max said, leaning down and grabbing the redhead by the arm and shoulder. Tom followed his lead and the two of them drug her in and flopped her onto the first bed. They did the same with Pole Cat, who, weighed about 75 pounds less and it was much easier.

"Well, that should do it! I better get out of here and find my own place to stay. After getting evicted from my camp looks like I'll be joining you guys in town here for a while."

Max started for the door. Exiting the room, he could hear and feel Tom right on his heels. He was suddenly worried he was going to take a blow to the head, but instead came Tom's quiet, apologetic voice.

"Listen, Max! I'm sorry I cussed at you. In our business, you can never be too sure."

Max turned around. "Hey. No problem Tom, just doing Pole Cat a favor. Regardless of what side we are all on, we have to look out for one another, right?"

Max studied Tom closely to see what his reaction would be to that statement. Tom didn't seem to care. He just looked at Max.

"So, I heard about your camp being discovered. What do you plan on doing?"

"I'm not sure yet," he said, trying to sound genuine. "I'll hang here for a bit until I figure it out. I know the well will be getting down to a critical depth soon, but definitely not worth getting hurt over."

"Yeah, I think that sounds wise. Too bad I never got a chance to go back there with you. But, hey, if you do go back in, I'd love to go with you." Safety in numbers, right?"

Max smiled and slapped Tom on the shoulder. "That does sound good. I'll let you know. Good luck with those roommates of yours."

Max turned and waved as he opened the door to his truck. He threw it into reverse, backed out, spun a doughnut on the frozen pavement and made a quick exit from the parking lot.

Max wasn't looking forward to heading back to his new camp this late at night, but at least he felt good about the fact that nobody would be following him. Before he headed down the lonely highway, however, he wanted to call Phil.

Max saw a pay phone on the side of a closed café, and pulled over and parked. He quickly jumped out and, without checking the phone for bugs, dialed Phil's number.

The phone rang several times before the sleepy voice answered on the other end. It was Phil's wife. "Sorry for waking you. This is Max. Just need to talk to Phil if he's available."

"Yes, Max, of course! Just one minute." Max could hear the soft voices through the phone.

"Hello, Max! What is it? Everything OK?" Phil said, sounding fearful.

"Yeah, yeah! All good. Look! Sorry, for waking you Phil, but thought you might be interested in what happened here tonight."

"Yeah! Go ahead Max, I'm listening." Max conveyed the information with excited exuberance.

Max gave Phil a detailed report on the events that had transpired and how it didn't look like the two bumbling scouts had any significant information on Black Gold's operation. Phil listened, intently.

"You done good, Max! Real good!" Phil replied. "I didn't expect to hear from you so soon, but your report confirms what I was afraid of."

"What's that, Phil"? Max inquired.

"I have the sneaky suspicion there is an inside leak at Black Gold. I still have some more due diligence to do, but that is what my heart and the circumstantial evidence tells me. I'll get with Wayne tomorrow and see what unfolds."

"OK, Phil. Good luck! I better let you get some sleep." Max was about to hang up, but Phil stopped him.

"Hey, Max, before you hang up. I am thinking of sending Rich Barnes up there. I know you like working alone, but this situation is about to boil over and I'd really feel better if you had someone else helping you, and watching your back."

Max was silent for a while. He really did like working alone and hated committee style decisions requiring a consensuses.

"I pretty much have everything under control, for now, but it's up to you, Phil," Max said, trying to reassure his boss.

"Everything may seem all right, for now, Max, it's what might happen down the road that scares me. Because of OPEC and soaring oil prices, who knows what people might do to ensure they win this project. It really could change the world."

Max knew there was nothing he could say to change Phil's decision. He truly did worry about the safety of his scouts and the Wolverine Hills endeavor was like no other. All bets were off with this one.

"OK, Phil. You're the boss. Keep me posted."

"I will thanks. Max! Good night!"

"Good night, Phil."

Max hung up the phone and jumped back in his truck. As he sat there staring at the closed café, he suddenly had the desire for a soft bed and a store-bought meal.

He laughed to himself. All it took was one café sign and a picture of steak and eggs on the window in front of him to convince him. Usually, advertising had no effect on him, but being in the field so long and living on his own cooking gave him cravings like no other.

Most of all, he wanted to feel the warmth and loving embrace of his wife. He knew that was impossible, however. Thus, he decided, he would treat himself to the next best thing: a comfortable bed and a hot meal. Max pulled out and headed back to find a motel.

As he drove, he thought about being joined by another scout. Rick Barnes was a capable, experienced scout, Max had no doubt, but he did prefer to work alone.

Perhaps that will continue to be the case, Max hoped. Either way, he'd worry about that in the morning. For now, it was time for sleep.

L. GORDON KESLER

CHAPTER NINETEEN

Max felt revitalized and ten years younger when he awoke the next morning. Despite all that was going on and everything that nagged and worried him, he finally had a good night's sleep.

It must have been due to fatigue and the fact that he felt the client was happy with his performance, thus far. Max laughed out loud. He knew the real reason, as he looked around the motel room. Lying in the over-sized queen bed, he let out a big smile and stretched.

Max leaped to his feet like a boy on Christmas Day. As he passed the mirror he checked his face for wrinkles. He was sure he had less than when he went to bed a few hours ago.

Time for a big breakfast, one I don't have to cook, he thought. Right after a long, hot shower, he decided. Max was almost giddy as he turned on the hot water. How amazing such little comforts can be when you forego them for so long.

At the café, Max pretty much ordered exactly what was in the picture on the window: steak, eggs, and hash browns. He did add an extra plate of bacon to the order, however, and scanned the room feeling guilty for being a pig when everything was placed in front of him.

Eating bacon and feeling like a pig. That's a funny one, Max joked to himself. Shit, he thought, maybe he was cracking up. Cracking like the eggs, Max laughed out loud at his string of puns. Hope no one is watching he thought, they will think I'm losing it for sure.

Max was a damn good bush cook, but this breakfast could have been the best in his life. Probably say that after every meal I have after extended field-work, he surmised. Regardless, he concluded, it was a very tasty change.

As he ate, Max eyed every table, trying to identify any other scouts or rig personnel that he might get to eavesdrop on. No one looked familiar and most of the talk was about the new pulp mill being proposed for south of town.

Same old shit; the community was up in arms over the possibility of shutting down the new pulp mill project before it even got started. As Max listened to the conversation around him, he heard a couple of environmentalist whackos chatting about the loss of trees. When will they fucking figure out trees grow back, Max questioned in his head with a chuckle!

Same damn leftists wanting to save trees at the expense of humans having jobs. It didn't make sense to Max.

He savored the last bite of toast and jam and motioned for the bill. The total came to $8.20. Max threw down a $10, grabbed his coat, and headed out.

Time to get back to work, he told himself. Suddenly, an anxious feeling began to consume every fiber of his being. It was a feeling familiar to Max each time he left a rig he was watching for an extended period of time.

The logging road to the cutline was holding up well, considering the warmer weather and the patches of melting ice. Normally, it was full of holes and extremely hard on the truck and the body. Today, however, with the softer conditions, Max was not bouncing around the cab as much. A nice break, he thought.

The only negative was the heavy logging truck traffic, which caused him to go much slower and pull over more often. The mills were scrambling to get all the lumber and pulp wood stockpiled before operations were halted during the warm spring months.

This made it a dangerous time to travel because most drivers drove fast and rarely slowed down for others. Max wasn't sure if that was because they rarely saw other traffic on these back roads or because the drivers knew the huge trucks they were driving, ones they didn't own, were much bigger than anything else out here. Probably a combination of the two, Max concluded.

He did respect them, however, because it was a tough job. When he saw a truck bearing down on him, he always pulled as far right as he could and came to a complete stop. It was still a nerve-racking experience each time a truck, loaded with 70-foot logs passed him at speeds of up to 60 mph.

As Max rounded another bend, he passed a sign that read: WARNING TRAVEL AT YOUR OWN RISK. So true, Max thought, as he saw yet another logging truck headed down the hill right for him. He again pulled over to the right shoulder.

The big purple Kenworth was moving to his side of the road, the bunk behind sliding back and forth across the road, shearing the overhanging limbs off the trees lining the road. The truck was hugging his side of the trail, coming right for him.

"Son-of-a-bitch," Max said loudly. Must be out of control, he thought.

It was barreling right for him. Unless the driver pulled hard to the other side of the road, Max would be squashed. Thinking fast, he quickly cranked his steering wheel hard to the right and stomped down on the gas pedal. He gunned the truck straight between two large fir trees.

Just as his Chevy bounced off the road, the bunk of the logging truck swiped the back end. Max's truck went spinning counter-clockwise into the forest. Snow, dirt, and broken tree branches went flying across the windshield and hood. The side eventually slammed into one of the fir trees and Max's body and head banged into the window.

Max's head hung low as he tried to collect himself. His shoulder and head hurt, but he was OK. He slowly looked up and took a deep breath. He couldn't see anything out of the windows. They were completely covered in snow and debris.

Thank God Carmen demanded he always wore a seat belt. Who knows what would have happened if he wasn't strapped in. Max wasn't a big believer in seat belts; he didn't like the government making decisions that were none of their business. He could tell however by the soreness across his chest that this time around they may have saved more serious damage.

After letting his nerves settle, Max tried to open the door. It didn't budge. He slid across the seat and tried the passenger door. Same negative result. The window was his next option and he hit the down button. It slowly lowered and a big clump of snow fell into his lap. Max was able to crawl out the window and fell into a built-up bank of muddy snow.

He stood up and stepped away from the truck to get an assessment. He was facing downhill, which meant the logging truck sent him into an 180-degree turn. The driver-side door was pinned against a fir tree and the passenger side against a bank of snow and broken branches. The damage didn't look too bad, however, but he'd have to dig part of it out to get a full diagnosis.

Like a snow badger, he frantically dug the dirty, white slush from around the truck. Unbelievable, he thought, absolutely unbelievable. Looking over his beloved Chevy, Max was elated.

The only damage was a small dent in the driver-side door and a gash to the rear-quarter panel. Sure the panel was smashed to hell, but it wasn't up against the tire. That meant he should be able to drive it. Course that would be after he somehow got back onto the logging road.

The shovel Max carried in the back of the truck had flown out during the wild ride, along with a bunch of other items. Max found it about 20 yards away and began the slow, painful task of getting his truck out. As he started shoveling, a surge of anger and rage suddenly overcame him.

Max replayed the accident in his mind. No way was that a fucking accident, he thought. He could vividly see the driver's face, just as he gunned his pickup off the road. The bastard was smiling, Max was sure of it. Max's heart was pounding like a jackhammer.

"That bastard was trying to take me out!" Max yelled as he looked up toward the logging road.

The note he read in Tom's briefcase flashed in his mind. Then the note found on the coyote carcass. Here it was, Max deduced. The gloves were off and Zephyr would stop at nothing to win the bid for the Wolverine Hills land parcel. Apparently, even go as far as killing him.

A chill crept down Max's spine. Maybe it was the cool breeze, but most likely the thought that this job could possibly cost him his life.

After two hours of digging and sweating, the 4X4 was back on the road. Several logging trucks had passed the scene of the wreck. Some gave a blast on the horn; others flew by oblivious to the accident.

His adrenaline was still racing as Max drove through the ditch and up the hill into the cutline. When he was close to his usual hiding spot, another surprise was waiting for him.

The teal Chevy glistened in the sunlight next to his Polaris. Apparently, the white camouflage tarp did not do its job this time, as Tom was standing right by it. Max saw Tom wave at him, as he pulled over.

"Be cool, Max, be cool," he told himself, stepping out.

Max was still upset and rattled, but he didn't want Tom to know that. Max was pretty sure Tom knew about the accident, and if he didn't, he would soon find out from his employers. Thus, in order to keep the upper hand, he needed to show he was in command of everything. Part of him wanted to walk up and punch the bastard in the face.

Calm, Max again thought, calm. The surprised look on Tom's face told the story. He knew what probably just happened.

"Uh, hey there!" he said, as Max walked up.

"So, you found it," Max said, trying to sound nonchalant.

"Yeah! I was waiting to see if you'd show. Wasn't sure if you decided to call it quits or not."

Max so wanted to let out his frustrations on Tom, but he kept it together.

"Yeah, still mulling it over, but I do need to go in and get the rest of my stuff," Max replied, lying.

"Sounds like the smart thing to do," Tom said, nodding his head. "You mind if I accompany you? I can help you take some stuff out."

Max eyed Tom closely. Out here, in the middle of nowhere, was the perfect place to take Max out. He was under orders to do just that, but did that mean actually killing him or just scaring him? If he was already planning on leaving, maybe Tom was being genuine and truly wanted to help him pack out?

Max wasn't sure of anything, at this state. He just knew he'd have to keep an extra eye open.

Max looked over at the teal Chevy and could see a snowmobile in the back. He thought it over, and then nodded.

"OK. I could use an extra hand. Let me help you get your snowmobile out."

"Great," Tom replied, then headed off toward his truck. Looking back over his shoulder, he added, "Shit, man! What happened to your vehicle? Looks like you got in a gnarly accident."

Accident, my ass! Max almost said it aloud.

"Tangled with a logging truck about a mile down," he said instead, "If you see a purple KW coming right for you, better head for the nearest ditch. I don't think he likes Chevys."

"Well, you were lucky. Don't know who your client is, but I'd damn sure send them a bill."

Tom laughed. Max was about to lose it. Of course, Tom knew who his client was. Hell, wasn't he supposed to be working for them, too? Max wasn't quite sure of Tom's false story. Nor did he care, at this point. The whole charade and his aloof act were getting comical, in his mind.

Max led the way. By now, he knew every bump, dip, bend, nook, tree, stump, etc., in the trail and he opened it up to see if Tom could keep up. Around one turn, Max knew there was thick, low-lying branch that was tough to avoid. Nearly took him out twice before.

Approaching it, Max slowed down to pull Tom in close. When he was just behind him, he twisted the handle to go full throttle down the straightaway leading into the turn. He was hoping Tom would do the same.

Tom saw Max take off and gunned it to stay with him. Just as the trail swerved around a large tree, Max turned hard left and knelt down just missing a large branch. Tom did the same but never saw the branch.

Just as he turned left, he stood up to keep his weight on balance. The branch hit him square across the chest, throwing him off the snowmobile and back into the white powder. Max turned looking back in time to see the wreck take place. He couldn't help but smile.

Max quickly pulled over and waited for him. About twenty minutes later, a visually ailing Tom came puttering up to him. Now, it was Max's turn to be aloof.

"What happened? I thought maybe I lost ya," he said.

Tom stopped and turned his machine off.

"No. I wiped out," he said slowly, rubbing his chest. "Didn't see a tree limb after one of those turns back there, knocked me clean off."

Max could see that it really shook him up. He started to feel bad for him. Shit, he thought, this dude may be out here to kill him, no time to feel sorry for the prick.

"Oh yeah, I think I know the turn. I should have warned you. Sorry! Used to doing this alone. We'll take it slower from now on."

Tom simply nodded to show his gratitude. Max was conflicted, part of him wanted to apologize for his actions. The other part of him wanted to do it all over again. Max shook his head and started his snowmobile. He led the way down the trail, this time going much slower.

As they approached Nose Creek, Max brought his Polaris to a sudden stop atop the small snow ramp he made. Tom coasted in next to him.

"Why are we stopping?"

"This is why," Max said, pointing downward toward the creek bottom. Tom followed his finger and looked straight down the canyon.

"Fuck me! You actually built a ramp down there? Holly shit!" The awe and respect were all over Tom's face.

Max didn't respond. He just smiled and fired the Polaris back up. Down he went. "Take it easy on the ramp, Tom!" he yelled back. "Make sure you idle it all the way to the bottom."

Max was enjoying himself. On the creek bottom, he gunned it about half way up the east side, before stopping to watch Tom. He looked like a snail going down and almost fell over the handlebars, but he finally made it and throttled up toward him. Max laughed and then continued on to camp.

A few yards from camp, Max stopped and hid the snowmobile. He took extra precautions to camouflage his new accommodations as much as he could with pine boughs and camouflage material Carmen had made for him years back. When Tom pulled up next to him, his face lit up.

"Damn man! You really take this shit serious!" he said with what sounded like genuine appreciation. "I can't believe how much trouble you went to get back in here. Incredible."

Max was meticulous, as he covered the Polaris.

"Better put some pine boughs over that Cat, the fancy fluorescent strips will show up for 200 yards even through the heavy timber," he said full of pride, but trying to conceal it. Tom didn't argue, he just did as Max asked and broke enough boughs to cover the bright colored machine.

The two started toward his camp. About 10 yards away, Tom finally saw it. "Sweet, Jesus! You did a great job concealing the camp! I'm just now seeing it!"

Again, Tom sounded purely authentic and Max again beamed inside with pride. Course, he suddenly wondered, is it really a compliment if it comes from someone as lazy as Tom who scouts from the comforts of the local hotel bar?

Max hurried inside his tent to make sure his best equipment, especially any evidence of the satellite phone invention, was well hidden. He wanted Tom to only see the standard scanners in operation.

Tom stepped up and stood in the doorway with the tent flap pulled back. "Mind if I come in"? He asked politely.

Max could hear the shrill squawking of the brakes on the drum as the pipe lowered inch by inch into the ground. The big Cat engines that ran the rig sounded like continuous low volume thunder in the distance.

"Sounds like they're still drilling, same as when I left. I'm going to walk into the rig and get a penetration rate before we head back, you want to come along?"

"Hell, yeah!" an enthusiastic Tom said. "About time I see what's going on!" Tom laughed. It actually made Max laugh, as well.

The scouts stood silently in the shadows of the black timber, looking off at the rig in the distance. Max checked his watch as he made a mental note of where the blocks were in the derrick.

A half hour passed, with neither man saying a word. Finally, Max broke the silence. "Looks like about ten minutes a foot," he said, as he checked his watch. "They should be pulling out for a new bit by tomorrow sometime, I would think."

Max looked over and Tom nodded, seemingly agreeing with him.

"All right! That's good! Let's get out of here." Max turned and headed back along the narrow trail toward the campsite. With Tom behind him, he had the sudden feeling he might get whacked over the head at any moment. Max sped up and, fortunately, the blow never came.

On arrival at his tent, Max turned to Tom. "I need to fuel up the generator. I'll be right back. Go ahead and make yourself comfortable."

Max motioned to the tent and continued on his way. He looked over his shoulder and saw Hughes quickly throw back the flap and enter. Once his head disappeared, Max waited a few minutes then slowly eased his way back, ensuring to be as quiet as possible.

Carefully, he placed each foot down making sure not to step on any twigs and lightly pushing the snow down to avoid the crunching sounds that comes with partially packed snow.

At the flap of the tent, Max peered through the crack. He could see Tom frantically checking under the bed and throughout his stuff. He was about to open the aluminum photo case when Max threw the flap back.

"A-ha! Find what you're looking for traitor?"

Tom spun around in the center of the room, his color the same hue as the outside snow. "Um, just...Just looking for a different antenna for the scanner," he said with a stutter.

"You're such a lying bastard, Tom! I know what you're up to!" Max couldn't contain his anger any longer. "You think this is my first fucking turkey shoot? You're fucking counter scouting me, ya chicken shit bastard!"

Tom said nothing. He was still too nervous and shocked.

"Get on that machine and get the hell out of here before I lose my fucking temper and hang your ass from a tree like you all did with that poor fucking coyote!"

Tom slithered past him like a snake. "Let's go! Move it!" Max yelled at him as he zipped past. Once outside, Tom ran straight toward his snowmobile.

"Hey! One more thing! If anything happens to my camp, I'm holding you personally responsible!"

Hughes didn't look back, as he straddled the seat of the Arctic Cat in the distance. "You'll be sorry, Max!" he yelled, starting it up and spitting snow and ice as he hit the throttle.

"Save it, Tom! People like you give scouting a bad, fucking name!"

Tom didn't hear him. He was already bouncing and sliding his way to Nose Creek. At the speed he was going, he was sure to go flying up the ramp on the west bank and right over the snow ramp, Max chuckled as he envisioned the wreck about to take place.

His laughter echoed in the timber at the thought of his nemesis landing on his back in the bush.

CHAPTER TWENTY

At Black Gold Resources, things were rapidly falling into place. With less than a month to go until the bids were due and the critical stages of the well just ahead, Joe had decided to fly to the rig and become an additional member of the field team.

He still found the field more exciting than the office and his decision to go was made easier by the fact that Val was there. Wayne and Gerry would handle any major situations at the office until the land sale was over.

The mood was upbeat, even Chuck, the bean counter, was more cooperative, as the escalating oil and gas prices were putting more of a shine on the perspective numbers.

Phil had been struggling with how to handle the apparent leak situation. He knew the delicate nature of the problem. How do you inform your client that someone inside his company may be working against them? There was still the chance he was wrong, but he knew in his gut that was not the case.

Phil picked up the phone and dialed the number.

"Good morning, Black Gold Resources," came the soft voice on the other end of the line.

"Morning, beautiful! Or is it, beautiful this morning"? Phil teased.

In reality, he was trying to lighten the mood because he was on edge and nervous about the conversation about to come.

"Who is this please"? The voice replied, more direct.

"Sorry about that! It's Phil Graves."

"Oh! Phil no need to apologize. I didn't recognize your voice."

Phil laughed. "No worries. Is Wayne in?"

"Yes. I'll put you right through."

Phil could hear the conversation in the background. "Phil Graves is on the line for you Mr. Stadwell. OK! I'll put him through."

"Yes Phil! What can I do for you today?"

Here it was. Phil could no longer avoid it. "Morning, Wayne. To be blunt, we need to have a meeting ASAP!"

Wayne was startled by the tone. "Um, sure, Phil. Want to come on over to the office?"

"Yeah. That would be great. Although, I think it's imperative you and I meet alone. So, maybe we can meet in your office instead of the meeting room?"

"OK, Phil. Can you head on over now?"

"Yeah. Yeah, I can. Be there in about an hour."

"No problem Phil. See you when you get here."

As Phil rolled the black Buick into the visitor stall at Black Gold's office, he was still feeling anguish over the situation. Phil decided the best strategy was to ask questions and listen closely. At this point, he was on a fishing expedition still and absolutely had no idea where the so-called leak could be.

Phil had seen it all in this business. One thing he knew was greed is a powerful motivator and can sometimes reach all the way to the top. He couldn't believe that Wayne was the source. As far as Phil was concerned, Wayne's character was without question. Hopefully, his judgment of character would hold true.

The elevators seemed to move at warp speed, which is always the case when you want to delay the inevitable. Why did Phil feel sick to his stomach, it wasn't his problem? It was the way things were and something he was paid for and skilled at trying to remedy. Perhaps it was because, in the end, he was human.

The young receptionist immediately relieved the tension with her flirtatious greeting.

"Hey, there, how's the number one rogue in the oil patch"? she said with a giant smile.

Phil's laughter was more out of apprehension over the coming meeting than it was at the light joke. "Phil Graves to see you Mr. Stadwell," she said still looking at Phil with a smile.

"Send him right in," came the reply.

Phil thanked her and headed down the hallway. As he rounded the corner, Wayne was standing in front of his office.

The two quickly entered and Wayne shut the door behind him.

"What's up, Phil?" Wayne asked as he motioned Phil to have a seat before sitting down himself.

Phil took a deep breath, as he positioned himself across the desk from the young looking oil executive.

Just as Phil was about to speak, the intercom crackled to life.

"Mr. Stadwell. Sorry to bother you, but Joe and Val are calling in from the field."

"Tell them I'm in a meeting and I'll have to..."

"Wait a minute," Phil interrupted, suddenly having an idea.

"Um, put them on hold, please. I'll be with them in a minute." Wayne looked at Phil, wondering what he had in mind.

"Take the call, Wayne," Phil instructed emphatically. "I want to ask them a few questions if you don't mind."

"Sure, Phil, if that's what you want."

Wayne leaned forward and hit the blinking light, then the speaker button. "Morning, Joe! Morning, Val!" Wayne said enthusiastically.

"Morning chief," Joe said robustly.

Val's greeting was more reserved, "Morning, Wayne."

"Listen, guys! Before we get into the daily stuff, I just want you to know that Graves is in the room, so be careful what you say." Wayne chuckled softly.

Phil was puzzled by the comment. Why would he say that he wondered?

"Oh, hey Phil," said Joe.

"Morning guys," Phil responded.

"We really don't have anything to report regarding the drilling operation," Val said. "I know we're not supposed to say anything on the phone, anyway. Joe and I thought you might be interested in another situation that took place last night. I know Phil will be."

"Go ahead," Wayne answered with curiosity, looking over at Phil with raised eyebrows. "Somebody nearly ran over Phil's security man about 3:00 am."

Phil sat more erect in his chair. "Say that again, Val?"

"Maybe you heard already, but some drunk came barreling up the road to the rig. Took out the gate and sideswiped the security trailer."

"Really Wow! Nobody's checked in with me yet," replied Phil. "Course, I have not been to the office, yet this morning. Was anybody hurt?"

"No. Everyone is OK. Did some serious damage to the gate, however."

"Any idea who did it?" Wayne asked.

"No idea. Looked like the same older red Ford that came by awhile back. I think I told you about that Wayne. At any rate, the security guard said the driver was most likely drunk."

There was a brief pause in the room as the two considered the news.

"How far did he make it down the lease road?" Phil finally asked.

"The guy drove clean to the rig! Did a few donuts in the snow and mud on the location, then turned and drove away. It happened so fast, only a few people saw it."

"Anyone get a license number?"

"Like I said, Phil, it happened too damn fast."

"Sounds like maybe a drunken rig hand letting off steam"? Wayne said, looking at Phil for confirmation.

Phil didn't say anything. He shrugged, letting Wayne know he may be right. He was pretty sure who it was, however, based on the truck description and the fact that he was drunk. He did worry about the safety of his security team, but his mind was still elsewhere. He would deal with the crazy driver at a different time.

"At any rate, we thought you guys would want to know," Joe chimed in. "We can discuss all the other stuff from a landline in town."

That comment piqued Phil's interest. "Joe," he suddenly asked. "How often do you all get to town?"

"I am not really sure, Phil. I just arrived here a few days ago," he responded.

"We don't go very often," Val said, helping Joe answer the question, "Maybe once a week to talk over a secure line."

"When was the last time you went, Val?"

"What's this, Phil "My own personal interrogation," If I don't answer correctly, I don't pass go and head straight to jail?"

Phil laughed with Val. He knew his questioning could raise suspicions and worry, so he needed to be subtle.

"No monopoly game here," he responded with a chuckle. "I just wanted to see how often you guys called in. Just making sure you are all following security protocol, that's all?"

"Ah," she responded. "Well, I believe the last time was last Thursday? So I'd say about 8 days ago. Does that sound right, Wayne"?

Wayne thought about it. "Yeah. Joe and I and Gerry were in the conference room. So, yeah, that sounds right."

"OK, thanks, Val. Hope you guys are doing well up there." Phil wanted to end on a light note.

Phil sat quietly while Wayne discussed issues unrelated to the intruder incident. It was obvious that the conversation was subtly coded to preserve the integrity of the ongoing activities at the rig. Wayne expressed some final pleasantries and hung up the phone.

"Now, Phil. Tell me what's going on." Wayne said it in a hushed tone, as he leaned across the desk.

Phil sensed that the always-considerate Stadwell might be mocking him a bit. That was all right, it made it easier for Phil to jump into the issue with both feet.

"I think you have an internal leak," Phil said forcefully.

The confused, agonizing look on Wayne's face was a sight to behold. He looked like a kindergartener who just dropped his ice cream cone.

After a few painful seconds of silence, words finally came to his tight lips.

"No way, that just can't be. You must be mistaken! I'd stake my life on it, Phil."

"Look. I could be wrong, but I wouldn't stake your life on it," Phil warned. "Let me tell you where I'm coming from before you say anymore."

Phil spoke with authority to make sure he had Wayne's full attention.

"I had lunch three days ago with a client. At that lunch, the guy starts spilling his guts about all the info he has on your well in Wolverine Hills. Wayne, the guy had specifics on stuff only you would know about - formations, gas kicks, oil shows, the whole damn works!"

Wayne was very pensive. He wasn't sure what all this information meant. He knew it wasn't good.

"But, maybe he's getting his information from someone scouting our rig. Maybe from Zephyr?"

Phil nodded his head. It was certainly a possibility.

"That's what I initially thought, too," he said calmly. "But Max has been following their scouting pretty closely and I'm pretty certain this information is coming from your rig hands or right here from this office."

Wayne said nothing. He was still trying to process the meaning.

"Max has been really monitoring the airwaves, and he says your rig is tight. Also sounds like they don't get to town very often, so I'm not really sure where the leak is coming from. I do know if any of the rig personnel were talking, though, Max would know."

Wayne was battling to keep up, but he understood what the last statement meant.

"Then, what you're saying is the leak is most likely coming from here."
It was slightly more of a statement than a question.

"That is correct," Phil said apologetically.

Wayne sat quietly and expressionless.

"You OK"? Phil inquired in a whisper.

The response came back just as quiet. "Yeah, I'm fine." After a long pause, he followed with: "What do we do now?"

The pain and disappointment were obvious. Wayne trusted everyone; it was his nature. It may be naïve to think that way as the president of a company, but it was Wayne's way.

"I need you to make a list of everyone in the office, including all those who might have access. From the cleaning staff all the way up."

Phil waited a while for an answer. It finally came. "No problem. I can certainly do that."

"Another thing, if you don't mind. If you can highlight who has access to critical information about the Wolverine Hills drilling operations that would be great, as well."

Wayne didn't say anything. He just nodded.

"Don't bother putting your name on the list, Wayne. If I can't trust you, this is all futile anyway."

Wayne looked Phil square in the eyes. "Maybe, But I don't plan on being exempt. Include me like everyone else."

Phil knew Wayne wanted to be treated just like everybody else. Thus, he knew not to argue with him on it.

"How soon you need the list"? he asked solemnly.

"The sooner we get it, the sooner we can start eliminating people."

Wayne again just motioned with his head.

"You hired Wildcat to do a job, I just want to make sure we do it right. I really am sorry to have to share that information with you, Wayne. I hope I'm wrong, but I don't think so."

Wayne again nodded to show he understood. This time, he managed to give Phil a smile with it. Phil got up to leave. Wayne stood up with him and walked around his desk.

"Wayne," Phil said as the two walked toward the door. "I don't need to tell you how imperative it is that nobody else knows about this."

Wayne patted him on the back, as he opened the door.

"I understand, Phil. I understand. I'll have that list to you as soon as I can. Thanks for coming."

Phil shook his hand. For once, Wayne was looking more to the ground, than he was in his eyes. As Phil walked passed the receptionist, he said goodbye and gave her a quick smile.

"Have a beautiful day," she yelled after him playfully.

Beautiful was hardly the case, Phil thought, as he stepped into the elevator. Things from here out were bound to get ugly.

CHAPTER TWENTY-ONE

It took Max several hours to unwind. He decided to get his mind off the day's events by focusing on monitoring the airwaves.

He sat down in front of the hypnotic flashes of neon green lights dancing across the front panels of his two scanners. Max worked quietly programming more channels into the scanners, hoping to hit the jackpot on some of Zephyr's private frequencies. He then retrieved the silver case from where Tom had found it, and opened it up. Max was disgusted he hadn't stored the case in the vault away from the tent. Just fucking careless he thought!

Good thing the bastard never saw it, he thought. Course, the dork probably wouldn't know what he was looking at. Max was deliberate and methodical, as he assembled the satellite monitor. It had taken months of research and making contacts in the communication world before he finally found the right person who got him what he really wanted.

To secure the receiver was a real coupe in the scouting business. Max was sure no other scouts had acquired the valuable monitoring device necessary to track and record satellite communication. He knew it was only a matter of time until others had this technology, but until then, he would relish the upper hand.

One last adjustment to the directional antenna and Max was ready for some serious eavesdropping. The airwaves were quiet. After several hours, Max finally picked up some domestic chatter, but nothing of interest. Once again, it all changed at 3:00 am.

There it was the familiar voice of the English geologist. Max was disappointed in Gil of late. He hadn't shed any light on the activity at the rig and kept his conversation to romantic gibberish. By 4:00 am, Max grew tired of the incessant small talk. He turned the volume knobs down and crawled into his down-filled sleeping bag. Within minutes, he was sound asleep.

In what seemed like only a few minutes, Max was suddenly wide-awake and nearly on his feet when the crackling sound woke him from his slumber. He immediately turned up the volume and looked at his clock. It read 5:00 am.

As he rubbed his eyes and cleared the cobwebs, he knelt in front of the satellite receiver. The initial reception was intermittent, as Max scrambled to adjust the antenna. Every muscle in his body was tense with anticipation. He could tell these voices were important. Max was totally oblivious to everything else until his eye caught the sudden movement over his right shoulder; Max whirled around ready to defend himself. It was just the tent flap, swaying in the early-morning air.

He chuckled, as he tied the strings more securely and once again focused on the voices.

He recognized one right away; it was Matt Crane, Zephyr's field engineer. Even at 5:00 am, he sounded like the biggest asshole in the industry. Max double checked the recorder to make sure he didn't miss any of the conversation.

"Roger, things are going along great! Should be no fucking problem reaching our final depth in time to core and test the well, especially if the damn office intellects don't throw a fuckin' monkey wrench into the works."

Crane paused for effect or to see if Roger had any reaction. He started right back up.

"We're currently drilling in the Leduc at 12,365 feet and we're making about 2 feet an hour."

"Matt! came the static-ridden reply. "How's the hole on connections"?

"Appears to be in good shape on connections and the last trip out only had a couple of tight spots; Nothing to worry about."

It was obvious that for some reason both these Zephyr employees felt their conversation was secure.

"Matt any sign of that scout?"

"No, but if he's still out there, I'll personally make sure he disappears. Don't sweat the small stuff, Roger. Me and my boys can handle him."

"Listen, Matt, just keep things low key. We got a scout working for us. He's on it for now. Just wanted to see if he was still making any cameo appearances."

"That's fine, Roger, but if I catch him around, I'll exterminate that bug myself and they'll find his bones when the snow melts. Oh! By the way, how's the little sting going?"

"What sting?"

"Don't play cat and mouse with me! This is Matt Crane you're talking to, not some fuckin' greenhorn," he snapped back. "I know we have a rat inside Black Gold."

Max's eyes and ears opened as wide as they could go. He again checked the recorder and leaned in closer. Ah, man, this link better hold up, he desperately thought.

"That's highly confidential, but you are right. Our source has been very resourceful. The fact is, we receive the same information across our desk almost as soon as they do. Might, as well be drilling their well, too!"

Roger laughed coldly. Matt joined him. It was the first time the two laughed together. Things must be going well for Zephyr if these two sorry bastards are getting along, Max thought.

"Guess that's good, since those scouts you hired are pretty much useless, right?" Matt said still chuckling.

"Nothing but a cheap diversion," Roger said confidently.

Max's blood pressure was reaching a boiling point. Phil was right on with his suspicions. The only thing he needed was a name. He knew he wouldn't be that lucky, but his excitement got the better of him and he leaned in further, hoping all the information would spew out.

Just as Max thought no such luck!

"All right, there, Matt. Thanks for getting up so early. I'll talk to you tomorrow." And with that Roger was gone.

The scanner was suddenly quiet, but what Max heard was reverberating loudly in his head. It was 5:30 in the morning and in the last 30 minutes the entire scouting job once again changed and not for the better.

By the time he had written everything down in his notebook, it was 6:00 am. Max was eager for the time to pass and for daylight to arrive. He really wanted to get back to town and report to Phil. That is if his truck was still intact when he got back. If Tom returned, he was sure to have slashed the tires or something worse. After all, his truck was right there for the taking. Or destroying!

The sun started its slow climb over the hills, illuminating the new day. Finally, time to go. As dangerous as things were becoming, Max knew it wasn't time to use his cell phone.

In the time between writing the report and waiting for reasonable light, Max had worked feverishly trying to secure his camp and his equipment from unheralded invaders. There was no carelessness this time in concealing all of the monitoring equipment. In fact, Max moved the storage case further away from the tent, making certain that all tracks were erased that might lead to the buried treasure.

As Max crossed Nose Creek, he was conscious of the hardness of the ice surface and was relieved that at least his escape route was still intact.

The trip over the crusted snow so early in the morning was nerve racking. Each muscle felt like a violin string wound too tight. Every shadow was suspicious and took on the form of a human. Finally, Max cautiously idled his way within eyesight of the Chevy.

Only two hundred yards away, Max took in a deep breath in a futile attempt to relax and gain composure.

As he closed in on the concealed pick-up, he suddenly caught the flash of the teal truck speeding off the cutline toward the logging road. Max brought the Polaris to an abrupt halt. He sat there, waiting for what seemed an eternity, for something to happen. There was nothing but silence.

The silence was broken by the distant rumbling of a logging truck heading for a load. It was quickly followed by more silence.

Max started the Polaris up again and slowly idled the last 100 yards to the truck hidden under the tarp. He suddenly realized what Hughes was up too.

"Son-of-a-bitch!" Max shouted. Right in front of him Max could see his truck flattened by two fallen trees. The bastard actually went to the trouble of cutting two large spruce trees and purposely dropped them on his pride and joy.

One tree fell directly across the hood and the other fell over the box of the truck. They had completely destroyed his beloved Chevy. Max felt his gut twisting into knots. Sure it was an inanimate object, but he and his truck have been through so much together. He truly felt as if he had lost a member of the family; or like losing an old friend.

"Fuck!" Max screamed out loud. Now, what? He stepped off the snowmobile and walked up to his truck to survey the damage even further.

His options were fairly limited. While it was something he hated to do, it was now time to use the cell phone. Max dialed the number. Three rings that seemed like an eternity and Phil finally answered the phone.

"Morning! Graves here!"

"Hey, Phil Max here! Am I glad to hear your voice!"

"And I yours, my good man."

"Phil, I'm going to need your help."

Max gave Phil a quick assessment of the situation regarding Tom and his destroyed truck. He also told him he had some news for him, but would reveal specifics when he got to a landline. He did give him a very good, clue, however.

"Let's just say I can confirm with 100% certainty that what you think is happening with our client is indeed the case."

Phil was eager for details, but he knew what Max was referring to and he also knew it was time to seriously go through that list of Wayne's staff members.

"Alright, Max," he finally said. "What do you need up there?"

"Better send me another 4X4 and I'll try to look after it better than my own. I think I can make it to the tiny country store down in Grovedale on the Polaris, but it's going to be one rough fucking trip."

"All right. How long will that take you think?"

"Roughly two hours or so, I believe. Still enough snow pack on the side of the road to make travel reasonable. Course, that is if I don't get taken out again by another logging truck."

"Deal, you get started and I'll get you the new truck. I am going to get Rich Barnes to drive it up. I know you like working alone, but things are getting too crazy out there, Max."

For once, Max did not contest. "Can you handle a Ford"? Phil laughed openly in spite of the situation. He knew Max needed to relax.

"Ha-ha," he said. "At this stage, even a Prius would do!"

The two shared a quick, nervous laugh. "OK, I'll fill you in on everything in two hours. Thanks, Phil!"

Max tucked the cell phone back inside his coat pocket to keep the batteries warm and set off on his long, slow ride back to civilization.

It was late morning when Max arrived at the pay phone outside of the country store. This time he took extra precautions as he checked the phone for bugs knowing that his call to Phil very well could be monitored. No bugs were found, so Max started to dial Phil's number.

As the phone rang, Max looked down and noticed a tiny board nearby on the side of the store slightly out of place. He quickly put the phone down and went to inspect it. He moved the board to the left, revealing a tiny crevice behind it.

"Well, fuck me!" Max said with surprise.

Sitting in the tiny nook was an FM transmitting device. Max quickly hung up the phone and inspected it closer. It was a brand he knew well and had used many times himself. Max quickly looked around the parking lot. Whoever set this up had to be close because the reception range was only a quarter of a mile, at best.

Max rose up and walked around the store. He could hear the tires burning rubber on the asphalt and slipping in the icy snow before he saw it. Flying out from behind the store and onto the main road, nearly taking out a smaller pickup truck was Tom's shiny teal Chevy.

Max watched him intently as he high-tailed it down the lonely highway. The back-end of the truck fish-tailed from side to side as it went. It quickly disappeared in a blizzard of ice and snow. Max shook his head in disbelief. He looked down at the small FM device in his hand.

"Hey Tom- if you can hear me, know that I'm coming for you! If I see you again, you're going to be unrecognizable! It's one thing to fuck with me it's another to fuck with my Chevy! If I were you I'd keep right on driving; right through Grand Prairie and straight to fuck out this part of the country!"

With that, Max slammed the device down and mashed it into the ground. He then spun around and returned to the pay phone to call Phil.

L. GORDON KESLER

CHAPTER TWENTY-TWO

With only three weeks to go until the April land sale, it was becoming difficult to contain the excitement around Zephyr's office. The drilling was on schedule for completion in the next ten to twelve days, giving a comfortable cushion for coring and testing operations.

Another factor hyping the enthusiasm and anticipation was the fact that the zones of interest were coming in higher than their estimated projections, which was an indication of productive pay zones.

Roger was in early every morning, making sure all the details for the final stages of the well were in order. Basically, operations had gone smoothly with only a few glitches along the way. This particular morning, Roger had some loose ends to tie up with his geologist, Nick Mayfield.

As he dialed Nick's number, he noticed the memo next to the phone. It was his secretary's handwriting: "Please give Mr. Wallace a call first thing in the AM."

"Fuck!" he barked, reaching toward the ashtray to find a cigar stump. "I have other important shit to deal with this morning. I'm not in the mood for the third degree from Wallace and his Texas losers!"

Roger had a habit of talking out loud when he was uncomfortable. Roger chomped down hard on the cigar butt. The meeting with Nick would have to wait.

"Shelley!" he yelled out.

"Yes, Mr. White"? She inquired without using the intercom.

"When'd you get this call from Wallace?"

"About 5:30 yesterday afternoon."

"I didn't think it was 5:30 this morning!" Roger's voice was dripping with sarcasm.

"Sorry, Mr. White, I..."

"Sorry my ass, did he say what he wanted?"

"No sir. He said to have you call first thing in the morning. It didn't sound pressing or serious."

"How would you know it's not serious? Anytime Mr. Wallace calls consider it serious, got that?"

"Yes, Mr. White," Shelley said, rolling her eyes.

"Listen! Give Nick a call. Tell him to come to my office in fifteen minutes." Roger paused. "No, make it half an hour!"

"Yes, Mr. White. I'll take care of that right away."

"Damn straight you will," Roger mumbled to himself, dialing the Houston number.

"Good morning, Zephyr Resources," the voice said.

"Mornin' there. How ya all doin' in TeX-ass"? Roger found great humor in mimicking the southern accents when he called the Houston office.

"We're all just fine, thank you. What can we do for you?"

"This is Roger White in the Calgary office. Put me through to Mr. Wallace, please."

"Yes sir. Hold on one second." She said.

Roger rocked back in the leather chair and nervously transferred the cigar butt in his mouth from one side to another.

"Hello, Roger. What's happening in our favorite northern Canadian town this morning?"

"Well, Al, it's still early here, we're two hours behind you guys, so not much going on yet here in the office."

"Understood, let me be more specific then," Al stated matter-of-factly. "How are things going on the Wolverine Hills well?"

Roger rolled his eyes and took a deep breath before answering.

"Things are great!, just tying up a few loose ends so nothin' goes wrong during these exciting final stages. The way I figure it we're about 10 to 12 days away from finishing all the drilling. We're getting mighty close to the big prize, Al, and the geologists are excited by the formation tops."

Roger thought he had done a nice job of not only recapping the situation but was positive enough to keep Al happy. He leaned back in his chair, waiting for the response.

"Roger, I've been in this business too long to count our eggs before the hen hatches 'em. But, you are right, it's a damn sight better than having everything coming in low."

Al paused for a second, then started right up. "At any rate, what I called about is my trip to Calgary next week. Along with a couple members of the geological staff, I plan on flying up in the company Learjet. We'll let you know the exact time of our arrival."

"Sure Al."

"What we would like to do is fly in the chopper up to the well site and spend some time at the rig; probably just a day trip. Can you work out the logistics on that, Roger?"

"No problem, at all," Roger replied, without much care. "What day you thinkin' about"?

"Wednesday of next week, that work for you?"

If Roger had his way, they would never come. It would be just a few days of being the dutiful "yes man," kowtowing to every one of Al's needs and remarks. It would not be a fun time, but if all went well, it was something he could easily accommodate.

"Perfect. We can go over the final stages of the well together."

Al didn't care for any small talk. "OK, Roger, see you next Wednesday." That's all he said, and then hung up the phone.

"Fuck!" Roger shouted loud enough for Shelley to hear. The last thing he wanted to do was cater to the Texas big wigs. He also didn't want them messing with any of the decisions he was making.

Pissed off, Roger punched the button on the phone. Before Shelley could even respond to the flashing light, Roger was yelling.

"Get Nick the fuck in here, will ya?"

Shelley didn't answer she simply picked up the phone to summon the geologist. Not a minute had passed before Nick was in front of Shelley's desk. He smiled nervously as he addressed her.

"Good Morning, Shelley."

"It is morning, Nick, but I'm not so sure it's a good one. Good luck in there. He's in one of his moods, yet again."

"When isn't he"? Nick said in a whisper, as he walked toward the double oak doors of Roger's office.

Nick knocked, and then slowly pushed the doors open before Roger could say anything. He slid into the large executive office. Roger continued his booming rage as he interrogated Nick about the status of the well. The young geologist remained calm, as he explained the recent data.

"Everything continues to look good," he explained. "The mud tech reports everything is holding up and the hole is in great shape. The samples continue to look very promising; the gas readings are still high and the samples have good oil staining."

Roger leaped out of his big chair and stepped up to the window. Still chewing madly on the cigar butt, he mulled over the latest news.

"Wallace is coming up next Wednesday and I want everything to go smoothly," he said with conviction. "I don't want to give him any reason to come down on our operation and I don't want to give him any reason to feel these big Texas bastards need to take over this project. This is our baby and that's the way I want it to stay. All I want is for them to fly in, see how great we're doing, and fly the fuck out!"

Roger suddenly turned and looked him in the eye. "You got that, Nick?"

"Yes, sir. I got it," he replied nervously. Roger looked him over and, satisfied he understood the gravity of the situation, nodded. He returned to staring back out the window.

"Roger," Nick said, suddenly feeling an urge to keep the conversation going. "Do you have any more updates on the Black Gold well?"

L. GORDON KESLER

Without turning, Roger immediately shot back: "What the hell is it with everyone wanting to know about Black Gold's well?"

"Just wanted to know how they were progressing relative to our well and the sale deadline, that's all," replied Nick defensively.

"For your damn inquiring mind, it appears they are having dumb luck and actually doing pretty well. The drilling is back on track and all indications are they will finish in time. At this stage, it's our job to make sure they get no data from our operations."

Roger mulled his own statement over as he looked down the long city street toward Black Gold's tiny offices.

"Well, that's too bad. But glad to know at least our scouts are getting you useful information." Nick wanted to end the conversation on a positive note and thought that would do it. On the contrary, this just riled Roger even more. He turned and stared at Nick to make sure he knew what was really going on.

"Scouts my ass! Those two morons couldn't get laid in a whorehouse if it was free! They are nothing but useless pricks. Thanks to me, we have a better, inside source at Black Gold."

Shelley's eyes widened, as she could hear Roger's loud, crass voice through the door. Shelley thought something else more than scouting was going on. Those must be the strange phone calls she was getting asking for Roger without leaving a name. Bet it's a Black Gold rig hand trying to make a fast buck on the side, she decided.

The door quickly opened and a nervous, timid Nick walked out. He turned and smiled at Shelley as he raced back to his office. As Shelley watched him, Roger suddenly emerged. He stormed right past her without stopping or looking at her.

"Take messages!" Roger said curtly with the cigar stub still gripped tightly between his teeth. "I'll be back in an hour or two."

Shelley sighed with relief as the door closed on the elevator and Roger disappeared. He was such a jerk. She knew she couldn't put up with him and his tirades any longer; the stress and anxiety were getting to be too much.

Time to make a change, she thought, glancing at the bottom drawer of the desk. That was where the oil company directory was and it was finally time to use it, she demanded of herself.

Shelley opened it up and took out the directory. She quickly scanned the companies under "B" until she came to the listing for Black Gold Resources, Inc.

What she was about to do was out of principle and, perhaps, a bit out of revenge. It certainly wasn't for money, which seems to be the one and only motivator in this God-forsaken town. She looked at the number and started dialing. Do it before you chicken out, she concluded.

"Good morning, Black Gold Resources. May I help you?"

"Yes, you can." Shelley's voice was shaky and her palms were sweaty. "Um, who is the president of your company?"

"That would be Mr. Wayne Stadwell. May I ask what this is regarding?" Shelley suddenly felt trapped. She wasn't sure what to do.

"Uh, um….No, thank you!"

She quickly hung up the phone. What was she doing? She looked down at her hands. She was trembling uncontrollably. I can't do this from here, she suddenly realized. The call could be linked right back to her through phone records, caller ID, whatever. Plus, someone could easily overhear her or walk in on the call.

She looked back down at her hands. They were still shaking. Shelley wrote the name Wayne Stadwell down on a sticky note and put it in her purse. She would call from home. Most likely after a few glasses of wine, she surmised.

The day passed slowly and Shelley talked herself into and out of her plan to call Black Gold at least a half dozen times. By the time she reached her apartment, she had talked herself back into it. She didn't owe Zephyr any allegiance. Everyone in Texas seemed nice, as did Nick, but she rarely talked to them. It was Roger she dealt with on a daily basis; an intolerable, excruciating day-in and day- out basis.

He had abused her long enough and it was time he got what was coming to him. She would quit in a week or so, any sooner and Roger might grow suspicious of her. The paranoid asshole was suspicious of his own shadow. It was 10:00 pm when Shelley took one more gulp of her large glass of Zinfandel and picked up the phone.

It was the fourth time she had done so that evening. Each time she would dial a few numbers, and then get cold feet. Maybe she shouldn't get involved in this whole mess. Nah, this was something she must do! It wasn't about Wolverine Hills; it was about social justice! That may have been the wine talking, but it sounded good.

This time around she actually made it to the end and the phone starting ringing. Her heart was coming out of her chest. It was beating like 100 times per ring. Her fear again got the better of her and she went to hang up. Just as she did, a man picked up.

"Hello"? Came the tired, sleepy voice.

She still wanted to hang up, but with caller ID now so popular there really was no turning back.

"Oh, I'm sorry! Is this Mr. Stadwell?"

"Yes, it is."

"Mr. Wayne Stadwell"? Again she asked. She was so nervous her mind was racing, trying to find the right words.

"Yes, it is. Who is this?"

"A...Um...Well, I really don't want to tell you who I am, but I'm calling to help you. Um, well, actually give you some information that, uh, might help your company. It is Black Gold, right?"

"Yes, it is, but to be honest I don't take sales calls at home and it is really quite late."

"No! No! This isn't a sales call!" Shelley said way too loudly and excitedly.

"Then what it is this regarding? I have to say I'm not really following." Wayne's voice was non-threatening and still surprisingly polite.

Shelley searched frantically for the right words.

"Mr. Stadwell you have a leak!" she blurted out. It was all that came to mind.

"A what?"

"A leak! Someone in your office is leaking information about Wolverine Hills!"

Shelley was again trembling. She suddenly feared she was doing the wrong thing.

"Say that again"? Wayne asked with a hint of alarm and wonder.

What if Roger had tapped her phone! The thought immediately popped into her head. She was crazy with panic. "That's all I can say!"

With that, there was a click and the phone went silent.

"Wait! Who is this? How do you know that?" Wayne desperately asked the questions, hoping for more information. The stranger was gone.

"Hello? Hello"?

Bewildered, Wayne hung up the phone. He sat quietly, hoping the caller would ring again. No call came.

Wayne's first impression was it was all a hoax; someone was playing a trick on him, knowing how big this project was. After all, the news about Black Gold and Zephyr competing on Wolverine Hills was the talk of the town.

Yet, he could sense genuine fear in the woman's voice. Plus, how many women would pull such a ruse? Not many, he concluded.

Wayne reached for the phone and dialed the only number he knew would help him get to the bottom of it.

Phil was just pulling the sheets back when the ringing started.

"Hello, Phil? Sorry to call you so late."

"Wayne, you can call me anytime. What's up?"

"I just had the strangest call," Wayne said.

CHAPTER TWENTY-THREE

Max waited patiently at the Grovedale store for Rick to arrive. He continued checking his watch: 8:00 pm. His new companion scout was two hours late. Perhaps he skidded off into a ditch like so many have done on these northern roads or perhaps the Ford he was driving broke down. After all, FORD did stand for Found On the Road Dead.

The thought made him chuckle. But it was an abbreviated one as boredom and anxiety were getting the better of him.

Max continued pacing. He had already consumed what seemed to be a gallon of coffee. Any more and I'd float away, he joked in his head. Max started a move to the pay phone to give Phil a call. No, he decided, he'd check in with his wife. It had been a long time and who knows when the next time would be. Just try to sound upbeat, as if nothing is wrong, he told himself.

"Hello, gorgeous!" Max said enthusiastically when his wife picked up.

"Who is this? Carmen teased.

"A secret admirer," Max flirtatiously answered

"Oh, that's nice. I need one of those since my husband disappeared months ago."

Max chuckled softly. "OK. OK. I get it."

"I'm still not sure who I'm talking to," Carmen couldn't stop giggling. "Just kidding, it is so great to hear from you! When are you coming home?"

"Hang in there, baby. The job will be over in a couple of weeks. Then we'll grab the kids and get away for a few days."

"Couple of weeks more? That sounds like an eternity."

"Well, Rich Barnes is coming up to help me, so maybe I can sneak away for a day or two. Not sure."

Carmen's suspicions were aroused. She knew Max liked to work alone.

"Why is Rich coming up?"

"The well is super critical now and the client is concerned about missing information," Max said, sounding as cool and confident as possible.

Max did not like to lie, but he didn't want Carmen upset.

"Be honest with me. Is everything going OK?"

"Yeah! Yeah! It's all going well!"

Max suddenly thought about his squashed Chevy. If Carmen knew what happened, she would immediately demand him to come home. He quickly digressed.

"How are the kids"? Max asked.

"Kids are fine. They miss their father."

"I miss them terribly, too. Tell them I love them and will see them soon. Are there any bills or mail I need to know about?"

"Nothing, honey! Everything is under control down here. Just focus on finishing and getting back to us."

Rich's timing was perfect. He drove the blue truck into the parking lot of the small convenient store and Max watched as it slid to a stop a few spaces away from the phone.

"All right, honey! I'll do that. I gotta go, now. Rich just pulled up."

"OK, sweetie! I love you and miss you! Be safe!"

"I love you, too! Talk in a few days."

Max hung up the phone and walked over. Barnes was already out of the truck waiting as Max approached.

"Where you been"? Max asked, trying to sound as cordial as possible.

"Sorry I'm late," he responded, sounding a bit out of breath. "Had water in the gas line, fucker froze up on me; took me forever to get her started again."

"Did you put gas line antifreeze in?"

"Yep! But there was none in Phil's truck. Had to flag down a big rig to get some. You know those SOB's, they don't stop for nothin'."

"Tell me about it," Max responded, thinking about the big logging truck nearly taking his life.

Standing close to Rich, Max could smell the booze on his breath. He thought about saying something but was just too damn tired. He didn't understand everyone's penchant to drink while driving to the job. Maybe it's stress, he concluded, and let the whole thing go.

"Well, should we get that Polaris of yours loaded up and head to camp?"

Max mulled that idea over. "It's pretty late and I've had a really long day. I think it would be wise to stay in town for the night. We'll head out at first daylight."

"All right! You're the head honcho on this one. Whatever you say."

Max was glad to hear that. Even though it was obvious, since he had been running the show for months, you never know how things will go when another scout comes on the scene. There was a lot of testosterone in the scouting industry with people always feeling they needed to prove their worth.

Despite the fatigue and the nice feather bed, Max did not sleep as well as he did the previous night. It was far better than most nights in the bush, however, since he was always constantly checking the scanners, but he felt an air of uneasiness.

Things were definitely changing and now that Tom knew he had been made as a turncoat, and knew where his new camp was, he had to really be on the lookout.

After a quick breakfast in the hotel restaurant, both men were on the road headed south. As they neared the Grovedale store, Max spotted the old red pickup pulling out onto the road just ahead of them.

"Slow 'er down, Rich"! Max said from the passenger seat.

"What's up"? Rich cautiously applied the brakes on the slick, icy pavement.

"You see that beater that just pulled out ahead of us?"

"Yeah"

"Recognize it?"

"No, should I?"

"I thought everyone knew that piece of shit. It's Bill, or Pole Cat," Max said, eyeing the truck closely.

"Ah," Rich said. "I should have known by the look of it."

Max glanced over at Rich and smiled. "Let's follow him and see what the grubby bastard is up to."

Rich followed the old rust bucket from a safe distance. Suddenly, the red taillights flashed in the distance. "Looks like he's turning, Max," Barnes said.

"Nah" Max replied. "He's just slowing down. Only got one brake light functioning on that beater."

Rich pulled the Ford over. Max quickly reached for a pair of Bushnell binoculars from the seat next to him and focused on the action ahead of him. "Why'd he just pull over on the side of the road?"

"Not sure," Max answered, adjusting the focus of the binoculars. "Maybe trying to pick something up on his scanner?"

An hour had passed since Pole Cat had parked the pickup on the side of the road. Nothing seemed to have taken place, as he continued to simply sit in his truck.

"Fuck! What the hell's he doing"? Rich's patience was wearing thin.

"Still just sitting there. Probably got a bottle between his legs and monitoring the airwaves."

Just then the one red taillight lit up and then quickly went off. The red truck did a U-turn and was now coming right for them.

"Oh, shit! He's turning around, Now, what?"

"Just take it easy," Max answered calmly. "I'll duck below the dash; you just sit there, as if you're reading something. There's no way he'll recognize this truck."

As the pickup passed, Rich continued to look down at a map he unfolded across the steering wheel. Pole Cat did slow down and strained to see if he recognized the driver, but Rich held his stare downward. Pole Cat hit the accelerator and drove off down the highway.

"Think he recognized you?" Max questioned from below the dash.

"Hell no!, That dude doesn't know me from a fence post."

"Now what, want to follow him to town?" Rich inquired.

"No. I got all I wanted to know. Poor ol' Pole Cat is nothin' but a harmless drunk. Not so sure about the big prick staying with him, however."

Rich wasn't sure whom he was referring to, but he let it go once Max ordered him to continue to the camp. Max gave directions as Rich left the main road and turned onto the cutline.

"Pull 'er up on the other side of my flattened Chevy over there," he said pointing.

Rich's eyes widened as the truck came into full view. "Holy shit! They really did a number on your girl!"

Max didn't say anything. He was still in mourning over the loss. The blue Ford came to a stop.

"I sure fuckin' hope they don't do that to Phil's baby here," Rich added.

"Hey, you can stay here and babysit it if you want," Max responded.

Rich clearly heard the sarcasm in Max's tone. He just nodded, realizing it was all part of the job.

"All right, let's just get these machines unloaded."

Max liked the answer and the two worked well together to get everything out of the truck. Soon the tandem snow machines were roaring in unison through the willows. Rich was a good snowmobile rider and was right on Max's tracks. As they approached the west bank of Nose Creek, Max coasted to a stop. Rich slide up right next to him.

"Wow! Looks wild, but I guess I have no choice, huh?"

Max just smiled. "Take it slow and follow my lead."

Rich's eyes were wide and wild as he watched Max idle his snowmobile down the steep ramp.

"That is one fuckin' crazy dude," Rich said, laughing. He then started down the ramp. It was slow going, but he managed it successfully and quickly hit the accelerator up the east side to catch up.

Coming over the canyon rim, Rich spotted Max. He was stopped, staring forward. He pulled up next to him and cut the engines. He looked over at a very distraught and anguished colleague. Rich looked at him, not sure what to make of it. He then followed Max's stare off into the distance.

"You OK"? Rich asked.

It took Max a few seconds to respond.

"See that?" Max pointed toward an unidentified item between two large branches of a giant fir tree.

Rich strained to see, but finally noticed something hanging.

"Yeah," he answered, quizzically. "Looks like a badly decorated Christmas tree. What the hell is it?"

"I'm afraid it's what's left of my camp."

Max looked solemnly at Rich, then dismounted. He grabbed his Magnum off the Polaris and slowly walked forward. A baffled and startled Rich followed.

As the two got closer, it became evident that the entire camp was ransacked and destroyed. There were pieces of equipment and clothes strewn all over the snow and hanging from tree limbs. The two continued their walk into camp.

Rich's mouth was wide open. He was astonished by the destruction.

"Damn it," Max said, quickly speeding up. As Rick stopped to take it all in, Max hurried past the camp toward a clump of fir trees 100 yards away. Max ran up to the base of one and dropped to his knees. He quickly pushed away some pine boughs and snow. His icy tomb, thankfully, went undetected, and the silver case was intact.

He pulled it from the hole and looked it over. A big smile fell on his face. In their zeal to destroy the camp, they never did find his secret hiding place. His satellite monitoring invention was still alive and well.

"Holy Shit!"

The shout from Rich immediately got Max's attention. "Look at that," he yelled toward Max. Max's eyes followed to where Rich was pointing.

Where Max's tent once stood was a black crater. Pieces of nylon, plywood, dishes, food, and metal were strewn all over. The smile on Max's face suddenly disappeared. The bastards had not only ransacked his camp, they blew it to smithereens!

Max's guts were in knots. He had worked years to acquire just the right kind of equipment and now it was all gone.

"Shit Max! You sure are lucky you weren't here when all this went down!" Rich's voice was one of both gratitude and shock.

Max said nothing. He, too, was in a state of shock. The two men didn't say a word for almost a full minute. Suddenly, Rich broke the silence.

"Max, I think we need to get the hell outta here! Before we get blown into little pieces; like your camp!"

Max looked over at Rich, and then back at what had been his camp. The numbness he felt gradually turned into rage. He put the case back in its hiding spot and quickly covered it up. He then turned and started marching straight toward his snowmobile.

Rich watched him with great intrigue. "What ya doing, Max? We leavin'?"

Max didn't say a word, as he continued his march. He was growing more and more, angry with each step. Finally, getting to his Polaris, he jumped on and stared at Rich.

"You get out of here! Try to salvage what you can from my camp and I'll meet you back at the truck in a few hours."

Rich was dumbfounded.

"What do you mean? Where are you going?"

Max started up the snowmobile and revved the engine angrily.

"I need to get a final check of what's happening at the rig before we go!"

With that, Max hit the throttle and was headed straight toward the rig. Rich couldn't believe it.

"Hey! Max! What are you doing? Get back here! I wouldn't go anywhere near that rig! Come on man!"

Max did not answer. He was too angry and determined. Rich watched as Max disappeared into the nearby forest. He stood, bewildered, as the roar of the Polaris faded in the distance.

CHAPTER TWENTY-FOUR

As the Dover elevator came to a stop and the doors parted, Phil checked the time: 9:00 am. Why, he wondered, did he feel like he was running late? Must be the fact that he always made it a habit of being early, thus, on time meant he was tardy – at least in his mind.

Before entering Black Gold's office, Phil instinctively patted the pocket of his blue blazer. Yep, the box was still there, as it should be. Sometimes this job required a degree of paranoia, he thought, chuckling to himself.

"Good morning, Mr. Graves."

"And good morning to you, Connie."

"I'll tell Wayne you're here." Connie pushed the button and announced Phil's arrival.

"He'll be right out, Phil," she added.

Phil took a seat and once again caught himself checking the blazer pocket, as he reached for the outdated Oil Week magazine. On the cover, in big, bold letters it read: "OPEC sends oil industry into pandemonium." Before he could open it, Stadwell appeared in the hallway.

"Morning, Phil! Come on down."

Phil threw the issue back down on the coffee table, making a note he should read that article later. The two men disappeared into Wayne's office. The door closed behind them.

"You want anything Phil, coffee, water?"

"No thanks, Wayne. Before we get into your strange call, I should let you know that I got my own call – from Max in the field. As much as it pains me to say, he pretty much confirmed there is a leak inside Black Gold."

Wayne nodded as if it wasn't anything new.

"We're not talking a leak from the rig or from town, either, Wayne. We are talking right here in this office."

Wayne looked glum, but it looked as if he had already come to accept this horrid news.

"I understand how disappointed you must feel," Phil went on "but at least now we can focus our efforts on your office personnel, which will greatly limit the time and effort needed to find the perpetrator."

"Phil, I hate to concur with your assessment, but after the call, I received last night, I'm going to have to agree with you." Wayne was quiet and somber.

Phil was intrigued. "Oh, really I'm all ears!"

"About 10:00 last night, as I was getting ready for bed, I received an anonymous call from a woman. Sounded like she was on the younger side, but I'm not really sure. She point blank told me I had a Wolverine Hills leak coming from my office. Then she hung up."

Phil was very curious and interested who this caller could be. Not many women in the oil industry, he surmised, and even fewer with any knowledge whatsoever on Wolverine Hills.

"I see. Did you happen to get the caller ID?" Phil asked.

"I did!" Wayne replied with a slight smile. "I tried looking it up online this morning, but nothing came up. Thought you might be able to do something with it."

Wayne leaned forward and handed Phil a folded up piece of paper. Phil nodded, as he took it and put it in his pocket. "I'll check this later."

Phil reached inside his blazer and pulled out a tiny black box. Wayne looked at it with intrigue.

"Now, what's that thing?"

"Essentially, this is what you call a bug detector." Phil pushed a button to activate it. The red light on the end of the box glowed steadily.

"I came prepared to sweep the offices, but I think I will do it tonight after everyone goes home; with your permission, of course."

Wayne looked perplexed. "Yeah, whatever you have to do, Phil. But what does it do?"

"There's a chance someone may have tapped your phones to monitor your calls and activity. If they are here, this little guy will let me know."

Phil held it up and they both examined it with a bit of investigative intrigue. Wayne thought for a moment and then nodded.

"All right, let me get you a set of keys." He jumped up and went to a filing cabinet in the corner and opened it up.

As he rifled through the contents, he added, "I'll also let security know you're coming this evening. I'll tell them you are doing a polishing job on the oak desks or something."

Phil was impressed. "That's good. I'll bring some cleaning supplies. If they ask, I'm spit-shinning the desks and tables."

They both nodded in agreement. Wayne shut the drawer, then stepped over and handed Phil a set of keys. "Here you go. The big one is the key to the office. Let me know what you find."

"I will," Phil said, standing up. "I'll come by tomorrow so we can talk in person again."

Wayne took a seat back down. He didn't look too thrilled about what was happening. Phil noticed Wayne's anguish.

"Don't worry too much, Wayne. We'll catch this bastard sooner or later."

Wayne simply raised his eyebrows and sighed. "That's what I'm afraid of," he remarked solemnly.

Phil understood now why he looked so sad. It wasn't because they might not catch the person responsible for the sabotage; he was upset that there was a saboteur in the first place. This guy truly cared about everyone who worked for him, Phil concluded, as he walked out. It was a very admirable trait, especially in this cutthroat industry.

"See you later, I hope," Phil said with a smile, as he headed past the receptionist."

She giggled and blushed. Phil hit the elevator button. Why am I being such a flirt, he thought. I'm a happily married man. Guess I'm just human, he concluded, feeling a bit guilty. Deep in thought, Phil simply stepped into the elevator the minute the doors opened. He stepped right into a pretty young brunette.

"Oops! Excuse me!" Phil said, embarrassed. "I'm really sorry! I totally didn't see you."

Phil thought he heard Connie, the receptionist, laughing as the woman simply nodded nervously and stepped around him. Phil boarded the elevator and hit the "L" button.

"What a moron," he said aloud, as the doors shut in front of him.

"Good morning, may I help you"? Connie said to the woman.

"Ummm, yes, my name is Shelley. I'm here to see Mr. Stadwell." Shelley looked around nervously.

"Is he expecting you?"

"We....ll, not really," she said again looking around.

"Mr. Stadwell is a very busy man, but let me check with him. Hang on." The receptionist hit the intercom button. "I'm sorry, your name again?"

"Tell him it's Shelley. Um, tell him we talked last night."

Connie was a bit confused but noticed the woman was not going to offer any more information. Thus, she rolled with it.

"Hello again Mr. Stadwell, I apologize for bugging you, but there is a Shelley here to see you."

"Shelley? Shelley who?" came the response over the intercom.

Connie pressed the button again. "I'm not really sure, she won't say, sir. She just said you guys talked last night?"

"Talked last night? I don't understand...." Wayne trailed off in a state of confusion. "Oh! Oh!" he quickly followed with enthusiasm. "Bring her down! Thanks, Connie!"

Connie escorted the mystery woman to Wayne's office without engaging in any further conversation. The woman looked extremely fidgety and kept looking over her shoulder. Wayne met the two women at the door.

"Thanks, Connie! I'll take it from here." Wayne motioned for Shelley to come into his office. He quickly shut the door behind her.

"Hello," said Wayne. "I'm Wayne Stadwell president of Black Gold, please have a seat."

Shelley was uncomfortable and nervous as she stepped over and sat down. Wayne quickly hurried around his desk and sat down opposite her. "Now, Shelley. It is Shelley isn't it?"

"Yes, Mr. Stadwell, it is."

"So, what brings you here today?"

After twenty minutes of explanation about what was happening at Zephyr and describing her boss, Roger, Shelley felt relief. It was if she was talking to a psychologist because as the words spewed out of her mouth, the weight went flying off her shoulders.

She was not one to blab on and on and talk ill of others, but by the time she finished, she was sure she did the right thing. She felt a sense of peace for the first time in months.

"Shelley," Wayne replied calmly and softly. "You have shown a lot of courage coming here today and giving me a heads up on this whole situation. It's something we were already investigating, but I really appreciate you confirming it. Now, my question is, if I may be so blunt – what's your price?"

"Mr. Stadwell, please understand I didn't do this for money," Shelley responded with nervous energy. "I just don't feel comfortable at Zephyr and felt I needed to let you know. In all honesty, if you have a position that comes available down the road or something that would be great, but I don't want any money. It's just the right thing to do, I believe."

Wayne thought about it and nodded to show he understood her. He could tell that she was extremely nervous and was taking a big risk to show her face around here.

"That seems like a reasonable request," he told her with confidence. "Black Gold Resources is always happy to have ethical people on board. However, if I may, I might suggest you stay at your current place of employment until we finish the Wolverine Hills project."

"Mr. Stadwell, I'll stay as long as I can bear it. It may not be until the end, but I'll certainly try. "

"I understand," Wayne replied, standing up. "I don't want you staying in a combative, dangerous workplace any longer than you have to. You do what you have to do, Shelley. Bottom line, be safe."

"I will! Thank you so much Mr. Stadwell." Shelley stood up.

"Call me Wayne," he said, coming around the desk and putting his hand on her shoulder to offer support. "By all means keep in touch. When this all blows over, please come back and we'll see what we can do about that job. Hopefully, we'll still be in business."

Wayne laughed nervously at that last statement. Shelley looked him in the eye and thanked him profusely. He then walked her out.

Wayne escorted Shelley to the private elevator that led to the underground parking. He thought it best she secretly leave the premises just in case some other oil executive may recognize her. Oil was a big industry here in Calgary, but in reality, it was a small, tight-knit community and most everyone knew each other.

Once his guest was safely out of the building, he returned to his office and fell into the large leather chair. "What a morning," he said, letting out a big sigh.

He checked the time on the brass oil derrick clock on his desk: 11:00 am. Felt more like 11 pm, he thought.

Wayne dialed the number to Wildcat Scouting. He wanted to give Phil an update on what just transpired and tell him he now had a name and face to go with the strange caller. He didn't pick up, so Wayne hung up. He'll let him know personally in the morning.

Phil arrived at the Sixth Ave office of Black Gold at approximately 9:15 pm. The uniformed rent-a-cop greeted him and dutifully asked a bunch of questions before allowing him to proceed to the 6th floor.

Just a bunch of programmed robots, Phil thought, as the questions were asked in a drone-like manner. Phil wasn't even sure the two guys listened to his answers. With Wayne already letting them know he was coming, what did it matter? They were ready to get back to their nap or surfing internet porn.

Phil walked briskly across the glass-like marble floor to the bank of shiny silver elevator doors. He stepped onto the elevator and hit the "6" button. On his way up, he shuffled through the keys looking for the big one that opened the front office doors. Hearing the ping indicating that he reached his destination, Phil stepped out and right into the big body of the janitor.

"Oops! Sorry about that," he said, finally looking up.

The big gray-haired, raw-boned night custodian didn't appear to be impressed with the collision.

"Be nice if you watched where you were going," he mumbled.

Phil watched as the large man wheeled his cleaning supplies into the elevator and hit the button to go to a new floor. He glanced at Phil as the elevator doors shut.

"Nice cleaning supplies," the man grumbled with sarcasm.

The doors closed and Phil looked down at his tiny plastic bucket with one can of Pledge inside. The janitor was right; the cleaning supplies were pretty pathetic. Next time, he concluded, it might be wise to be a bit more prepared if he was masquerading as someone else.

Might also be nice to start walking with his head up, he joked. That's the second time in one day I've walked into someone. Phil laughed to himself, then continued to the Black Gold office.

The place was pitch black when he stepped in. There was nobody around, but empty offices at night have an eerie feeling about them and Phil wasn't comfortable. He would whip through this and be on his way. Phil fumbled for the main light switch and finally found it against the sidewall. With everything now illuminated, he felt a bit better.

He knew the other scouts, especially Max, would laugh at him if they knew how uneasy he felt in the dark of an empty office. Some scout I am, Phil mused.

Wayne's office was the first to get a sweep. The red light on the bug detector remained a constant red glow. That meant that everything was clean. Phil decided the best attack was to sweep all of the offices for electronic devices first and then check each office again for hard wiretaps.

The sweep went extremely fast since everything turned out negative. Phil figured the electronic bugs, especially wireless FM bugs, wouldn't be used because they were too easy to detect. But it had to be done, nonetheless.

Actually, as he thought about it, he should have told Wayne to check and run a sweep the day he was hired. And every week thereafter!

"Idiot," he said aloud, knowing it was shoddy work on his behalf. Guess he was too focused on getting Max out into the field where the real action was.

Phil decided to be more methodical in his second sweep through each office, partially because it was needed and partly because he was trying to make up for his earlier screw-up.

Even though Wayne insisted that his office be checked out, Phil knew that it was a waste of time. After doing a routine check for hardwire taps, he left feeling confident the office was clean.

The first office down the hall from Wayne's was the drilling engineer, Joe. Phil knew he was in the field and had been for a few days, so any recent internal leaks couldn't be attributed to him. It needed to be checked anyway. Looking around the room, Phil couldn't help but be impressed by how neat he kept everything.

Each pile of paper was meticulously scanned for any telltale notes. After 30 minutes, Phil decided it was time to exonerate Joe and he moved on to the next office.

For convenience, Val and Joe had adjoining offices. This was because they worked so closely together and it saved having to always step in and out of the hall when constantly dealing with calls from the rig.

Like Joe, Val had gone to the drilling site to deal with the geology directly herself. She had left weeks before Joe. If the leaks were currently taking place, as they still were, Val couldn't be the culprit.

Looking around, Phil did observe one big difference between the offices. Val was a slob compared to Joe. The piles of paper, maps, charts, etc., were all over the place and nothing seemed to have semblance. It took longer for Phil to rifle through the paperwork, but after a while, he concluded that she, too, was squeaky clean.

Chuck's office was next. Chuck was the bean counter and an unlikely suspect, but Phil knew that sometimes the one you least suspect can be the guy you're looking for. Still, as the Black Gold accountant, he was last on Phil's list, since the information everyone was after was drilling details and geological data. In this project, nobody cared about financial records or company numbers, which is all Chuck dealt with.

Still, he had to be officially investigated and cleared.

The office was in shambles. Each office and employee were getting worse and worse in terms of appearances, Phil noted with a tad of humor. Papers were all over the desk, the nearby coffee table, and piled high on the floor. Phil dropped to his knees to make sure it was indeed a coffee table under all that mess. It was, and funny enough there were papers and binders under it, as well.

This was going to take forever, he concluded. After 45 minutes of searching and coming up empty, Phil decided that if evidence was in fact buried somewhere in this paper pigsty, it would remain buried.

With a bit of guilt for not continuing into the abyss of papers, Phil mentally scratched Chuck off the list. Chuck had enough to worry about without further complicating his life with clandestine operations, Phil concluded, as he turned out the lights to the office.

Time had gotten away from Phil. He really didn't mean to take so long on this fishing expedition, as he called it. Two more people and places to check: Gerry's office and the receptionist area. Connie's desk was tiny, so Phil opted to start there.

A good receptionist is worth her weight in gold, but are often underpaid and underappreciated. They also often have access to sensitive information since they are usually directly helping the president and talking to everyone who comes and goes.

The temptation to get rich quick is omnipresent and the more mundane and monotonous a job is, the more one thinks about it. Thus, despite Connie being a sweetheart in his eyes, she needed to be investigated.

The sweep through all the stuff in the desk literally took 10 minutes. There really wasn't anything personal or complicated present. It was mostly generic: a calendar, a Rolodex, various directories, letterhead paper, and lots of office supplies.

A quick scan of her computer emails showed she rarely communicated in a digital manner. Too busy on the phone and dealing with visitors, Phil thought. Phil left the reception area and headed back down the hall.

Good news and bad news, he thought. He was glad to be able to scratch all these employees off the suspect list, but with only one more to go, Phil felt worried he may not ever find the mole.

Phil suddenly felt punch drunk after all of the paper he had gone through and it was late. When he stepped up to Gerry's office, the word "Geophysicist" was written in big, bold letters on the door. Everyone else had their name, but for some reason, Gerry went with his occupation.

The door was closed and, surprisingly, locked, when Phil turned the knob. "Damn," Phil said, knowing he had to go through the wad of keys to find the right one.

On key eight, or maybe it was nine, he found the right one. It slid into the hole, turned, and the door pushed open. All right, Phil thought with a smile. The room was neat and well kept. He could tell that even in the dark. Phil hit the light switch and scanned around. He'd start with the desk.

The top of the desk had geophysical data carefully lined up matching formation markers that were hi-lighted with an array of colored felt pens. To Phil, none of the lines made any sense. It was all gobbeldy-goop, to him.

The walls had brightly colored charts hanging everywhere. It looked like a room of a grade-schooler proudly presenting all his artwork, Phil surmised. This was one area Phil knew he couldn't work in. He wasn't good at coloring, he joked to himself. Maybe he was drunk with fatigue.

Phil's mind was wandering. He was tired and he knew it. He opened the top desk drawer, glanced inside, and went to close it. Nobody in his or her right mind would leave any damning evidence in such an obvious place. As he pushed it shut, however, he stopped. A stapled report on top caught his eye. He opened the drawer back up and took it out.

On the top page of the "Black Gold Daily Field Report" was scratched or doodled in pencil, the word: Zephyr. It was faded and looked as if someone tried to erase it. They didn't do such a great job, however, as it was plain as day. Next to it, also partially erased, the remnants of a phone number. Why would a Black Gold well report have Zephyr on it, unless it was to indicate it was the report to go to over to their office.

Maybe, Phil thought, it was a copy left for someone to pick up or photograph. Any of the scenarios was possible.

Phil held the paper to the light, but could only make out the last two digits. Not significant enough to take and show Wayne, so Phil opted to place it back in the drawer where he found it.

A picture is worth a thousand words, however, so Phil did take a photo of it. The cell phone was a great invention, especially with the few extra bells and whistles that came with it, like text messaging, email, and, of course, the built-in camera. Phil snapped a few pictures and closed the drawer.

He checked the other drawers but found nothing of interest. A clue, and potential suspect, Phil thought, but he'd need more than just this before going back to Wayne. Phil sighed loudly. He was tired.

He turned out the light and shut the door. He stepped away, before turning back. He opened the door, reached in, turned the little lock, and then shut the door. Don't want the "Geophysicist" to know someone was snooping around his office, Phil decided.

With slouched shoulders, he picked up his tiny bucket of cleaning supplies off the receptionist's desk and headed for the door. Phil needed a plan to somehow expose this rat. "But how?" An idea suddenly popped into his head. As he locked the office doors, he smiled with confidence.

The morning meeting with Stadwell would be interesting, as well as disappointing. Phil had already begun to formulate a plan in his mind as to how he was going to expose the rat. He would need access to the office one more time after hours.

CHAPTER TWENTY-FIVE

Rich was getting nervous. It had been four hours since he watched an angry Max ride off into the forest. It was now blacker than the inside of a cow, he thought, and that meant something must be wrong. But, what should he do? There was no way he could navigate the ramp at Nose Creek at night. But standing around here doing nothing was driving him crazy.

Maybe he was jumping to conclusions and Max was simply busy gathering information at the rig. Perhaps they started tripping the pipe out of the hole? That would account for his absence. It took a while to get an accurate pipe count when that occurs, Rich deduced.

"No need to panic," he said aloud to himself and the darkness around him. Rich lay back down on the uncomfortable truck seat and pulled a blanket over him. He nervously adjusted his makeshift pillow of sweatshirts and coats. Listening to the hum of the scanner on the dash of the pickup was relaxing, and soon he drifted off to sleep.

He awoke to the sun shining through the windshield right into his eyes. The warmth felt good and he smiled slightly, enjoying it.

The sudden thought that Max was still missing caused him to throw off the blanket and quickly sit up.

"Shit," he said, looking all around the truck for any sign of life. He opened the door and stepped out into the snow. The sun was above the nearby mountain range, completely illuminating the trees around him.

"Damn it, Max! Where are you?"

Rich walked down the cutline, searching for tracks, anything that would indicate that Max had returned during the night. There was nothing. Rich was right back where he started; unsure where Max was and unsure what to do. His mind was racing with possible situations and ideas. Despite the cold temperatures, he found himself sweating.

Maybe it was time to use his cell phone and call Phil. Maybe he should call the Royal Canadian Mounted Police. He started to pace.

Finally, he stopped. No, he concluded, the first thing he should do is go back to Max's camp. It was the last place he saw him and maybe, just maybe, he returned there to rest and salvage what he could from the mass destruction.

He would figure out his next move once he got to camp, he decided. One step at a time, he told himself in an attempt to keep calm.

Rich checked the fuel gauge, one-quarter of a tank. That should be enough to get to the camp and back. He quickly grabbed some snack items, a bottle of water, some backup clothes in case he got wet, and some equipment that may prove useful, including his handheld Bearcat scanner and his 60-power Redfield spotting scope.

The trail on the cutline was well packed now and required little effort from the 80-horse power engine. Rich kept his eyes intently focused on the trail ahead of him, hoping to see Max riding toward him. There was still no sign of him as he coasted up to the canyon rim of Nose Creek and turned off the Polaris. He looked around, still no sign of Max, or any other human activity for that matter. The forest was eerily quiet.

Rich took a deep breath and turned his snowmobile back on. He slowly idled down the ramp and, without pausing, revved it up the east bank.

Rich was sweating profusely, as he rolled into what was left of Max's camp. He stood up on the Polaris for a better view. Still nothing, he turned off his snowmobile and dismounted. He spent the next ten minutes or so searching the camp and studying the snow.

Rich was a pretty good tracker and was certain everything he was seeing was there prior to his leaving the day before. Max had not returned, thus, it was time to come up with the next step in his plan.

In the distance, he could hear the steady soft roar of the two big cat engines coming from the rig.

"Still drilling," he whispered to himself.

Rich took a deep breath. He boarded his snowmobile again and slowly and as quietly as possible advanced forward, following the same tracks Max left behind the day before. He puttered through the forest, turning with fear at every movement, or perceived movement. He periodically stopped to listen to any sound that might be out of place.

Still no sign of him, suddenly, he saw something in the snow about 20 yards in front of him. Rich immediately shut off his engine and jumped off. Crouching low to the ground, he inched forward.

As he got closer, he could clearly see deep gouges and skid marks in the snow. Some were so deep the dirt below was exposed. Rich looked all around him, expecting to be ambushed at any second.

It looked as though two bull elk had engaged in battle. Just to the right of the deepest gouges, Rich noticed fresh tracks of a snowmobile headed toward the rig location, had to be Max's.

Adjacent to the ski tracks were a bunch of footprints and two long skid tracks. Looked too Rich like something most likely Max, was being dragged through the snow. Four, maybe five, people in total, he figured.

Rich crept forward through the forest. It was slow going, but he was so nervous and focused, he didn't notice. He weaved his way through the forest until he was close to the lease. A large mound of snow and debris blocked most of his view, purposely put there by the rig hands, but he could still see some action.

He placed his camouflaged backpack carefully in the soft snow and retrieved his high-powered spotting scope. He peered through it. There was some movement, but he'd have to get further up that wall of debris to see it. At this early hour, that would mean exposing himself and most likely being seen. He would wait until the cover of darkness, he decided.

He leaned against of the spruce trees, out of sight, and turned on his handheld scanner. "Hope the batteries aren't dead," he muttered softly.

Chances of getting a call were slim to none, but rig personnel were known to get excited and boastful after catching a scout. The four green lights began to dance across the listening device. He checked the volume and placed the device on a perfect shelf between two branches. He then sat there, pondering his next move.

As darkness fell, Rich still sat huddled against the tree, mulling his options. The scanner picked up nothing, so he turned it off and placed it back in his backpack. In the fading light, he might not be seen from the rig, so he decided to chance it and crawl to the top of the manmade hill.

With his white camouflage backpack on, he edged his way forward. It took him a good ten minutes to navigate his way to the top of the 45-degree incline. Once on top, he peered over.

He slowly removed his backpack and took out his scope again. With the 60-power lenses, he would be able to read the names on the hard hats of the crew. Rich made the necessary adjustments and zoomed in on the activity on the drilling location. The first scan failed to produce anything of interest, but on the second sweep, he found what he was looking for.

"Bingo," he said, looking right at the nose of the Polaris partially hidden behind the boiler building. No sign of Max. No sign of anybody for that matter. Where the hell was the crew? Rich desperately wanted to know.

"Somebody should be scrubbing or cleaning up around the rig and the lease," he mumbled it to himself with a slightly panic tone.

Suddenly, he caught some movement. The door to the engineer's shack flew open and four boisterous, jovial crewmembers appeared. Another large man appeared behind them but stopped in the doorway. He yelled something at the men and Rich could barely hear it over the drilling noises. He strained his ears to make out the conversation. No such luck.

Three of the men went one way, far enough away from any structures, and lit up cigarettes. The other man walked by himself over to the boiler house. He opened the door just as the large man screamed something from the engineer's shack. The man waved and nodded to show he understood, and then disappeared inside.

Rich turned the spotting scope to the activity on the other side of the lease. The three were still enjoying a good smoke, laughing the whole time. Rich continued to move the scope back and forth, looking for any sign that might tell him where Max was.

Ten long, excruciating minutes passed and the only activity Rich could see was the lighting up of another round of smokes. Rich suddenly felt exposed and vulnerable. He turned around to see if anybody was sneaking up on him. There was no movement; no indication he was about to have company.

The only sound coming through the green veil of the forest behind him was the sound of Grey Squirrels, arguing over some unseen edible prize. Rich turned his attention back to the boiler shack. It was good timing, as the door suddenly flew open and the one roughneck came walking out.

He appeared to be carrying something rolled up in a wad under his arm. Looked like cleaning rags to the naked eye, Rich surmised. He grabbed the scope and zoomed in. He suddenly felt nauseous. Those weren't rags, those were Max's clothes!

Time to call the police! Rich reached into the backpack and extracted his cell phone. He looked at it to make sure he had reception, then started to dial. He suddenly stopped. What the hell were they going to do? By the time they got there, Max would most likely be beaten up and left naked somewhere out in the forest. Or maybe even killed and left out there for Ravens to fight over.

Even if they did get there in time, the rig hands would get word from the security shack down the road and get rid of any trace of Max. Rich put the phone down. He knew he would have to do things himself. He again felt nauseous and defeated.

He quickly looked inside his backpack. There was an extra pair of pants, a coat, and waterproof boots. Rich smiled. In this cold, it was always smart to bring an extra pair of clothes. Thank God he remembered to bring them along.

It was completely dark when Rich peaked over the mound again. The crew had started tripping out of the hole and would be occupied for the better part of the night. This was the perfect time to act, he knew.

Rich had mapped out his route to the boiler shack and went over it several times in his head. The goal was to stay in the shadows as much as possible. The first 200 feet would be the hardest. In fact, that would most likely be the make or break of his whole plan.

The first and closest hiding place was behind the D8 Caterpillar. Most likely the equipment responsible for the big mound Rich currently used for cover. From there, it was a quick jaunt to the safety of what looked like spare drilling equipment, then on to the shadows of the shack.

Problem was the 200 or so feet to the dozer were all lit up by lights coming from the rig. That meant for five seconds or so, he would be exposed to all eyes on and around the rig. Fortunately, all snow had been removed, so once he climbed over and down the earthen wall, it would be a straight, unobstructed, all-out run.

Rich once again peered over to make sure nobody was standing around or taking another cigarette break. He took one, deep breath and went for it. Getting up and over was easy, but going down the backside was clumsy and slow due to the large chunks of ice, splintered timber, and the steep incline. He slid and tripped twice. He thought about turning and going back, but he held to the plan.

With the light bearing down on him, he thought for sure he would be spotted and expected the men to start shouting at any second. Faster you fuckin' idiot, he thought.

He finally reached the flat surface of the lease and without hesitation, continued straight for the D8. He heard something in the distance and thought for sure it was someone screaming. Maybe it was, but it must have been hollering about the drilling because when he reached the shadows, nobody was running toward him.

He could literally feel the heart coming out of his chest. He desperately looked all around to ensure nobody was barreling down on him. There was no shouting, just the loud roar of engines pulling the pipe out of the ground.

He was safe – for now.

Hidden in the dark silhouette of the large tractor, he took long, deep breaths to try to calm down. "Fuck it!" he said aloud and darted for the safety of the mud materials stacked high on wooden pallets. For whatever reason, Rich ran right passed them and kept on going to the side of the boiler shack. Perhaps thinking the shadows were not big enough to hide him or perhaps his adrenaline got the best of him, whatever it was, he found himself leaning against the boiler shack, safely out of sight.

He slowly peered around the corner and eyed the front door. There was a heavy steel bar braced against it. Must be their makeshift, cheapo lock to keep Max in, he figured. The large man, who Rich expected was the engineer, would probably not be impressed with this shoddy work.

Rich returned his head to the shadows and embarked on another set of long, deep breaths. Maybe there was something to this breathing thing, Rich thought to himself, trying to get his mind off things. Maybe I'll take up yoga if I survive this, he joked without laughing.

Time for the final assault, he decided, and peaked out again to make sure the coast was clear.

He quickly darted for the door. Running up to it, he grabbed the metal piece with all his might. The damn thing didn't seem to move at first, but his adrenaline was pumping more than it ever had in his life and Rich was able to slide it a few feet and drop it out of the way.

He then quickly opened the door and shut it behind him. Good God, he suddenly thought, I hope nobody is in here.

With wide, crazed eyes, Rich looked around the room. His eyes immediately fell onto the lifeless, naked body tied to a chair next to the big boiler. Rich ran to him and knelt down. His bloodstained, bruised body was a sight to behold. At first, Rich thought he might be dead.

Sensing someone was next to him, Max's head quickly sprang up.

"Took you long enough," Max said slowly with a hollow laugh.

"Funny, Max! Let's just get the fuck out of here!"

Rich immediately started untying the ropes that held him to the chair. He was about halfway done, when to his horror, the boiler door flew open.

He and Max turned, expecting the man to start screaming for help. The brown-haired, middle-aged rig worker simply stepped in. Rich quickly looked for something to use as a weapon, but couldn't find anything. The man slowly took a few steps closer and stopped.

Rich frantically searched the room for anything that might help them escape. Again, he came up empty. Dejected and defeated, Rich and Max looked back at the man, waiting for the worst.

But it never came. The man stood there, silently. He then simply gave Max a smile, turned around, and exited. Rich was dumbfounded. He couldn't believe it, the man did nothing.

Max, on the other hand, knew exactly why. It took him a few seconds, but he finally recognized him as the man he rescued in the rig explosion many months prior. Max smiled, knowing just how fortunate he was.

"Shit, man! We gotta get outta here before that dude returns with reinforcements." Rich finished untying Max and he quickly grabbed his backpack. He threw it over his shoulder and ran to the open doorway.

A naked Max, shivering from the cold, was right on his heels. Rich slowly peered out. He could see the man slowly walking back to the rig with his back to them. Odd, Rich thought, why isn't he doing or saying anything? The thought left his head almost as soon as it entered.

"OK! Max! We'll run straight for the forest and get the hell out of here! Sound good"? Rich said nervously scanning in all directions. Looking up at a few nails just to the right of the door, Max spotted a bunch of keys. One was his Polaris key.

"No. We're not running anywhere?"

"Huh"? What are you crazy?" Rich said, spinning around to face Max. Max simply smiled and reached up and grabbed the key.

"They already took my pride and joy truck away from me, they're not taking my custom snowmobile, too."

Rich looked at him as if he was insane.

"You serious, they'll hear us!"

"Good!" Max calmly said. "Then they'll see my nice big, fat, bare ass as we ride out of here."

Rich couldn't believe his ears.

"What? I don..." Rich started to protest, but Max slapped him on the shoulder and cut him off.

"Let's ride!"

Max ran out of the boiler shack and over to the nearby Polaris. He jumped on the machine and started it up. Rich jumped on the back.

Max couldn't believe his luck, the 300 was still in the scabbard. Dumb bastards he thought.

"Hold on!" Max yelled at Rich.

"Do I have to," a cautious Rich replied, putting his hands around Max's bare mid-section. Max hit the throttle and the two rode off on the hard packed snow toward the forest.

"Kiss my ass!" Max yelled toward the rig. As they headed for safety, Rich couldn't help but feel excited, too. He held up his left hand and gave the rig his middle finger.

Max maneuvered around the debris mound and headed out of the lit-up lease and into the dark shadows of the forest. The ride was wild and rough in the dark. The Polaris spent more time air born than it did with the skis on the ground, but Max simply followed the earlier trail in the snow. About 100 yards into the forest, Rich tapped Max on the shoulder and pointed to his left. Max could barely make it out but knew what he was telling him and made a quick turn into the trees.

Within seconds, they pulled up to Rich's Polaris. Rich immediately jumped off. The two suddenly stopped and listened intently. The only thing they could hear was the sound of the engines still pulling pipe, and Max's teeth chattering.

"You're not cold, are you?" Rich asked with a big smile.

"No! I feel right at home being naked in zero-degree weather! Throw me a beach towel and some sun-tanning lotion will ya?"

Rich laughed harder.

"Of course I'm cold! It's fuckin' freezing!" Max quipped. "How about sharing your coat there or something, before I lose everything to frostbite?"

Rich laughed a little more, before taking off his backpack.

"I'll do you one better there, Max," he said, throwing him the backpack. "Why don't you put on your own set of clothes?"

Max caught it. "You mean to tell me you had clothes in here all along and you made me ride out of there buck naked?"

Rich started laughing harder. "Hey, if I'm going to risk my life to save you, I deserve a little bit of fun at your expense, don't I?"

Max started pulling out the clothes as fast as he could.

"I guess! But if my dick falls off, I'm holding you personally accountable."

"From the looks of things, it already has. Guess it's true what they say about shrinkage factor."

The two shared a good laugh, as Max added layers of much-needed warmth to his body.

CHAPTER TWENTY-SIX

At Zephyr Petroleum, the news continued to be positive. With the way the drilling was progressing, it would be only a day or two until the crew reached the coveted Granite Wash formation at 13,950 feet.

Knowing his team was almost finished drilling, Roger had an air of arrogance like no other. He even upgraded his brand of Cuban cigar to the most expensive on the black market.

Taking one out of his new box, Roger held it to his nose and gave it a nice, big, glorious whiff. He closed his eyes and relished it. He then hit the intercom button.

"Shelley come on in here for a minute!" he said in a normal voice, before taking a second long sniff of his hand-rolled, illegal delicacy.

She took a deep breath, before grabbing her notepad and pen and heading to Roger's office. Shelley was just biding her time and was counting down the days until the land sale. Unlike everyone else in the office, however, she was anticipating the big event for other reasons.

After another deep inhale, she stepped into his office.

"Yes, Mr. White. What can I do for you?"

Shelley watched him as he continued to stare at his cigar. "Just wondering if you would like to go to lunch with the most high-profile oil exec in town?" he said smugly.

Shelley was immediately disgusted. She was trying not to throw up her coffee and Danish all over the carpet.

"Um, thanks for the invite, Mr. White, but I am way too busy. With all that is happening with Wolverine Hills, the paperwork is really piling up."

She was really hoping he would accept that excuse and not push the matter. It was true, she did have a lot of filing to do, but she was still planning on taking a lunch. Just not with this sexist jerk.

"Never mind all that! You can get to it later. You deserve to go to lunch with me," he said, still looking over his cigar. "Consider today your lucky day."

Roger smiled and lowered his cigar. He rose out of his chair and walked over to the window. He gazed out at the town below.

"No, really, I can't make it," Shelley pleaded. "Besides, you're a married man and I don't go to lunch with married men, even if it's strictly business."

Roger abruptly turned on his heel and gave her a wicked stare. "Is that right?"

"Um. Yes, sir, it is."

Roger's calm countenance turned ever so slightly to anguish. His face blushed slightly.

"Well, then, what are you standing around here for? Better get to back to fuckin' work!"

"Pardon me?" Shelley said with astonishment.

"If you have so much work to do, you best get at it! Go on! Scram." Roger waved his hand to motion her out.

Annoyed, Shelley just shook her head and retreated back to her desk. No matter how much she knew Roger was a jerk, the things he did and said still surprised her.

She sat down at her desk and paused. There was a mound of paperwork in front of her, but she just stared at it. Why even bother, she thought. I'm so done with this place. The statement echoed in her head.

The ringing of the phone snapped her out of her trance. She picked it up and answered it in a tone that was a tad too cold and curt. It was Al Wallace from Houston. Shit, Shelley, thought.

"Uh, yes sir! I will pass you through to Roger right away."

Shelley tried to calm herself. She may be out of here soon, but she couldn't start showing signs of disinterest and distress - especially not to her bosses in Texas. She needed to leave Zephyr with no questions or concerns from management.

"Roger," she said as calmly as she could. "Mr. Wallace is on the phone for you."

Roger said nothing and Shelley hung up the phone.

"Hey Al, What's shaken?"

Shelley could see he picked up successfully since the blinking red light on the intercom was now solid red. Hopefully, her anger wasn't overly evident to Mr. Wallace, she thought.

"Oh good, good!" she heard Roger say through the open door. Phew, Shelley thought, the boss in Houston didn't say anything about her bad phone etiquette. Next time, she concluded, I'll try not to let Roger rile me so much.

Shelley eavesdropped on the entire conversation. It was all about Al's trip to Calgary and arrangements for the trip to the rig up at Wolverine Hills.

Near the end, however, Shelley's ears perked.

"What was that, Al? The scout?"

Shelley stopped what she was doing and listened intently.

"Yeah, guess I forgot to update you on that situation. Sorry about that," Roger said.

Shelley thought about quietly picking up the phone and hitting the red button so she could listen in. She looked over at the light and a chill immediately went down her spine. If she made a noise and they heard her listening in, who knows what would happen? Her heart started pounding and she quickly looked away from the phone.

Not worth it, she thought, as her mouth went dry and her palms got sweaty.

"That Black Gold scout somehow managed to escape. Pesky little bastard, but my guess is we scared the hell out of him and he's still running even as we talk!"

There was a long pause. Shelley stared at Roger's office door, frozen with anticipation.

"No, Al. He was not hurt. We just scared him a bit and then he was gone."

Again, there was a long pause. Shelley again glanced back at the solid red light. What was Al saying? Maybe it was some valuable information that Wayne would love to hear. Shelley thought again about picking up the receiver but just couldn't do it.

"Everything was by the book. Nobody is going to get sued or arrested. All is good, Al."

Shelley slowly took a sip of her coffee and continued to strain her ears. There was no need, as the conversation quickly ended.

"OK, Al! Yup! Me too! See ya in a few days!"

With that, the red light on the speakerphone went off. Shelley took a deep breath and went back to attacking her paperwork. Only a few seconds into it, Roger yelled out the open door.

"Hey, Shelley, if you're not too busy, get Nick in here!"

Ah, the nice combination of anger and sarcasm. I'm sure going to miss it, Shelley mused to herself.

"Yes, Mr. White," she calmly and politely hollered back.

Shelley exited and walked down the hallway past the elevators to Nick's office to alert him that the high-and-mighty wanted to see him. She quickly returned and went right back to organizing the papers on her desk for filing.

She just assumed Nick had gone into Roger's office, but after ten minutes, the shout came out again.

"Damn it! Can you please get a hold of Nick and tell him to get his ass down here?"

Standing at the filing cabinet, Shelley placed a bunch of papers on top and turned again to get Nick. It wasn't necessary, as she immediately saw Nick scampering down the hallway. Guess that time Roger yelled so loudly even he heard it clear on the other side of the office building, she surmised.

Behind the tenacity and vanity was a scared, sad man. Or at least that is what Shelley concluded in her head.

"Sorry Roger! Was getting some info together from the well that I assumed you wanted." The words came from a nervous Nick, as he disappeared into the big corner office.

"You're right about that! Sit your ass down and give me an update."

Shelley again listened intently. Nick started to give Roger an update on drilling location, core samples, and other geological findings and once again Shelley found herself frozen at the filing cabinet not wanting to make any noise and miss something important.

Holy shit, she suddenly concluded, I'm acting like a scout myself now. Or a mole, or a traitor, or whatever you want to call it. Wayne never asked for anything. He simply told her to be safe and when the project was over, to check in with him about potential employment.

Yet, here she was, desperately trying to listen in on Roger's conversations to find some little tidbit to feed Black Gold. Was it because she hated Roger so much or was it because she was trying to secure her next job?

She wasn't sure. Either way, she decided it didn't matter and she returned to filing away all the paperwork from Wolverine Hills that kept showing up on her desk. Just then, a nervous Nick came out and headed down the hallway to his office. Seconds later, Roger came out.

"You sure you don't want to go to lunch with this here top exec?" Roger said, stepping up to her desk. "I can do this…"

Roger slid his wedding ring off and put it on the desk. "Huh? Huh? Will that change your mind?" Roger said with a giant smile and wink.

Now she really was about to lose her breakfast. She stood there with papers in hand in complete shock by what she just witnessed.

Roger laughed at his own joke, although he probably was dead serious. He put the wedding ring back on and headed for the door.

"All right, Suit yourself! This married man is off for a stellar lunch!"

Roger walked to the elevators and hit the button. He started whistling to himself, as he waited. When the doors opened, he did a little jig and danced his way in. There was a woman in the elevator when he sashayed in.

As the doors closed, she heard Roger say "Well, hello there beautiful! Got any plans for lunch?"

With mouth agape, Shelley was once again standing in disbelief at the filing cabinet.

CHAPTER TWENTY-SEVEN

Wayne was uneasy all day, as the hands on the fancy drilling rig desk clock seemed to move in slow motion. Earlier in the day, he received a phone call from Phil wanting to meet in his office at 5:30 that evening.

It wasn't like him to be so unsettled, but this was a situation he had never confronted before in all his years in the oil business. He so wanted Phil to be wrong about his suspicion about the leak, even though in his heart he knew better.

The reports from Val and Joe were beyond promising and it appeared as though this well might be the oil discovery of all discoveries. Still, he couldn't relax.

Finally, the working day concluded and all office personnel had left for the day. Sighing deeply, Stadwell glanced at the clock again before rising up and walking over to the window. The magnificent tower that had ZEPHYR in lights across the top of it immediately garnered his attention.

How on earth can we compete? It was the only thing that Wayne could ask himself. The streets below were cast in long shadows as the spring sun slowly vanished behind the Rocky Mountains to the west of the city.

"Sorry to interrupt you, looks like you're deep in thought."

Wayne immediately turned around. "Phil! How the heck did you get in here?"

"Door was open, so I let myself in."

Wayne chuckled, "So much for security around here!"

Wayne slowly made his way to the small bar in the corner of his office. "Like a drink?" He asked.

"Think I'll pass, but thanks!"

"Hate to drink alone, but this occasion warrants it. So, how much shit are we in?"

"Not sure," Phil answered. "Guess that's all up to how you take it."

"All right, I've got my big boy pants on so let er rip," Wayne said, as he turned around with his freshly made drink in hand.

It didn't take Phil long to apprise Wayne of what he had found.

"Gerry!" came the quick, loud response, as Wayne flopped into his chair.

Phil gave him time to let that discovery settle. Wayne sighed loudly, before slowly sipping his drink.

"Funny. That guy was always against us hiring a scout from day one. And here you go and expose him, "Pretty ironic."

Wayne again stared out the window deep in thought. He sipped his drink again, as Phil remained quiet.

"I suppose I'll have to confront him in the morning?" He said solemnly.

It was now time for Phil to speak.

"Not so fast Wayne. I have a few other details to try and iron out in this matter and if you'll just give me access to the office one more time, hopefully, I can get it nailed down for sure."

Wayne was deep in thought still. He simply nodded and waved his approval toward Phil. Phil could tell he was deeply disheartened by the news and thought it best to give him time alone. He quickly rose and thanked Wayne, leaving him in his chair, staring out the window.

At 10:30, Phil decided it was a good time to make his rounds again at Black Gold. The three cups of coffee he had down the street at the local coffee shop were more than enough, plus he had no choice because they were closing.

"Guess that's my cue," he laughed to himself, as he looked up at the last two remaining workers staring at him. He quickly made his way down 6th Avenue and to the security desk at Black Gold. A few questions at the security desk, questions he could answer in his sleep, and once again he was headed up the elevators with his cleaning supplies.

The "ding" sound announced his arrival and he briskly stepped out into the hallway. Despite all the caffeine, he was tired and wanted to get this last operation over with as soon as possible. Just as he turned, he looked up to see the big, grey-custodian close the door to Black Gold's offices.

"Working late?" Phil asked with a smile, as he walked up to him.

"Always work late that's what most night custodians do," he said sarcastically and curtly. Without looking at Phil, he wheeled his cart toward the elevators.

Phil watched him go. What a sorry, grumpy prick, Phil decided. He shook his head, as he watched him enter the elevators and disappear. He then grabbed his own keys and opened up the doors to Black Gold.

Once inside, Phil headed straight to Gerry's office or to the "Geophysicists" office, he joked to himself. Phil walked directly to Gerry's desk and opened the top, left drawer again. He was sure he was going to find more incriminating evidence and there it was staring back at him.

He lifted up the report, trying not to disturb any other items. The report was unmistakable with the heading of- Black Gold Daily Geology Report. This time it had more doodling with arrows and bright yellow hi-lighting over several lines of information, but it also had the word "compare" in several places. Compare with what Phil thought?

None of what he was looking at made sense, but he started shooting pictures anyway. He knew Wayne could figure it out. Phil put the documents back in the drawer, making sure to do exactly as he found them. He shut the door and checked the one below it.

Phil lifted a few loose papers and quickly scanned them. Nothing too interesting caught his eye. He decided to try the drawers on the other side. The very first page stopped him in his tracks. It read: Zephyr Morning

Report. Why the fuck would Gerry have the morning reports from Zephyr's well? Phil couldn't make sense of it but knew Wayne would have a field day with all of it.

Phil decided he'd seen enough. This was enough to confront Gerry with, so he vacated the office, making sure both doors were locked before heading to the elevators.

As he waited there, he again started thinking about the grouchy janitor. Poor guy must really hate his job, he deduced. Suddenly, the cleaning cart the guy was pushing flashed in Phil's mind. There was nothing but rags and blue rubber gloves. How the hell can you clean an office without supplies?

"Shit!" Phil said out loud. He also remembered the small black box on the cart. It was a damn camera, Phil knew. What the hell did a custodian need a camera for?

The light went on and Phil not only realized that was not a janitor but was pretty darn sure he knew who it was. Barry Stein!

Phil hadn't seen him for years, so didn't recognize him until he seriously thought about it. The last he heard of Barry, he had started an oil field security company. Barry Stein was one bad dude with a reputation for violence. That, Phil, knew through many years of reports from his colleagues.

Phil was all excited and full of questions. He quickly sped up, wanting to get to his car and call Wayne. He stepped up to his new black Buick parked in a stall marked for Black Gold employees and inserted his key. Just as he did, a sizzling sound caught his attention.

What the hell, he thought? Sounds like a fuss on a string of firecrackers, he surmised. Phil realized what was going on just in time and dove behind a nearby metal garbage container, as flames instantly shot out from under the hood of his car.

The smoke and flames were gone in seconds; the only damage was a small heat blister on the fender. Phil slowly climbed to his feet to inspect the damage more closely. Stein could have turned the black beauty into scrap metal, but thankfully he just gave him a warning.

Phil shook his head and very cautiously walked around his car and once again inserted the key. He looked around to see if anybody was watching him; then drove off.

The next morning huddled in the corner office, Stadwell and Graves reviewed the information and the pictures recovered from Gerry's office. It was obvious what had to be done.

Wayne picked up the phone and hit the direct line to Gerry's office.

"Come on down to my office, please," he said softly. "I have something I would like to discuss with you."

Wayne hung up the phone and leaned back in his chair. Phil did not envy Wayne at all and decided to step out of the way and gaze out the window at the town. Gerry appeared in the doorway after a few long minutes.

"Sit down, Gerry."

Walking to his seat, Gerry noticed Phil for the first time. He looked at him quizzically and sat down his mind filled with anxiety.

"So, what's so important I need to leave all my work and come to chat with you, Wayne?" Gerry's tone wasn't as harsh as expected. Must know something is up, Wayne concluded.

"As you know, Gerry, Phil was hired to scout the Zephyr well, but that is only part of his duties. The other side of his commitment is to run security in the field and in town for us."

Wayne paused to make sure Gerry was following. Gerry looked very confused and he kept glancing at Phil over by the window.

"Through multiple sources, it came to our attention that there was a leak here in Calgary and we happened to narrow it down to right here in this office."

Instantly, Gerry recoiled and flew out of his chair. "So, you fucking think I'm the leak?"

Wayne was seething mad, but he knew he had to stay in control or the entire situation could get out of hand.

"The information we have gathered indicates that you may very well be involved, yes."

Gerry again looked from Phil to Wayne. His face was red and he was slightly shaking.

"Well, you can stop accusing me because I have done nothing wrong! You have the wrong fucking mole, Wayne!"

Wayne simply watched him for a few seconds and then opened the folder on his desk with the pictures Phil took. Wayne turned the file around and pushed it toward Gerry.

Gerry scanned it quickly. "So that's your incriminating evidence? I have to say you have it all wrong! You really do, Wayne?"

"Well, then," Wayne simply continued. "We're all ears."

Wayne waited patiently for an explanation. After several long seconds, Gerry stood and walked to the window. He looked down 6th avenue at Zephyr's office in the distance.

"You see that fucking fancy-ass tower down there," he slowly and methodically said. "Well, let me tell you something about them. When I started out as a young kid just out of school, Zephyr hired me. I worked hard to fit in, but management didn't think I was the right fit and so they fired me. Made up some lame sexual harassment, bull-shit story and canned my ass."

Gerry turned back to face Phil and Wayne.

"There isn't enough money in the world that would make me work with Zephyr, Wayne. I am dedicated to Black Gold and making sure those fuckers over there get what's coming to them."

Gerry was very much deflated. It looked as though the weight of the world came off his shoulders with that confession. He contritely looked at Wayne, waiting for a reply.

"Just answer me one question, Gerry. Why do you have Zephyr's reports in your possession and how did you get them?"

Gerry quickly glanced at Phil, then back at Wayne. He walked up to his desk and looked him in the eye.

"I have them to compare their well to ours and coordinate all our information. As you know, this helps us determine just what's down there. I have to say, our well is way more promising than theirs."

Gerry let out a quick, but fading smile. Wayne was still suspicious.

L. GORDON KESLER

"That is nice to hear, Gerry, but you still haven't told us where you got them."

Gerry continued to look at Wayne. "I know I haven't Wayne because quite frankly I don't want to reveal my source."

He turned to Phil. "That's what they say in the scouting business, don't they, Phil?"

Phil thought about it for a few seconds and nodded to show he understood. Wayne looked at Phil to try and get a reading of what he thought of the conversation.

Phil finally pushed himself off the window sill. "I think he's telling the truth, Wayne. I really do. And I believe I know exactly how, or rather who, they are getting their information through."

A huge feeling of relief befell Gerry and he slumped ever so slightly in his chair. He let out a big sigh.

"OK, So now what, Phil?"

"Here's what has to happen. First, all locks have to be changed every five days. I know that may sound extreme, but in these circumstances, I believe it must be done. Second, all critical documents must go into a safe at the end of the day. No important geology information is allowed to sit out. Understood?"

Phil looked at Wayne to make sure he got it. Wayne nodded profusely.

"And third, I will come here and sweep for bugs every couple of days until the land sale. It's something I should have been doing from the start, but certainly, will do so going forward."

Everyone looked at Phil and shook his head to show they completely agreed.

"Good," Phil suddenly said. "Zephyr may get all the information they need, but it's not going to be from us. Not from this point on, that's for sure!"

They all looked at Phil excitedly. Wayne then turned and looked at Gerry. He beamed with relief. Gerry could see it in his eyes and despite being accused, he now had more faith and fondness in Wayne than he ever did.

Phil said goodbye to both men and said he'd be in touch. On his way out, he noticed a locksmith on his knees, replacing the locks on the main double doors to Black Gold's office.

Phil laughed out loud. That Wayne was sure on top of things.

CHAPTER TWENTY-EIGHT

The blue Ford moved slowly over the slippery, icy logging trail north to Grand Prairie. The only sound in the truck was the radio playing some top 40 country hit. Finally, after 30 miles, Rich decided to break the silence.

"Hey Maxy, sorry I didn't tell you about the clothes sooner. I thought it was funny, but maybe not so much when the temperature is freezing cold."

There was no response, as the lead scout was deep in thought. Another 10 miles passed before Max interrupted the country crooning.

"Let's get a room for the night," he said quietly and unequivocally. "I've got some calls to make and need a good hot shower and a shave. Can't get this damn chill out of my bones."

Rich simply nodded.

"Where you want to get that room?"

"The GP Inn is just fine," Max replied.

As the Ford pulled into the parking lot, Max spotted the teal Chevy and the beat up red bucket of bolts but said nothing to Rich. He wasn't sure what to say or what he was going to do to the two enemy scouts. Max so wanted to walk up to Tom and punch him in the face. He also wanted to do something to his truck. But, the most important issue at hand was the job, and he didn't want to do anything that might jeopardize its success.

Thankfully, Max knew the two dopes would not recognize their Ford. Max instructed Rich to get the room, as he headed to the phone located in the lobby.

He definitely checked it for bugs since it was the only payphone in the popular motel. He then dialed Phil's number.

Max spent the best part of an hour explaining to Phil what had happened. The call could have been twenty minutes, but Phil was so full of questions and concern for Max's safety, he didn't want him to get off the line. He left it up to Max to decide how to proceed but did suggest he might want to return home.

The thought was not just for Max's own health and welfare, but because Phil wondered if the operation with Max as the lead had been compromised.

Max's response was simple and clear. "Screw that!"

Phil loved the dedication and resolve but was worried.

"Here's what I want. First I want you to pull Rich out of here! I like the guy a lot and he actually saved my bacon, but when the time comes, and believe me it's coming, I can't have any dead weight holding me back."

Phil was not too excited to hear that. This was no time to be the hero. In fact, Phil was mulling over the idea of sending another scout to help.

"Hold your horses there Max Cordova," Phil said calmly, but sternly. "You're the best man in the business and I can't afford to lose you. Life is too short and you have a beautiful family. The most important thing is to stay safe."

Max said nothing.

"You there, Max?" Phil inquired.

"Sorry, Phil, But this is personal now."

"Max, I understand how you feel. But remember, you still have a job to do. I need you to stay cool and make smart decisions. If you can't do that, my suggestion that you return home will be an order."

Max was again silent. In his history of working with Phil, he has never had his boss warn him like that. Of course, the circumstances have never been this intense.

"OK, Phil. You're the boss," he said as calmly as possible. "But if you don't mind, I'd like to rent my own truck and send Rich home."

Phil was a mildly upset by the request. He was all set to demand his employee forget the notion of working alone; he also thought about pulling him. It was obvious; Max was still too stubborn to think clearly.

Yet, in the end, Phil trusted Max. He really was good at what he did and in all their years of working together, he had zero problems with his work. He certainly sounded selfish, but Max always put his client's interest ahead of his own. Most likely, he would calm down with a good night's rest and come to his senses.

"OK," Phil said with a giant sigh. "I am going to go with my gut and trust you on this Max. But you have to promise to call me with an update in two days' time. That is not a loose request! That is an order. Understood?"

Max was slow to respond but finally said, "Yes. You got it, Phil."

"All right, Max. Good luck and be safe. If you see any sign of trouble I want you out of there! Not just out of Wolverine Hills, I mean out of town and right back to Rocky!"

"Understood," was the clear, concise answer.

The phone was suddenly silent. Max called his wife to check in on the family and give her an update. Of course, the number one question came up again, "How much longer, Max?"

Max knew it was coming down to the final last few hectic days, so promised it would only be another week or two before he was back in her loving arms. It was a good conversation – loose and relaxed.

Despite what had happened Max was feeling good. His wife had a way of doing that, and fortunately, most of the talk was about the family. That took pressure off Max, who never liked lying to Carmen and helped him feel less stressful regarding what may be coming.

Sunshine pouring through the one crack in the blinds told Max that he had slept well past the break of dawn. It was time to get another big breakfast under his belt. That could very well be the best part of staying in town. The bacon and eggs were such a delicious way to start the day; he really enjoyed savoring every bite. The bed and the hot shower were pretty nice benefits, as well, Max knew.

This breakfast may not be so delightful, though, since he had to tell Rich he wasn't needed anymore. Max wasn't sure if he should say it was Phil's decision or his own. After being rescued, it was an odd time to tell him to leave, but he just worked so much better alone. And, he vowed, this time I will not get caught again.

As expected the news didn't go over so well. Rich didn't quite understand why he was leaving, and he didn't quite like the idea. Leaving Max to do the job alone just wasn't a wise thing to do and he couldn't live with himself if something happened to him. The rebuttals Rich was throwing back at him all made sense and made Max start thinking he was doing the wrong thing.

Maybe it was idiotic to send his backup home, he suddenly thought. It was followed by the notion that he was being selfish. He stuck to his guns, but Rich was definitely wearing him down. He was also making the bacon and eggs not taste so good.

The two went back and forth for a while before Max grew tired and ended it. "Rich, you are being pulled from this project and have been ordered to head home. That's the end of it."

The scouts finished their breakfast in silence. Rich dropped Max off at a car rental outlet and the second Max shut the door, he hit the accelerator and sped out of the parking lot. Max watched him go, feeling like an full-fledged idiot. He really did like Rich and was very grateful, but this was his project and he was going to do it his way.

I will be sure to stop by his house after the project is over and buy him some drinks to apologize, Max concluded, as he turned and went inside.

Max ended up renting a white Chevy 4x4. It wasn't his beloved baby, but at least it was a Chevy. Everything was right where it should be, Max thought. The place was called Speedy Rentals, but the two hours it took to finally drive off the lot made Max think it should be Not-So-Speedy Rentals.

Max laughed at his own joke. It was a bad one; he knew and was probably just laughing to get his mind off Rich's abrupt departure. He drove to the cutline without thinking about anything in particular. He told himself he'd come up with a plan on his way back to his Polaris, but, for some reason, he thought about mundane things instead.

As he boarded the very cold vinyl seat, Max jumped off and returned to his truck. He opened the door and pulled out his Sako 300 magnum rifle. He stared at it and nodded. Grabbing several boxes of ammunition, he then threw it over his shoulder and went back to the snowmobile and slid the gun into the scabbard.

The trip to Nose Creek didn't take long. All the trips in and out over the last two months had created a nice, hard-packed trail to follow. Max decided that he would not make the trip down the ramp. He would leave the Polaris on the west side. It was vital to remain quiet and hidden.

Max pulled the big sled into the bushes and made an extra-long effort to camouflage it with snow and pine boughs. When Max made it down the creek, what he saw further substantiated his decision to leave the Polaris.

It had warmed considerably in the last few days and the water was running about 6 inches deep over the surface of the ice in the bottom of the raven. He carefully navigated his away across the thinning ice and started up the east side. As he made his way to the rim, he could already hear the drilling sounds of the mud mill in the distance.

"Mud mill," Max said aloud with a laugh. He wasn't sure who had coined the term referring to a drilling rig, but it was apropos. Max removed his parka and put it in his backpack. All this trudging through the snow was causing him to sweat.

The rifle felt light over his right shoulder, as he walked toward the intermittent belching of the black smoke and the roar of the engines at the rig. Nearing the brightly lit lease, Max slowed and ever so slowly crept forward. He knew the rig hands were preoccupied with tripping out of the hole, but, after what had happened, he wasn't going to take any chances.

By the time he got settled behind the debris mound, the day had turned to night. The bright rig lights lit up part of the forest behind him, but he had great protection from the shadows of the man-made hill.

Sliding stealthily to his right, Max finally found the spot he was looking for. It was the perfect window between two high spots, he thought, as he removed the magnum rifle from his shoulder. Motionless, he watched as the crew latched and unlatched the elevators, as the pipe was lifted skyward one more time.

They must be finished drilling or they needed a new bit to finish drilling, he concluded. Max was pissed he hadn't arrived earlier in order to get his client that vital information. There wasn't much more to do on this hole before the final stages kicked in, which meant time was running out.

Max watched the activity for an hour longer and he could feel his body relaxing and his eyes getting heavy. He raised the rifle and adjusted the Leopold scope to his eye. Perfect line of sight – nothing between him and the big C15 Caterpillar engine; belching black smoke into the air.

Max focused on his target – a 4x5-foot radiator on the Cat's engine.

The roughnecks were all bent over, latching the elevators to the pipe. Max held his aim steady and then pulled the trigger. The sound was barely audible over the roaring engines, but he crouched lower in the shadows watching anxiously for some reaction.

The workers all hesitated momentarily, not knowing what had just happened, then went back to work. Strange noises were just a part of drilling operations.

Again, Max raised the scope and focused on his target to assess the damage. Yes!, he thought, mission complete. Coolant was spewing from the huge radiator on the main Cat engine. Max knew it was just a matter of time and the engine would shut down from overheating. He smiled as he surveyed the area.

This would set them back a couple of days, maybe even more, depending on how much work they would need to do to the internal components of the engine. The other option, they could get another big C15 on site, but Max knew that would take days. "My work is done here," Max said to himself, then flung the rifle over his shoulder and slowly crept back into the darkness of the forest.

The walk back to the west side of the Nose Creek was more like a stroll in the park. Max was thoroughly enjoying the peace and quiet and made frequent stops to hear if the sounds of tripping pipe had changed. He also stared to the heavens amazed by the beauty of the Big Dipper and the North Star.

Max descended the east bank and struggled to climb the ramp to his waiting transportation. On the rim of the west side, standing next to his snowmobile, Max again paused to listen. No engines roaring and no black smoke billowing in the night sky. Nothing but silence! He smiled, then started up his Polaris and headed back down the cutline.

Arriving at his rented white Chevy, Max placed the ramps up against the tailgate and eased the Polaris into the back. It took another hour to load the remaining tarps and other gear. He paused to look over at his trusty old truck still lying in the same spot where the two trees had fatally crippled her. "Goodbye ol' friend I'll be back," he said, as he slowly drove back to the logging road.

The drive north would be short, Max knew. Several weeks earlier, he had noticed another potential cutline that should have good access and was most likely close enough to the rig to get good reception for reports coming over the scanner.

Twenty minutes and Max pulled off the road and onto the new cutline. He drove between groves of trees for camouflage and immediately went to setting up the scanner. Within minutes, the scanner lights were dancing on the dash and the recorder was placed next to it ready to record if any calls were picked up. No camp needed this time, the truck would do for now, he concluded.

Just as Max lied down on the seat and closed his eyes, the call he was desperately hoping for came in loud and clear.

It was Matt Crane. He was angry; more than his usual crabbiness and explaining to Roger how one of the Cat engines had sprung a leak in the radiator. Matt explained it would have to be replaced and with any luck, there wouldn't be any internal damage to the engine.

"I fuckin' have no idea how it happened?" He continued. "The hole is huge! It makes no fucking sense! We are definitely sunk for at least two days until we can get 'er fixed! With luck, there's no internal damage."

"What the fuck?" came Roger's reply. "We don't have time for this! Al is coming in from Houston! Damn it!"

Max smiled, and then pulled the eiderdown sleeping bag over his head. Within minutes, he was sound asleep.

CHAPTER TWENTY-NINE

Overnight, the temperature had dropped to 20 below zero and the arctic front was accompanied by heavy snow. Max squirmed, to get comfortable under the goose down sleeping bag. After several tries to escape the bitter cold, he rose up from the truck seat.

The windows were partially frosted over and the snow blanketed his vehicle. So much for that warming trend, Max thought.

Max fired up the truck and tried to lower his window. It took several attempts before the frost-crusted window slowly started going down. The light reflecting off the freshly fallen snow was blinding. Max decided to roll it back up, so the blasting hot air from the heater could fill the cab.

Rolling the sleeping bag up, Max suddenly realized the scanner wasn't operating.

"Piss," he said aloud and he started tinkering with it. Somehow the plug got pulled from the power outlet. Must have rolled over and kicked it loose or something, Max concluded.

It took a few seconds to get it back on, but the nagging thought of potentially missing a whole night of talk hung on his mind. He moved the dial left and right and nothing came across. The power outage had de-programmed the Swedish-made apparatus.

"Great," Max said, as he started the long, monotonous task of reprogramming the proper frequencies.

He finally got it all running to his liking and immediately went into maid mode. He had to have things organized around him or he became nervous and agitated. Probably some sort of phobia, he knew. Shit, these days they had a phobia for everything.

With the truck clean and everything in its rightful place, Max put on his parka and stepped outside for a little fresh air. Just as he stepped into the fresh powder and stretched, he saw the glimpse of a teal colored vehicle. Appeared to be going at least 80 mph up the logging road, way too fast for these snowy conditions.

"Hughes!" he said loudly, as it disappeared from sight.

Must not have seen me, Max concluded. With the freshly fallen snow, all tracks and sign of his entry into the cutline would be hidden. Max knew the bastard was probably looking for him. Most likely saw he had taken everything out of the other cutline – everything but his fallen beloved truck.

Max ran to the logging road to see if Hughes' was turning around but all he could see was the blizzard of snow and ice swirling from the back of the truck as it faded in the distance.

"Bastard," Max said, thinking about his crushed truck again.

At the speed Tom was going, it was obvious he was in a hurry to find Max. Crane had probably inspected that hole a bit closer and figured out exactly what made it-and who, Max thought with a smile.

If so, the hunt would be on for Max and Tom would have orders to find him as soon as he could. Then who knows what he was supposed to do? Turn him in? Kill him where he stood? A chill went down Max's spine and it wasn't because of the arctic breeze.

Max jumped into his truck and threw it into 4x4 mode. He eased to the edge of the cutline and checked both directions for traffic before entering the snow covered trail that led to town. It was time to disappear for a couple of days.

CHAPTER THIRTY

At Black Gold, spirits were high. The drilling in the bottom section of the well had gone without a hitch and there were only about 60 feet of left before they would penetrate the Granite Wash formation. The good news was even if the main hope, which was the Granite Wash coming back with incredibly high oil and gas showings, there was already optimism for what might be available from the other formations.

The geological team and Chuck had run the numbers and the consensus was the well would be a financial success regardless of what came at the bottom. The big question remaining was just how successful?

All along, it was Wayne's intuition that Wolverine Hills was one of the last untapped great North American oil discoveries. The numbers were pointing in that direction, but only the Granite Wash would prove it.

The next big question on everyone's mind, one that nobody talked about and tried not to think about, was could they compete with Zephyr at the land sale? The answer was, questionable.

Wayne contemplated flying to the rig for final testing. He would love to be on site when those core samples came in. He also felt a bit useless. Everyone was so busy with his and her own particular assignment, while he simply sat in his office, waiting for details.

The intercom came to life. "Mr. Stadwell, Phil Graves is on the line."

Wayne was excited. Something to do, he thought, with a smile. "Thanks, Connie! Put him through."

Wayne picked up the phone the second it rang. "Morning Phil," he said jovially. "Haven't heard from you in a few days."

"Yes. Thought I'd give you some breathing room after the last adventure," he said with a quick laugh.

"Well, we really appreciate it. Without you on our side who knows what would be happening around here?" You really are worth your weight in gold - black gold that is." Wayne chuckled at his play on words.

"I appreciate that, Wayne. I really do. Speaking of which, any sign of tampering or break-ins since we tightened things up?"

"Not that we are aware of. We are all on high alert and on the lookout for anything out of the ordinary. But, looks clean – locks still in place and nothing looks messed with."

"Great! Great," Phil responded. "Have you heard from Max at all lately?"

"Yeah," Wayne was quick to reply. "Coincidentally, he called this morning with some information. Apparently, Zephyr had some kind of a mechanical malfunction to one of its big Cats, which will set them back a day or two. He estimates they have another 100 feet of drilling to go."

Phil smiled widely. He could only guess what had gone on.

"That's fantastic news, Wayne," Phil said with genuine enthusiasm. "Glad Max is doing well and able to touch base with you."

The two men spent the next half hour discussing what would most likely come next and the best way to protect vital information from getting into the competitions hands. Phil made a few more suggestions and hung up the phone.

Wayne's next item of business was to call Joe at the rig. It was time to line up the service companies that would be required for coring, logging, and testing. He still wasn't convinced that coring was a good idea, especially with time running short. Coring a formation could be a long tedious process, and having to pull 14,000 feet of pipe in and out of the hole could lead to issues that could set them back.

It was important to have all the information and data possible in order to submit a genuinely competitive bid. Since Joe and Val were at the rig, they would have the best idea of which operations would be the most beneficial in such a limited time frame. Wayne knew Joe would also know the companies that had proven themselves the best in the past.

"Screw it!" he said, standing up. "I'm going to the rig."

No sooner had the words escaped his lips did Wayne sit right back down. He couldn't leave the office. The rig was already in good hands, but there was nobody to run the ship in Calgary. What was I thinking, Wayne laughed hollowly to himself?

Wayne let out a big sigh, then went back to sitting and waiting. He thought to himself, "You are one lucky man." Wayne knew his decision to pursue the Wolverine Hills project could have destroyed the company if there had been any major glitches.

Maybe a glass of wine was in order, Wayne started toward the bar in the corner of the office just then the intercom came to life.

"Wayne, Joe is on the line," Connie's voice had a sense of urgency.

Wayne turned back to his desk to take the call.

"Hello Joe, how are things going?" He asked with hesitation in his question.

"Hi Wayne, got some bad news for you."

"So what's up Joe?"

The line was quiet.

"Come on Joe, give it to me!"

Joe started slowly, "Wayne I should have called you sooner but I thought we could work through the problem we're having without getting you involved. The bad news is, we are stuck in the hole and it doesn't look good. We have been trying to get pipe movement for the last 4 hours and the most we have gotten so far is 2 feet. It really looks bleak."

Silence consumed the line.

After several seconds Wayne responded to the devastating news. "So what do you recommend going forward?"

"We have ordered a load of crude oil out to the rig and we are going to try to spot some oil to see if we can get the pipe moving, if that's ok with you?"

Wayne knew Joe had the expertise to make the right decisions and he would do his best to resolve the problem.

"How far are we off bottom?" Wayne asked

"We were coming out of the hole on the last clean- out trip and got to 12,200 feet and the driller pulled into a bridge, looks like he walked into it pretty hard. He tried to get unstuck for about 30 minutes before notifying me. I had just laid down for a little snooze when it happened."

Wayne hated to ask the most important question but he knew it was inevitable. "So Joe what does this do to our prospects of getting information on the Granite Wash before we have to submit our bid?"

Joe was quiet; softly he gave the crushing response. "We're not going to be able to log or test in time Wayne."

Darkness filled the room as Wayne dropped his head on the desk.

The sound of Joe's voice sounded a million miles away, "Wayne we're not out of options, remember we still have Max. He is one great scout and I feel he'll come through for us!" Joe stated with as much enthusiasm as he could muster.

"Thanks for you encouragement Joe, I better let you get back to work."

"Wayne I'll let you know if there are any changes." The line was suddenly silent.

Wayne's head dropped slowly again to the desk top. He was numb.

CHAPTER THIRTY-ONE

It had been three days since Max had outmaneuvered his nemesis – Tom Hughes.

Max had driven numerous logging roads, looking for just the right place to lie low and he had found the perfect spot. The site was about five miles from the Zephyr well and it was surrounded by heavy timber.

Perfect, he thought. The fact that it kept snowing meant his tire tracks would be covered. If they found him, it would be like finding a needle in the haystack, he concluded.

Max had plenty of fuel left in his tank and even had an extra 70-gallon gas tank in the back of the pickup. He could lay low for days on end, if need be, living on a scout's rations of Ritz crackers, cheese, canned chili beans, and water. He had been through it so many times before it wasn't even a sacrifice. Max became quite fond of crackers and cheese.

The hi-powered Swedish scanner had been working overtime, trying to pick up any calls coming from the Zephyr rig. He was pretty far away, but close enough as the crow flies to get a pretty good signal.

Max rolled the goose-down bag out on the seat and prepared to get one more night of rest and monitoring. The information coming over the scanner was hit and misses and Max knew that he would begin a plan of action starting in the morning.

He had heard that Black Gold had reached their optimal depth of 13,980 feet, which was great news. He knew, however, that Zephyr had to be back in business by now and most likely very close to the same goal. The hypnotic hum of the electronics rocked Max to sleep.

Max woke early and was lying on the seat in a semi-conscious state thinking about his next plan of action. It was 5:30 in the morning when Max reached over to slap at the alarm clock. Looking over, Max suddenly realized the rolling blue lights on the scanner were vacant and the familiar hum of the scanner was absent.

"Damn it," he said loudly, springing up off the seat. He knew he must have accidentally pulled the plug from the power source again. Max fumbled for the cord. It was still in the outlet.

What the hell is happening? Now the damn cell phone started to ring.

Max checked the number, it was Phil. What could be wrong this early in the morning, he thought, must just be worried about my good health, Max chuckled.

"Howdy Phil, worried about my health?"

There was no humor in Phil's voice as he responded to Max's light hearted comment.

"Got some bad news this morning", Stadwell called me. "I guess they pulled into a bridge at about 12000 feet and they are still stuck in the hole, doesn't look like they are going to get any information on the Granite Wash formation before sale day."

"Holy shit!"

"Phil I haven't heard a thing about it. This piece of shit scanner quit working sometime while I was sleeping and I didn't get any calls this morning.

Phil was quiet, then emphatically reminded Max of how important it was to get as much information as he could.

"One more thing Max, anything you could do to impede Zephyr's progress would be a bonus and greatly appreciated by Black Gold!"

"Be careful Max!" Phil was suddenly gone as the cell phone went silent.

Just what I need more fucking pressure Phil, Max mumbled to himself.

Max spent the next hour trouble shooting his expensive piece of Swedish shit. That's what he now called it since he knew he might very well be missing the exact information he was hoping for to put his next plan of action into motion.

Nothing he did brought the scanner back to life. It was dead. Max looked at the clock: 7:00 am. The fucking report would have already gone out. It was too late. Max couldn't believe his bad luck.

With no scanner giving him information, he would have to do it the old-fashioned way – by sneaking onto the lease and getting it firsthand. It was the most dangerous and challenging part of scouting and with what Max had done to the big Cat engine, Zephyr would be more than a little pissed with him.

By now Tom would have given up on finding him, thinking for sure he had put the fear of God into him. Max knew this would take some pressure off and he should be able to travel without being caught.

After a quick breakfast of water and crackers, Max started up his truck and slowly headed back down the logging road toward the Zephyr location. He decided to go into town first, as there were a few items he needed. One of which was more Ritz crackers.

Driving back down the lonely road, Max saw a sign that immediately brought back old memories. It read: "Explosives Keep Out."

Fresh out of high school, he had gone to work for a seismic company and his first job was to cut five-pound sticks of dynamite into half-pound sections, then push them down into holes that had been previously drilled. Once the 40- to 60-foot holes were loaded with the explosives another crew would follow up and detonate the dynamite.

The explosion would cause shock waves and the information from the waves was recorded on special instruments for geological purposes.

Occasionally, for fun, he would tie a chunk of the dynamite to a large tree and detonate it, causing the tree to shatter and come crashing down. Damn dumb, Max surmised, as it could have killed someone. Max chuckled. He had certainly done some stupid shit when he was young.

Thinking more about it, Max suddenly stopped. Phil's last conversation echoed in his head. He threw his truck into reverse and backed up to the sign. The bright orange sign was there to warn all passersby that there were explosives in the area. To Max, he knew it meant there was a Powder Mag nearby, which was a metal trailer or small metal structure used to house any extra dynamite the seismic companies needed for their work deep beneath the surface.

Max threw the truck back into drive and headed down the old snow covered dirt trail adjacent to the sign. Sure enough, about half-mile in, there it was – the familiar looking red and white trailer.

Fumbling through the outer layers of his parka Max located the small pouch that had once held Carmen's manicure set. It now contained the small intricate handcrafted tools that Max had made for just such a job.

Max wasn't the best lock-picker, but he knew a thing or two. The lock was an old Slaymaker, the exact kind Max used in his youth. Forgetting keys was an unfortunate, but normal occurrence back in his youth, so one of his colleagues was, on occasion, forced to pick the lock. Over time, with additional research, Max picked up this skill and now he was going to put it to good use.

In two short minutes, the lock popped and Max was opening the door to the trailer. He knew how to handle explosives and very carefully removed two five-pound sticks. Wrapping the two sticks of hi-glycerin TNT in his sleeping bag, Max placed it gingerly on the back seat.

The next items, the explosive caps, could be even more deadly than the dynamite itself. This kind of dynamite didn't have a fuse; it had to be detonated with small metal caps that were inserted and then set off with a small electric current. Each cap had two blue lead wires with protective plastic ends on each wire. This was to protect against an inadvertent setting off from static electricity.

Many a seismic worker had lost his hand in this manner and it wasn't something Max wanted happening to him. He placed the caps into the glove compartment with extreme care.

Max quickly locked the trailer back up and drove to the logging road. Seeing the sign and garnering the explosives now; put a new plan of action into Max's mind. He knew when the seismic crew did its inventory and discovered the missing dynamite it would report it to the authorities. Max would be long gone by then.

There was no time to waste. If Max was going to give his client the advantage going into sale day, he had to act now.

It was almost 20 miles into town and there was no use driving with excessive speed. The roads were treacherous with the new fallen snow and the last thing Max needed was to hit a rut or hole with the hazardous cargo and go flying into the ditch.

The logging road had become very familiar and he tapped the breaks, as he approached the upcoming hairpin turn. Right away he could see the deep tire tracks leading straight into the ditch on his right. Max slowed down even more and surveyed the tracks heading toward the timber and bush.

He spotted the red Ford lying on its side; it was Pole Cat's red Ford.

Max brought his truck to stop and stared for any sign of life. Nothing moved. He then saw the arm hanging out the open window.

"Shit," Max yelled, flying from behind the steering wheel and charging for the old pickup. It was a struggle getting through the heavy deep snow and Max had to engage every muscle as he plowed forward.

He managed to finally reach the driver's side door and he peered in. There, lying motionless half on the steering wheel and half on the seat was Pole Cat. The overwhelming smell of whiskey permeated the air.

"Hey! Pole Cat! You OK Bill?" Max yelled through the open window.

Pole Cat slowly started to move. He mumbled something, but Max couldn't make it out. He was able to jar the door open and he looked down at a bruised and battered scout.

"What the hell happened, old timer?"

"Fuck you KID!" Pole Cat mumbled.

"Oh! I guess with that attitude I'll be seeing you later.

Max turned and started to make like he was leaving.

"Don't leave me here," he shouted with fear. "Shit, man, it's 20 below! I'll freeze to death!"

With a wry smile, Max turned back and started digging the snow away from the truck. Max pried the door open a bit more and grabbed Pole Cat by the upper torso. He carefully and slowly pulled him out.

It was difficult, but he managed to drag him through the deep spring snow and back to the logging road. Pole Cat was mumbling to himself the whole time. He was very woozy still, Max wasn't sure; it could be from the crash or all the whiskey.

Max was able to get him up into his truck, he was moving as quickly as he could because he knew all the freshly fallen snow would never slow down the maniacal logging truck drivers.

Max jumped behind the wheel and started forward through the tight turn. Max glanced over at the blood stained scout. It looked like he had fallen asleep. Or maybe he had passed out. Max turned up the heat to help him out.

"Fuck, Tom Hughes!" he finally mumbled with his eyes closed.

"Huh? What about Tom?" Max asked intrigued.

"That fucking bastard left me there- Left me to freeze to death!"

It was slow going, and Max thought he had fallen asleep twice, but Pole Cat manage to tell Max how Tom was driving right behind him when he lost control of his truck and spun out into the ditch. According to Pole Cat, Tom stopped and stared at the accident for several minutes, then drove off.

"Just left me, sorry prick didn't even bother getting out," he slowly muttered.

"Maybe he went to get help?" Max said, knowing it didn't make much sense this far out in the bush. This made Pole Cat laugh and grimace with pain at the same time.

Max noticed his fingers. They were dark at the tips. Most likely frost-bite, Max concluded. To what extent he was unsure, but he suddenly felt sorry for the old scout.

Max drove straight to the Grand Prairie Inn. When he pulled into the parking lot, there was no sign of Tom's truck.

The two men spent the next half hour in Max's Chevy discussing the operations at the wells. Most of it was general and Max laced his updates with a few white lies.

"Fuck, Max! I don't have shit on Black Gold's well," Pole Cat suddenly said. "Not sure what the purpose in sending me out here was anyway. All they told me to do was make myself known to Black Gold and be a nuisance. That's it! My guess is they never wanted or cared if I got any real information on their well."

It was an odd request, Max knew, but it suddenly made sense. Zephyr had what it wanted elsewhere. Bill was simply a decoy.

"You know, Pole Cat. I really should get you to the hospital to have those fingers looked at."

Pole Cat simply opened the door and stepped out. "I got it from here Max! Thanks for your help. If you need anything, and I mean anything, you let me know. That's twice now you've saved my bacon."

Max chuckled and nodded, as Pole Cat turned to walk to his motel room. He suddenly had an idea.

"Hey, Pole Cat you serious about that offer?"

"Serious as a heart attack," he said, looking like he may topple over at any second.

"OK, then. I may need your help on a little project. Don't go anywhere. We'll discuss it all tomorrow."

Pole Cat nodded and waved, then turned and limped off toward his room.

L. GORDON KESLER

CHAPTER THIRTY-TWO

The joy and excitement at Zephyr Petroleum had recently morphed into despair and apprehension.

Roger's disposition was ugly in the best of times, so now it was on a whole new level of awfulness.

"Shelley, get your ass in here, NOW!" He screamed out the open door.

Shelley had formed a plan of escape from Zephyr in her mind and his demanding demeanor only made her more confident and sure about the decision. It also made her numb to his rudeness.

"Did you call Jack Watts over at JW Scouting?"

"Yes, sir, I told them to be here at 10:00 am sharp."

Just then, Jack stepped into the office and up to Shelley's desk. He was accompanied by Barry Stein.

"Oh, he's here, Mr. White."

"'Bout friggin' time, Send him in!"

Shelley forced a smile and motioned with her hand toward Roger's office. Jack looked a bit tired and red in the face, Shelley thought. The other guy just looked plain mean.

"You're late!" Roger screamed as Jack and Barry walked into his office. "Who the hell's this?"

"Roger, this is Barry Stein," Jack said nervously. "He's the guy who's been getting your daily reports from Black Gold."

Roger was suddenly irate.

"So, this is the guy you called one of the best in the business, huh?" Roger's voiced dripped with sarcasm. "What's his fuckin' name again? Did you say Inspector Clouseau? Or was that Inspector Clue-less? I guess that fucking hi-powered camera wasn't so hi-powered after all now was it?"

Barry simply looked over at Jack, then back to Roger.

"What the hell am I even paying you for, Jack? The only thing I have gotten is my ass chewed off from my superiors in Houston!"

Shelley had completely stopped what she was doing. She was intent on listening to Roger berate the two men. Other staff, including Nick, had walked over to listen, as well.

"Let me be straight with you, Jack. We've got some major issues going on at our rig right now and who knows if we'll be able to log, core, and test in time. At this point, it's lookin' pretty shitty! So, we need some quality information on Black Gold's well and we need it yesterday! So far, I've gotten Jack shit! Pun fuckin' intended!"

Roger put emphasis on the word Jack to make sure he knew that was directed at him. Jack sat in the chair opposite Roger and took the verbal insults. He'd been through this before, although not quite this bad.

"Look, Roger," he finally chimed in. "From the beginning, you demanded that you call the shots on how to proceed. Not only did you want Bill Emerson to be nothing but an odd distraction, but you also wanted to have my other scout, Tom Hughes, act as a counter-scout. This meant that nobody was watching the Black Gold well. I told you this may be an issue if Barry here couldn't gain access to their offices."

"But, he did gain access, Jack! And we were getting some great information, until about ten days ago! What the fuck happened?"

Jack tried desperately to remain calm. In any business, the client is always right, and it's definitely the case in the oil business. Jack truly wanted to explain his position without jeopardizing a client. This time, he knew, saving the client might not be possible.

"Roger, I'd like to start by reminding you, again, that you wanted to call the shots. Things were going very well until that field engineer, Crane, kidnapped and beat the shit out of the Black Gold scout. Once that happened, everything changed. I even had to pull Barry here from the job in case the cops got involved. Course - that also became the case once Black Gold found out they had a leak coming from their offices."

"Who told you to do that? Just because they knew they had a leak wasn't a reason to stop! Shit, man! You just said I was calling the shots!"

Jack took a deep breath. He knew reasoning with Roger was most likely futile. But he was desperate to try.

"Roger, I had no other option. Not only was Barry here recognized, but they changed their locks! We had no way of getting back in, so we had no other option but to pull out."

"That's straight bullshit!" Roger fired back.

Jack knew this working relationship, at least with Roger at the helm, was most likely not going to last. The goal now was to ensure he and his scouts got paid for the job.

"I'm sorry that we have a difference of opinion on how everything went down, but at this stage, we have fulfilled our contractual obligation."

"What the hell are you talking about?"

Roger's face was the ash color of the end of one of his cigar butts. He flew out of his oversized chair, the cigar butt rolling frantically from side to side in his mouth.

"That's crap, Jack! You have done nothing of the sort. This has been nothing but a fuck-up because you and this sorry blond prick can't do the fuckin' job!"

The words had barely escaped his lips when Barry reached across the desk and back-handed Roger alongside his head. Instantly, Roger began to sputter and cough and then he began flailing his arms like a wild man.

"He....he....lp," he muttered in a grotesque-sounding low moan. His faced turned bright red and a shade of purple. Finally, it occurred to Jack what was happening. The sorry bastard had swallowed his cigar stub and he was choking to death on the Cuban contraband.

Jack Watt was paralyzed by the sight.

"Do something Barry!" he yelled.

Barry nonchalantly stepped around the desk and grabbed Roger like a rag doll. He spun him so his back was to him, then put his large mitt in his midsection and started the Heimlich maneuver. With each push, Roger looked like his head was going to come off. He flopped back and forth.

After several attempts, the cigar dislodged and shot across the room. It hit the floor and bounced like a ping pong ball finally ricocheting off the wall coming to rest clear across the room.

Barry let go of Roger and he slumped down into his chair. He gagged and grunted for air. Both Barry and Jack watched Roger for a few seconds as his lungs slowly got back some much-needed oxygen.

He slurped and made sounds unknown to humans. This caused Shelley and Nick to rush into the doorway to see what was happening. They saw a crimson-faced boss gasping desperately in his chair.

"Ge...Ge...the fu' o' m' oveece..."

Still breathing heavy, Roger stared at the floor while holding his throat. Barry and Jack looked at each other, unsure what he said.

"What's that?" Barry asked.

"Get...Get out of my fuckin' office," Roger said slowly and painfully, pointing with one hand toward the door.

Barry simply shrugged and walked out. Shelley was quick to get out of the big man's way. Jack turned to follow, but looked over his shoulder at Roger, knowing he had just lost a valuable client.

"One more thing," they all heard Roger grunt, as they walked toward the elevators. "JW Scouting better hope Zephyr gets that fucking land at sale!"

CHAPTER THIRTY-THREE

Max woke early in anticipation of the work that lay ahead. He had dropped off his scanner the night before at an electronic repair shop and he needed to pick it up, along with Pole Cat.

Successful or not, this was to be his last mission into Wolverine Hills. With only 48 hours until bids were due, time was just about up.

The old red Ford was back in front of Pole Cat's room when he pulled into the parking lot. For a guy as lazy and drunk as Pole Cat was, this impressed Max.

How the hell did he get his old beater back here so fast? The last time he saw him, he looked like he was either headed to bed or the hospital. Knowing ol' Pole Cat, Max joked, he probably did neither and headed to the bar.

There was no sign of Tom's teal Chevy, which was a relief to Max. He didn't want to deal with him right now. Max tapped lightly on the motel door. A voice inside responded, but it was too female-sounding to be Pole Cat's.

A minute later, the door opened and the naked body of the crusty old scout was standing in front of him. Behind him, lying on the bed was Red. Max quickly raised his hand, "Oh, jeez, Pole Cat! How 'bout puttin' some clothes on?"

Max turned to look back out to the parking lot. Pole Cat just laughed.

"Hey Red, better put some clothes on before this young pup comes in here and jumps your bones! It's been a while since he's been home."

Pole Cat continued to laugh, as he held the door open. This time, Max laughed lightly with him.

"I'll go get some coffee and give you a few minutes."

Pole Cat shut the door, as a smiling Max walked down toward the lobby.

Max got two coffees just in case. He leaned against the hood of his white Chevy enjoying the cold, sunny day. He stirred and took a sip when the door opened and Pole Cat stepped out. Red, still buck naked stepped out with him and gave him a kiss.

For an older, overweight woman, she actually didn't look too bad, Max thought. He quickly realized he was staring and looked away. Damn it, Pole Cat was right, I have been gone too long.

"All right, woman! I'll see you later. Not sure how long I'll be. Who knows what ol' Max has planned for me?"

With that, Pole Cat headed toward the truck. Max grabbed the coffee off the hood and offered it to him.

"Not unless you spiked that coffee with whiskey or rum, No Thanks!"

Max just laughed and shook his head. As he did, the raspy, hard voice of Red rang out.

"Take care of my man, there!" she said still standing naked in the doorway. Max found himself shooting her an extra glance before she shut the faded blue door.

"Don't even think about it there, Maxy! That's my girl!" Pole Cat laughed, as he punched Max jokingly in the shoulder. Max felt his face slightly blush.

The two men stood there in the parking lot talking. Max got the run down on how Pole Cat was able to get his truck out so fast. Turns out, Red is very connected in town and has a friend who owns a tow company. He was more than happy to help out. Which is very fortunate, this far north and so far off the grid. Quite often if someone breaks down or has an accident, their vehicle remains right where it lies never to be moved again until Spring break up. Just like his poor demolished Chevy, he thought.

Max explained what he was thinking and thanked Pole Cat for helping out. To emphasize his appreciation, he called him Bill. It seemed to Max that Pole Cat was very eager to help.

"Sorry, I didn't have time to thank you appropriately the first time around," Pole Cat joked. Remembering him running off the lease just before he pulled the rig hand from the truck did make Max laugh robustly.

He then turned to Pole Cat with one request.

"Bill," he said. "What I have planned is very risky and I need you to be sober." Max looked him directly in the eyes and to his credit Pole Cat did not waver. Staring right at him, he nodded. "That I can do, Max."

Max smiled and then told him to follow him in his truck. Fortunately, the damage was not bad enough to impede his driving and the beat-up red Ford was up for the task.

Max jumped into his truck and started it up. He looked at the scanner on his dashboard and smiled at the blue lights that danced hypnotically across the front panel. Max had his doubts about getting repairs up here so far north, but that technician knew exactly what he was doing.

This was a huge relief because he would now most likely get some badly needed updates of both wells.

Max was going back to his original entry, which meant there could be people waiting for him when he got there. Pulling off the logging road, his worries were immediately allayed. There were no tracks in the fresh new snow. That meant nobody, not even Tom, had pulled up in the last day or two to check the cutline.

Max pulled alongside his beautiful old, flattened Chevy. He sighed again looking over at its sad demise, before turning off the engine and stepping out. Pole Cat pulled up next to him. Max rolled his eyes because he knew what was coming.

"Holy Shit, Bill said, I knew he crushed your Chevy, but I had no idea!" Pole Cat's voice was one of utter dismay and he stared at it in amazement. He then turned to Max and could tell he was pissed.

"Sorry, Max," he said quietly.

"It's OK. Just help me with my snowmobile," Max said.

Pole Cat helped Max get the ramp into place against the bumper, then Max hopped on and attempted to fire her up. There was intermittent ignition, but the Polaris 800 failed each time to keep running.

Max lifted the hood and looked it over. Cool, he thought, a spark plug wire had worked itself loose. Must have happened after all that bouncing around, he reasoned, as he tightened it up. He jumped back on, and sure enough, it sprang to life.

He rode it down the ramp and then told Pole Cat to hop on. Poor Pole Cat, Max thought, has no idea where I'm taking him. Max was only going to the west side of Nose Creek; he had no intention of getting any closer to the Comanche rig during daylight hours.

There were only five things Max needed to take on this trip: his snow-white tarp for camouflage, a small propane heater, two sticks of dynamite, and two dynamite caps. Oh, yes, he quickly remembered, and one alarm clock.

Max had prepared the sticks of TNT earlier in the day and gingerly placed them in the built-in toolbox on the Polaris. The ignition caps were another matter; they would go into Max's parka pocket.

It was an easy ride into the creek, although he could feel Pole Cat squirming on the back. He really must be wondering what the hell was going on.

Max turned off the Polaris and walked to the edge of the rim. Pole Cat stepped up next to him and immediately gushed with admiration.

"Holy Crappola! Did you do that Max? Did you honestly build that so you can get access to the rig?"

With wide eyes and mouth agape, Pole Cat stared at Max. Max simply bobbed his head slowly up and down. He, too, looked back down at it. Now that the job was almost over, he looked at it with newfound pride. He was proud of his work, but he always worried the ramp would not hold. One more trip and that worry would be over.

Max looked back over at Pole Cat. As the old scout stared at the ramp, he suddenly looked a little forlorn. Maybe he was marveling at how hard Max was working, while he was sitting at the bar drinking the days away. Max poked him in the shoulder and motioned him back to the snowmobile.

With his help, the two scouts were able to hang a nice white tarp between two jack pines and remove all the snow from the ground. This would be their shelter for the next day or two. It wasn't much, but maybe Pole Cat would feel secure with it. It was a good shelter and perfect place to set up the propane heater. Fortunately, the gas wasn't gelled and it fired right up.

"What now?" Pole Cat asked.

"I'll show you," Max replied, walking over to his snowmobile. He quickly removed the stick of dynamite and held it up.

"What the fuck ya gonna do with that?" He asked alarmingly.

"Again, I'll show you," he said with a nervous smile. He sighed deeply then headed for the canyon rim.

What he was going to do next required nerves of steel. Max's chest was rising and falling faster, as he climbed part of the way down the ramp. The dynamite had to be placed perfectly. Finding a spot between the middle tree and the one next to it, he found a hole big enough to place it where the skis of the snowmobile wouldn't hit it.

Next, the cap had to be placed into the dynamite. Carefully, ever so carefully, the cap was pushed into the sawdust and glycerin. Max then gingerly separated the cap wires and ran them all the way back to the shelter. Once there, Max tied the wires to a low hanging branch.

"Phew," Max said loudly, looking over at Pole Cat who was sill dumbfounded.

"So"? asked a clueless Pole Cat.

Max looked out at the canyon rim and at the forest around him. He then looked at Pole Cat. "Now," he quietly said, "we wait."

L. GORDON KESLER

CHAPTER THIRTY-FOUR

Max could tell Pole Cat was going through mini withdrawals because he was fidgety and paced back and forth around the makeshift camp. Max watched him for a while before asking.

"Pole Cat, you have any booze on you?"

"Fuck no," he quickly snapped. "I knew you'd be pissed if I did!"

Max was pretty sure it was a lie, he never went anywhere without a pint of something. But it was evident he wasn't sneaking off for drinks and he was doing what was asked of him.

"You know what to do right?" Max asked once more. "You have the two nine-volt batteries, right?"

"Yes! Yes, I have them," he snapped back with an agitated snarl.

"OK. I just want to make sure. It may mean my life if you misplace them."

Max went over the instructions a second time just to make sure Pole Cat knew exactly how to handle his job. At midnight, Max suddenly smacked his partner in crime on the shoulder.

"All right, I'm outta here. Wish me luck."

"Go get 'em, Max!" Pole Cat said with a big, confident smile, Max smiled back before jumping on and firing up the Polaris.

"And don't worry! I have everything under control here!" Pole Cat shouted.

The only thing Max could think was, sure you do. Max waved and was off. He headed up the hard pack snow that lead to the ramp and slowly disappeared over the side.

Pole Cat waited until the sound of the engine was a safe distance away, then quickly reached into his coat and pulled out a pint of cheap vodka. He twisted the cap off and took a long, satisfying drink.

"Ah," he said with great satisfaction.

Max listened carefully for any sign of activity coming from the rig. It was quiet, except for the steady purr from the big Caterpillar engines. Cautiously, the Polaris was eased down the ramp. On this trip, Max was straining his eyes trying to make sure the skies didn't catch the package tied to the underside of the center timber.

This night had two objectives and if one failed, the mission failed. It was imperative that no information leave the Zephyr location before the land sale bids were due. This would give Black Gold better than equal footing with their competition.

Max knew there were only three ways to get the goods delivered: one was by way of the satellite communication system and another would be to transport the geological data by road and finally the third was by helicopter. Max was confident that by the time they got a chopper involved it would be too late.

Max had to eliminate the first two possibilities.

This trip would take Max back through the timber toward the access road that led to the Comanche rig location. After working his way through the thick underbrush, he was finally able to see the high-grade access road that wound between the massive timbers to the Zephyr well site. Max parked his snowmobile.

He placed the other stick of TNT into his knapsack and, with flashlight in hand, Max began the 2-mile or so hike to the Grayling Creek Bridge.

It took more than an hour to reach his destination. Max wasn't sure why they called it a creek. In summer months it was a wide, fast-flowing rush of water. Definitely resembled more of a river, Max thought.

It probably didn't matter where Max set the explosives, but he decided the far side of the river would be best.

Crouching down, Max ran to the far side of the temporary steel bridge and disappeared over the side. It wouldn't take long to set the dynamite, but the work was nerve-wracking nonetheless.

Max pulled the material from the bag. Alarm clock, explosives cap and stick of glycerin.

The dynamite was tied to the steel beam that met the crossbeam next to the road grade. Next Max placed the cap into the dynamite. Max released the pent-up oxygen from his lungs. He could breathe. He didn't blow himself up, yet.

One more tricky part, connecting the batteries and lead wires to the alarm clock, then he was done. He set the blast to go off at 5:30 am, then hauled himself back onto the bridge. It was pitch black and Max turned off his flashlight. He stood there motionless on the bridge, enjoying the absolute silence. Time to move, he thought, and jogged down across the bridge and disappeared into the forest.

The walk back to his Polaris seemed to go by much faster than he thought it would. He was always relieved when he made it back successfully. Walking in such darkness and utter silence can start to weigh on you mentally. Throw in the ominous shadows created by the flashlight and Max knew it just got downright eerie. After a while, it sometimes felt as if one would never escape the cold, dark underworld.

The only saving grace was the clear, star-studded sky above. Like a beacon of hope and beauty, Max never grew tired of it. One look up and a smile would come to his face. The smile vanished abruptly as the piercing howl put him on notice that wolves would be stalking prey at this time of night. The hair on Max's arms suddenly came to attention.

After a very brisk thirty-five minute trudge through the snow, his flashlight reflected off the back of his snowmobile. He quickly jumped up on the seat while peering into the dark timber for any sign of his furry friends. The Polaris started right up, thankfully!

Awesome, Max thought. In such a remote location, in such cold weather, relying on machines and the technology of combustion engines were always risky.

Surrounded by darkness and the stars above, Max followed his snow tracks back the way he came. As he neared the east side of Nose Creek he turned right and headed straight for the rig.

Max had taped over the front and back lights of the Polaris to cut down on any reflection from the rig lights. Just as he started for the rig, he turned off his flashlight so nobody could see him approaching.

He neared his old camp and hung a U-turn. He wanted the ride out to be as quick as possible. Max had left his parka with Pole Cat and was only wearing his special white-camouflage coveralls. With his 300 Sako rifle over his shoulder, he proceeded toward Zephyr's rig. Max knew the rifle could be a handicap if he had to make a hasty retreat but leaving it behind was not an option.

Everything was eerily quiet, as Max crawled up the debris mound to the edge of the well site. He peered all around for any sign of movement. The satellite communication dish was in position on the logging van and another one was located atop the engineer's shack. Lined along the edge of the location to his right were the living quarters. The entire location was roughly 100 yards by 100 yards, Max knew from his many years of experience.

At one end of the engineer shack, Max noticed something that seemed out of place. He raised his rifle and peered through the scope. Upon further examination, Max could see that next to one of the trailers were three hi-powered Arctic Cat snowmobiles. One was bright orange and the other two were fluorescent green. Looked like some of the roughnecks went a bit overboard and spent a ton of cash on some fancy new toys, Max concluded.

Scanning the entire lease, Max saw a few rig hands busy scrubbing the buildings. Scrubbing the rig before a move was a ritual for most drilling companies and it starts as soon as the drilling concludes.

A large bright red logging van with the words HI- TECH etched across the side was backed up to the rig. Its back was open and the large reel containing steel cable was exposed. To the front of the reel was the instrument cabinet where the technicians would track the feedback, as the steel cylindrical logs were hoisted from the bottom of the hole.

This is where all the precious data would be recorded and stored, Max knew. He focused the spotting scope on the cable that ran from the big reel and over the orange pulley hanging in the derrick.

The cable was slowly moving downward. It would continue to do so, Max understood until it reached the bottom of the hole at roughly 14,000 feet. Once on bottom, the slow process of reeling the logs to the surface would begin.

These highly sophisticated metal cylindrical recording tools were used to gather downhole information and in the oil industry they were called "logging tools". Essentially they were long, metal cylinders with highly sophisticated electronics built inside to record and assess the porosity and contents of the formation. As the cylinders were slowly reeled to the surface, the information was electronically recorded on long scrolls of special paper; these were called "logs".

This was the best source of information any company could gather to truly understand what exactly existed deep beneath the ground, and it was the only information Zephyr would have prior to the Wolverine Hills land sale.

Moment of truth, Max silently said to himself.

He watched intently as the long metal tube was brought to the surface and broken down. He knew once this was loaded onto the truck, another one would go down into the hole and the process would begin again.

The side door on the instrument cabinet opened and the technician stepped out. As he did, he rolled up a large paper scroll and dropped it into a five-gallon pail on the ground beside the red van.

Instantly, Max's eyes opened wide and his pulse began to race. Did he just see what he thought he saw? How could they be so careless? This was the best break any scout could get. If he could get his fingers on those electronic reports, it would provide all the information his client could hope for.

It wasn't the first time he had seen someone throw away such vital information, it was just a shock to see it happen on a project of this magnitude. The thought suddenly came to him that maybe he was being baited. This would be like dangling a nice big chunk of stinky cheese in front of a rat.

Funny, Max joked, scouts were considered by many to be nothing but rats. Was this scroll, placed in clear view, the bait? It certainly could be the way he blatantly rolled it up and tossed it away. The only other explanation was the man tossing the material, was a green technician.

Max hunkered down closer to the ground to ponder his options. Rising slowly to scan the lease one more time, Max wondered what to do. His plan all along was to sneak onto the lease and try to covertly garner whatever information he could. Thus, this changed nothing. In fact, it only made him more convinced his plan of action was the right one.

"Screw it," he mumbled. He again peered over the mound at that five-gallon garbage can.

In his mind, the big challenge would be getting there without being spotted by the hands on the rig. Slowly, Max slid back down the mound into the safety of the dark shadows. Lying on his back, his breath visible in the cold night air he was suddenly at peace, staring up at the stars. Max calmly gathered his thoughts and planed his strategy.

The first conclusion was; he would come from the other side of the lease. There was just too much open area on this side to advance without being exposed. Moving to his left, Max slid from tree to tree until he finally reached the opposite side of the rig.

He dropped to his belly and crept up to the edge of the lease. The pipe racks were piled high with the casing that would eventually be run in the hole for the production of the black crude – if the well had any oil and gas at all. The piles of casing created dark shadows, ideal for hiding. They also ran almost up to the red logging truck.

Max checked his pocket. This was a two-fold operation. He could feel the cable cutters tucked away in the deep pocket on his off-colored brown and white coveralls.

Lying on his belly next to the edge of the lease, Max estimated the casing racks to be only thirty feet away. Should be a piece of cake, he concluded and raised his upper torso for one last check of activity.

Holy shit, he suddenly thought. Right in front of him, not six feet away, was a rig hand. Max immediately dropped his head, hoping he couldn't be seen in the darkness.

Max held his breath and froze on the ground. He would not have seen the roughneck if he did not suddenly light up a cigarette. The red blaze came out of the recovery tank shadows right when Max was going to spring into action.

Max ever so slowly raised his head and surveyed the situation. He was not spotted. He could barely make the rig hand out but could tell by the fact that his head kept going in and out of the light around the tanks that he was nervous about being spotted. Must have snuck off for a smoke without permission, Max deduced.

"Where the hell's Johnson!"

The voice rang out from across the lease. The red glow of the cigarette suddenly dropped to the ground and was out. The man stomped on it and quickly jogged back toward the rig.

That was close; too close. Max sighed with relief. Max immediately jumped up and ran through the dim light and safely into the shadows of all the casing. He then dropped to his belly and did a military crawl to the end of the casing racks. Peering out, he could see the red truck, not fifteen feet away.

Another 15 feet of exposure through the rig lights, Max realized. Seeing nobody, Max darted forward and quickly did a tuck and roll to get under the vehicle. He stopped and listened. To his delight, there was no shouting.

"Safe," he slowly joked to himself.

On his belly, he slowly pulled his body toward the far side of the van. He could hear the cable being reeled out of the hole. Max could also hear talking going on in the instrument cabinet above him. They were in a heated discussion on why part of the last logs had been so distorted and poor in quality. Interesting, Max thought.

He slid some more until he was adjacent to one of the back tires.

The five-gallon pail was now only three feet away from his reach. Carefully, he reached around the tire and out to the pail. Just as his hand was on the side handle, the door on the instrument cabinet was thrown open. Run is all Max could think of, but instead, he froze; hand still on the can. He didn't dare move.

Instantly, Max heard the sound of someone clearing his throat and hacking up a green monster from his lungs. He spit and then slammed the door shut.

The disgusting yellow and green snot ball landed right on his wrist. Ewww, Max thought staring at the nasty slime slowly sliding down his arm. Yet, he kept his cool and kept his hand motionless on the handle.

Slowly, Max tipped the five-gallon pail downward toward the tire. With his other hand, he reached up and blindly reached in. He felt his hand on a scroll of paper. Bingo, he thought, pulling the precious material out, while slowly tipping the pail back into place.

His heart beat madly. He was waiting for someone, anyone, to see the pail moving and cry out. No such holler came and Max quickly pulled both hands back under the truck.

He quickly rolled over onto his back and unzipped his coveralls. He slid the scroll inside, then zipped it back up. Rolling back over, he quickly shimmied back the way he came.

Max quickly looked around again. He couldn't believe his luck and his good fortune, but another pressing issue was still nagging at him.

At this point, communication from the rig to Zephyr headquarters was enemy number one. Max still wanted to take out the satellite dish on top of the truck and the other one on the engineer's shack. And he needed to do this before the reports started being transmitted back to management in Calgary.

Taking a deep breath, Max slowly crawled out from under the truck and turned around. Seeing a few places to put his feet, he cautiously climbed upward. He had to not only be stealthy, but he had to move quietly enough so the technicians in the recording cabinet of the truck did not hear him.

Each step was measured in inches and it seemed like an eternity to get to the top of the Hi-Tech vehicle. Once he did, he was now in full view of anybody on the rig. He quickly dropped to his belly and squirmed his way forward. Like an inchworm, he made his way to the satellite dish. He quickly reached into a large pocket on his coveralls and pulled out his cable cutters.

In one quick move, he snapped the cable leading up to the dish. The sound it made was as if a 9mm pistol had gone off. Max was sure the sound and the interruption in communication would bring some sort of chaotic reaction. But to his surprise again nothing. Must be too busy looking over the instrumentation problems still, he concluded.

"One down, one to go," he whispered.

Max crawled to the side of the truck facing the pipe racks and the casing and slowly slid off, dropping to the ground landing softly. He quickly made his way to the shadows of the steel casing, and then jogged down the back side into the safety the timber lining the rig site.

The slightly graying sky indicated dawn was rapidly approaching. Max checked his watch: 5:05 am. "Fuck", panic shot through his veins, only 25 minutes until this whole place would explode with activity.

It looked to be only 50 yards to the engineer's shack. Fifty yards straight across, wide-open fully lit snow and dirt was too far. Max continued working his way through the timber toward his destination. It was only 20 yards now to access the dish on top of the shack, shouldn't be too difficult he reasoned nervously.

"Go time," he said aloud and sprinted straight for it. Running across the wide-open lease, the shiny, new snowmobiles again caught Max's interest. Top of the line hi-powered machines, Max realized.

He continued to the shack and immediately slammed his body against the wall. He worked his way around the corner to a tiny make-shift ladder welded on the side of the building. Very convenient, he chuckled and started his ascent to the top.

Max extracted his cutters and reached over and snipped the cable in two. Time to get the fuck out of here, Max concluded. Just as he took his first step down the ladder, the loud snarling growl of a dog shattered the silence.

Max looked across the yard. Standing next to one of the shacks, even from this distance, Max could see the white fangs flashing in the dim light. No time for the ladder Max knew and dropped straight to the ground. In an instant, he was running at full speed for the forest.

The dog continued to howl as it went after him. Max quickly reached the end of the lease and jumped with all his might into the deep snow between two trees. He immediately rolled over, sprang to his feet, leaping and plowing his way through the snow.

The dog was much faster and Max could hear it snarling right behind him. He grabbed a dead piece of timber from the snow and whirled around and swung blindly. He hit the dog square in the side, sending it flying off into the darkness.

Max didn't pause to relish his good fortune; he kept right on running through the snow. The barking and growling right behind him meant the damn dog didn't stay down long and was already back in hot pursuit.

Right in front of him another dead branch. This time at shoulder height, Max grabbed it with both hands and prayed.

"Break, Dam It," he shouted, as he took two more hard steps forward, before turning. Just as he did, the dead timber broke off and Max swung it with all its might. The guard dog again yelped in pain, as it went flying off once more into the shadows.

Again, no time to rejoice, Max whirled back around and continued running toward the Polaris.

In the distance, he heard the loud sound of snowmobiles. Shit, he thought, should have dismantled those fucking toys when I had the chance.

Max saw his Polaris in the distance. Just 50 yards or so to go, looked more like 500 yards, to Max. Just as he felt that he may make it, a gunshot rang out in the distance. The thud on a nearby tree told him it was off the mark.

He jumped onto the Polaris as another gunshot rang out and he felt the bullet whiz by his head. Way too close for comfort, he concluded, starting up the snowmobile and cranking down on the throttle.

Speeding away for his life, the thought of the dog somehow entered his mind. Where the hell did it come from? Had Max known they had a fucking guard dog, he never would have approached the rig. Thank God the German Shepard didn't smell or spot him sooner. For whatever reason, Max made a mental note to alert Phil about having client's hire guard dogs. It really was a great idea and made total sense.

Another bullet whiz by over his head bringing, him immediately back to reality. Max headed for Nose Creek. The screaming engines of the brand new colorful snowmobiles were ominously loud, and as Max turned and looked over his shoulder; the orange one zoomed out of the forest and was almost right next to him.

"Son Of a Bitch," Max yelled.

The rider pulled his gun and pointed it right at him. Max immediately turned to his right, screaming full throttle between two trees, then he turned back left. Navigating at high speeds in this darkness was not a good idea, nor was covering his lights, Max concluded.

Through the trees, Max could see one of the fluorescent green snowmobiles zig-zagging toward him. The third one was right on its heels. In the shadows, they looked like ninja warriors in full combat, as they darted through the dense timber.

Max suddenly flinched with the sound of the loud noise. The explosion in the distance rang out loudly and the early morning sky was quickly illuminated with a bright, but ephemeral light. The sight made Max smile. At least they couldn't get the valuable data out by the road, he knew.

The smile disappeared, the second the bullet shattered the tree next to his head. Max flinched again and immediately hit the throttle and peeled off to the right. The three were closing in on him.

"Fuck! These boys are serious!" Max yelled to himself.

Max rolled to the left just as his windshield shattered in front of him. Options were getting short. He knew if he was going to survive he had to get into the heavy trees. The opening ahead of him between the two jack pines was hair-splitting narrow, but it was the only route he could see that would give him a chance.

As Max split the pines, the orange cat was right on his tracks. Fortunately, the rider behind him wasn't so lucky and the sound of a large crash told Max, the Arctic Cat jockey had straddled one of the trees; he had to deal with one less dangerous prick.

"One down, two to go," he said, as he looked over his shoulder. Through the trees, the light from the gun blast was the first thing he saw. Again, a branch just above him exploded into a thousand splinters.

Max again cranked down hard on the throttle and shot forward toward his escape route down to the creek. Once again he heard the pop of a pistol and this time he felt a burning sensation on the right side of his head.

Upon reaching the canyon, Max didn't slow down and he soared high into the air. The nose of his Polaris hit the ground first, causing him to almost flip over. The back came back down and he managed to gain control, as he continued to the bottom of the creek.

Despite his good fortune and driving skills, the roaring engines behind him told Max he still had company. He had never tried his ramp while going full throttle, but with two guys with guns right behind him, the thought brought on an instant shot of adrenaline almost as soon as it entered.

He screamed up the ramp, too nervous and focused to look over his shoulder.

"Now Pole Cat! Now!" he yelled at the top of his lungs.

Pole Cat, who was woken up just seconds prior from the gunfire, jumped to his feet. The empty vodka bottle fell to the snow, as he ran over to the hanging wires and quickly touched them to the 9-volt battery.

Just as the two riders made it to the creek bottom and started up after Max, the ramp disintegrated into a million pieces. Both snowmobiles went flying high into the air and the two hired thugs somersaulted backward, crashing violently onto the river ice and snow.

The flying debris came raining down in hypnotic slow motion on top of the makeshift camp, sending Pole Cat diving for cover. Chunks of timber landed all around him.

Max bailed from his Polaris and immediately ran back to the canyon rim. What he saw brought a smile to his face. Both of the Zephyr rig hands were alive on the east side, stumbling around, dazed and confused.

Max relished the moment, then walked over to the camp to find Pole Cat. He was still lying face down in the snow. This image was very similar to the earlier one when the rig exploded months before. Max laughed hysterically at the sight.

"You can come up for air now tough guy the actions over."

Pole Cat slowly lifted his head up from the snow and debris. He looked around to make sure all was good.

"Did it work?"

Max just laughed harder.

"Ah, Pole Cat. Let's go get you a drink."

That statement made Pole Cat smile widely and he jumped to his feet. The two men mounted their snowmobile and rode off feeling a great sense of exhilaration and satisfaction.

L. GORDON KESLER

CHAPTER THIRTY-FIVE

The sun was coming up when Max pulled the white Chevy into the motel parking lot. As Pole Cat slowly exited the pickup he turned and gave Max a solemn look.

"You little prick, he said, with a chuckle; I'm just an old drunk and I can't do this anymore. I just want you to know it has been a pleasure working with you. This is my last job and I can't think of a better way to go out, thanks."

"Bill I'm just glad it worked out and we're not just a couple of missing scouts!"

Pole Cat pondered Max's statement before laughing, "You know for a low life scum sucking scout you're really not a bad guy. Take care, Max".

Thanks and don't forget that old bucket of bolts that wouldn't start back on the cutline.

Pole Cat gave Max thumbs up without looking back.

Max watched as Pole Cat limped toward the open motel door where Red was waiting to embrace her old scout. She gave her man a big kiss and hugs and disappeared behind the blue door.

Max knew Pole Cat was going to be ok.

Max arrived at the chopper pad and checked his watch 7:45 a.m. Phil should be arriving any time now.

What he couldn't figure out was why he wanted him to leave the rented 4X4 in the "park and fly" lot. Max was glad to simply drive it home. The other thing troubling him was Phil's instruction to secure all of his equipment.

At least there wasn't much equipment left after the roughnecks had their way with it all. Well, almost everything. Max knew he was fortunate they never found his prized scanner in its hiding place away from camp. Like everything else, it too could be replaced, but it would take a lot of time and several thousands of dollars to do so.

Max stood there anxiously waiting to tell Phil the latest news from the Zephyr location. It was confirmation of the best possible outcome and he just picked it up while driving to the airport.

In the distance, he could hear the unmistakable "thump, thump, thump" of a helicopter. Looked like Phil was going to be right on time, Max concluded, as he spotted it coming straight for him over the Kakwa River to the south.

The pilot wasted no time getting the bird on the pad. Phil ducked under the whirling blades and strolled briskly to Max, extending his hand and offering him a huge smile to go with it.

"Got to hurry, Max! I'm sorry, but they are in a panic at Black Gold's office in the city!"

Max reached under the parka and passed the valued charts and information over to his boss.

"Great job Max, Incredible Work!" Phil said widening his smile. Phil began running his thumb and index finger down the scrolled parchment, as he did the countenance on his face changed to a look of concern.

"You look at these logs, Max?"

"Shit, no! I've been too busy running for my life." Max continued to study Phil's facial countenance. It looked like what he delivered had no value. His heart immediately sank. Damn it, he thought, I failed.

Phil continued to scroll down the parchment, viewing the recordings for each distance beneath the surface. He continued to frown.

"Sorry Phil." Max couldn't help but mutter his apologies.

Phil said nothing. He continued to read. Max glanced at the ground, then off to the distance. When his eyes came back to Phil, his huge, beaming smile once again returned to his face.

Phil suddenly jumped up and down and twirled around, looking like Michael Jackson in concert.

"Maxy! You son of a bitch! You did it!"

Max had no idea what Phil was talking about.

"There was nothing! I mean nothing on these logs down to 11,000 feet but at the bottom, at the Granite Wash, jackpot!" Phil slapped his fellow scout on the shoulder and laughed ecstatically.

Phil was no geologist, but even he could recognize the massive hydrocarbon imprint Zephyr found at the end of its drilling. He was as giddy as a teenage girl asked on her first date.

"Got more good stuff if you want it?"

"What else you got you little awesome prick?"

Max started to laugh. "You been hanging out with Pole Cat?"

Phil didn't know what that meant, so Max continued. "Just kidding! On my way over here I heard on the scanner that there was no satellite communication to or from the rig, so Zephyr sent a helicopter out to the site. Guess what?"

Phil was in no mood to play games.

"What, Max? What? We got to get these to Wayne and Black Gold ASAP!"

"Apparently, their logging tools got stuck. Bastards bridged off!!! They couldn't get the logging tools back to the surface."

Phil's mouth opened in amazement.

"Are you shitting, me? Are you saying that Zephyr may not know the full extent of what they have down there?"

It was now Max's turn to smile. He grinned broadly ear-to-ear and nodded to Phil.

Phil couldn't believe it. He slapped Max on the back vigorously almost knocking him down.

"Let's get these where they belong. Come on Max, no time to spare."

Phil turned and ran back to the helicopter. A confused Max hesitated, but quickly joined him. Both men boarded the helicopter with their heads bent low.

Once settled in their seats, the helicopter quickly rose off the pad and headed back south.

"Phil, I was hoping to get a tow truck and see if I can salvage my Chevy. Can't you bring the information to Wayne solo?"

Phil was slow to respond, but then turned around from the front seat and said, "No can do, Max! I hate to say this but I have another job for you!"Max looked as if he saw a ghost. All energy and joy left his body and he turned pale. His mouth dropped and he sat there too tired and annoyed to say anything.

CHAPTER THIRTY-SIX

The ride south on the chopper was quiet. Max was suddenly over-whelmed with fatigue. Just as he was about to drift off to sleep, Phil turned around and talked into his headset.

"Hey, Max! I heard a report this morning that someone blew up the Grayling Creek Bridge. Know anything about that?"

Max was about to come clean, but once again felt some things must remain a secret – even from his boss.

"Can't say as I do," Max said with a slightly wry smile on his face. "Maybe it was the work of those fucking eco-terrorists we keep hearing about."

Phil studied his employee, then nodded. He was pretty sure who was responsible but decided to let it go.

He turned back around and the two rode in silence for a few minutes. He then turned back around and talked to him through the headset while looking at him.

"I know another job is not what you want to be doing right now, but it will be quick, I promise!"

Max's fatigue suddenly turned to anger. He looked at Phil like he was plumb crazy.

"Seriously Phil, This better be an emergency! I just spent three months in the bush! I really would like to get home!"

"I understand," Phil calmly replied. "This won't take long."

Phil slowly turned back around. Max just shook his head and mumbled his displeasure to the back of his Phil's head.

He then turned and stared out the window. He was dog ass tired. The scenery below, to Max, was beautiful, but he simply stared at it without much thought. The wilderness was nothing but thick timber and a checkerboard of cutlines. On occasion, there was a rig busy at work drilling for oil and gas.

Max could feel his eyelids closing. The sound of the chopper engine was hypnotic and soon he drifted off to sleep. What felt like only seconds later, he was suddenly roused awake.

"Hey, Max! We're almost here!" Phil said.

Max slowly opened his eyes to see Phil looking back at him. He turned to look down at his watch. They had been flying for just over an hour. Max looked out at the open fields below as the helicopter slowly descended.

Phil removed the headset then turned to look back at Max.

"I am afraid we only have time to simply drop you off. Your ride should be here any second now. You'll get everything you need to know then, got it?"

Max was too tired and annoyed to respond. He simply nodded slowly to show he reluctantly understood.

"All right! I have to get these reports to Mr. Stadwell, ASAP. Today is the sale day and they need to get everything they can get for the bid."

Max didn't say anything. He simply opened the door and stepped out. Running with his head down, the helicopter took off. Max turned around and looked back. He thought for sure he saw Phil laughing. That was odd, he thought.

Suddenly, he looked around, for the first time, he recognized this place, it was his own acreage. Phil had dropped him off in the middle of the field behind his barn.

"You sorry sneaky little bastard," Max said, his glum face turning into a face filled with joy. Max watched intently the helicopter, as it disappeared in the distance. He again smiled and nodded toward Phil.

Just then, all that mattered in life could be heard in the near distance. Max turned to see his wife running through the pasture straight for him. Carmen ran into his open arms and hugged and squeezed him at the same time kissing his face all over.

"Welcome home," she said, as she stepped back to admire her man. The two then embraced for a long time.

Max then scooped her up and carried her home.

The front door was still wide open and Max carried the love of his life directly to the master bedroom laying her gently on the bed.

"Just going to jump in the shower and I'll be right back."

As Carmen waited for Max, in anticipation of the lovemaking to come, she watched the gorgeous silhouette of her ruggedly handsome man through the glass doors of the shower.

Max emerged with a towel wrapped around his waist.

Carmen motioned him toward the bed; she had already removed her outer garments.

Max dropped the towel and gently caressed the woman who meant the world to him. Carmen's body was still so beautiful after all their years together and after five kids.

"Oh, Max, I have missed you every day," Carmen purred.

Slowly Max responded, kissing and caressing Carmen's neck and shoulders.

The reunited lovers engaged in tender love making until the sound of children's voices ended the bliss.

Making love to Max was always special and exhilarating but Carmen couldn't remember it being so good.

L. GORDON KESLER

CHAPTER THIRTY-SEVEN
(ONE YEAR LATER)

Calgary had come alive in the last year. There were new companies filling all the vacant office buildings and even new construction was taking off. It was something the old "cow town" had not seen in years.

In the tallest tower in town, Roger White stood looking out his window. It was not so high up as before and he stared at a lot of brown, dusty buildings in his way. Through a gap between buildings, he could barely see a part of the Rocky Mountains.

He looked indifferent as he stood there. His face turned gray when his gaze went skyward to the old Sun Rise Resources tower down the street from him. He continued to stand there motionless, chewing on the end of a cheap domestic cigar; one he picked up at the newsstand across the street.

Roger rolled the skinny cigar from side to side and then chomped down clinching the butt between his teeth.

"Laura, get your ass in here!" he yelled through the open door.

Into his office quickly bounced a sleazy-looking, big-breasted blonde woman. Her nipples were hard and easily visible through the blouse. The short white skirt was hiked up, exposing the bottom part of her buttocks.

Chewing gum extra loudly, she glided across the room and rubbed up close to the crusty, old oil executive.

"Not now!" he said sharply. "I need you to take a message."

Laura simply shrugged and walked over and plopped into his tiny, cheap office chair by the almost as tiny desk. She found a notepad and pen.

"All right, Roger, sweetie. I'm ready."

"After many years as an employee of Zephyr Petroleum, I have made the difficult decision to resign. Please sign it, Sincerely, Roger White."

"Ya serious about all that stuff?" Laura asked very informally.

"Yes, I'm fucking serious! Type it up, if you're capable, and send it out today!"

"All right! All right! Hold your horses," she said with extra smacking on her gum. She headed out the door with broad sweeping hip action.

Roger continued to stare out the window. His gaze again fell onto the tower down the street. On the top floor, Roger could see the gold glow of a digital sign illuminating everything around it. The sign lit up one letter at a time.

Roger stared at it as it spelled out, "B...L...A...C...K...G...O...L...D" across the side.

"Fucking gnats," he muttered sadly. He then dropped his head toward the floor.

Starring out of the 48th-floor window looking east was the conservative blond president of Black Gold Resources. Wayne had a slight smile and look of amazement on his face. How the hell did they pull this off, he thought! The small fish in the big pond had landed quite possibly the biggest land deal in North American history.

His smile grew ever so slightly larger.

Across town, the red lettering of Zephyr Petroleum continued to shine but didn't seem so bright. At this height and with things the way they were, Wayne knew it didn't look so intimidating anymore.

"Mr. Stadwell?"

Wayne turned to see Shelley standing in his doorway.

"Yes, Shelley?"

"You have guests," she said.

"I do?" He asked quizzically.

"Yup!" she responded. "And, whether you like it or not, we're all coming in."

With that, Shelley stepped out of the doorway and let all the Black Gold employees pour in. Connie was first, carrying a cake, and a few others, including Chuck, came in carrying balloons. Val and Joe held a few bottles of champagne and cups. Gerry and Nick followed, with Phil and Max coming in last.

"What's this?" Wayne said surprised.

"Don't you know," an excited Val asked?

Wayne stepped away from the window. He was still very confused.

"No. No, I don't," he said still bewildered.

"Come on! And you call yourself our president!" Joe said, laughing. "Come on! It's the one-year anniversary of Wolverine Hills!"

"Time to celebrate our victory over Zephyr," someone yelled from the back.

"Amen to that," Shelley said loudly and proudly.

Wayne beamed with joy and pride.

"Let's open that champagne, Val," Joe said again.

Val was already working on it. The cork came flying out, bouncing off the ceiling and the wall. Everyone was ecstatic. Joe opened another bottle, as Val filled up the plastic, clear cups and handed them out. She handed one to Wayne.

"Toast!" someone shouted. "Toast."

Wayne was reluctant to oblige the request, but everyone else chimed in asking the same of him, so he blushed and raised his glass.

"I just want to thank you all for such hard work and dedication. Without each and every one of you, this would never have panned out. Not in our wildest dreams!"

Everyone raised their glasses.

"To Black Gold and many, many, more years of success!"

"To Black Gold," everyone repeated before drinking up.

Wayne spotted Phil and Max in the background.

"I'd also like to thank Phil and Max from Wildcat Scouting! Without all their help and, of course, all their information, especially that last giant tidbit from Zephyr, this all wouldn't have happened."

"To Wildcat Scouting!" everyone repeated before again exuberantly partaking of more champagne.

"Just have one question for Max, "how's that new black and gold Chevy running?"

Max blushed, "It's running great, thanks, I appreciate it, but want you to know I'm still working to repair my old battered friend."

Everyone cheered.

It was Gerry's turn to chime in.

"Scouts rule!"

Everyone laughed loudly.

"And who would have guessed Gerry; that you had your own little scout in Nick over there at Zephyr, "Clever man, Clever Indeed!" Phil said to the crowd.

Gerry turned to Nick who was standing next to him and gave him a one-armed hug. Nick looked up at everyone slightly embarrassed.

Laughter and joy permeated the 48th floor of the offices of Black Gold Resources.

THE END